I0742823

Meet Me in Berlin

A contemporary sapphic romance

Samantha L. Valentine

SAPPHIC
stories
PUBLISHING

Copyright © 2024 Samantha L. Valentine

All rights reserved.

The moral right of the author to be identified as the author of this work has been asserted.

This book is a work of fiction. Names, characters, places, and incidents are the product of the author's imagination or are used fictitiously. Any resemblance to actual events, locales, organisations, or person, living or dead, is coincidental.

No part of this book may be reproduced in any form or by any electronic or mechanical means, including information storage and retrieval systems, without written permission from the author, except for the use of brief quotations in book reviews.

No AI training: Without in any way limiting the author's exclusive rights under copyright, any use of this publication to 'train' generative artificial intelligence (AI) technologies to generate text is expressly prohibited. The author reserves all rights to licence uses of this work for generative AI training and development of machine learning language models.

Developmental edit: Sophia Blackwell

Copy edit: Penny Carroll

Cover design: Samantha Sanderson-Marshall

Paperback ISBN: 978-0-9756111-0-4

Ebook ISBN: 978-0-9756111-1-1

Also by Samantha L. Valentine

Novels

Normal Functioning Adult

King Love

Short stories

Eternal Love (Romance Writers of Australia Sweet Treats anthology, 2024)

Five Circles of Love (Romance Writers of Australia Diversions anthology, 2025)

Author's note

Hello!

Thank you for your interest in my novel. Although one of the main characters is British, and this book is partly set in Berlin and London, I am an Australian author publishing in Australia; therefore, this novel uses Australian spelling and publishing standards. This means you might see words with 's' instead of 'z' or an '-our' instead of '-or'. Different words for the same item may also vary depending on which character's point of view you're in.

Two real paintings are referenced in this novel: *Italia und Germania* by Johann Friedrich Overbeck and *Sappho and Erinna in a Garden at Mytilene* by Simeon Solomon. The galleries I've referenced that house these paintings are also real. However, in the real world, *Italia und Germania* is not on display at the Alte Nationalgalerie, and while *Sappho and Erinna* is part of the Tate collection, I don't believe it's on display in the gallery.

My British main character, Casey, is biracial and the novel

also features other characters of colour. Because I am not a person of colour, I engaged a sensitivity reader.

If you're a reader who likes content warnings, you'll find the list on the next page, if not – skip ahead to chapter one.

Happy reading!

Sam x

Content Warnings

Coarse language, drug use, sex scenes, infidelity, dementia, parental death.

To three of my favourite cities – Melbourne, Berlin and London. But mostly to London, a city where I spent eight years and that changed my life forever. East London. Angel. Notting Hill. Selfridges Foodhall. Forever part of me.

have met again after being apart for so long. It's the pain of separation in their expressions.'

'Oh,' I breathed. 'Yes. That.'

Casey gave a satisfied smile and gestured to the doorway. 'Want me to take you around the gallery and show off more of my art knowledge? There's an Aesthetics of Resistance exhibition on.'

I picked up my bag. 'I have no idea what that means, but defo up for a tour guide.'

She hooked a small backpack over her shoulder and started walking. 'You're Australian, yeah?'

'Yep. From Melbourne,' I said, falling into step beside her. 'And you're a Londoner?'

Casey raised a surprised brow. 'Very good. How'd you tell? Please don't say *EastEnders*, otherwise I'm going to have to compare you to someone from Ramsay Street.'

I chuckled and shook my head. 'No. British parents. My dad's Welsh and my mum's from London. She grew up in Wanstead.'

'No way!' She stopped and faced me. 'That's near me.'

A little thrill shot through me that this beautiful stranger and I had some kind of link, albeit a tenuous one. But I didn't want to come across as too keen. 'Cool,' I said and continued walking.

A beat of awkward silence followed, then Casey asked, 'Why are you in Berlin? It's a long way from home.'

'Student exchange with Berlin Tech for a semester.'

'Same, but at Berlin Arts. What degree?'

'Creative Arts.' I held up my small camera bag. 'Photography's my favourite, though.' We entered the next gallery, and I took a step closer to her. 'But I'm taking German art this semester, so here I am.'

Casey's arm brushed mine, making my skin prickle. 'I can help with that, if you like.'

~

Two weeks later, we found a patch of grass under a tree in Monbijoupark. It was early evening, but the late summer sun hadn't yet started its descent.

Casey laid her jacket on the grass and patted it. 'I've made you a bed.'

I held my camera at eye level and twisted the focus ring to sharpen the image, keen to capture the dappled light that shone through the leaves and fell across her face. 'You're sweet,' I said, shifting a few steps to the left so that she was off-centre.

She stretched out and propped up her head with her palm, her warm brown eyes gazing into the lens. 'Romantic is the word you're after.'

The shutter whirred as I held my finger down for a few seconds. I checked the images on the monitor, tucked the camera into my bag and flopped on the grass beside her. 'You are romantic.'

She pressed her mouth to mine, forcing me to sigh, the way I always did when she kissed me. When we broke apart, Casey said, 'You know, people always think Paris is the most romantic European city, but I think it's Berlin. It has this understated romantic coolness, yeah?'

'Uh-huh.' I brushed my nose against her neck and inhaled her scent – fresh and earthy from the cedarwood shower gel she used. 'You believe in love and romance, then?'

'Totally.'

My heart swelled. We hadn't talked about the intensity of what had passed between us since we met, but the way Casey pressed her ear to my chest and told me that our hearts beat to the same rhythm had to mean she felt the same. Still, I wanted to hear her voice it. 'What happens next?' I asked.

She slid her hand across my waist, her fingertips grazing the bare skin between my T-shirt and jeans. 'We go to your room.'

'I don't mean now. I mean after semester finishes. You go back to London. I go back to Melbourne...'

'Fuck, Holly,' Casey said with a laugh. 'We only met a couple of weeks ago.'

The sting in my chest was hard to ignore. 'And it's been the most incredible two weeks I've ever experienced.' Not that I'd experienced many relationships in my twenty years – sex a few times with a male classmate in year eleven, a brief relationship with a woman in my first year at university, and a healthy amount of pashing and fumbling here and there over the years. 'I can't be imagining this between us,' I said, slipping my hand up the back of her shirt and running my palm over her soft skin. 'It's too real, like the women in the painting.'

Casey considered me for a long moment, then said, 'You're not imagining it.'

Relief coursed through me. 'Maybe I could go to London after the semester finishes? I have a British passport and family in London. They're in Wanstead, too. You said that's near you.'

She sat up, a flash of irritation sparking in her eyes. 'Whoa, Holly. And drop out of university?'

'I can apply to a London uni – get credit for what I've already done.'

'And pay stupidly high international fees?'

'I'll pay domestic fees with my citizenship. I don't care about that – I'll get a student loan or something.'

'You can't leave Australia and get yourself into debt for me. That's huge. And what about your family? Your friends?'

I shrugged. 'I'll miss them. But we'll have each other.'

Casey shook her head. 'I can't make promises about the future like that.'

I fell silent, blinking to hold back tears.

She gave a remorseful groan and grabbed my hand. 'I didn't mean for that to sound so blunt. Please don't get upset.'

'I'm not asking you to make promises,' I said quietly.

The light breeze blew a strand of hair across my face and she gently brushed it away, letting her fingertips linger on my cheek. 'I think we should just enjoy the moment, yeah?'

'But what if we lost one another right now? In this huge city?'

She lay back and pulled me down with her. 'I know where you live.'

I sat up. 'I don't know where *you* live.'

'I told you. I'm staying with my aunty.' Her face softened. 'We do have each other's phone numbers.'

'Okay, but what about other ways to contact you? You're not even on social media.'

'Because I've got a shitty temporary phone and a shitty laptop – it's a hassle. Can't we just call each other?'

I stretched out beside her and fiddled with the sleeve of her T-shirt. 'But what if one of us loses our phone or something?'

'Then I'll sit by your door until you turn up.'

I searched her face, looking for signs that she meant what she said. It was unreadable, so I dug for more. 'What's your last name?'

Casey nuzzled my neck. 'If I tell you, it takes away from the mystery and romance of this amazing time we're having.'

I pulled away, narrowing my eyes at her. 'Seriously? You won't even tell me your last name? I told you mine the first day we met.'

Her brow creased, as though she was trying to recall that conversation. 'Right. Mine is ... Vassell.'

'Vassell,' I repeated.

'Mmhmm.'

'Spell it.'

She gave an exasperated huff. 'V-A-double-S-E-double-L. Okay? Can I snog you now?'

'See, that wasn't so hard.' I shuffled closer. 'And yes, you can snog me now.' Her lips pressed against mine, sweet and warm, making all my worries melt away.

When we stopped for air, I laid my head on her chest. 'Sorry. That was too much. I just ... I haven't felt like this before.'

There was a long silence, and I was about to ask if she was okay when she said, 'I tell you what. If we lose each other, then we'll come back to this spot, on this day, at this time, every year until we find each other.'

'Right here, under this tree?'

Casey nodded, peeked at her watch, then closed her eyes, a band of sunlight falling across her face. 'Yeah, 6 pm under this tree.'

'But this park is huge; you won't remember what tree.'

Her eyelids slowly opened. 'Big tree right in the middle of this grassy area.' She sat up and pointed towards the river. 'The Bode Museum is there.' She shifted her arm to the left. 'The Berliner Fernsehturm is there.' She twisted behind her. 'The fountain is there.' Then she waved her hand in the distance. 'And the Alte Nationalgalerie, where I met the prettiest girl I've ever seen, is over there. I'll remember. This spot. On this day. At this time.'

The idea that either of us could travel to Berlin every year was unrealistic, I knew, but the fact that Casey had even suggested it made me weak. 'That is the most romantic thing anyone has ever said to me.'

She shrugged and lay back down. 'It's the Berlin air. Has that effect on me.'

I ran my finger down her torso, stopping at the waistband of her jeans. 'I thought it was the effect I had on you.'

'It's *defo* you. See – I even sound Australian now.' She smiled, but her eyes didn't glisten like they normally did.

I jumped up and pulled her to her feet, eager for us to be alone and carefree again. 'Let's go.'

We left the park and took the S-Bahn four stops to my dorm room. Although Casey stayed close to me on the journey, she was quiet, and the regret for coming on so strong sat heavy in my gut.

Inside my room, I dumped the pizza we'd picked up on my tiny desk and tugged her down onto the bed, holding her close. 'Are we okay?' I asked, running my hand through her short curls.

She nodded.

'I didn't mean to say all that stuff. I don't know why I did.'

Casey reached for the small silver H that hung around my neck and pressed it between her fingers. 'I do care about you, Holly.'

The 'but' that hung in the air was deafening, and I scrambled for something, anything, to say to shift the focus from the pressure I put on her. 'You seem worried. Is it that exam next week?'

Her brows furrowed. 'Exam?'

'That renaissance art exam. You said you haven't studied for it.'

'Oh, that. I'm a bit stressed about it, yeah.'

'Okay, well, you should study then. I can leave you alone,' I said, rolling away.

She pulled me back to her. 'Not now. Can we just be together tonight?'

I kissed her in response, long and deep, delighting in her soft sighs and warm hands on my skin. We took our time removing each other's clothes until our naked bodies were fused together, silky skin, gentle fingers, hot tongues, and just when I thought my heart couldn't hold any more affection for her, her tenderness made my chest ache in a way it never had before.

After our heart rates had slowed and we'd untangled, we ate, shared a beer and smoked a joint on the balcony. Then I set up my tripod.

'We having a photo shoot?' Casey asked, draped against the pillow dressed in underwear and one of my singlets.

'I need to practise low-light shots.'

I turned off the overhead light and angled the lamp on my desk so that a gentle buttery glow shone over my bed, then set a low ISO and a wide aperture. I adjusted the lens using Casey as the focal point, set the timer and jumped back in bed. We lay on our sides gazing at each other as the camera snapped a series of shots. Her face carried an intensity I hadn't witnessed before, and in the dim light I could see the tiny cinnamon flecks that marked her dark brown eyes. I set the timer again. This time, Casey kissed me softly, holding my face close to hers.

I scrambled off the bed to check the photos and gasped. What I wanted to see was there – our connection, solid and electric, evidence it was real and captured forever. 'What do you think?' I asked, passing Casey the camera. 'I'll edit and fix the exposure, but they're good.'

Casey stared at the digital image for a long moment before thrusting the camera back to me. 'They're ... um ... they're nice. I-I like what you did with the lighting.'

I took the camera from her and tried to meet her eyes but she turned away. 'We look good, too. Together, I mean.'

She nodded.

'Casey, please look at me.'

She slowly turned, her eyes misty.

'Are you crying?'

She kissed my forehead. 'They're beautiful photos. I just get emotional over art sometimes.'

I tossed my camera to the side and clung to her, desperate to wind back the clock so that our conversation in the park never existed. 'The London thing was too much. I won't make any plans. I can't imagine saying goodbye to you, that's all.'

She didn't respond, just buried her face in my neck and held me tight.

The next morning, the quiet click of a door woke me. I stretched and reached for Casey, but my eyes shot open when I felt an empty space. 'Casey?' I hopped out of bed and checked the bathroom. Empty. I grabbed my phone from the desk. No calls or messages. I opened the door to the small balcony. Nothing. I leant over the iron balustrade and spotted a thin figure with short, black hair rushing along the concrete path below. 'Casey?'

She stopped and peered up.

'Where are you going?'

She pulled her phone from her hoodie pocket, tapped the screen and looked back up, a pained expression on her face.

My phone buzzed and I quickly opened the message.

Sorry xx

My blood ran cold. 'Wait!'

But Casey turned and ran.

Chapter 2
Casey, London
Eleven years later

I lean against a department store pillar and check my work emails while Eva drums her glossy, manicured nails on the shelf of a display unit.

'I can't decide,' Eva says to Dante, the wedding planner. 'I love the decanter, but we'd probably get more use out of the glasses. We should use our gifts, right?'

'Oh, absolutely,' Dante says. I glance up from my phone as Dante picks up a tumbler, examines it and says, 'And these are gorgeous. Look at the detail in the crystal.'

'Hmm,' Eva says, tapping a fingertip against her bottom lip. 'But that decanter...'

This back-and-forth has lasted for at least five minutes and if I'm ever going to get back to work today, it needs to end. 'What the fuck are we going to use a decanter for, Eva?' I say.

Dante clears their throat and replaces the glass.

Eva faces me, a faint scowl marking her brow. 'It would be a wedding gift, Casey. Something nice to have. It's a Louis the Thirteenth from France.'

I smirk at the retort that's popped into my head and can't

resist voicing it. 'Well, I hope he blew the fucking glass himself for that price.'

Eva's scowl deepens. 'Do you have to swear in the middle of Selfridges?' Her plummy accent has become more pronounced.

I narrow my eyes at her. She knows I hate the little digs that serve as a reminder she's a step above me in the society food chain – or thinks she is. But then I check myself; maybe I'm overreacting. I have been a mardy cow today. I give a conciliatory sigh and push myself off the pillar. 'Sorry. Work is full-on at the minute. My head's a mess. Do you want the decanter?'

'Not if you don't,' she says exasperated, and shifts her attention back to Dante. 'We'll go for the glasses.'

My eyes widen when I clock the price tag of said glasses. 'They're over two thousand quid!'

Eva turns back to me, one dark eyebrow raised. 'They're Waterford crystal. What do you expect?'

'I expect our wedding guests to have affordable options.' I soften my tone. 'You know my friends and family can't afford anything like that, and even if they could I wouldn't want them to spend it.'

She sniffs. 'Well, these will be the gifts for *my* guests to buy then. If I can't have the decanter, I want the glasses.'

Dante's eyes dart between us, finger poised over their iPad. 'We're going for the glasses?'

I stare at Eva, dumbfounded that she can be so dismissive of my concerns. I shake my head and return to my emails. 'I guess.'

'Do you want this cutlery set on the gift registry?' Eva asks me.

'Sure,' I say, typing out a reply to an email on my phone.

'Casey! Will you please stop working. This is important.'

I hit send, slip my phone into my trouser pocket and peer

down at gold-plated stainless-steel cutlery. 'Isn't normal stainless steel good enough?'

Eva places her hands on her hips, green eyes blazing, while Dante glances around the shop floor awkwardly.

'I'll take that look as a no,' I say. 'Then, yes. Put them on. They're nice.' An image forms in my head of the two of us years from now, sitting across from each other, eating with our gold cutlery, silent and miserable, and a heaviness lodges in my chest.

'Gold-plated cutlery...' Dante murmurs as they tap their screen. 'Splendid. That's the gift list done.' They slip the iPad into a leather satchel. 'I've got to dash to another client, sweetie, but we'll catch up on the weekend to go over the menu and table settings.'

'Thanks, Dante,' Eva coos. 'Oh, does that homewares company still want us to do a paid partnership on Insta for the reception?'

I inwardly groan at the idea of our wedding being splashed all over Instagram. I only agreed to it because the reception is going to be in the art gallery where I work. Not only did I love the idea of being surrounded by art while we ate and danced, I thought it would be a good opportunity for gallery exposure.

'I think so,' Dante says. 'I'll confirm tomorrow. See you both soon.' They kiss Eva, then me on both cheeks and scurry off through the maze that is the lower ground floor.

Eva shoots me a glare, snatches up her handbag and struts off, her short dress swaying.

'Eva, wait,' I say. 'Why are you storming off?'

'Oh, let's see...' The low heels of her strappy summer sandals click on the hard floor. 'Maybe because I'm organising this entire wedding myself.'

Because you *wanted to get married.* The thought bursts into my head, but thankfully I'm a think-before-you-speak kind of person. 'I'm here, aren't I?'

'Physically, yes. But you argue every point and then leave it all up to me. We're getting married in seven weeks and you don't even have a wedding outfit!'

I shrug. 'I'm wearing a suit. I have a wardrobe full of them.'

She steps onto the ascending escalator and makes a face at me. 'You can't wear a work suit to your own wedding.'

'Why not?' I hop onto the step behind her. 'They're good quality, expensive suits.'

She grunts and throws her hands up.

'Okay, okay. I'll buy a new suit.'

'When?'

'Um ... at the weekend? I'll sort it with Jaz now so she can help me.' I pull out my phone and tap out a message.

> Help me find a wedding outfit this weekend?

Three dots appear, followed by a string of eyeroll emojis.

'Was that Jaz?' Eva asks. 'What did she say?'

I slip the phone into my pocket. 'Yeah. She's dead excited about it. We good now?'

We step off the escalator and Eva's face softens. I take her hand. The large solitaire diamond of her engagement ring shimmers under the downlights. 'Besides, you're all over this wedding stuff, and you've got that side biz going on with your influencer thing. I'll just mess everything up.'

She pouts as she fiddles with my belt buckle. 'Well, that's true, I suppose.'

I give her the sexy smile and sultry eyes that win her over every time.

She tuts but stretches up to kiss me. 'You only get away with this because you're so hot, you know that?'

My smile widens; I absolutely know that.

'Have lunch and a glass of champagne with me at the oyster bar?'

I raise my brows. 'Champagne and oysters? I have to be back at work in half an hour. A sarnie and coffee will do.'

She huffs a defeated sigh. 'Fine.'

We stroll into the bustling Selfridges Foodhall. It's noisy with chatter and customer exchanges, and the scent is coffee, sweetness and spice. We wander past counters brimming with luscious cakes and glossy pastries, deli meats and cheeses, and vibrant displays of fruits and vegetables. Eva stops at the chiller cabinet and I head for the small café by the exit to order a Reuben sandwich and a latte.

With my order in hand, I grab two free seats by the window overlooking Orchard Street and give Eva a wave. By the time she sits, I'm already biting into my sandwich and moaning as the warm, salty beef mingles with the tangy sauerkraut and nutty cheese. 'These sarnies are the best,' I mumble through my mouthful.

Eva picks at her salmon buddha bowl. 'Oysters and champagne would've been nicer.'

'Nicer than a Reuben? Are you for real?' I take another huge bite.

She rolls her eyes, jabbing her fork through a piece of salmon, and I gaze at the flurry of pedestrians passing by while I chew. A woman with honey-coloured hair falling loose around her shoulders stops in front of the window. I feel a wave of nostalgia as I scan her body, take in her clothing, the way she moves, searching for something familiar.

'What are you thinking about?' Eva asks.

I take another bite and home in on the woman's face.

'Casey!'

I twist in my seat and gulp down my mouthful. 'Sorry. Work. I was thinking about work.'

Eva sips her sparkling water and eyes me thoughtfully. 'You work too hard.'

'That's because I'm curating exhibitions in two countries.'

'Well,' she says, running her hand up my thigh. 'There will be zero working when we're on our honeymoon.'

'None?' I say, only half-joking.

She leans closer with a coquettish smile. 'None. Because we'll be too busy doing honeymoon things.'

I lick a drop of Reuben sauce from the crust. 'Drinking cocktails and smoking loads of weed?'

She sits back and scrunches her face. 'You are not taking weed to Bora Bora.' She resumes the flirty smile. 'I meant *other* honeymoon things.'

I swallow the last bite and wipe my hands on a napkin. 'We shaggin' every minute of every day for two solid weeks? We can do that in our flat here.'

She huffs and fixes me with a deadpan expression. 'Yes, we're shagging every minute of every day for two solid weeks. That's what newly married couples do. And they do it in a location that's not their home.'

I grin. 'You're so easy to wind up. Okay. No weed and no working on honeymoon. But it goes both ways — no constant social media updates either.'

'Babe. Influencers don't get paid holiday leave. My job is twenty-four seven.' She clicks her fingers rapidly as though that correlates with the pace of her online presence. 'I'm always on the pulse.'

'I'm sure you won't lose all your followers if you don't post for a few days.' I finish my coffee and glance at my watch. 'I really need to go. See you at home tonight, yeah?' I lean forward to kiss her goodbye, but she places a hand against my chest.

'No, not at home. We've got the cake tasting, remember?'

I groan. 'Fuck, Eva. I've got to finish a funding application today. I probably won't even leave work until seven.'

'I know. That's why I made it for seven-thirty and in Soho, so it's close to the gallery.'

My shoulders slump. 'I'll be exhausted and hungry and I don't want cake for dinner.'

She pouts and walks her fingertips up the inside of my thigh, stopping a centimetre from my crotch. 'It won't take long. I've already narrowed it down to seven cakes, and then we can go home and' – her eyes flick downward then back up to my face – 'have an early night.'

I clear my throat and peer about, my face warm. 'Fine. Text me the address. I really need to go.'

'Go on, then. I have to get home to do a live feed of some new make-up I'm trialling.'

I give her a quick peck and exit the heavy glass doors, waving at her through the window as I pass, but she's busy snapping a photo of a new gold bracelet that appeared on her wrist this morning. I merge with the throng of people heading towards Oxford Street. It's mid-August and the crowds are lapping up the warm weather in their T-shirts, shorts and summer dresses as they amble along the wide footpaths and stroll in and out of shops. I jump on the number 139 bus and pull out my phone to message Jaz.

> Wedding doing my head in.

Not only is Jaz my best mate, she's the only person I've been honest with regarding my conflicting feelings about Eva and marriage. Feelings that began as a tiny spark of uncertainty a few months ago, but as the date has drawn closer, have quickly gathered oxygen and ignited a fire that's hard to ignore.

Eva and I had only been going out a year and living together for a month when she proposed at our housewarming party. And because Eva always needs an audience, she popped the question in front of the forty people spilling out from our kitchen into the tiny garden and live streamed it to her 100,000 Instagram followers. It was a mild May evening, and I had a nice buzz from hours of drinking. I was in the garden chatting with friends when Eva appeared in front of me, her cheeks flushed from the champagne.

'Hello,' she said, slipping her arms around my waist and kissing me.

I let our mouths linger before asking, 'Having fun?'

'Mmhmm.' She swayed a little as she gazed up at me. 'I really love you.'

I kissed her again. 'Love you, too.'

'We get on well living together, don't you think?'

My mind quickly recalled the two barneys we'd had since we'd moved in, but it had mostly been good, so I said, 'It's only been a month, but yeah, we do.'

'It feels right, though, doesn't it?' Eva loosened her grip on my waist and reached for my free hand.

'You okay?' I asked. 'Are you drunk?'

'A little bit...' She glanced at her friend Leila and gave a quick nod. Leila held her phone up, directing it at us.

My eyes darted between them, suddenly very sober.

'Casey, the year we spent together' – Eva's voice rose and a hush fell among our guests – 'before moving in together was one of my best.'

I sought out Jaz and spotted her by the kitchen door, eyes wide, mouth hanging open. When she caught my eye, she mouthed, 'What the fuck?'

Eva looked up at me, eyebrows raised expectantly.

I took a swig of lager before I replied. 'Um ... good. It's been fun. I mean, it's been a good year for me, too.'

She beamed. 'I didn't think we could get better, but waking up beside you every morning has made me love you more.'

The arguments, I wanted to say, *what about the arguments?*

Eva dropped to one knee and a collective gasp rippled around the garden while panic rippled through my body. 'Marry me? I don't have a ring because you're not a ring person, but if you want one...'

My mouth opened and closed but no words emerged. The romantic garden decorations suddenly made sense – fairy lights, torch lanterns, glittery champagne flutes. I became aware of the piercing silence and Leila still pointing her phone at us. I helped Eva stand and whispered in her ear, 'Is Leila recording this?'

'I'm live streaming it,' she whispered back.

I stared at her, hoping the shock wasn't splashed all over my face. Her eyes flashed with panic, her cheeks grew red, and I crumbled. I forced a smile and said, 'Of course I will.'

Eva squealed and threw her arms around me. The party erupted with cheers and whoops and the pop of champagne bottles. From the back door, Jaz winced at me, but who could say no in that situation? The following day, Eva was so caught up in the romance of it all that she swept me along with her, suggesting we hold the wedding reception at an art gallery – just for me – and I told myself that maybe it wasn't all bad. We loved each other, so why not?

The days became weeks and weeks became months, and now here I am, getting married in seven weeks, a permanent knot in my gut and the thought of admitting that maybe, just maybe, I should've said no, makes my throat seize. Because, what do I say without destroying her? *Sorry, Eva, I didn't want to upset you on the night because I love you and getting married is important to you, but it's not important to me, and I should've said no and I'm sorry I didn't, but let's call off the wedding and see if we can still have a relationship.*

No, that won't do. I shake my head, disappointed in myself, and jump up ready for my stop. I hop off the bus and head along Regent Street until I reach the side street that houses my gallery. My phone pings with a reply from Jaz.

It's getting serious now mate. We need to debrief. Meet you Friday after work. Put on your dancing shoes.

Chapter 3
Holly, Melbourne

I dish up the last of the vegetables and carry the plates to the dining table. 'Dinner's ready,' I shout.

'Right,' Tom shouts back from somewhere in the house.

I grind salt and pepper over my food and let a few seconds pass before yelling again. 'Tom! It's getting cold!'

'Okay,' he says behind me. 'Calm down.'

My lips press into a tight line and I release a long, tired sigh through my nose.

'It's boiling in here, Hols.' He taps the digital panel on the wall that operates the heating.

'It's pleasant in here and freezing outside.'

'We don't need it on twenty-four degrees. Keep it on twenty. It's the ideal temperature for cost efficiency.'

Tom sits opposite and I glare at him, not only for telling me to calm down but for schooling me on the heating every night.

'Here I am. Panic over,' he says.

'There's no panic. I've made us a lovely meal, and it would be nice if you appreciated it and came when I called you.'

His lips twitch – his standard response when he thinks I'm

overreacting. 'You know I appreciate it. Smells great,' he says, zigzagging gravy over his dinner.

I wait for a thank you, but he cuts through the chicken breast and shoves a chunk in his mouth. There's a sting in my chest that he can't voice his appreciation with two simple words, but last week's argument about dinner is still fresh in my mind, so I quickly take a bite, not trusting myself to speak.

Once he swallows, he asks, 'How was your day? Work busier?'

I nudge the carrots with my fork. 'It's quiet, but a new project will come in soon.' My workload has steadily decreased over the past few months, and rapidly decreased in the past few weeks, but I don't want to worry Tom. He frets if I buy the expensive milk; he won't cope if he thinks my job is at risk.

'Isn't your campus planning a revamp of the Swanston Street building? That will go to your department, won't it?'

I work for the Melbourne University of Technology as a project manager, and that revamp *has* been given to my department, except it's gone to the newly formed team that focuses on buildings and physical spaces. A team I'm not part of because I didn't apply for one of the new roles, despite my manager urging me to do so.

I nod and take a mouthful. 'Mmhmm.'

Satisfied with that response, Tom scoops a mix of potato and peas into his mouth and chews while his eyes drift from his meal to me and back to his plate. I watch him, waiting for the date to register, or for him to question why we're having a roast on a Wednesday night, but his face is blank. I take another bite and give him a moment longer, but the only sounds are the clink of cutlery against crockery, the gentle hum of the ducted heating blowing through the vents and the noise of my own chewing.

I relent. 'Anything you want to say to me?'

A flicker of surprise crosses his face, like he's just realised I'm in the room. 'Um ... this is nice?'

I stare at him, my fork carrying a bite of roast potato paused in mid-air.

He continues eating, watching me with a creased brow.

'You don't want to say, "Happy anniversary"?' I ask, my tone tart.

His eyes widen. He places the cutlery down and dabs his mouth with a napkin. 'It's our anniversary?'

I nod, dropping my fork and gulping down some water, like it will diffuse my rising body temperature.

'Shit, Holly. I'm sorry.' He reaches across the table for my hand. 'You know I'm no good with that sort of thing. Why didn't you remind me?'

Because the date should be scorched into your memory. You should message me all day about how much you love me and come home with flowers or wine or chocolates or puppies, just fucking something.

'I thought you might have remembered,' I say.

He adjusts his glasses and hangs his head. 'I'm sorry. Happy anniversary.'

I retract my hand. 'Do you even know how many years?'

He gives a short laugh. 'Course I do. Two...' His eyes dart around the kitchen as he searches that part of his brain I call his relationship black hole. It's where everything about us being together falls, never to be seen again. 'Yeah, two ... *incredible* years.'

My jaw tightens. 'Three. We've been together three years, Tom.'

He scrunches his face, the lines around his eyes deepening. 'You sure? Feels like we just met. Well, it's been a great three years, hasn't it?'

I frown.

He reaches for my hand again, but I pull it back. 'I really am sorry. I'm terrible with dates, but you know how much I love you.'

I do know that. And he has been stupidly busy at work lately, so he's more forgetful than usual.

'You want me to make it up to you?' he continues. 'Maybe ... an early night?' He winks, or tries to wink, but he's one of those people whose eyelids lack the coordination and it presents as a blink.

I inwardly groan. A ten-minute poke that leaves me frustrated and him satisfied is not how I want to be appreciated tonight. I pat his hand and give a conciliatory smile. 'How about you buy me some nice chocolates from that place near your office tomorrow, hey?'

He grins and mops up the last of his dinner. 'I can do that. Just send me a text to remind me before I leave work.'

I huff and shake my head, but it's lost on him because his head is tipped back, draining his glass of water.

He places the glass on the table. 'So, Jack's back tomorrow,' he says, nerves coating his words.

Jack is Tom's son, who's started living with us every second week since Tom's ex-wife decided that he needed to parent more. Prior to the new arrangement, I'd met Jack a total of five times and struggled to get a hello from him.

I carry my plate to the sink. 'How do you feel about that?'

Tom follows and puts his dish on the side. 'Looking forward to seeing him, but a bit worried how it will go. Glad you're with me for this. Don't think I'm very good at handling an eight-year-old.'

'I'm not either,' I say, rinsing the dishes and placing them in the dishwasher. 'Jack is definitely not a fan of mine.'

'Not at all. He's a kid. He likes you.'

'He's going to need to like me a whole lot more if this living arrangement continues.'

'He'll come round.' Tom gives my shoulder a gentle squeeze. 'Thanks for dinner. It was lovely. And happy anniversary.' He pecks my cheek and points towards the lounge room. 'Do you mind if I watch *The 7.30 Report*? The treasurer's on tonight talking about the national debt. I don't want to miss it.'

I glance at the pile of dishes and the leftover food scattered across the bench.

'Leave all that,' he says. 'I'll tidy it up later.'

'It's easier to do it now and I was going to...' But he's already walking away. 'Go for a shower,' I murmur to his retreating back. My hand tightens around the dirty cutlery. That thread of patience holding me together is about to break. I go to call him back but decide against it because he'll stack the dishwasher wrong and won't pack the leftovers properly. And to be fair to him, he started work at seven, whereas I didn't go in until ten, left at four and had a two-hour lunch break.

Once the kitchen is clean, I head down the hallway, the soles of my slippers scuffing the floorboards, and retreat to the bathroom. I switch on the ceiling heat lamp and run the hot water, then peel off my dress, thick tights and underwear and pile my hair on top of my head. When steam starts to fill the shower recess, I step in and tip my head forward, letting the warm flow massage my neck and shoulders.

The non-event that was our anniversary sits sour under my skin. But I'm not sure what I expected – for Tom to suddenly be this person he isn't and never will be? It's not his fault he's forgetful, and partners always take each other for granted now and then.

I run the soap over my thighs.

Maybe I was too hasty turning down that early night. I was

hoping for more than dinner tonight, and the sex isn't awful, not at all. It doesn't blow my brain apart, but I'm not always left frustrated either. Besides, who's having brain-blowing sex when they've been together for years? At least he tries to give me an orgasm.

I grab the scrubbing brush and vigorously wash my back.

Maybe he'd make more of an effort tonight – I could even get some oral. The reality of that thought registers. *Unlikely.* Unless I ask, and there is no way I'll ask. He knows I like it so he should just do it. But he's not really a going-down type of guy. I guessed that the moment I met him, with his glasses, smart-casual clothing, clean-shaven skin and practical haircut. Not that how he looked was the sole reason. It was that combined with something missing in his hazel eyes. They were kind and loving, but they lacked fire, passion, a desire to devour me.

'Get over it, Holly,' I mutter and turn off the taps. I can't choose a life partner based on their ability or willingness to devour me. I step onto the soft bathmat and dry myself under the warmth of the heat lamp, then slather my skin with an almond milk body butter. I swipe my hand through the mirror steam, let down my hair to run a brush through it and wrap the towel around me.

When I walk into the lounge, Tom's gaze shifts from the TV. 'Better?'

'Mmhmm.' I hold out my hand. 'Maybe I'll take you up on that early night.'

He grins and clicks the remote. 'Rightio, then. I'll just put that on pause for ten.'

Chapter 4
Holly, Melbourne

I unwrap my scarf, shrug off my coat and walk the wide, carpeted corridor of the care home to the lounge area. Mum and my brother are seated on the far side of the room by the fireplace. I weave through the recliners and couches, offering hellos to the residents who smile up at me.

'Hey, Hols,' Adam says with a tired smile and weary eyes.

'You okay?' I give his shoulder a rub, dump my bag on the floor and take the free chair on the other side of Mum.

'Yeah. Long day.' He gestures to the fire. 'And that's putting me to sleep.'

I lean down to kiss Mum's cheek and breathe in the familiar rose scent of her face moisturiser. 'Hi, Mum.'

'Hello...' Confusion skates across her pale blue eyes. 'Erm...'

'Hol—'

'I know your name,' she says, her voice tinged with irritation.

My eyes cut to Adam and he replies with a worried frown.

'Holly.' Mum places her hand on my cheek, soft and warm

against my skin. 'Sorry, my lovely girl. It's Holly,' she says, her English accent still strong even after forty years in Australia.

I give her a reassuring smile. 'That's right.'

'Ooh, you're cold,' she says, letting her hand linger on my cheek.

'Uh-huh. It's icy out there and I walked from the tram.'

'The nearest tram's a good fifteen-minute walk,' Adam says. 'Why didn't you call me to pick you up?'

I shrug. 'Felt like a walk.' I turn to Mum. 'It's cosy in here, though. The fire's nice.'

'It's okay.' She glances furtively around the room and lowers her voice. 'It would be better if everyone wasn't so old.'

Adam and I exchange a bemused look.

'I reckon a lot of them are around your age, Mum,' Adam says.

Her eyes widen. 'They aren't!'

'That's why we chose this place,' I say. 'So you'd be with people around the same age.'

'I don't even know how old I am these days. I started forgetting that even before' – she points to her head – 'I started forgetting.'

I grin. 'You're only sixty-seven, Mum.'

Her eyes widen again. 'Only? Well, who wants to remember that?' She pats Adam's knee. 'Now, how's your little one getting on at school?'

As Adam tells Mum about his youngest son, I take in the other residents, wondering how they came to be here and whether any of them have similar stories to Mum. We moved her in about three weeks ago but she'd been struggling on her own for months, her short-term memory slowly deteriorating over the years. Possibly the consequence of a stroke she'd had after Dad died, according to her doctor. Eventually diagnosed with vascular dementia and the early stages of Alzheimer's, she refused to leave her home or to accept that she needed more care, until – all in one day – she left the gas burning on the stove, the iron switched on and the front door unlocked overnight.

Adam stands. 'I need to get going. Walk me to the car, Hols?' He bends down and kisses Mum on the cheek. 'I'll see you soon.'

'Okay, love. I'd like to see my grandsons, too.'

'You will when you come to my place for lunch on the weekend. How does that sound?'

She beams. 'Splendid.'

I grab my coat. 'I'll be back in a couple of minutes, Mum.'

'I'll stay here by the fire,' she says, picking up a magazine from the table by her side.

Adam and I navigate our way through the lounge and back along the brightly lit corridor.

'Have you spoken to any of the staff today?' I ask.

Adam nods. 'About an hour ago. They said Mum hasn't eaten much the past couple of days. They think she's had a bit of gastro, but thought she seemed brighter today.'

I tug on my coat before Adam opens the door and the cold wind hits me.

'You think she's getting worse?' Adam asks, zipping up his jacket and slipping on his beanie. His blue-grey eyes are fatigued and heavy, and the harsh lights above the entrance make the lines around his eyes more prominent. He's only four years older than me, but running his own construction company, looking after two young sons, worrying about Mum and dealing with his youngest child's learning difficulties are all aging him fast.

I tuck my hands into my pockets. 'I don't think she's any different than when we brought her here. She still remembers us – it's just our names she's struggling with.'

The unspoken fear of how long it'll be before she forgets us completely hangs in the air, but we've had that conversation countless times and it drains us both.

'How are you, anyway?' Adam says. 'Things any better with Tom?'

I release a heavy sigh and the cold air vapour swirls between us. 'We're okay. We haven't argued for a week, so that's something. Jack's back with us tonight.'

He grimaces. 'I take it he's not warming up to you?'

'Nope.'

'It's a big change for him. He'll come round. How's work?'

Adam always does this – he feels guilty for not contacting me so he squeezes all his questions in at once. 'Boring. Everything is going to the new team.'

'Maybe time to look for a new job? You've been there ages.'

'Kind of like it there. When I've got work to do, that is.' I shrug. 'This has happened before. It'll pick up soon. Anyway, you've got enough going on without worrying about my job and relationship.'

He smiles and ruffles my hair. 'Always worry about my little sister.' He gestures to his car. 'Better get going. Meg's just home from work and I've got to help with dinner and the kids.'

I hug him goodbye. 'Tell them hi from me. See you on the weekend.'

He jogs over to his car and jumps in, waving as he drives off.

I hurry back to the lounge and spot Mum heading for the dining area. I collect my belongings and catch up.

She brightens when I appear beside her. 'Hello, you're back.'

'I am,' I say, pleased she's recalled that I was just with her. 'Where are you going?'

'We're being rounded up for dinner, like cattle in a

paddock. Someone will probably give me a prod if I don't get a move on.'

I laugh. 'I think you're safe from prodding, Mum.'

In the dining room, small round tables are dressed with fresh white tablecloths and centrepieces of mint-green vases filled with plastic flowers. A couple of wall-mounted televisions play the six o'clock news and staff members walk around with trolleys.

'I'll stick around so I can spend more time with you,' I say, pulling out a dining chair for her.

She sits and pulls herself closer to the table. 'I do like it when you visit.'

A staff member approaches and places a tray on the table. 'There you go, Elaine,' he says, lifting the silver cloche to reveal a bland-looking white meat covered with a drizzle of gravy, a sliver of crackling, a scoop of mashed potato and a medley of carrots, peas and beans.

When he walks away, I lean forward to take a closer look. 'Looks like roast pork.'

'Ugh,' Mum says. 'I don't want pork.'

'Aren't you hungry?' I unwrap the cloth napkin from around the cutlery and set the knife and fork by her plate.

'I want pie and mash.'

'Pie and mash?' I say, surprised.

'Yes. My dad brought a pie home every Saturday when he finished work and Mum would make the creamiest mashed potato and mushy peas. It was my favourite meal. He was a fishmonger, you know, at the Billingsgate Market.'

As her Alzheimer's has progressed, she's talked more and more about her past. I know she's referring to London, but I want her to latch onto a memory and keep talking. 'In London?'

Mum's eyes light up. 'That's right.'

I cut the meat for her since she doesn't appear inclined to

do it herself. 'You've told me about growing up there' – I pass her the fork – 'but I'd love to hear more.'

She takes a small bite of pork and chews slowly. 'Hmm, it's all a bit hazy now.'

'You remembered your dad and your favourite meal.'

Her brows rise. 'I did, didn't I?' She scoops in a spoonful of mashed potato, and after a few seconds she says, 'And it was nicer than this.' She reaches for the salt grinder.

As the salt crystals fall onto her food, I gently say, 'Mum, that's a lot of salt.'

She shoots me a glare. 'I like salt.'

'I know, it's just your risk of another stroke...'

She cuts me off with a wave of her hand. 'A bit of salt never hurt anyone. My parents lived until...' Her forehead creases. 'Well, I don't know, but they were old and had plenty of salt their entire lives.' Her words come fast – a sign she's getting distressed.

I rub her back. 'Sorry. I just worry.'

Her face softens. 'I know you do, but I feel okay.'

'That's good.' I'm eager to return to the topic of London, hoping it'll put her back in a nice place. 'You were telling me about growing up in London. I'd like to go back there.'

'Would you?'

I shift my gaze to the winter darkness outside the large windows. 'I'd like to find someone,' I add softly.

'Then why don't you?' Mum says matter-of-factly.

I face her and give a short laugh. Such a simple perspective. 'It's not that easy.'

'Isn't it?'

'I can't just up and leave. I have a job and a partner. And you.'

She points to herself. 'Me?'

'Yeah. I'd miss you.'

'Well, that's lovely of you, but don't worry about me.' She waves her fork around. 'I have all these people, and your brother and his family. You're far too young to spend your days sitting here with me.'

'I like being here with you, Mum.'

She pushes her half-finished dinner to the side and picks up the small bowl of apple pie and custard. She breaks off a piece and spoons it into her mouth. Her eyes soften as she chews, the way a baby's do when they taste something sweet for the first time. 'Who do you want to find?'

'Sorry?'

'You said you wanted to go to London to find someone.' She points her spoon at me, eyes narrowed. 'Some things I remember.'

That makes me smile. 'Do you remember when I went to Berlin for Study Abroad at uni?'

Her brows knit. 'Hmm, I think I do. It was for a semester in...' She stops eating and peers into the distance, deep concentration on her face, then shakes her head. 'No. It's gone.'

'It was my second year. Eleven years ago now.'

'Eleven? Goodness. Where has the time gone? Your father was so proud of you for doing that.' Her voice has turned wistful, and an ache expands in my chest at the mention of my dad. Not only do I miss him, but everything changed for Mum when he died.

'I know he was.' I pause in case she wants to talk more about Dad, but she takes a big bite of apple pie and looks at me expectantly, so I continue. 'I told you about that girl I met when I was there?'

She shrugs. 'Maybe.'

Mum holding me as I sobbed over the girl in Berlin is a vivid memory for me, but it would've faded into the background for her. 'She was from London and I've always wondered what happened to her.'

She keeps chewing, her eyebrows raised with interest.

'Not that I know how I'd find her. She's just always been in my head.' I pause. 'And my heart.'

'It sounds like you loved her.'

'Oh,' I say. 'I guess I did, in a way. As much as you can when you're twenty and have only known someone a short time.'

The spoon clinks against the side of the bowl as she chases the last of the custard. 'Well, I always said nothing worth having comes easy.'

I grin and shake my head at the random things her brain recalls. 'You did always say that.'

Chapter 5
Casey, London

Milky coffee spills from the spout of my takeaway cup as I burst through the gallery doors. It's Friday morning and I didn't get to bed until after midnight because Eva insisted that we finalise the reception seating arrangements, which meant her sorting it while I lazed on the sofa watching telly, giving 'uh-huh' and 'whatever you think' replies. Whenever I tried to sneak off to bed, she'd fetch me tea and chocolate hobnobs then massage my tense shoulders, and I'd cave and stay put.

'Oh, Casey, there you are,' Michaela says from behind the counter.

'Sorry I'm late,' I say, rushing past.

'Your ten-thirty's postponed,' she calls after me.

I walk back to the counter. 'You're jokin' me?'

Michaela shakes her head. 'She was struck by a sudden burst of creativity and couldn't ... hang on, I wrote it down.' She shuffles about the desk and holds up a Post-it. '"Break the flow of divine creativity", so she'll be here around two.'

I lower my voice so a couple on the far side of the gallery don't overhear. 'Fuck's sake. Again? This is the third time she's cancelled.'

'Postponed,' Michaela corrects me.

'And this divine flow's going to stop in time to get here for two from Sussex? Remind me why we want this artist?'

Michaela wrinkles her nose. 'Making waves in the art world with her fresh perspectives on social justice?'

I sigh. 'Right. I've got heaps of other stuff to do anyway, but I swear if she does this again she's out of the exhibition. We don't have time to be messed about.' I stride off across the gallery floor.

'And Josanne's looking for you!'

I acknowledge Michaela's comment with a wave and head for the staff access door in the far corner, swiping myself in. My office is a tiny, windowless room at the back of the gallery, but it means I don't have to squeeze into the open-plan area with four other people. It's painted a crisp white to give the illusion of space. On the wall to the left of my desk is a large oil painting of a pristine beach in the north of Jamaica, close to Montego Bay, where my paternal grandmother is from. A single palm tree leans towards the ocean, shading a section of sand. One of our regular artists, who specialises in depth perception, gifted it to the gallery after discovering she and my grandmother were from the same town. Whenever work is stressful, I lose myself in the translucent turquoise sea and pure white sands, imagining sun and salt on my skin, gazing up at the silky blue sky. It always calms me and puts everything into perspective.

I dump my bag, take a swig of coffee and fire up my laptop.

Within seconds, my boss strolls in. 'Morning, Casey.'

'Hiya, Josanne. Sorry if you were chasing me.'

She waves away my apology. 'No problem.' She sits and crosses her legs, smoothing her floral dress over her knees.

My eyes flick up from my screen, curious about why she's settling in.

'So, I know you've got a lot going on at the mo...'

'Not more work for today,' I groan.

'Not today, no. But I do need you to help out with the Berlin exhibition.'

'Berlin?' I lean back in my chair. 'I'm already helping.'

'I mean, more hands-on. As of this morning, they're down two staff with illness. Felix is in an absolute tizz trying to sort it on his own.'

'Well, I'll be there for the opening. S'pose I could go the night before.'

'You'd probably need to go earlier than that. Be there for a couple of days.' She pauses. 'A week, max.'

'Oh. You want me to go there to work?'

She fiddles with the bright pink beads hanging low on her chest. 'You helped curate it, so you're more across it than the rest of us.'

'Um...'

Her dark eyebrows draw together. 'I thought you'd jump at the opportunity. You normally like going over there.'

'I do. It's just that I need to crack on with our winter exhibition. The artists have to be firmed up in the next few weeks and—'

'Delaying a week won't hurt, and Michaela can help out in your absence.'

'It's, erm...' I search my brain for another excuse. 'It's the wedding. Eva's got us doing all sorts every night.'

The truth is I love the Berlin gallery, and the *Queer Perspectives* show we've curated is incredible, plus it'd be a chance to see my aunt and uncle, but Berlin in August has a strange effect on me. A couple of years before I met Eva, I went there in August and found myself sitting under that damn tree in Monbijoupark, as though doing so would magically throw me back in time and reverse my idiotic decision to cut ties with Holly. I ended up crying for an hour and breaking it off with my girlfriend at the time because my feelings for her didn't come close to what I felt for Holly. And right now, with all this confusion about Eva and the wedding, it's best I fly in, attend the opening and come straight home.

'Ah, the wedding, of course.' Josanne presses her lips together, her disappointment palpable.

'And it's my dad's birthday that week,' I quickly add. 'We always go to Carnival...'

She stands. 'Okay, well, I don't want to put pressure on you when you have a lot going on. You were my first choice because our Berlin gallery was the main reason you came to work here.'

I narrow my eyes at her because she's trying it on. '*One* of the reasons – you're the main reason.' I loved that this gallery had a Black female director who transformed it from a failing, stale art house to a thriving contemporary gallery that champions diversity in all forms, supports artists of colour and exhibits progressive works of art in all mediums. The fact that it had a collaboration with a Berlin gallery was a bonus.

She grins. 'Sucking up will get you very far in your career.'

I laugh.

'Have a think about it over the weekend. I don't want to ruin your dad's birthday if you have plans or get in the way of the wedding, but it would be good to send someone to help them out. You're the best person, but if you can't go, you can't go.'

Telling me to take the weekend to think about it is Josanne's way of saying she needs me to do this. What she's not saying is that I'm head of exhibitions, which means I sometimes need to fulfil that role in both galleries.

'Let me check what I've got on here for the next couple of weeks and chat to Eva and my dad. Let you know by Monday?'

She beams. 'You're a star. I knew you wouldn't let me down.'

'Oh, I haven't decided—'

But she's already left my office.

Chapter 6
Casey, London

The workday has finally ended and I've been looking forward to a bevvy with Jaz all week. I lock the gallery doors and cross the narrow street to the pub opposite. A light mist of rain falls, and despite the warm weather earlier in the week, the air carries a damp chill that signals summer will soon be gone. The wet tables outside are empty but inside it's crowded and noisy with an end-of-work-week buzz. In the far corner I spot Jaz's tight, black curls. She sticks her hand up then points to a full pint on the table in a 'I've got you sorted' way.

'Alll riiight,' she drawls as I reach her. Her dark eyes are framed by black liner, her lashes thick with mascara and her brown cheeks shimmer with a glittery blush.

'All right, Jazzy Jaz.' I take the seat opposite. 'You're all dolled up.'

She pouts, the overhead lighting making her glossy lips shine, and gives her curls a bounce. 'I like to look good on a Friday night.' She gestures to the glass in front of me with an upward nod. 'You sounded stressed, so I got your pint in.'

'Cheers, mate.' The crisp, cool ale slides down my throat as

I take a slow sip. 'Ah.' I place the glass down and slump against the back of the chair. 'I needed that. This week has been so fucked.'

Jaz shakes her head, her dangly gold hoop earrings swinging from side to side. 'You need to stop letting Eva run your life.'

'She's not.'

'She is. And you let her because…' Jaz leans forward, her eyes sparkly and mischievous. 'You're whipped by the pus-say.'

I screw up my face. 'What? Don't do that.'

She grins. 'Do what?'

'Say "pus-say" like you're some geezer from an eighties porno.'

She laughs, loud and unapologetic. 'I'm totally an eighties porno geezer.'

I laugh too, not because it's particularly funny, but because her laughter is infectious. Even the people at the next table look at us and chuckle. 'That you are,' I say. 'And I'm not whipped by anyone's vulva.'

Jaz shudders. 'Ugh. I hate that word. Sounds like you're about to jump in and go for a drive in the countryside. At least say vag.'

I smile. 'Okay, I'm not whipped by Eva's *vag*. It's just the wedding. There's a lot to do.'

'Fuck, mate. You still haven't told her you don't want to get married?'

'I can't. She'll be devastated if I call it off. She's like, really into it, excited about her dress, spent heaps of money.'

'You mean Mummy and Daddy have spent heaps of money.'

It's true that Eva's parents are paying for the wedding. I tried to dissuade them – Eva and I can afford a nice enough wedding – but they insisted. I shrug. 'That's what they want.'

'Still, I don't think they'll be too pleased when you get divorced in a year's time.'

I sip my pint. 'You're such a sceptic.'

A waitperson appears and places a large basket of chips and a silver pot filled with tomato sauce in the middle of our table.

'Cheers,' Jaz says. She dips a chip and points it at me, a blob of sauce landing on the wooden table. 'I'm a realist. And you're not in love. Divorce is inevitable.'

I reach across and wipe up her sauce mess with a napkin. 'I love her and getting married is important to her, so what's the problem?' I shove a few chips into my mouth and wait for the latest reason I shouldn't marry Eva.

'Yeah, you love her. That's different to being *in* love. And the problem is you're giving up the chance of being truly happy, finding the one.'

I ignore her and grab more chips. Jaz's eyes flit behind me and I turn to see a curvaceous body saunter past, accompanied by a flirty smile Jaz's way.

'They're probably my soul mate,' Jaz says, leaning towards me so I can hear her low voice over the crowd.

I wash down the chips with a gulp of ale. 'You'll have about ten soul mates tonight.'

Jaz laughs and picks up her glass. 'Totally. See what you're missing?'

'I'm not missing anything.' But as I say it an emptiness expands in my chest and I have the overwhelming sense that I am, in fact, missing something.

Jaz frowns, assessing me, no doubt picking up on the dip in my mood. She's intuitive like that. Although she's often brash and blunt, underneath is a soft centre filled with loyalty, and she just wants what's best for me.

'You know I love you and I'll be there no matter what,' she says. 'It just makes me sad because I don't think you're right for each other, and inside there' – she points to my heart – 'I think you know that, too.'

But I don't know that, not for certain. 'Why aren't we right?' My tone is defensive when I meant for it to be a genuine question. I soften my voice. 'Seriously, why aren't we?'

Jaz shovels in more chips and narrows her eyes at me as she chews. She takes a sip of wine, calmly places her glass on the table, her mouth curving into a wicked grin. 'Because she's not *her*.'

I groan and roll my eyes. 'You bangin' on about that again?'

A group by the bar become animated and Jaz raises her voice. 'Yeah, because you're getting married when you don't want to, and you've been in love with someone else for the past however long.'

I scrunch my face like it's the most ludicrous thing I've ever heard. 'Haven't.'

'Have.'

I shake my head and drink.

'Look me straight in the eye and tell me you haven't thought more about that Australian bird now that you're getting married.'

I dip a few chips into the sauce. 'Haven't thought about her in ages.'

'You're not looking at me.'

I jam them into my mouth and look her dead in the eyes.

'Now say it.'

'Eating,' I mumble.

She slaps the table. 'Ha. I fucking knew it.'

It's pointless trying to get one past her. I give a defeatist shrug. 'Course I've thought about her more. Getting married is scary, innit? It's like, bringing shit up.'

'You need to search for her harder online. Put your mind at ease. You'll never settle until you know what happened to her.'

'I've looked, mate. There are loads of Hollys in Melbourne and none I recognise. That's even if she's still in Melbourne, and I've no idea if I'd recognise her now anyway.' But that isn't entirely true because the vision of her has never left me. The Berlin summer sun highlighting the honey tones of her hair. Sharp blue-grey eyes, curious and intelligent. The tiny mole to the right of her nose. The freckle on her bottom lip. God, those lips – soft and sweet and delicious...

Jaz snaps her fingers in my face. 'Hello,' she singsongs. 'Where have you gone?'

I blink. 'Sorry. Just thinking.'

Jaz smiles slyly. 'About *Holly*?'

I shrug and take the last mouthful of my pint.

Jaz swirls a chip around the sauce pot. 'You think she's looked for you?'

I frown. 'Doubt it. Never told her much about myself and I gave her your last name. We had each other's German phone numbers and that was it.'

Jaz shakes her head. 'For someone so smart, you're really fucking stupid sometimes.'

'Give me a break. I was twenty and hadn't felt anything like that before. I didn't know how to handle it.'

'You're still fucking stupid when it comes to women.'

'I'm a Gemini; we avoid shit.'

Jaz rolls her eyes. 'You need to go back to Berlin.'

I throw my head back and let out a frustrated groan. This is why I didn't message her as soon as Josanne left my office. 'That's not going to help me find her.'

'Maybe she's there? Maybe she's been there this whole time, waiting for you.'

I raise my brows. 'What fairytale land do you live in?'

Jaz watches another curvy body stroll by and flashes a flirtatious smile. 'Queer fairytale land. And it is fab-u-lous.'

I laugh and reach across the table for a sip of her wine, since she got herself two drinks.

'Isn't the date coming up?' Jaz asks.

'What date?' I say, feigning ignorance.

'Don't pretend you don't know what I'm talking about. *The* date. You have to go to that park.'

'And you say *I'm* stupid? You think she's going to be sitting in a park waiting for me eleven years later?'

Jaz shrugs. 'Stranger things have happened. And last time you did that, it helped you sort what to do about whatshername – that one you dumped when you were there.'

'Bethany. And don't remind me; I still feel guilty about that.'

'Aren't you going to Berlin in a couple of weeks for the opening of the new exhibition anyway? You're head of exhibitions, go earlier.'

I sigh, knowing I can't keep it from her any longer. 'Josanne wants me to do that. Sick staff and Felix can't manage everything on his own.'

'No way!'

I frown. 'I don't think I want to go. I'm a bit stressed, with work and Eva. I'm confused about everything. Stick me in Berlin at this time of year ... it's a bit much, know what I mean? I'm worried I'll get there and something weird will come over me. I don't want to hurt Eva.'

Jaz gives a sympathetic smile that also tells me she knows to back off, although it won't last long. 'Yeah. I don't want you to hurt her either. I'm just messin' with you. Do what's right for you.' She necks her wine. 'Let's go to a queer bar. It's too straight in here.'

'Too straight? You've just eye-fucked two women.'

'I need more than an eye-fuck, mate.'

'How about I leave you to it and go home?'

'No!' she says. 'I need you to pull the fems for me.' She waggles her eyebrows. 'You know how much I love the fems.'

I grin. 'I do.'

'Fems love you,' Jaz continues. 'They don't go for me; I'm too pretty. I need you to reel them in with' – she waves her hand in my direction – 'this thing you got going on and those eyes – they love them eyes, mate. Then I snag 'em with my prettiness and patter, yeah?'

I can't help but laugh. 'Okay. Whatever makes you happy. Let's go before I change my mind.'

We weave through the pub crowd and head outside. The rain has eased and the grey sky from earlier has darkened. I zip up my jacket as we turn into Brewer Street, busy with Friday night revellers. A couple of women pass and one of them shamelessly runs her eyes over me before flashing me a coy smile.

I nod politely in return, and Jaz nudges me with her hip. 'That's what I'm talking about. I need you to help me get the pus-say.'

I tsk. 'Goodness gracious me.'

Jaz freezes on the footpath outside the bar we're about to enter, her mouth dropping open. 'I'm sorry, did you just tsk me and say "goodness gracious me"?'

I press my lips together to suppress the smile and wait for the bollocking coming my way.

'For fuck's sake, man,' Jaz says, fists on hips. 'Eva is sucking the life out of you.' She prods my chest. 'You get to your ma and da's this weekend and get some bad fucking language back in that vocab, yeah?' She pushes me towards the bar entrance. 'Now stop being a posh cunt and get your round in.'

I laugh, fling my arm around her neck and kiss her temple. 'Oh, Jazzy. What would I do without you keeping me real?'

'Get off,' she says, cackling. 'I'm not going to pull with you hanging off me.'

Inside it's busy and dark. We push through to the bar and I raise my voice to be heard over the music. 'A pint of pale ale and…' I turn to Jaz. 'What do you want?'

'A glass of white wine.' She steps onto the footrest and leans over the bar. 'Make it an Australian wine.' She gives me some side-eye. 'I'm in the mood for a bit of Australian.'

The barperson tends to our drinks and I shoot Jaz a look. 'Give it a rest.'

Jaz smirks and moves her hips to the music, scanning the crowd. 'Oh yeah, I'm definitely finding my soul mate in here. I've got a big night feeling.' She looks down at my feet. 'I hope you've got your dancin' shoes on.'

My limbs start to loosen, the week's stress dissolving, the beat of the music working in rhythm with my body. 'I have, mate. I have.'

For the next couple of hours, we dance, talk shite, drink and flirt – with other people, not each other. Jaz takes her flirting to the next level, but I keep mine light, innocent and fun.

I'm chatting to a couple when Jaz detaches herself from the woman she's snogging and yells in my ear, 'Toilets'. She grabs my hand and drags me to the bathroom, where she pulls me into a cubicle and slides the lock across.

I glance at the lock and then at her. 'No, Jazzy. No.'

She reaches into her bra, pulls out a small plastic sleeve and waves it. 'Go on,' she whispers. 'Just a little bit.'

'We're too old for that shit, and I'll feel like crap tomorrow.'

'Too old? What are you on? We're thirty-one, and it's my birthday.'

'It was your birthday three weeks ago.'

'Yeah, and this is left over from my birthday, innit? You

weren't too old then to get stuck into it. Besides, this is quality – no drug hangover.'

I grimace. 'I've got things to do this weekend.'

Jaz reaches into her bag and pulls out a tiny compact mirror and a ten-pound note. 'Like what? More wedding stuff? Eva's family stuff?'

'I've got to find a wedding outfit, remember?'

'For fuck's sake, Casey. Again, she's sucking the life out of you.'

'Not wanting to snort coke in a toilet cubicle in a Soho bar hardly means Eva's sucking the life out of me.'

Jaz grins. 'You know what I mean.' She opens the compact, places it on the cistern and sprinkles on the white powder. Using a credit card, she separates the small mound into two fat lines.

I gaze at it longingly. It has been a hell of a week. I deserve to relax and to forget about weddings and work and Berlin romances from years ago.

Jaz offers the rolled-up tenner and raises a questioning brow.

'Go on, then,' I say, taking it. 'One line and that's it. Maybe two.'

Closing one nostril, I hold the tenner to the other and run it along the line, quickly inhaling. The chemical taste hits the back of my throat within seconds. I pass the note to Jaz, who turns it around and does the same. She cuts another two lines, which we quickly snort before dabbing our fingers on the mirror for every last grain to rub along our gums.

'Just takes the edge off,' Jaz says.

'Totally,' I say. A gentle buzz floats through my body and I'm already looking forward to it peaking and more later.

We head back to the bar where Jazzy orders us rum with orange, and we push our way through the crowd until we're in the middle of the dancefloor. My rush is heightened by the drum and bass pulsing through me. I close my eyes and let myself go.

I have no idea how long I'm dancing alone, because by the time I open my eyes, I'm off to the side, Jaz is sexy dancing with the woman she was snogging earlier, and a pretty blonde is headed straight for me. I neck my rum and place the empty glass on the narrow ledge just in time for her to thrust a glass at me. I take a sip. It's rum and orange and I lift my brows in surprise.

She leans in close, breath warm on my ear. 'I saw you at the bar and asked what you'd ordered.'

I give her a smile. She reminds me of another pretty blonde I spent half the night talking about and that's enough to keep me welded to the spot. We chat for a bit – her name is Emily and she's a vet nurse. We finish our drinks and I buy another round. We flirt and I don't step away when her hand rests against my hip. When she goes to the bathroom, my pocket vibrates, and I pull my phone out to find a message from Eva.

> Missed you tonight. Sorry I've been so caught up in wedding stuff lately and haven't had time for us. I'll make it up to you. Home now and going to bed. Love you xx

My chest tightens. What am I doing? Am I so tormented by Holly's memory that I'm imagining the vet nurse is her?

Jaz dances up beside me. 'You all right, mate?'

I stare at her, the coke peaking proper now.

'You're looking a little cosy with that woman, so I thought you might want to get home?'

I hold up my phone. 'That was Eva. What was I doing? If she hadn't messaged me—'

Jaz puts her hand up to stop me. 'I've been keeping an eye

on you. You were just talking, and I would've stopped anything else, but time for you to go now, yeah?'

I nod. 'I'll call you tomorrow.'

Outside, my clammy skin and lungs welcome the cool air. I hail the black cab moving towards me and jump in. The quiet, dark cabin helps regulate my breathing, but my body feels disjointed. Waist down, I'm buzzing, like I could take on anything, but my brain is scrambled about what just happened, and my chest is hollow about what it all means.

Chapter 7
Holly, Melbourne

I open an old computer file and search through documents, looking for something to do. The office is almost empty – maybe I should leave early. I'm keen to wander the city with my new camera before the afternoon light fades. I've neglected photography for months because I've been occupied with sorting out a care facility for Mum and Jack coming into our lives, but now that Mum's settled, I'm desperate to get back to it.

I forget about finding work to do and open a photography website. Just as I start reading about camera settings for architecture shots, my manager's name flashes in the bottom corner of the monitor. I slip on the headset and click the call answer icon. 'Hi, Sasha.'

'Hi, Holly,' she says. 'If you're free, would you mind coming to my office?'

'Sure,' I say, relieved that I'll finally be given a project to take on. 'On my way.' As I pass my colleagues' desks, it dawns on me that one of them left mid-morning and didn't return, and the other went for a late lunch.

When I knock on the office door, I'm surprised to see Sasha talking with Maria, the HR manager. 'Holly. Come in,' Sasha says, standing and pulling out a chair for me. 'You know Maria, don't you?'

'I do,' I say warily.

Maria gives me a quick smile. 'Hi, Holly.'

Sasha clicks the door shut and sits back in her office chair. 'Thanks for coming at such short notice.'

'No problem.' I glance between them. Maybe this is about a role in the new department.

Sasha rests her elbows on the desk, laces her fingers together and holds them to her mouth. Odd body language for someone who's about to offer me a new job. It must be something else. 'Is this about my leave?' I ask. 'I know I've got too much. I was about to book some time—'

Sasha holds up a hand. 'No. Not about your leave.' She clears her throat and looks at Maria, who gives her a nod. 'It's, um, it's about your job.'

Her sombre tone causes my stomach to clench. 'Oh.'

'You might have noticed that the workload in your area has reduced since we've developed the new buildings and physical spaces team?' Sasha says.

She poses it as a question, and I reply with the first thing that enters my head. 'I hope their first job will be to come up with a new team name, because "buildings and physical spaces" is a bit of a mouthful.' They both stare at me and my face warms. 'Yes, I have noticed, but since we won the tender for the Swanston Street building, I thought there'd be something for me to do.'

Sasha audibly swallows, Maria looks down at her notepad, and I suddenly feel quite foolish.

'That project's gone to the new team, being a building,' Sasha says.

'And a physical space,' Maria adds, quickly turning away when I shoot her a look.

'I'm not sure why you didn't apply for one of the new project manager roles, Holly?' Sasha says.

The pity in her eyes unnerves me. 'Oh, um...' What can I say? Finding a care home for Mum, visiting her most nights, trying to catch up with Adam and his family, and looking after my man-child partner, the house and now his eight-year-old son every second week has sucked away my life. But I simply say, 'I guess I didn't realise the restructure would take so much work from our area.'

Sasha's sigh carries the weight of bad news. 'Due to budgetary restraints, we won't be able to retain all positions, which means we have no choice but to make some redundant.'

The ball of dread in my stomach unravels and spreads through my body. I rub my arms, feeling a chill through my thin jumper. 'Redundant. Wow. Those ... poor ... people.' A piece of fluff on my tights catches my attention, and I pick it off.

'Holly,' Maria says softly.

I lift my head.

'Your position is one of them,' she says.

'Me?' I look at Sasha, but she closes her eyes, her brow creased. 'Oh.'

'I'm sorry, Holly,' Maria says. 'I know you've given so much over the years, and you've been – you are – a valued employee, which is why we're sorry you didn't put in an application for one of the new PM roles. These redundancies aren't about anyone's capabilities; it's business. The additional project management roles are no longer tenable.'

'I have no job,' I say.

'We've calculated your redundancy package,' Maria continues, bulldozing over my feelings with her rehearsed spiel. 'I'll email you the details, but given you've been here seven years, it's generous. Certainly enough to give you time to find a new job. And of course, you'll receive an excellent reference.'

'Um…' I shake my head. 'How much will I get, exactly?'

Sasha blinks at me, her eyes watery, then taps the keyboard and twists the monitor my way. 'We need to give you eight weeks' paid notice, plus twenty-one weeks for your seven years' service, and an additional four months. You'll also get paid out your annual leave, and the long service leave you've accrued to date. So, around sixteen months in total.'

Maria interjects. 'The first four weeks of the notice period you can work if you like, and you can either come in here or work remotely.'

'What do you expect me to do for the month if my position is redundant?' I snap.

Maria's cheeks turn pink and she glances down at her notepad.

'Finding another job like this will take ages,' I say.

Sasha twists the monitor back. 'You have excellent skills and experience, Holly, and people always need project managers.'

'Except this office,' I say, a little more sharply than I intended.

She gives a regretful sigh. 'Look at it this way – it could be a fresh start. A chance for you to do something you've always wanted to do. A career change?'

'I wasn't really looking for a career change,' I say. 'I like it here. I've been here since I finished my master's.' I screw my eyes shut and pinch the bridge of my nose. 'Okay. So, what happens now? Do I leave and not come back?'

'That's up to you,' Maria says. 'You can take the weekend to think about what you'd like to do for the next four weeks. We understand this is a difficult and stressful situation, so do what's right for you. You can speak to a support person now – we have someone waiting – and we want to ensure that you have friends or family available to you outside of work this evening. If you don't, we can—'

'It's fine. I live with my partner. Do I have to speak to a support person?'

'You don't have to, no,' Maria says. 'But we think it might be helpful.'

I stand, suddenly too warm and struggling to catch my breath. 'I need fresh air and to walk. I just want to walk.'

'Do you mind if I call you later to check in?' Maria asks.

'I'd rather you didn't. I won't be working for the rest of the afternoon.'

'Of course,' Maria says.

I head back upstairs and stare at the contents of my desk. I have very little to pack up since I had a clear-out when I was bored last week. I go to switch off my PC and spot the email with my formal notice already waiting. I ignore it, grab my bag and camera and head for the lift, but Sasha is racing towards me.

'Holly,' she gushes. 'I am so, so sorry.'

'Have you known about this for ages?'

She shakes her head. 'No. I wasn't sure what was happening, which is why I urged you to apply for one of those jobs. I found out yesterday. I fought to keep your position and have you moved to the new team, but they wouldn't budge.' The anguish on her face is genuine and she's always stood by me.

'I'm sorry I didn't listen to you,' I say.

She frowns. 'I am too.'

'They really expect me to work the next month?'

She huffs. 'Fuck them. Don't do that. You've got more than a month's sick leave, right?'

I nod.

'Go to your GP, tell them what's happened, get a medical

certificate for stress and take all your sick leave.' She waves her hand in the direction of my desk. 'If you don't want to face anyone next week, come in over the weekend and do anything you need to do. Email us the certificate on Monday and tell HR you won't be back.' She gives another regretful groan and throws her arms around me. 'I'm sorry we're losing you. List me as a referee, won't you?'

I return the hug and step away, my chest hollow. 'Bye, Sasha.' I take a last look around the office where I've spent the past seven years and leave.

Outside, the city bustles with trams, buses, cars and pedestrians. Everyone getting on with their lives with no clue that the person who has just exited this building has lost their secure, decent-paying, good-benefits job. I walk along Queen Street, welcoming the winter sun and cold air on my face. Instead of taking the normal route to my regular tram stop, I turn down Little Bourke Street to escape the noise and try to process what's happened. But my only thought is, *I have no job.*

An old building on the corner of a laneway catches my eye. Chairs and tables are set up outside, Parisian-style, the overhead heat lamps aglow. Inside, behind the large windows, a few people nurse wine glasses. The aged concrete and uneven shape of the building automatically make me reach for my camera. I check the settings, which I fixed last night ready for architecture photography, and adjust them slightly to suit the soft light. So that the asymmetrical structure is prominent, I focus on the west-facing side of the building, snapping a series of shots until I have a few I'm satisfied with. I slip the camera away and move closer to the door. The plaque above it reads Caleb's Wine Bar. A glass of wine is exactly what's needed right now.

Inside, jazz plays on low volume and the space is warm from the overhead heaters. A staff member behind the bar is on the phone with a fed-up expression that vanishes when he notices me. As I approach, he gives me a 'won't be a sec' finger-raise. He hangs up, huffs a little and says, 'Sorry about that. Things always happen on a Friday arvo, don't they?'

'Ha, they certainly do.'

'What can I get you?' he asks.

A wine list is written in white marker on the blue tiled wall behind him, which I scan quickly. 'Something white? Any recommendations?'

'Depends on what you like. And your mood.' He wipes his hands on a towel and pulls a glass from an overhead rack.

'I like crisp and dry. Nothing too sweet or heavy. And my mood...' I frown. 'I've just been made redundant, so...'

He winces. 'Oof, that's rough. Worse than my little dilemma.' He gestures to a small table in the far corner. 'Take a seat. I'll bring you something.'

I weave between the wooden tables to one by window, get comfortable and dig out my phone to message Nat.

> In a wine bar in the city. Just been made redundant.

Nat and I met at work, starting our jobs a week apart. We bonded over being the new employees and quickly became good friends. She left to go on maternity leave but didn't return. Instead, she found a part-time job closer to home. Her husband works with Tom, which is how Tom and I met.

As I wait for my drink and Nat's reply, it occurs to me that there are zero expectations on me right now because everyone thinks I'm at work. It's strangely freeing and my body loosens.

The barperson appears with a tray and places down a carafe of water, a glass of white wine and a small bowl of green olives. He points to the wine. 'Thought you might need a large.'

I give a short laugh. 'Thanks. I think so, too.'

'This is a fumé blanc from Tasmania. It's fresh but has a creamy texture and a warm aftertaste. Good for a winter's day.' He tilts his head sympathetically, his kind eyes taking me in. 'And for soothing the soul.'

I lift the glass to my nose and breathe in a delicate citrus scent. I sip and let the tangy flavour swish around my mouth. 'Mmm. Lovely. Exactly what I needed.'

'Let me know if you want anything else. Olives are on me.'

I pop one into my mouth as he walks away. Free olives and an expensive glass of wine on a weekday afternoon – already my life is different.

My phone buzzes with an incoming call and Nat's name flashes on the screen. 'Hey,' I say.

'Shit, Hols. What's happened?'

I sigh. 'Restructure, not enough work for all of us, and I stupidly didn't apply for the new PM jobs when they came up, thinking I'd be okay.'

'That is so crap. Please tell me you got a decent pay-out at least?'

'Sixteen months.'

She gives a low, impressive whistle. 'Well, that's something. Takes a bit of pressure off. What did Tom say?'

'Haven't told him yet. I only found out half an hour ago, left work and stopped in here. I don't want to tell him on the phone – he's going to hyperventilate about me losing the seventeen per cent superannuation benefit.'

'Fair enough. Hey, I've got to run to a meeting, but I just wanted to check you were okay. I'll phone you tonight. I won't say anything to Marc until you've told Tom.'

'Thanks. Chat later.'

I end the call and casually glance at the two people who came in while I was on the phone. They're on bar stools facing each other, knees touching. One runs her finger along the hem of the other's skirt, then rests her palm on her knee. My job woes are momentarily forgotten as a pang of longing flares. I miss those tiny actions that carry such loving sentiments, and in moments like this, I miss my ex-girlfriend Lily, or at least, what we had in the beginning. I thought I might've found it with Tom, but it's obvious now that I chose him for all the wrong reasons. Still bruised from Lily's infidelity a year after we split, I wanted a safe relationship and Tom provided it – older than me, sensible, his own home, a trusting energy. My love for him grew as our relationship developed, but it was never a love that fully consumed me.

Would I ever meet someone who would fully consume me long-term? There was someone once who might've done that, but she never gave us a chance. I grab my phone and open Instagram, then type 'Casey Vassell' into the search field like I've done countless times over the years. It brings up no one familiar, so I type 'Casey Vassell London'. That changes the results, but I still don't recognise anyone, and the few accounts I do check are set to private.

I've asked myself so many times why I didn't find out more about Casey or why I didn't tell her more about myself, but we lived for the moment and I thought we'd have plenty of time for that. She wasn't on socials, or so she said. Besides, the big social media platforms that are popular now either hadn't started then or weren't for our age group. She talked about art and her best friend – I recall her name was Jaz. She didn't say a lot about her family, but neither did I because we were young and trying to find our place in the world independent of our families. Talking about them just made me miss them more. Maybe it was the same for her.

I gaze out at the narrow street. What would I do if I found her anyway? Send a DM and say, *Hi, remember me? I'm the one you spent an incredible two weeks with in Berlin when we were twenty. The one you ran away from and cut all contact with. The one who turned needy and tried to move to London to be with you and has forever regretted speaking those words. Oh, and by the way, I've never forgotten you, my heart has never healed, and you ruined me for every relationship that followed. So, how have you been?*

'Another?'

I spin around. 'Sorry?'

The barperson points to my glass. 'You've finished. Would you like another?'

I look at the empty glass. 'Oh, so I have.' I shake my head. 'No, thanks.' I pick up my camera bag and hold it up. 'I'm going to take some shots around the city before the sun disappears.'

'You're a photographer?'

'In my spare time.'

'Are you any good?'

I shrug. 'It's been a hobby for a long time, and I studied photography at uni.' I open my Insta profile and pass my phone. 'Judge for yourself.'

He scrolls through my feed and nods appreciatively. 'You do events?'

'It's not my speciality, but I'll do it for friends. I mainly do architecture and street photography. Sometimes portraits.'

He passes my phone back and pulls his own from his back pocket. 'What's your username? I'll give you a follow.'

'Oh, sure. It's Holly Craddock Photography. That's C-R-A-double D—'

'Found you.' He smiles. 'You've got yourself a new follower, Holly Craddock Photography. We're actually looking for a photographer for an event tomorrow night. What do you charge?'

'Oh,' I say surprised. 'Like I said, events aren't my speciality.'

He scrolls through his phone. 'Well, I'm looking at your feed now and you've got some good people and food shots here, wherever this was.' He turns his screen towards me.

It's a photo of Nat holding a large knife, the tip sunk into a layered chocolate cake. Her dark-blue eyes glint and I've captured her mid-laugh. 'Ah, that was my friend's thirtieth birthday. Thanks, but you don't need to feel sorry for me because I lost my job.'

He grins. 'I do feel sorry for you, for sure, but that phone call I was on when you came in was the photographer cancelling. I don't have time to find another one by tomorrow.' He gestures to my camera. 'That looks like a shit-hot camera. You take great photos, and we need a photographer, fast.' He shrugs. 'It's a small event. Just some snaps of guests, some wines, food. It's for our new website and our socials.'

I open my mouth to say no but catch myself. *Why am I saying no?* 'Can I get back to you about the fee?'

'Great! Of course.' He opens his arms wide and for a moment I think he's going to gather me into a hug. 'I could hug you right now, but that would be inappropriate, so...' He sticks his hand out. 'I'm Caleb.'

I shake his hand. 'Nice to meet you, Caleb.'

He gestures to some customers who've just walked in. 'Work calls. We'll message in the morning through Insta and sort out details?'

'Sounds good.' I pull out my purse to pay for the wine.

'Leave that. It's on me,' he says and rushes back to the bar.

I slip on my coat and head outside. Such a strange afternoon, and it's unearthed something in me – a glimmer of possibility. I swing the camera strap over my shoulder and start walking in search of my next photo subject.

Chapter 8
Casey, London

I stretch out my limbs as I slowly wake. My eyelids open and Eva comes into focus, perched on the end of the bed, arms crossed, lips pursed. 'Jesus,' I say. 'You scared me.' I grope around for my phone. 'You're awake already? What time is it?'

'I'm awake because it's eleven and we need to be at my parents' by one.'

I groan. 'It's Saturday morning, Eva. I need more sleep.'

'Well, you can't, because we need to leave soon.'

'No.'

'Yes, Casey, we arranged it.'

'*You* arranged it. I didn't have a say – as usual.'

She scoffs, her arms still tightly crossed. 'What's that supposed to mean?'

'Nothing. I don't want to go.'

She glares at me.

'You never come to my parents' when I ask you,' I say.

'That's different.'

My defences rise. 'How? Because my parents' house isn't as nice as yours?'

Her arms relax. 'That's not what I meant. It's different because today we're going over the speeches, finalising the menu...'

I throw the pillow over my head. I can't deal with weddings at this hour. 'You don't need me there,' I say, my voice muffled.

She rips the pillow off me. 'I do! I need your support.'

'Tell them I'm sick. It's not untrue.'

'Well, if you hadn't been out drinking and taking drugs all night with Jaz, you'd be able to do things with your fiancée.' She hops up and opens the curtains. The late morning light floods the room and I glimpse some blue sky, the grey from yesterday gone.

'We weren't taking drugs *all* night.' I throw off the duvet and head to the kitchen, Eva on my tail. I flick the switch on the kettle and grab the cafetière, scooping in some ground coffee beans.

'Oh, so you were taking drugs, then?'

'We had a few lines, some drinks, and danced.' The vet nurse materialises in my mind, but I quickly banish the image and bury the guilt. 'I was having a good time with my bestie. It was a stressful week. I'm allowed to have fun, Eva.' I fill the cafetière with boiling water, plunge it and pour two coffees, handing one to her before shuffling back to the bedroom.

'I bet Jaz got off with someone,' she says, following me.

'She did.' I sip the coffee, the strong, bitter flavour satisfying my tastebuds, and climb back into bed.

Eva places her mug on the side table and slides in beside me, fiddling with the hem of my vest top. 'I worry when you go out with her.'

I laugh a little too hard. 'Why?'

She watches me for a few seconds. 'People must try it on with you.'

I quickly turn away and put my own coffee down before

she can clock my guilt. 'Sometimes, but it doesn't mean I do anything about it.'

'But it might turn into a bender and you'll sleep with someone else again.'

About three months after Eva and I met, we had a massive barney and split. Jaz and I drank too much, took way too many drugs, and I woke the next day in a strange bed with a strange woman. Eva and I reconciled a few weeks later and I told her what had happened. But last night was the first time I've come close to crossing that boundary.

I slip my arm around her, drawing her in. 'That was a different situation that had nothing to do with Jaz. You also slept with someone then, and I don't give you a hard time. And we had split up,' I remind her.

'I only slept with someone else to pay you back,' she says sulkily.

'So, we're even. Leave it now,' I say, kissing her forehead.

She frowns. 'Okay, but can you please ask Jaz to behave herself at the wedding? I don't want her getting off with the other bridespeople.'

I grin. 'She's totally going to cop off with someone. You know how much she loves to pull at a wedding, especially if it's one of the bridal party – she gives herself extra points for that.'

Eva runs her hand across the bare skin between my vest top and pyjama shorts. 'I'm just saying, I don't trust her. She doesn't like me, and I feel like she's trying to take you away.'

'Of course she likes you. She's just...' I shrug. 'Jaz.'

She pouts. 'You might've got off with someone in the toilets last night.'

I roll my eyes. 'I didn't get off with anyone in the toilets, okay? It's been a long time since I've done that.'

She gives a delicate little grunt. 'So common.'

I bristle. She knows I hate that phrase – about anyone – but I don't rise to it. Instead, I shrug and say, 'Well, that's me.'

She walks her fingers along my bare arm. 'I don't mind a bit of rough.'

I give a short laugh. 'I'm hardly a bit of rough, Eva. Besides, everyone's rough compared to you.'

Her fingertip trails my chest and my nipple hardens under the thin fabric. 'Oh, I don't know ... your tattoos and cropped hair. Your androgynous charm and East London accent. It does it for me.' She slips her hand under my top and runs her palm over my breast.

I sink down into the bed, a heat spreading between my legs, and I hate that she has this power over me. She jumps up, closes the curtains and strips off her T-shirt. I moan as my eyes roam her naked body. 'Eva, I'm exhausted.'

She straddles my waist and bends down to kiss me, soft lips and hot tongue against mine. I sigh and run my hands up her thighs. She sits up, reaches behind and slips her hand inside my pyjama shorts. 'Are you really too exhausted?'

'I need to chill,' I say, but can't help pushing against her hand.

'Please come with me this afternoon?' she pleads.

'Oh, Eva,' I whine.

She shuffles her knees up and places them either side of my head. My eyes drift down before meeting her gaze.

She smirks. 'I'll make it worth your while.'

'Fuck, Eva,' I say, and press my mouth between her legs.

Eva and her friend Leila are set up at Eva's parents' dining table with laptops, notepads, champagne and a platter of figs, cheese and nuts. Dante is on FaceTime and the three of them are gushing over table settings. I'm on a stool at the island bench, chatting to Eva's mum about the long-standing barrister career she's about to retire from. I warmed to Rosa as soon as we met and I love that she always asks about my family, my job and the art in the gallery.

Rosa tops up my red wine and calls across the kitchen to Eva. 'Oh, sweetheart, good news. That chef you wanted for the reception has confirmed.' She recorks the wine. 'I can't remember her name – your father arranged it.'

Eva squeals. 'What?! Are you serious?'

'Of course I'm serious,' Rosa says. 'You know I don't joke.'

Eva clamps her hands to her head as though it's about to explode. 'You mean the French chef, right? Margot Laurent?'

'Yes, that name sounds familiar,' Rosa says.

'Oh. My. God,' Dante screeches from the laptop screen. 'This wedding just gets better and better!'

'Oh, Mum. Thank you.' Eva runs over and throws her arms around Rosa.

'Thank your father. He's the one who called in a favour,' Rosa says, returning the hug.

'Thanks, Daddy!' Eva yells through to the next room.

Rosa covers her ear. 'Goodness. I meant when you see him.'

Eva giggles. 'Sorry. I'm just so excited.' She turns to Leila, seemingly unaware I'm in the room. 'Can you believe it?'

Leila shakes her head. 'No. Her food is incredible, and she rarely does weddings.'

I stay silent, waiting for some kind of acknowledgment that I'm part of this wedding. Like Eva's read my mind, she spins to face me. 'Babe, did you hear that?'

I nod. 'I'm sitting right here, and people in Scotland would've heard your squeal.' I tilt my head. 'Remind me why we need another chef? I thought that was sorted.'

Eva walks over to me and places her hands on my thighs. 'I didn't confirm because I wanted Margot.'

'You've never mentioned her to me, and what about that chef we spoke to a few weeks back? I liked her and she had some Jamaican dishes lined up. My gran was dead excited about that,' I say. 'Jazzy's grandparents, too.'

Eva's face falls and Rosa says to her, 'I thought your other options fell through?'

Her eyes dart between Rosa and me, her cheeks growing pink. 'Well, we hadn't confirmed, and Margot's been my first choice right from the start.'

'Why do you want a French chef anyway?' I say, struggling to keep the irritation from my voice. 'I thought you wanted Italian for your family, along with a Jamaican and British menu. We were going for a fusion-type thing. That's what we talked about.'

Rosa shakes her head. 'Oh, Eva.' She turns to me. 'I'm sorry, Casey. I had no idea you'd already discussed menus with other chefs.'

'I'm sure Margot can do whatever we want,' Eva says. 'She's one of the top chefs in Europe.'

A vein in my neck throbs. A top chef means nothing to my family or me. My mum's idea of fancy food is buying a Victoria sponge from Waitrose instead of Asda. My phone vibrates on the bench and Jaz's image flashes on the screen. 'Just taking this. It's Jaz.'

Eva walks back to the dining table, but Leila looks up. 'Jaz? Tell her I said hi.'

My brows lift in surprise – this is new. 'Sure.'

Rosa points to a door on the other side of the kitchen. 'Go into the sitting room, if you like, Casey.'

'Thanks.' I grab my glass of red and move to the other room, closing the door behind me. I place my wine on the side table before sitting so I don't splash on the cream sofa, like I've done before, then slide the call answer icon. 'Hiya. I'm in wedding hell.'

Jaz grunts. 'I'm in zone six hell. How the fuck did I end up in Epping last night?'

'Epping?' I laugh. 'Hope she was worth it.'

'Oh, she was,' Jaz purrs. 'But I won't be trekking all the way out here for visits. My soul mate needs to live in zone one. It's going to take me hours to get home.'

'It'll take you, like, an hour.'

Jaz groans with the effort of it all. 'I'm stopping halfway at your ma and da's for an afternoon fry-up and a strong brew. There's no way I'll make it back to Islington on an empty stomach.'

'Why don't you stop at your own ma and da's for a fry-up?'

''Cause your parents have the best black pudding in all of East London.'

This is true. Mum and Dad own and run Stratford Meats, a local butcher that's been in Mum's family since her dad was a child. Customers queue every Saturday morning just for the black pudding.

A sudden craving gnaws at my belly. 'God, that sounds good.'

'Oh, come! We'll stuff our faces with greasy food and slob on the couch for the afternoon.'

I consider it, questioning whether it's worth the earache I'll cop from Eva. 'I'll never hear the end of it if I leave now. Not that what I have to say matters much.'

'No, because you're just her fucking lapdog.' Jaz's voice rises over the rumble of a train.

'I'm not *totally* her lapdog,' I say, fiddling with the stem of my wine glass. 'I stood up to her this morning. Told her I wasn't coming here today.'

'And yet, you're there.'

I hear the train doors slide open. 'She kind of ... persuaded me.'

'How?' Jaz says, and then she laughs. 'Oh my God. You are like, proper pussy-whipped.'

'Well, she was naked, and it was in my face. How do you say no to that?'

'Hmm. True. I know she's your fiancée and all, but she's well fit, so I don't reckon I'd say no in that situation either.'

I laugh. 'Nice, Jazzy. Glad I can trust my best mate.'

Jaz snorts.

I lower my voice. 'Seriously, though. I don't think I can do this. Each day my feet get colder. Look what I did last night – I was so close to snogging that woman. Why would I do that?'

'Don't beat yourself up. You were flirting a bit. Chill, yeah.'

'Still. It's a sign something's up, innit? I can't work out if it's wedding nerves or the relationship. I'm so confused. Eva's in there talking about top chefs and I'm just like, fuck, what am I doing? It's just ... really overwhelming.' My breathing becomes laboured.

'Jesus, mate, don't hyperventilate. If this is how you feel, then you're going to have to deal with this – and soon.'

'I do love her, though. Like, I think I do.'

Jaz sighs. 'Course you do. You have a good life. She's a beautiful woman. And you were good together, for a while. But you're not happy. Look, if you're a spare part there, come and meet me at your parents'. We'll have a nice fry-up. Chill for the afternoon. Go and meet my dad at the King's Arms for a pint when he finishes work. Give yourself some space to think about what you want.'

'I just feel bad, guilty like. I don't want to hurt her. Her parents have put so much effort into the wedding and I feel like I'll hurt them too.'

'But this is your problem, Case. You never want to hurt anyone. It's sweet, but you make it worse in the end. You can't get married just because you don't want to hurt her or her parents.'

'I know, I know.' I press my fingertips to my temple and massage, an attempt to ward off the throb that's intensifying. 'I'd better go. Oh, before I forget, Leila says hi.'

'Leila? Who the fuck is Leila? Have I slept with her yet?'

'I have no idea. She's Eva's friend. Small, long brown hair. Well pretty. She filmed the proposal, and you met at our place again a few weeks back.'

'Hmm...' She pauses. 'Ohh. Leila. Amazing boobs.'

'Erm ... I guess. She's quite friendly as well.'

'Oh yeah, that too. Well, hel-*lo*, Leila. Tell her I said hi right back.'

I shake my head at her womanising. 'Later, Jazzy.'

I end the call and take advantage of being alone for a few more minutes. I long to be at my parents' right now, dipping buttery white toast in runny egg yolk and eating greasy bacon and black pudding. Instead, I'm in a multimillion-pound house in South Kensington, planning a wedding I don't want to a woman I'm no longer sure I'm in love with. I glance at the artwork over the mantel – a piece from our gallery that I sold to Eva's dad at an exhibition opening. It's an impressionist work in vibrant oils of two lovers kissing on a tree-lined path that he bought because it reminded him of meeting Rosa. Eva was with him that night, bored by the exhibition but interested in me. We swiftly became caught up in each other, our differences drawing us together.

I try to pinpoint the moment the cracks began in our relationship. After that first mini-split, we fell in love all over again. Until we moved in together, maybe even a bit before that, if I'm truly honest with myself. The traits we once found endearing about each other weren't so appealing when they were on constant display. Her bossiness and plummy accent, a turn-on at first, quickly became a turn-off when she started controlling everything in our shared home and began correcting my English.

I look at the lovers in the painting and run my palm over a tattoo on my upper arm. My mind drifts to Berlin and how much a kiss under a tree in that city meant to me, how it's never left me. Maybe Jaz is right – space from Eva might be good. Being in Berlin helped me figure out what to do about Bethany. I grab my phone and tap out a message to Josanne.

Up for Berlin if you still need me to go.

I hesitate a second then hit send.
She replies immediately.

Yes! Thank you.

I drain my glass and head back to the kitchen.
Leila looks up. 'How's Jasmine?'
I give a bemused smile. 'Jasmine?'
'Oh. It's such a pretty name,' Leila says, dipping her head coyly. 'It suits her better than Jaz.'
My smile broadens. Jazzy will love that comment. 'She's good. She said to tell you hi.'
Leila's hazel eyes widen. 'Really? She's part of the wedding party, I take it?'
Before I have a chance to reply, Eva jumps in. 'You are not getting off with Jaz.'
'Why not?' Leila asks innocently.
'Um,' Eva says, 'because she sleeps with someone different every week.'

'Not every week,' I say. 'And she is single, so...'

Eva rolls her eyes. 'Well, that makes it okay, then.' She jumps up and walks over to me. 'So, next week, you need to keep every night free. I've already arranged tasting sessions at Margot's restaurant for the main meal, and on Wednesday night a rehearsal dinner.'

I guess we're not discussing the choice of chef. 'Rehearsal? For what? Eating?'

Eva folds her arms, the familiar scowl forming. 'We need to get everything right.'

I shake my head. 'Can't. I'm going away for work.'

She pulls her head back in surprise. 'Since when?'

I break eye contact. 'Er ... Josanne asked me yesterday, but I didn't ... I wasn't sure what was happening. Until now.'

'She contacted you on a Saturday about a work trip?'

I clear my throat. 'Yeah.'

'Where are you going?'

'Berlin. You know the exhibition I've helped curate for their gallery?'

She nods.

'Well, I was going to the opening anyway, but they're short-staffed, so they need help to finalise everything.'

'And it has to be you who goes? You're going to miss your dad's birthday and Carnival?'

'Dad will understand.'

Eva places her hands on her hips. 'Josanne *knows* the wedding is coming up.'

'She does, but this is my job, Eva.'

She glares at me, but she has no argument for that. 'Fine. I'll sort the menu myself.'

I grab my bag off the bench. 'Also, I'm going to head off now.'

Her face darkens. 'Where are you going? To meet Jaz? She calls and you go running?'

'I'm going to Mum and Dad's. I haven't seen them for ages and now I won't see Dad for his birthday.'

'But—'

'You don't need me here.'

Eva pouts. 'That's because I was busy organising. I'm finished now and I want to make some content of us doing wedding prep together.'

I shake my head. 'No way. I draw a line at that.' I give her a quick kiss before she can persuade me to stay. 'I'll see you later. Nice to see you, Leila,' I add.

I leave the kitchen, head down the long hallway and out the front door, closing it quietly behind me. I gulp in the warm afternoon air, my chest cresting and falling, then text Jaz.

> Tell Mum to set a place for me. On my way.
> And going to Berlin next week.

Jaz's reply is instant.

> WTAF!

Chapter 9
Casey, London

I walk at double speed to South Kensington tube station, the desperate need for space propelling me forward. The cool change yesterday didn't last long; today is warm and sticky, but it doesn't prevent a cold clamminess creeping over my skin. I duck into Waitrose to pick up a Victoria sponge for Mum before descending underground.

As the train zips through the dark tunnel, I gaze at my reflection in the window and imagine that person isn't me – it's Jazzy or my sister. What would I say to them in my situation? I'd tell them to end it; I know I would. The carriage rocks as we round a bend and I close my weary eyes. I can't shake Holly from my mind. Apart from some internet and social media searches over the years, I haven't done much to try and find her. Stale regret swells in my chest and the same old questions swirl in my head. *What if I hadn't run away? What if I'd answered her calls or responded to her messages? What if I'd told her more about myself? What if I'd listened properly the first day we met when she told me her last name? Am I just obsessing about her because my current relationship feels too permanent?*

The train stops and I open my eyes to see we're at Holborn Station. I jump up and make it through the doors just as they slide closed. I walk the long corridors to the Central Line, where I take the tube to Stratford, ride the steep escalator to the street and begin the twenty-minute walk to my parents' house. Already I'm calmer, returning to where I grew up makes me feel more like me.

The area around the train station has changed since I was a kid, gentrification for the Olympics starting when I was in my late teens. Mum and Dad's shop was far enough away from the Olympic village and train station not to be pushed out, and the regeneration of the area has been good for their business and their house value.

When I let myself in with my spare key, loud cackles drifting from the kitchen greet me, and I find Mum and Jaz at the table, cradling mugs.

'Here she is,' Mum says, standing and opening her arms. 'Hello, darlin'.' Her blonde hair is pulled back off her face and she's wearing her favourite tatty old apron that says, 'Love thy butcher'.

I place the cake on the side and pull Mum's short frame into a tight embrace. 'All right, Ma.' Then I ruffle Jaz's thick curls, transformed from glossy and textured last night to frizzy today. 'You look rough, mate.'

'Get off,' Jaz says, brushing my hand away. 'That's your fault. Making me go out all night.' She looks up at me, make-up smudged under her eyes.

'Sure it is.'

'Want a brew?' Mum asks.

'Yeah, ta.' I give an upward nod towards the shopping bag. 'Got you one of those cakes you like.'

Mum drops a teabag into a mug and tops it with boiling

water, then peeks in the bag. She tuts. 'Almost six quid, those cakes. Don't be spending your money on that.'

I collapse onto a chair and twist behind me to open the window. 'I can afford to buy you a cake, Mum.'

'That's not the point.' She grabs the milk from the fridge and splashes some into the brewing tea. 'I can afford to buy me a cake too, but I can get the exact same thing at Asda for a pound eighty-five.'

'It's different quality,' I say.

'All made in the same factory.' Mum places the mug in front of me.

'They're not, Wendy.' Jaz gets up and pulls the cake from the bag. 'Ooh, I love a Waitrose sponge. We having this now?'

Mum slaps her hand away.

'That's a no, then.' Jaz grins and joins me back at the table.

I sip Mum's magic tonic tea and the remaining tension inside me loosens. 'Ah. You make the best tea, Mum.' I stick my feet up on a chair. 'Where's my sis?'

The thunk of the front door opening and closing echoes through the house and Mum gestures to the hallway. 'That's her home from work now.'

My sister shuffles in, frown in place. 'What you two doing here?' she says to Jaz and me, plonking a package wrapped in white paper on the bench. 'There's your black pud, Mum.'

'Nice to see you too,' I say.

'Yeah, hiya,' Chandice says, then focuses on Jaz. 'Fucking hell, mate, you look like you've been dragged under a train.'

'Cheers,' Jaz says. 'You're looking good, too, with your butcher get-up and bags under your eyes.'

'And you've got a face like a wet kipper,' I say to Chandice. 'What's up with you?'

She drops onto a chair. 'Shut it, you two.'

At twenty-eight, my sister decided she was going to do a

second degree in creative and professional writing and move back home so she could be close to the University of East London campus. The downside for her is that if she wants free rent, she has to do shifts in the butcher, which she hates. The downside for our parents is that Chandice being at home again has regressed her to a fifteen-year-old state.

Mum puts a mug of tea in front of Chandice. 'You want a fry-up, love?'

Chandice screws up her face like Mum has offered her a plate of human body parts. 'A *meat* fry-up? I'm vegetarian, Mum.'

'Just have eggs, then,' Mum says.

'Did you get any vegetarian black pudding the other day when I asked?' Chandice says.

Mum gives her a look. 'What's that? The blood of a mushroom? Don't be daft.'

Chandice rolls her eyes. 'I'm starving.'

'There's some leftover veg in the fridge – grab it out, I'll do you a bubble-n-squeak,' Mum says.

I shake my head and mutter, 'Spoilt brat.'

Chandice hops up and opens the fridge. 'Spoilt? I've been hacking up meat since 6 am.'

'For free rent,' I remind her.

She ignores me and nudges Jaz. 'Go on, then. What you get up to last night?' She points to Jaz's short, black dress. 'That's obviously last night's outfit.'

'It's too steamy for you,' Jaz says. 'You couldn't handle it.'

'Oh, I can handle it. I'm writing steamy romances now.'

I laugh. 'Is that so?'

'Too right,' Chandice says. 'I need some material.'

'I've got plenty of material,' Jaz says. 'But I'm not telling you about it. Do your own research.'

'I will,' Chandice says defiantly.

'Don't think you're doing it here,' Mum says, lighting the hob.

'As if. I'll go to their place.'

'Good. Give me and your dad a night to ourselves. We like to do our own research sometimes too, you know.'

Jaz and I laugh, but Chandice makes a gagging motion. 'Mum! No need. Oldies having sex ain't right.'

Mum's eyes widen. 'Oldies? We're mid-fifties! People still have sex in their *eighties*. Put that in your steamy romance.'

'I don't reckon it'll be that steamy,' I say. 'You're a bigger geek than Dad.'

'Mum, Casey called me a geek,' Chandice says.

I roll my eyes. The inner fifteen-year-old's out and proud today.

'She's got a point, love. I can't see you out doing much' – Mum does air quotes – 'research.'

'Well, excuse me for not being a cool, tattooed lesbian like your favourite daughter over there,' Chandice says. 'Or not sleeping with a different bird every night like this one.' She jabs her finger in Jaz's direction.

'We are pretty cool,' I say, laughing.

'Totally,' Jaz says.

'Stop winding her up, you two,' Mum says, pointing the spatula at Jaz and me.

The afternoon sunlight filtering through the kitchen window highlights the fine lines on her face and makes her blue eyes shine. She steps behind Chandice and wraps her arms around her in a hug, pale skin and blonde hair pressed against Chandice's brown skin and black hair. There's something about the contrast of them together that always makes my chest swell, and I love that Chandice and I are such a solid mix of both our parents, despite external appearances.

'Don't you go changing,' Mum says to her. 'We love you

exactly the way you are. You write whatever you want.' Mum kisses her temple and turns back to the hob, tossing bacon and black pudding into the frying pan, filling the kitchen with the delicious smell of sweet fat and cooking meat.

Chandice gives me a smarmy smile. 'Where's your fancy piece, then?'

Mum swats her across the arm with a tea towel. 'She's got a name.'

'*Eva* is at her parents',' I say.

'Our place not good enough for her?' Chandice says.

Jaz smirks and I suck in my cheeks, trying not to bite. I can say it, but I don't like it when others do. 'I didn't invite her because she's busy with her parents.' I cradle my mug and gaze out the window to the back garden where purple dahlias bloom along the fence. 'But I'm glad to be here.'

'I'm not liking the sound of all this wedding stuff, Casey,' Mum says, raising her voice over the sizzle. 'Jazzy's filled me in.'

I raise my eyebrows at Jaz.

'What?' Jaz says. 'You were struggling to breathe. I was worried about you getting into that overwhelmed state you get into sometimes.'

I push my fingers against my temple, the throb from earlier returning. 'I don't know what to do, or even how to have the conversation with her.'

Mum turns to me. 'You just say, "I'm sorry, Eva, I can't marry you. I love you and we were good in the beginning"' – she's waving the spatula to match the cadence of her words, like she's a conductor – '"but we've grown apart and getting married isn't going to fix that".'

Jaz angles her head towards Mum. 'See. Easy.'

Chandice's brows shoot up. 'Oh, hello, wedding of the year's off, is it?'

I groan and drag my hands over my face. 'I don't know.'

Mum scoops vegetables into a separate frying pan. 'Well, you're going to have to tell her something soon, Casey. You don't want to break it to her on the bleedin' wedding day.'

'I just … I feel bad.' I pause. 'And stupid for letting it go on this long.'

Mum cracks the eggs into the pan, tossing the shells into the empty carton. 'No break-up is easy, love. But if she's not the one for you, it's best she knows that sooner rather than later.'

'I'm not sure I want to break up. I just don't want to get married. We're kind of settled in a way, with the flat and all.'

'It's just a flat,' Mum says. 'I know you love Notting Hill, but you can always stay here.'

'Where?' Chandice says. 'On the floor in your office? I'm not sharing a room.'

I jump up and wrap my arms around her, tickling her ribs. 'Oh, go on. It'll be like we're kids again.'

She squeals with laughter. 'Get off.'

I go to pull away, but she grips my arms and holds me there, pressing the side of her face against mine. She smells like raw meat.

'I'll let you stay tonight if you want,' she says. 'You can tell me what's gone wrong with your fancy piece.'

I kiss her cheek. 'Maybe.' I step over to Mum and lean against the kitchen counter. 'I know you and Dad aren't keen on Eva.'

'That's not true, darlin'. We like her enough; she's just different from your other partners, is all.' She tweaks my chin. 'You're a beautiful person and you deserve to be happy, yeah?'

'What she said,' Jaz says.

Mum pushes me towards the toaster. 'Now, you're on toast. Jazzy, you sort the table. Chandice, you make more tea.'

We all do as we're told and then tuck into the fry-up, chatting about the week. It's loud and chaotic and joyous. After the meal, Chandice heads upstairs for a shower, Mum goes to do some invoices and Jaz and I tidy up before moving into the front room.

'So, Berlin, hey?' Jaz says, switching on a pedestal fan and slumping next to me on the sofa.

I nod. 'Yep. Kind of couldn't say no, even though Josanne pretended I had a choice.'

'Uh-huh. The date's coming up, isn't it?' She nudges my knee with her foot. '*The* date.'

'Yeah, but ... I don't think it's a good idea to go to that spot.'

'But the park is right there, innit? Right near the gallery? I mean, you could just stop by. No harm done.'

'Not sure I want to, because...' I shrug. 'Hurts.'

Jaz picks up her phone. 'We have to look for Holly again. She was from Melbourne, yeah?' She taps her phone screen. 'I'll check Instagram first.'

'I've looked,' I say. 'Plus all the other social media platforms.'

'But people are always on and off socials, changing their usernames and pics and stuff. And you've not looked for ages, right?' She scoots closer and shares her phone screen. 'Recognise any of these?'

I squint. 'There are a lot of Hollys right there.'

'What about TikTok?' Jaz opens the app and navigates to the search function.

We search different platforms, but who are we kidding that searching 'Holly Melbourne' will find her?

Chandice walks in, fresh from the shower, flops on the single recliner and flips up the leg rest.

'What would I say if I found her, anyway? "Remember me? The one who followed you around an art gallery because you were so beautiful and shagged you for two weeks, told you fuck all about myself because I was trying to be mysterious and thought I was too cool for all that stuff. I knew you were completely in love with me and I was completely in love with you, but I felt overwhelmed and homesick, so I ran away, and by the time I got my head together and contacted you, your German phone number was dead."'

Jaz grimaces and pulls her legs up onto the sofa. 'Yeah, mate. I see your point. That's tragic.'

'Tragic, all right,' Chandice says. 'You're a total saddo.'

I throw a cushion at her. 'Shut it. You don't even know what we're talking about.'

'I bleedin' do. That one from Berlin you never got over.'

My phone buzzes with a message. I stretch to grab it off the coffee table.

> Going for dinner with Leila. Meet us?

Before I have a chance to reply to Eva's message, my phone rings.

'Hiya,' I say.

'Hi, babe,' Eva says. 'Are you on your way back yet?'

'No. I've not long been here, and...' I take a deep breath. 'I'm going to stay the night.'

Eva's silent for a moment. 'I'm sorry about the chef, okay? I should've talked to you.'

I soften, but I don't want her to be nice to me because it thickens my guilt. 'It's not that. I'm tired from last night. I'm full from the huge meal we just ate, and I'd like to spend time with my family since I won't be around next weekend for Dad's birthday.'

'But I'll be all alone.'

'Leila can stay with you, can't she?'

'She's not my fiancée, and I wanted to post some content of

us together. You never let me post about you, and no one can follow you with your account on private.'

'I don't want people to follow me,' I snap.

'Okay, no need to bite my head off!'

I sigh. 'Sorry. I'm just really exhausted, yeah?'

'Fine,' Eva sniffs. 'Well, we're going out, so I can't promise I'll be home if you change your mind.'

'Go out. Have a good time. I'll see you tomorrow.'

Once I've hung up, Jaz gives me a slow clap. 'I am dead impressed with you. Although I totally would've come with you so I could get off with Leila.'

'Didn't you get enough last night?' I ask.

Jaz shrugs. 'I'm just looking for my soul mate. Because I want to feel for someone the way you feel about *her*.'

I shake my head. 'I don't feel—'

'She's the only person I've ever seen you cry over,' Jaz says.

'What we talking about?' Mum says, walking in with the sponge cake. She places it on the coffee table and sits in the other recliner.

'Holly,' Jaz says.

Mum raises her brows at me. 'Holly? The one from Berlin? You still pining over her?'

'I'm not pining,' I say, a little pine-y. 'I just ... I'm curious about what happened to her, is all. How her life turned out.'

Mum shakes her head and switches on the telly with the remote. 'You're going to get yourself in so much trouble one day.'

'She's already in trouble, Wendy,' Jaz says.

Mum points the remote at me. 'I didn't raise you to sleep with two people at once. Sort things with Eva before you go chasing after more minge.'

Jaz cackles and Chandice yells, 'Mum!'

'Oh my God,' I say. 'For a start, don't say "minge" to me,

please. And I'm not sleeping with two people at once. I've just been thinking about Holly and where she might be now. Am I not allowed to wonder about someone?'

'I'm just saying, you've done this sort of thing before,' Mum says.

'Then don't say. I'm having a night off from Eva so I can work out some shit in my head. Okay?'

Mum clicks her tongue and flicks over to the *Coronation Street* omnibus.

'Why don't you just look her up online?' Chandice says.

I give an exasperated huff. 'Do you really think I haven't done that?'

'Well, no, but you're not that clued-up when it comes to online stalking, are you?'

'I can't be arsed with it, that's why.'

'Have you looked up where she went to university?' Chandice asks. 'Like her degree, year of graduation, that sort of thing?'

Mum throws a cushion Chandice's way. 'Oi, you, stop bloody encouraging her.'

'She's not going to stop wondering until she has answers,' Chandice says. 'She's got a bloody tattoo reminder, for God's sake. I'm just trying to speed up the process.'

'I looked up her university a few times, like the year after we were in Berlin and again a few years later, but I couldn't find anything. I've tried to remember her last name, but it won't come to me. All I remember is that it was different, not a common name.'

It was the first day we met that Holly told me her last name. After spending hours wandering the gallery, we went for a walk along the river. She told me a story about one of her lecturers who always used the students' full names when he was frustrated, then she mimicked him, using her own name as an example. As she talked my eyes drifted to her lips, and all I could think about was how beautiful she looked with the sinking sun behind her and how much I wanted to kiss that mouth.

'What was the Melbourne university?' Chandice asks. 'And what degree?'

'Um, it was a tech. Melbourne technology or something? Creative arts. It had a lot of photography in it, though. She was always taking photos and studying photography for her course.'

Jaz and Chandice both tap their phone screens.

'Hmm,' Chandice says. 'There's a stack of universities in Melbourne.'

'Melbourne University of Technology?' Jaz asks.

I nod. 'Maybe, yeah.'

'There's a University of Melbourne, too,' Chandice says.

'Mmm, no, it definitely had technology in its name.'

They keep tapping and scrolling.

'I found a Holly Morris, did arts and law at a Monash University,' Chandice says.

'No, she definitely didn't do law. And Morris doesn't sound familiar.'

Chandice keeps scrolling. 'Here's a Holly Craddock. She's a project manager at Melbourne University of Technology.'

'Hmm, Craddock ... that's vaguely familiar.'

Chandice taps some more. 'Her work bio says she did creative arts at the same university, followed by a master's. Graduated from the undergraduate degree ten years ago.'

My heart rate picks up and Jaz looks at me, wide-eyed.

Chandice scrolls some more. 'This page isn't that old. You looked for her in the past year and a half?'

I shake my head. 'Not since I've been with Eva.'

Chandice turns her phone screen to me. 'That her?'

A tiny image stares back at me from across the room. I can't see the facial features clearly, but the long, honey-coloured hair is achingly familiar. I jump up and snatch Chandice's phone, zooming in on the tiny image. 'Holy fucking shit. It's her.'

'No way!' Chandice and Jaz both say.

'It's totally her.' I fall back onto the couch, my legs weak.

'My phone, please,' Chandice says. 'God knows what you'll do with it.'

'Give me a look at her first,' Mum says.

I throw the phone to Mum and snatch up mine, typing 'Holly Craddock' into Instagram. Jaz squishes up beside me.

Mum lets out a heavy sigh. 'You're a goner if you ever meet up with her again.'

Chandice squeezes in on the other side of me.

An account called Holly Craddock Photography shows up in the search; the profile pic looks like street art of some kind. My finger hovers over the username.

'What you waiting for?' Jaz says.

I glance at her. 'Photography ... it's got to be her, yeah?'

'I'd say so, mate. Want me to do it?'

I nod and pass Jaz the phone.

Chandice rests her chin on my shoulder, watching on, as Jaz clicks the username. The bio doesn't say much – just that photography is her passion – and it's a personal account, so there's no business contact information.

I retrieve my phone and scroll. The grid is full of incredible, arty shots. I click into the first image and start scrolling. 'It's all Melbourne,' I say, skimming the captions. 'She's still there.' I keep going until I find a photo of Holly and the shock of seeing her up close sucks the air out of me. She's laughing into the camera, eyes crinkled, sunny smile, and my body aches with the memory of her.

'Ooh, she's well pretty, mate,' Jaz says. 'No wonder you've never forgotten her.'

I reach for my water and take a gulp. She was so much more than that. She was smart and fun and kind and natural. But most of all, she made my heart thump every time I looked at her, in a way I never knew was possible. 'I was such a fucking idiot.'

'You have to message her,' Jaz says.

'What did I just tell you?' Mum says. 'You are not doing that until you sort things with Eva.'

'I won't, Mum. Don't fret.' I look at the profile again, but the message icon isn't there. 'She's got her messages on private anyway.'

'Good,' Mum says, leaning forward to slice up the sponge cake. 'Now pipe down, you lot, and let me catch up on *Corrie* and enjoy my overpriced cake.'

Jaz shuffles back to the other end of the sofa and I scroll through image after image of arty street shots, heritage buildings, random people, until I come across a photo of Holly all cosy with a good-looking lad called Tom and my stomach plummets.

Chapter 10
Holly, Melbourne

Caleb's bar is busy and I've just circled the crowd, testing out my new flash unit under the dim lighting. 'How good is this?' I say to Nat, topping up my wine glass from our shared bottle.

Nat takes a gulp of wine before she answers. 'It's excellent you've got a paid photography gig, and this wine is delicious.' The pile of thin silver bangles on her wrist slips along her arm as she drinks.

'I think Caleb will like these.' I show her the camera screen and flick through some images – wine bottles, charcuterie boards, guests captured mid-chat.

She brushes a strand of hair from her face and takes a quick look, nods her agreement then drains her glass.

I place my camera back in its bag and pick up my own glass. 'Tough week?'

'Just full-on. Work, day care, housework, cooking. It's relentless,' she says with a heavy sigh.

'At least Marc helps you.'

Her face softens, the way it always does when her husband is mentioned. 'He does.'

'Tom does fuck-all.' I slice off a wedge of brie and squish it onto a cracker.

'He mows the yard,' Nat offers.

'Mmm.' I finish chewing. 'That takes about fifteen minutes because it's so small.'

'Everything okay at home?' she asks.

I sip my drink and glance out the window at the bustling laneway as I think about the best way to answer that. 'Has Tom said something to Marc at work?'

She shakes her head. 'No. Not that he's mentioned, anyway. You said you'd been arguing a bit, and...' Her eyes fill with concern. 'You just seem really down lately, Hols.'

I stare into my pinot gris. I haven't told Nat the full extent of my feelings about my relationship, but she knows me too well not to pick up on it. 'I guess I am a bit.'

'Are you unhappy? With Tom, I mean.'

'He's just ... not what I want. He's lovely. But our lives are so bland. We hardly go anywhere because he never wants to spend money. I feel like I do everything and he takes it all for granted. Never a *thanks* or *let me help with that* or *let's go out for dinner*. And now there's his kid. His *kid*, for fuck's sake.'

Nat frowns as she listens to me vent.

'I don't want to be a stepmother to an eight-year-old who hates me. Or even to one who likes me.' I sigh. 'Tom's a good guy, and he looks after me. He makes me feel safe, but it's not enough. I need passion and someone who can't get enough of me and brain-shattering sex. At least for some of the time.'

Nat lifts a brow.

'I'm being unrealistic, aren't I? I should be happy with what I have.'

'Well, to have that stuff all the time is a little unrealistic, but it's okay to want more from a relationship.'

I peer into the crowd and a woman at the bar meets my gaze. She's attractive, with smouldering eyes, thick, dark hair and glossy red lips. She gives me a sultry smile and turns her attention back to her friend.

'Jesus, how sexy is she?' Nat says. 'I think you've got a fan.'

'She smiled at me. I don't think that means I've got a fan.' But I sneak another glance at her as I sip my wine.

'Do you miss being in a relationship with a woman?' Nat asks, following my gaze. 'Is that it?'

'Sometimes,' I admit. 'I miss Lily. The way we were before it fell apart.'

Lily, the one who helped me trust again. The one I was ready to spend my life with, until she started pushing for marriage and children. 'We're too young and my dad is so ill, let's wait,' I'd said. But she was a few years older and didn't want to wait, so she found someone else. She just forgot to break up with me first.

I brush the thought away and change tack. 'Tom's already hounding me about finding a new job.'

Nat rolls her eyes. 'Christ. You only lost your job yesterday, with a year-and-a-half pay! Take some time out. Now's the perfect opportunity for you to think about what you actually want.'

'I have thought about it.' I fiddle with the H pendant on my necklace. 'I want to pack a bag, take my camera and go somewhere.'

Nat loads some prosciutto and oily artichoke onto a crispbread. 'Like, for a couple of weeks?'

I shake my head. 'Like a one-way ticket and see where it takes me.'

Nat stares at me, wide-eyed, until she finishes chewing. 'You really are unhappy.'

An emptiness unrolls in my chest. 'Yesterday afternoon was the best I'd felt in a long time. I spent hours walking around the city, finding the most interesting things to photograph. I was so focused that I didn't even think about losing my job. It reminded me how much I loved taking photos when I travelled. Then on the walk home, it hit me that I could travel again, if I wanted to.'

'You walked all the way to Hawthorn from the city? It was freezing yesterday.'

'I needed the thinking time. I can't breathe here, Nat. I don't think I can be with Tom anymore. I can't look after his child, and it's breaking me to watch Mum deteriorate. My whole twenties were spent helping to look after Dad until he died, then Mum, and then that horrible break-up with Lily. Now I have to look after Tom and Jack?' I shake my head. 'I'm thirty-one and I feel like I'm fifty-one.'

Nat gives a sad smile. 'Then you have to do it.'

I feel a swell of gratitude that she gets where I'm coming from. 'You think so?'

She nods. 'I hate the thought of you not being here, but if you don't go, you'll always think about it, and you'll become more resentful.'

'But Mum ... I worry about leaving her.'

She gives my hand a squeeze. 'She might be like this for years yet. And you can't sit around and wait for her to completely go. Maybe talk to Adam and see what he thinks?'

'He'll tell me to go.'

She releases my hand and picks up her glass. 'Well, then. It's decided. So, where will you start?'

I drink the last of my wine and splash in some more, then top up Nat's. 'Germany, maybe. I'd like to go back to Berlin.'

Nat's eyes widen. 'Berlin? Oh, you mean an open ticket overseas? I thought you meant to Perth or something.'

'Nope, Europe. I've been a few times, but there's so much to see and capture on film.'

Nat narrows her eyes suspiciously. 'I remember you telling me once about a Berlin fling when you were there for uni. Are you still in touch with her?'

Heat rises in my cheeks. 'No. I never saw her again.' What I don't say is that experience affected me in ways I can't explain, and I need closure if I'm going to get on with my life and find someone to be truly happy with. 'But she hurt me badly,' I continue. 'And I couldn't enjoy Berlin after that. I want to create new memories and enjoy the city again. Kind of reclaim it, you know?' I shrug. 'Then I'll go somewhere else. Vienna. Paris. London, visit Aunty Carol and my cousins. Might even go to Wales to see some of Dad's relatives.'

'Then go. It might help you put things in perspective.'

'Thanks, Nat.' I survey the bar crowd, suddenly remembering why I'm here. 'Oh, shit.' I grab my camera. 'I'm getting paid to take photos. Back soon.'

Just as I stand, Caleb appears and puts another bottle of wine on the table for us.

'Another one!' Nat says. 'Someone is going to have to carry me out of here.'

Caleb points to a buff bloke behind the bar. 'Have you seen the muscles on my hubby? He could carry both of you at the same time.'

Nat laughs and tops up our glasses. 'In that case...'

'I've got some great shots so far, Caleb,' I say, flicking through the images.

He grins as he looks at the monitor. 'I knew you were the right choice.' He gives me a wink and heads back behind the bar.

The woman from earlier watches me as I move into the crowd. I hold her gaze and lift my camera. She stares down the barrel of the lens, her mouth curling into a sexy half-smile, and I shift to the right so that the low light above falls across her face in a soft shadow. I press the shutter several times and walk away, not trusting myself to speak to her when I feel a longing in my soul and a fire between my legs.

I pull three plates from the cupboard and clatter them down onto the benchtop.

'I can't find my work shirt,' Tom calls from the hallway.

'Look in the laundry,' I shout back, pulling the frying pan off the hotplate.

'Not in there,' he yells.

I toss the steak onto the plates. 'I'm busy here, Tom!'

'I'm hungry!' Jack says from the table.

I clench my jaw and take a slow, deep breath. 'It's coming, Jack. I'm serving it now.'

'Mum gives me dinner at seven.' He points to the clock on the wall. 'It's half past seven. I'm hungry!'

'Tom!' I call. 'Dinner!' The TV blares and the cacophony of noise grates on me.

Tom shuffles into the kitchen and sits at the table – the table that isn't set. 'Not in the laundry.'

For fuck's sake. I grab the cutlery, stomp across the tiles and drop it in the middle of the table, along with the salt and pepper, then turn off the TV.

'No!' Jack yells.

'It's loud, Jack. And we're about to have dinner,' I say.

'I want it on! Mum lets me have it on.'

I look at Tom for support, but he just gives a 'kids, hey' shrug.

I grit my teeth and switch it back on but reduce the volume, then place the plates on the table and sit down.

'Oh. Um...' Tom says.

I cut into my steak and glare at him.

'No mustard?' He peers at the contents on the table, moving his head from side to side as though the mustard will reveal itself if he looks hard enough.

I look over my shoulder at the fridge, which is only about four steps away, three with Tom's long legs, and then back at him. 'You know where the fridge is, don't you?'

He stares at me a beat. 'Oh. Right. Yes.' He hops up, grabs the mustard and slathers it on his steak in less time than it took to ask me where it was.

Jack gazes at the TV while he mindlessly shovels in small bites of meat, leaving the salad. Tom occasionally glances my way while he eats, accompanied by a quick smile. I watch both of them as I work through my own meal, seething over the ingratitude, and with each passing second, my soul withers.

Within ten minutes, Tom snaps his cutlery together in the middle of his empty plate. 'Thanks, Holly. Lovely.' He yawns, not covering his mouth in time to disguise the food stuck in his teeth. 'Sorry. Such a long day.' He rests his hand on my shoulder. 'I don't suppose you could find my work shirt?'

I stiffen. Now that I have no job, I'm even more of a housewife.

He takes his dirty dishes to the sink, gives them a quick rinse, places them in the dishwasher and heads back to the lounge. Jack jumps off his chair and rushes after him.

A sourness curdles in my belly, deep in my core, and I blink back tears. 'I'm done,' I whisper. I ignore the kitchen mess, find

Tom's shirt and place it on the ironing board, then head to the bathroom for peace and a hot shower.

As the warm water soaks my skin, my mind shifts to the conversation with Nat last night. An open ticket across the world sounded like a good idea with my camera in hand, heady from bottomless wine. This morning the guilt and fear took hold. I told myself that it was irresponsible to travel when I have no job and that I shouldn't leave a good relationship or Mum. But when Adam and I were in his back garden this afternoon, warming ourselves in the winter sun, he told me to go.

'Shit, Hols. If I were you, I'd be gone,' he'd said, face tilted to the sun.

'You don't think it's a bit irresponsible?'

He shrugged. 'You've basically been given a year off with pay. There'll be heaps of time to look for jobs down the track.'

'It's Mum too, though.'

He glanced back at the house where Mum was playing cards with Meg and the kids. 'It's not like you can do anything to change her situation. Besides, you can call and FaceTime as much as you want. The world's small these days, and it's not like she remembers much of the day-to-day convos anyway.'

'I guess so.' I paused. 'Then there's Tom.'

He raised his eyebrows. 'You can't tell me you're happy with Tom.'

'No, I'm not. But I don't know how to end it.'

'Mmm. Not sure I can help with that one. I've always been the dumpee,' Adam said.

I laughed. 'Me too.'

'I reckon you make it quick and leave. He talks you round a lot – he'll talk you out of breaking up with him, and he'll definitely talk you out of travelling. Just rip off the bandaid.'

I hung my head. 'It makes me feel so guilty.'

He slipped his arm around me and pulled me close, his

body warm in the cold air. 'I know. But go and live, Hols. Tom's a grown man and we're here for Mum.'

That conversation was four hours ago and it's all I've thought about since. Out of the shower and dressed in flannelette pyjamas, I grab my laptop and crawl into bed, then rummage in my bedside table for a photo. A wave of longing washes over me as I look at it. It's one of the photos I took of Casey and me on the last night we spent together. There's an intensity to the image, a contrast of buttery yellow light and grey shadows. We're facing each other, our heads on the pillow. She's gazing at me, her eyes tender with what looks like love. But art is subjective and that's what I want to see.

I touch my fingertip to her face. 'What happened to you?' I whisper.

The date on my phone reads 18 August. I drum my fingers on the laptop as an idea germinates. If I'm going to do this, then I want to be there on 23 August – *the* day. Before I lose my nerve, I flip up the screen, fire up a travel website and within fifteen minutes, I've booked a flight to Berlin.

Chapter 11
Casey, London

Sunday afternoon, back in Notting Hill, I walk up the concrete steps of the Victorian terrace that houses our flat. I slip my key in the lock and pause, my hand on the brass door-knob, as a flutter of nerves burst in my stomach. *It's just a conversation. Open your mouth and say what's on your mind.* I give myself an encouraging nod, head into the foyer of the building and open the door of the flat.

'Hello?' I call out, pulling off my trainers and socks. I throw my keys on the sideboard, duck my head into the sitting room to find it empty, then head along the short hallway to the kitchen. Eva's at the dining table staring at her laptop, leg bent and heel up on the chair, resting her arm on her knee.

'You didn't hear me come in?'

'I heard,' she sniffs.

'You couldn't say hello back?'

She purses her lips.

I pour myself a glass of water. 'Don't, Eva. I'm allowed to spend the night with my family.'

Her jaw tightens. 'I didn't say you weren't.'

'Then why so frosty?'

She gives a snarky one-shoulder shrug.

'Fine. Be like that.'

I move to the sitting room and flick on the telly to drown out the uncomfortable silence. This conversation won't go well if she's in a mood. I drop onto the sofa, sinking into its velvety softness, and glance at my precious artwork above the mantel. It's a painting that was part of my first exhibition at the gallery. Eva wanted to hang it in the bedroom, but the neutral tones with splashes of plum and fuchsia blended better with this room. It's of two women in bed, legs tangled, one with her head on the other's chest, gazing up at her partner. I imagine the gentle thud of a heartbeat in her ear, and it triggers that old memory of me telling Holly our hearts beat to the same rhythm. The other reason I didn't want the painting in our bedroom.

I shake my head, disappointed in myself. What am I doing, thinking about Holly – someone who would've forgotten me long ago. My focus needs to be on my current relationship and whether or not I want to be in it. But now I'm home, I'm reminded that I'm in a flat I'd never be able to afford on my own, or even with a partner who earned the same as me, and I do all right. Suddenly the 'I'm not sure about this' conversation sticks in my throat. I lie back on the sofa, thinking about what Chandice said last night before we drifted off to sleep.

She'd rolled onto her side and faced me. 'Do you think that maybe – and don't have a go, right – but do you think part of you is staying with Eva because of what she gives you?'

'How do you mean?' I said, deluding myself that I didn't know what she was talking about.

Her dark eyes were gentle and probing in the low lamp-light. 'Your lifestyle, the flat. Money to do things.'

Her voice was loving, unaccusing, but it prodded at something underlying – that knowledge I carry around but never want to admit, that I've become used to how Eva and I live, and how her privilege extends to me – but I was still quick to defend. 'That's not why I fell for her. I still love her. It just feels different now.'

'I know you love her, but sometimes people get used to things, don't they? Especially in relationships. They put up with stuff because it's easier than the alternative, and you love that flat.'

'I do love the flat,' I said. 'I like having sex regularly, too.'

She gave me a playful kick under the duvet. 'I don't need to hear about your sex life, thanks. Besides, I know what you and Jaz are like when you're out. It's not like you can't pick up whenever you want.'

I frowned. 'I don't want to be out picking up. I want to be with someone I love and who loves me.'

'And that's not Eva?'

'I don't think it is,' I said sadly. 'When did you become such an expert at relationships anyway?'

'Doing lots of research for my steamy romances.' Chandice rolled over and switched off the lamp. 'Night, big sis. Just think about what I said, yeah?'

I'm still turning over the conversation with Chandice when Eva walks into the lounge room and sits on the end of the sofa.

'Talking to me now?' I ask.

'Mmm,' she says. 'I'm angry at you for leaving like that yesterday.'

'I'm sorry. I know it was sudden. But it was freaking me out, Eva. It's just a lot sometimes.'

'But it's a wedding, and I want a nice one. I only plan on getting married once.' She runs her hand up my shin.

I jerk my leg away. 'It's all a bit stressful. Maybe, we could, like, you know, postpone the wedding for a bit?'

'Oh, God. You're not serious?' Her eyes water and her chest heaves up and down.

'Um ... maybe ... yes?'

She jumps up and begins pacing. 'You're finishing with me? Why?' She buries her head in her hands, her shoulders jerking.

'Eva, please don't cry.'

'But ... everything,' she says though a sob, 'is ... planned. My dress ... the guest list ... the chef!'

'It's just ... I'm not sure about this,' I try again.

She drops her hands and glowers at me, her cheeks stained with mascara. 'You're seriously cancelling the wedding? After all the effort I've put into it? After what my parents have spent? After I've promised my followers the best lesbian wedding they've ever fucking seen?'

'Erm...' I swallow.

She stamps her foot, actually stamps her foot. 'No, Casey. You will not fucking treat me like this. We're not postponing. Either marry me or don't marry me. But do not fuck me around.'

I put my hands up. 'Okay. I'm sorry. Work is stressful and I'm a bit overwhelmed, is all.'

She rushes back to the sofa and grabs my hand. 'I know you get overwhelmed sometimes. That's why I'm doing as much as I can. And wedding nerves are normal. But we love each other, don't we? Once it's over, we can go back to being us again, but married.' She leans forward to kiss me.

I give her a quick peck, but when she clutches my face and tries to deepen the kiss, I pull away. 'I'm not in the mood right now. I might go for a bath.' I stand. 'You know what Mum's like with the hot water – I was in and out there.'

Her mouth drops open and I race to the bathroom.

I turn on the taps, squeeze in some bath gel and sit on the

toilet while the tub fills. That was a fucking car crash. It'd be just like Eva to burst in here any minute, so I jump up and snib the lock. That'll give me space for a bit. *Space.* That helped me last night. I dig my phone out of my pocket and check my flight to Berlin – Wednesday morning. That's still three days away. Eva will try to bring me round with sex before then, and she'll succeed, which will mess with my head even more. I tap the 'change flight' link and rebook to leave in the morning.

Chapter 12
Holly, Melbourne

Jack shouting from the other end of the house wakes me with a start. I sit up, glancing at the clock on my bedside table, ready to get up for work. Then I remember I don't have a job and I booked a flight to Berlin last night, leaving tomorrow. The thought fills me with equal measures of excitement and dread. I can't believe I actually had the courage to do it. But I couldn't find the same courage to tell Tom. After he fell asleep, I spooned him, breathing in his freshly washed skin one last time.

I swing my legs out of bed, waiting a few seconds to see if the nerves in my gut settle. They don't, so I take a deep breath and head to the kitchen to make lunches for Tom and Jack. Just as I'm finishing, Tom appears, clean-shaven and dressed for work. I catch the spice of his cologne. It's nice, and my heart squeezes.

'Morning,' he says. 'Ooh, sandwich today. That looks good.'

I place an apple and his sandwich in a lunch bag and push it across the bench towards him. 'Chicken, avocado and salad on that grain bread you like.'

'Great, thank you.' He stares at me expectantly, like he deserves a round of applause for showing some appreciation.

'You're welcome,' I say and flick the switch on the kettle.

He gestures to my laptop on the dining table. 'Ready for a day of job hunting?'

My cheeks warm and I turn away, grabbing the milk from the fridge and holding the door open a few seconds longer than necessary so the cold air cools my face. 'Well, I'm still technically employed for another month, so I don't have to start looking today.'

'True. But it could take a while to find something,' he says.

I roll my eyes at the milk carton.

'Okay, we're off. Come on, Jack.'

Jack picks up his schoolbag, shoves in his lunchbox and heads for the back door.

'What do you say?' Tom says to him, resting his hand on Jack's small shoulder.

He gapes up at Tom, his little face scrunched with confusion.

'What do you say to Holly? You won't see her for two weeks.'

Jack looks at me. 'Bye.'

I give him one last smile. 'Bye, Jack. Have a good day at school.'

He slides the glass door across and runs out to the garage.

'At least he said bye,' Tom says.

I walk around the island bench and lift my face to kiss him. He has soft lips and I always liked kissing him. 'You smell nice.'

He grins. 'You like this one?'

'I do.' I swallow and pat his chest. 'Have a good day at work.' It comes out strained, and for once I'm grateful he's not good at picking up on my emotional cues.

He slips his arms into his coat sleeves. 'See you tonight.'

My gut twists, and I push him towards the door before I change my mind about leaving. 'Bye.'

As he reverses down the driveway, I let out a pained groan. 'Sorry, Tom, but I have to do this.'

Settling at the dining table with my laptop and a mug of coffee, I email a medical certificate citing stress to Sasha and HR and let them know I cleared out my desk on Saturday morning and won't be returning. Then I search accommodation in Berlin, booking a studio flat in Mitte for two weeks. I'll choose the next country when I arrive. With nervous adrenaline coursing through me, I rush into the bedroom to pack, pulling summer clothes from my wardrobe and dumping the contents of my underwear drawer onto the bed, then hit Nat's number for FaceTime.

'Hey,' she says, her face coming to life on the screen. She's still in her pyjamas, her light brown hair mussed from sleep. Her baby squeals and gives her a huge gummy grin before she scoops porridge into his mouth.

'Hello, Archie,' I coo.

'You're calling early for your first Monday off work.'

'That's because I have something to tell you.' I flip my screen towards my open suitcase. 'I did it.'

Nat gasps and places the cereal bowl down on the kitchen table. 'Oh. My. God. You booked a ticket?'

'Yep. Last night.'

Her eyes bulge. 'Wow. I didn't realise you'd do that so soon.'

I hop on the bed and cross my legs. 'I didn't either. But last night, I snapped.' I tell her about yesterday: waking up hungover and not being able to get any peace because I was expected to help with Jack and the house was a mess; about Adam encouraging me to go; then cooking dinner with no thanks and Tom hassling me about his work shirt. Voicing it makes me sound irrational, but at the time it's all it took to make me want to leave.

'So, Tom just got up from the table and walked off?' Nat asks. 'Didn't do the dishes or anything?'

'He rinsed his plate and a few other things and stuck them in the dishwasher, but that's what he always does.' I suddenly feel bad for dissing him and back-pedal. 'I shouldn't have let it happen. I haven't raised things with him because of his long workdays, especially the past few months when I've had it so easy at work. I should've told him how I was feeling. He would've helped me.'

Nat scoffs. 'He has eyes. He can see that you're rushing around doing stuff all the time. Why is it up to you to tell him?' Nat gently pulls the spoon from Archie's mouth and smiles at him as he opens his mouth for the next bite.

'He doesn't mean it; he just doesn't think sometimes,' I say.

She gives me a look, her mouth a tight line. 'I hope he hasn't invited himself along on your trip.'

I prop my phone against a couple of pillows and fold T-shirts into my case. 'Um...'

Nat winces. 'You haven't told him?'

I mirror her wince. 'I couldn't do it last night, and you know what would happen if I told him this morning. I'd get Mr Sensible talking me out of it. I have to do this.'

'I get it, but you might want to tell him before you hop on the plane,' she says gently.

'I'll tell him when he gets home from work because...' I clear my throat. 'I'm leaving tomorrow.'

'Tomorrow!'

I release a shuddery breath. 'Yep. I'll stay at Adam and Meg's tonight.'

Her eyes well. 'I didn't expect it to happen so quickly.'

'Oh, Nat, please don't cry. I didn't either. But what am I staying here for? The longer I stay, the unhappier I'll be.'

She nods and leans across the table for a tissue, Archie gazing at her as she dabs the corner of her eye. 'You have to go. I'll run you to the airport if Adam or Meg can't do it.'

I shake my head. 'You don't have to do that.'

'I do. What time's your flight?'

'One.'

She smiles through her tears. 'Okay, brunch at the airport it is, then.' She tickles Archie under the chin, making him gurgle. 'You want to take Aunty Holly to the airport tomorrow?'

'Thank you,' I say. 'I'd better get this packing done. Then I need to visit Mum and do a million other things. I'll call you tonight when I'm at Adam's.' A wave of nausea rolls through me. 'Ooh.'

'Are you okay?'

'The reality hits me every now and then.' I look furtively at the bedroom door, half expecting Tom to walk in any minute. 'I'm dreading the convo with Tom.'

Concern creases Nat's face. 'You want me to be there with you?'

I give a grateful smile. 'I'd love that, but I need to be an adult and do this on my own.'

She holds her hand up in a wave. 'Good luck.'

I spend another half hour packing then race down to the local cheap shop for storage bags. Once they're filled with my heavy winter clothes and some other belongings, I lug them to the car to drop at Adam's on the way to visit Mum.

Mum's sitting on a bench partly shaded by an elm tree when I arrive. Her eyes are closed, and the sunshine that peeks through the leaves highlights the soft creases in her skin. The temperature is a few degrees above average today, but it's still cold, and she's dressed warmly in grey woollen pants and the pastel pink jumper I gave her for Mother's Day. She looks so serene that I can't stop myself snapping a photo on my phone.

'Hi, Mum,' I say, sitting beside her.

Her eyes open slowly, and she stares at me a moment before she breaks into a smile. 'Hello...' She pats my thigh, mouth open, waiting for her brain to catch up. 'Erm, hello ... Holly. Yes, it's Holly.'

I beam at her. 'That's right!'

She bumps her shoulder against mine. 'One of the nurses gave me a tip. She said my daughter's name is just like "hello" and if I can say hello when I see you then I might remember "Holly". I can't promise it will always work.'

'I'll take it for today.' I slip my arm around her shoulders and show her the image on my phone. 'I just took a nice photo of you.'

Her eyebrows rise when she sees it. 'That's what I look like when I'm sleeping, is it?'

'You look beautiful.'

'Mmm. If you say so.'

I slip my phone into the pocket of my jeans. 'How are you?'

'I'm enjoying this sunshine and those birds,' she says, pointing to a shrub a few metres away. 'They have a lovely sound. I recognise them but can't think what they're called.'

'I think they're a type of honeyeater.'

She nods. 'Honeyeater. Yes, that's it.'

'Can I get you anything? A cup of tea?'

She shakes her head and points to a mug on her left. 'I just had one.'

I'm stalling telling her my news, but the emotion associated with leaving her is building in my throat and it's hard to get the words out. I take a deep breath. 'I've got something to tell you.'

She twists to face me. 'You're having a baby?'

'What?' I laugh, and it's exactly what I needed to loosen me up. 'No.'

She chuckles.

'I booked a flight overseas.'

Her brow crinkles. 'Overseas?'

'Uh-huh. We spoke about it yesterday – when we were at Adam's for lunch.'

She frowns. 'No, I don't recall that conversation. I do remember we were all there though, and we played cards, so that's something, isn't it?'

'It is.'

She links her arm in mine. 'A holiday will be lovely. Where are you going?'

I'm about to say it might be longer than a holiday, but then decide against it. She probably won't remember, and maybe it's better this way. 'To Berlin first.'

'Berlin. You've been there before. When you were at university.'

'That's right,' I say, but don't let on that we talked about this last week. 'I'll go to London too and visit Aunty Carol and Katie.'

Her pale eyes spark with recognition at the mention of her younger sister. 'Oh, lovely. She'll be so happy to see you.'

'And I'm going to make good use of this.' I reach into my bag and pull out my new camera.

'Ooh, that's a beauty.' She takes it from me, inspecting it closely. 'You were always so good at photography, just like your dad. He gave you your first camera, you know. I can't think when exactly, but you were young.'

'It was my tenth birthday,' I say. 'It was a little digital one.'

It was the most extravagant present I'd ever received – more than Mum and Dad could afford. 'You and Dad took us to the botanic gardens that day. We had a picnic, and you named all the birds and trees, and Dad taught me how to use the camera. It was the best birthday I ever had.'

She smiles wistfully. 'You kids were everything to your father.'

'You were everything to him, too.'

She stares into the garden, a faraway look on her face. 'Yes. I miss him terribly.'

I rest my head on her shoulder. 'I miss him too, Mum, and I'm going to miss you.'

~

'Tom, I love you, but...' I pace the kitchen, wringing my hands. 'Tom, I've been unhappy...'

Through the kitchen window, the glow of headlights appears in the driveway, and I press my hand against my stomach like it will somehow quash the rising nausea. The engine cuts and I hear the beep of Tom's car key fob. My heart rate quickens. The side gate clicks and the security light flicks on. I sit at the dining table as Tom slides open the back door, his face brightening when he sees me.

'Hello. Waiting for me?' His gaze drifts to my suitcase and his smile falters.

'Something like that,' I say softly.

His Adam's apple bobs. 'What's going on? Everything okay with your mum?'

'Oh. Yes. Mum's fine.' I gesture to the chair beside me. 'Sit down, Tom.'

He places his keys on the bench and shrugs off his coat, throwing it over the back of a chair, and tentatively sits.

I grab his hand in both of mine. His skin is cold and I instinctively rub it to warm it up. 'I need to go away for a while.'

His brows knit. 'Go away? With friends? Girls' trip?' He looks at my case again and barks a quick, nervous laugh. 'That's a big case for a few days away.' He shakes his head. 'Women. Always have to take so much stuff. I bet Nat's case is just as big. That's funny, Marc didn't mention anything about Nat going—'

'Tom. Please listen to me.'

He stares at me, his eyes wide with worry and uncertainty.

'It's not a trip with Nat. I'm going overseas.'

The crease in his brow deepens. 'Overseas? Where?'

'I'm going to start in Germany and take it from there.'

He rips his hand away. '*Start* in Germany ... *start*? I don't understand.'

I hang my head. None of this is coming out right. 'I'm leaving, Tom. I'm unhappy and I need to do something for myself.'

'But that's just because of the redundancy. You're not feeling like yourself. You'll get a new job and—'

'I don't want a new job,' I say. 'This isn't about losing my job. This is about me not being happy and needing to do more with my life.'

'But we're happy.' He reaches for my hand. 'We have a good life.'

'No, Tom. You're happy. I'm not.'

He shakes his head. 'You've never told me that.'

That's fair. I hadn't talked to him because I didn't understand it myself, not really, not until now. But like so many relationships, the truth often remains hidden until something forces it out. 'You're right. I didn't, but I should have.'

'Well, yeah.'

'I'm sorry,' I say in a small voice. Empty words that only serve to help me feel better and him feel worse.

'But overseas? That's a bit drastic, isn't it? I mean, it will cost so much, and you don't have a job, and—'

'That's why now is the perfect time, while I have some money and don't have to worry about working for a while.'

'You could easily get a job at another uni. Seventeen per cent superannuation, Holly. No one else pays that, and if you got a job now, you could use that money for something important. Put it towards your retirement or the mortgage.'

I gaze at him unblinking and feel vindicated for not telling him sooner. 'I'm thirty-one, Tom. I don't want to think about retirement. It's different for you, you're in your forties and work in finance – you constantly think about it. And this is your house, in your name. You never put me on the mortgage.'

'That's only because you moved in not that long ago. We haven't got round to it. Besides, that's just official stuff. You've contributed financially. Of course it's your home, too.' He places his hands on my knees, eyes pleading. 'It's our home.'

I shake my head. 'No. It's not. And I moved in a year ago.'

He sits back and runs a hand through his hair. 'What about Jack? He's just started staying here. He's had a lot of upheaval.'

'I can't be responsible for Jack. He hates me, and I don't have the energy or the inclination to make him like me.'

A flash of anger crosses his face. 'That's a bit harsh; he's eight.'

'I hate doing this to you, Tom,' I say, bringing the conversation back to us. 'But if I stay, I'll end up resenting you, and I don't want that.'

'But right now? Can't we talk about this? If you need space, then stay at Adam's or Nat's for a while. Please.'

My resolve starts to crumble but I force myself to stay firm. 'I leave tomorrow. I'm staying at Adam's tonight. The stuff I can't take is packed in the spare room and Adam will collect it on the weekend. Nat's going to use my car for now.'

His mouth drops open. 'Tomorrow? You've been planning this and you didn't tell me? Way to make me feel like a complete idiot, Holly.'

I breathe through the guilt and try to ignore the prickle behind my eyes. 'I haven't been planning it. I booked a flight last night and organised everything today.'

He removes his glasses and pinches the bridge of his nose. 'Then why didn't you tell me last night? Three years. I thought we'd go longer than that, a lot longer.'

I brush a tear from my cheek. 'I didn't know how to tell you, and I didn't want you to change my mind.'

'But ... I love you.'

I stand because if I stay a minute longer, I might not leave. 'I love you too, but not like I should.' I kiss his soft lips one last time, grab my case and head for the front door.

He hurries after me. 'Holly, please.'

'Sorry, Tom,' I say, my voice breaking as I rush along the hallway. The wheels of my suitcase rattle over the floorboards, and all I can think about is how that sound will haunt him.

'Please,' he repeats as I rush through the gate and heave my case into the boot of my car. He swiftly moves to the driver's door and puts his hand on it.

'Let me get in the car, Tom.'

'Can't we talk more?'

'Please let me in the car.'

He hesitates but drops his hand and steps away.

I climb in and start the engine. He walks back to the footpath, hands shoved deep into his pockets, shoulders hunched. He hasn't put his glasses back on and it makes him look so vulnerable that I choke out a sob. My vision blurs as we stare at each other through the windscreen. His face is pleading, but I take a deep breath, mouth 'sorry' and drive off.

Chapter 13
Casey, Berlin

Immersing myself in the Berlin gallery for the past four days has been exactly what I've needed. When I'd finally emerged from the bath on Sunday and told Eva I'd brought my flight forward, a range of emotions crossed her face – confusion, then anger, then hurt. She asked if it was because of the way she'd acted the day before at her parents. I assured her that wasn't the case, which was mostly true, and told a white lie that Josanne wanted me to go early because Felix was drowning. Are little white lies wrong if they protect someone's feelings? I couldn't bring myself to hurt her any more than I already had, so it seemed the right thing to do.

Since I've been here, other than a quick visit with my aunt and uncle who still live in Berlin, I've crammed my days with work and put in a couple of hours on my normal job at night, which has left no time to dwell. Whenever I have spoken to Eva, she's slipped straight back into wedding planning, and I've tuned out.

My eyes flick to the time in the top right corner of my laptop screen. Almost five-thirty on August 22 – *the* day. I spin on my chair to face my colleague. 'Felix, did we secure that final work for the exhibition?' I say, switching to English since his English is better than my German. Especially at this hour, when my brain can't function in another language after I've spent all day attempting to speak it.

'Yes, Katarina confirmed earlier. Sorry, I got caught up and forgot to mention it. I've arranged collection for tomorrow afternoon.'

I let out a relieved sigh. 'Brilliant.' It's a key piece for the exhibition that we almost lost after some confusion with the artist and dates.

'And I fixed the issue with the installers,' he says. 'They've agreed to come in on Sunday.'

'Well done. Least they could do after messing you about. Are you still doing that radio interview tomorrow?'

He nods. 'That's at eleven. I'm also on the art weekly podcast that will be released over the weekend.'

'Okay. We're almost there.' I peek at the clock on the wall above his head. 'Anything else you need me to do?'

'Nothing that can't wait until tomorrow.' He smiles and brushes his floppy, sandy hair from his face. 'I'm glad you're here. It's been a huge help.'

I return the smile. 'No problem. It's a nice change, actually. Done me good to get away from London this week, and I love this exhibition.' I set my laptop to sleep and slip it into its bag. 'Mind if I get going?'

'You don't want to come for a drink with me and Matias? There's a good bar a few doors down; we're meeting there. We'll probably grab something to eat, too.'

'I don't want to take you away from your new husband.'

He grins. 'We get plenty of time together at home.'

I sling the strap of my laptop bag over my shoulder. 'It's okay. I was up late last night working, so I'm pretty tired.

Thanks, though.' This isn't untrue, but the park is calling me, and I'm jittery that six o'clock is nearing and I'm not there yet.

'Planning a wedding is tiring.'

'Oh, erm ... yeah.' I've known Felix for years now, but I don't recall talking to him about Eva or the wedding in any recent work conversations, and I've intentionally not mentioned it this week.

He tsks himself. 'Sorry, that sounded like I'm in your business. I follow Eva on Instagram and she posts about it a lot.'

'Ah.' I nod. 'Right. Well, you probably know more than me since I don't bother looking at her feed much.' My words have an unintended bitter edge, and I throw in a quick smile to put him off the scent.

He cringes. 'Sorry, have I said the wrong thing?'

I forget how perceptive he is sometimes. 'No, not at all. It's just a bit ... well, a bit complicated.' I head for the office door. 'Have a good night.'

'*Tschüss*,' he says as I pass.

'*Tschüss*.'

I leave the gallery, walking at a fast pace and glancing at my watch every few seconds. I turn onto Tucholskystrasse. It's thrumming with peak-hour traffic – people exit buildings and swarm to the S-Bahn, hop on bikes or scurry along the footpath. At the corner of Oranienburgerstrasse, the bars and cafés are busy outside despite the heavy grey clouds and patchy rain.

After another minute's walk, I'm at the entrance of Monbijoupark. My mouth turns dry and I dig in my bag for a bottle of water, downing a few gulps before stepping inside the park boundary. I pass the fountain and head along the concrete path that runs through the centre, then turn onto a dirt path. It's wet from the rain and the heels of my boots sink into the muddy earth. People laze on the grass – alone, reading books, chatting in groups or throwing balls for their dogs. Music floats up from the river and it helps to relax me for a minute until I spot the tree and my body tenses. I was only here a few years ago – when I first got this job and Josanne sent me to Berlin to see the gallery. Back then, I walked from tree to tree, searching for the right one, but once I found it, I knew.

I sit on the damp grass with my back pressed against the trunk, legs stretched out, my mind filling with an image of Holly and me lying here. So much has become hazy over the years, but that afternoon has remained vivid. Wanting to reassure her that I really did care but not knowing how, and instead giving her a ridiculous plan to find each other. *The Bode Museum is there. The Berliner Fernsehturm is there. The fountain is there. And the Alte Nationalgalerie, where I met the prettiest girl I've ever seen, is over there. I'll remember. This spot. On this day. At this time.* At least I told her one truth that day – that I'd remember. I press my hand to my heart, the regret burning thick, mingling with the constant ache of what-if and the grief of cutting all ties with her.

I glance around, but no one looks like Holly. Of course they don't. She's in Melbourne, taking photos of the city, busy in her project manager job, living life with a handsome lad called Tom. Is she happy? Has she had a good life? Has she thought about me or tried to find me? What did she do with those photos of us from that final night?

I pull out my phone and bring up Holly's Instagram profile. Her last post is from Saturday night, at a wine bar with someone called Nat. Holly looks incredible. Her hair still has the same honey tones and falls loose and wavy past her shoulders. Her smile is wide and genuine, her pale blue eyes glimmering with warmth. My gaze shifts to her throat and I zoom in for a closer look. It's the same necklace – a silver chain with a tiny H pendant. I can still feel the smooth silver between my fingers.

My fingertip hovers over the 'like' button. Is receiving a like on a post from a ghost from your past creepy? Would she respond? Mum's voice is in my head: *Don't contact Holly until you sort things with Eva.* Then I hear Chandice: *Stop stalking, you total saddo.* I exit the app and slip my phone away before I can do anything stupid.

Closing my eyes, I try to focus on the present, tuning into the sensations of the park. The birdsong above me, the warm air on my face, the voices floating on the breeze. But it doesn't work; the past continues to haunt me because I'm in the exact spot where I felt such intense emotions for the first time in my young life, emotions that overwhelmed me so much that I had to run. And if I'm honest, emotions I've never experienced again.

Emotions I've never experienced again.

My eyes open. Everything is sharper. I have to end things with Eva, like, completely. Not half, not 'maybe we should delay the wedding but stay together'. I'm in a park thinking about someone else. That's not fair on Eva, and it makes me feel like a shitty person. I give a silent cheer to Holly and head in the direction of my hotel.

Back in my room, I kick off my boots and settle on the bed with my pizza and bottle of Warsteiner, then FaceTime Jaz.

'All right,' she says, her face filling the screen. 'Did you go?' She shovels a forkful of noodles into her mouth. A few strands stick to her chin and she slurps them up.

I take a bite of pizza and nod.

Jaz frowns. 'She wasn't there, I take it?'

'Nah. Nor did I expect her to be, but I wanted to be there again to...' I shrug. 'Be there again.'

'And you were close by, weren't you? So you'd kick yourself if you didn't go.'

'Mmhmm.' I swallow my bite of pizza. 'I checked Holly's Insta, too.'

'Oh yeah. What's occurring in Oz?' She slurps another mouthful of soupy noodles.

'Sod all since Saturday night. I nearly clicked "like" on that post, but all I could hear was Mum nagging at me not to contact Holly, and Chandice calling me a saddo.'

Jaz grins. 'It is a bit tragic, mate.' She dabs sauce from her chin with a piece of kitchen towel.

'Totally. And if I contact her and she doesn't remember me, I'll look like a right twat.'

'You are a right twat.'

'Fuck off,' I say with a laugh and swig my beer.

She laughs too, picks up her bowl with both hands and tilts it up to her mouth.

I grab another slice of pizza. 'Being at the park cleared up something for me, though.'

'Yeah?'

'Me and Eva. It's not going to work. We don't get along anymore and we want totally different things. Not that I'm sure what I want; I just know it's not the same as her.'

'You had to get there in your own time.' Jaz fills her water glass from a jug beside her. 'I don't envy the conversation you're going to have tonight.'

I grimace. 'I can't tell her tonight. We've got a huge day tomorrow finalising the exhibition. I have to be up for seven at the latest. You know what will happen. There'll be tears for hours, demands for me to go home, or she'll want to come here.' I shake my head. 'No. I need to get tomorrow out of the way and get things clear in my head before I talk to her.'

'I get that, mate, but you don't want to put it off too much longer.'

'I'll call her tomorrow night after work. Felix and I are having Saturday off to give ourselves a break before next week, so it won't matter if I'm up half the night dealing with it. I know it's shitty not telling her in person, but I won't be home for almost a week. It doesn't feel right to wait when I'm sure.'

'Do whatever you think is right.' She jumps up and returns within a few seconds, cracking a Chocolate Orange on the table. She unwraps the orange foil and sticks a wedge in her mouth, narrowing her eyes at me, the way she does when she thinks she has me worked out. 'Hey, I'm sorry your one true love didn't show.'

I lean my head back against the wall. 'She wasn't my one true love. She was my one true what-might've-been.'

Jaz puts another wedge of chocolate in her mouth. 'That too.'

I hold my hand up in a wave. 'I need some sleep. Later.'

We hang up and I head for the shower, stripping off my T-shirt and catching sight of the tattoo on my upper arm. It was my first. The needle pricking my skin temporarily shifted the unfamiliar ache from my heart and it gave me a rush knowing that if I couldn't be with Holly physically, I could at least keep the memory of us stamped on my body forever.

Chapter 14
Holly, Berlin

The air in the Lustgarten is fresh after the rain, and sunshine has replaced the grey skies. I find an empty bench in the shade to finish my coffee and soak up my first Friday afternoon in Berlin. After two days, my jetlag has lifted, along with some of the heaviness of the past few months. My body feels lighter and I can breathe easier.

After I left Tom on the footpath, vulnerable and broken, I drove to Adam and Meg's, sobs jerking my body. They rushed me inside and let me fall apart, while Eli and Cooper, my young nephews, patted my wet cheeks. The following morning, trying to ignore Tom's pleading messages, I spent time with Mum before Nat took me to the airport. By the time I boarded the plane, the crack in my chest was deep, and I was questioning my decision. But as the distance grew between home and me, a sense of calm took hold and that glimmer of possibility I felt the afternoon I left Caleb's bar spread.

The moment I stepped out of the doors at Brandenburg Airport into a grey Berlin morning full of foreign sights, sounds and smells, a rush of memories hit me. First, being here three years ago with Adam and Mum and her excitement at being somewhere new, then my university exchange semester. The shock of suddenly being in Berlin almost made me run straight back into the terminal, but I reminded myself I came here to form new memories and to fall in love with the city again. So, I took a deep breath, jumped in a taxi and headed to my accommodation, forcing myself to stay awake for the day as I wandered Mitte.

Since then, I've rediscovered a small part of the city with a fresh lens, visiting the places that had darkened for me eleven years ago. I spent a chunk of my twenty-seven-hour plane journey reading psychology magazines, absorbing tips on 'how to let go' and learning how events from the past, no matter how small, can scar us. The advice was to feel the emotion, release it, then replace it with a positive experience to form new neural pathways. I've been to the suburb where my dorm room was, past both our campuses and a few bars, and to the spot by the river where we shared our first kiss. I've allowed myself to enjoy the memory of Casey and the experiences we had together, then focused on new things to like about those places, mainly through my camera. I've photographed incredible art along the wall, old buildings covered in plant life, food from around the world, lush city gardens and local people doing everyday things who were more than happy to let me photograph them.

Worrying about Mum is constant, but Adam has bought her a new phone and we've spoken a few times. She carries it everywhere, not always remembering why until I call. It takes her a moment to register I'm away, but then she wants to know everything, and she has some memories of being here. The hurt on Tom's face is still fresh in my mind. My head tells me it was a heartless thing to do, but when I ignore those thoughts and listen to my gut, I'm certain I did the right thing.

I place my coffee on the bench beside me and scroll

through my photo app, choosing an image from earlier today that doesn't need editing – a close-up of plants in the Tiergarten, fat, glistening drops of rain balancing on forest-green leaves. I've held off posting photos because I didn't want to rub Tom's face in it. Not that he uses Instagram, but Nat's husband might show him at work without thinking.

I feel a surge of anger. Why am I worrying about Tom? This is my trip, and I want to share my travels and promote my photography. Before I can change my mind, I upload the photo with a simple caption, slip my phone away and think about what's next on my 'letting go' tour, because it's 23 August – *the* day. Time to release more memories.

I leave my shady bench and venture through the park until I reach Bodestrasse and take the path to the Alte Nationalgalerie. I glance up at the sandstone building with its Roman pillars, extravagant stairwells and the equestrian statue guarding the entrance. The scene is the same as it was eleven years ago, although I didn't appreciate the beauty of the building as a twenty-year-old.

Inside, the visitors have thinned out being late afternoon, and I'm alone as I head to the upper galleries. On the top floor, I pause for a few seconds to get my bearings, then make my way to the room I want, taking a sharp intake of breath when I see it. The bench seat with the same dusty pink cushioned top is still there. I see a younger version of myself gazing at the painting, naïve, hopeful and focused on my studies, no clue that the person who was about to talk to me would leave a scar. Casey had told me she'd followed me from the gallery below, watching me tilt my head at paintings trying to figure them out, and waiting for an opportunity to talk to me.

I walk to the middle of the room, my sandals making a soft thud on the parquet floor, and sit in the same spot I had that day. *Italia und Germania* is long gone, in a gallery in Munich now. I take in the painting in my line of sight. All I see is a house among some trees. It looks rushed, like something my nephews would paint at preschool, but if Casey were here, she'd talk about the significance of the brushstrokes, the symbolism in the art, and how it reflected society at the time.

I shake my head to clear the thought. I'm not here to dwell on what might've been. I close my eyes and let that day swirl in my mind – walking through the different galleries, Casey showing off her university-level art knowledge, all cockiness and swagger. The way she gazed at me, dreamy-eyed, as I spoke. And later that night, our first kiss. My stomach flutters at the memory. I've never experienced a first kiss like it. The way we both sighed when our lips pressed together, her warm tongue tentative against mine, her mouth as soft as it looked, and the way my fingers tingled when they brushed her skin. I hold a hand to my chest, reluctantly let the memory go and say a silent goodbye to her.

I head outside, unsure if that exercise has made any difference, so I do what always helps – set up my tripod, adjust the camera settings to architecture mode and line up the building. I snap image after image. Different angles, shifting light, the contrast of sandstone against the expanse of blue sky and feathery white clouds. The edges of the building are sharp in the summer sunshine and the starkness of the different textures is striking. I snap some with my phone, send one to Adam and Mum, and upload another to Instagram. I stroll along the busy walkway to the Bode Museum where I take more shots, focusing on the way the sun casts a sheen across the magnificent copper dome.

Once I'm happy with my photos, I pack up my gear and slowly turn around, my stomach clenching. Across the small body of water is Monbijoupark. I check the time – 5.40 pm. My legs have suddenly become heavy but I force myself to move, cross Monbijou Bridge and descend the concrete steps to the park. Crowds are gathered along the promenade, lounging in deck chairs, soaking up the late afternoon sun and live music.

I head towards the centre of the park and take the dirt path. It takes a few minutes to orient myself, but then I'm certain I've found the right spot because the Berliner Fernsehturm antenna is peeking over the treetops. I know the tree by the width of its trunk; I'd measured it against my body when I first returned looking for Casey so I'd never forget.

I sit cross-legged on the grass and let the memories surface. My head on Casey's shoulder, her mouth on mine, my fingertips brushing her silky skin. *I'll remember. This spot. This day. This time.* My mind shifts to our other conversation that day – me pushing to go to London, trying to force a situation where we'd be together – and deep regret flares in my chest. I release a heavy, shuddering breath, hoping it will rid me of this hurt and confusion I've carried for so long.

'Time to move on,' I whisper. Opening my eyes, I look around the park. Nothing has changed. No one has magically appeared in front of me. But I feel a shift, a willingness to let it go, and that's a start.

I pull out my camera and take some random shots. Maybe I'll go to a bar tonight and find myself a new Berlin romance – create new, amazing-sex neural pathways, test whether this letting go stuff has worked. I flick through the images I've just taken and consider my own invitation to go out. Too much effort. Maybe I'll just get some nice food, a bottle of wine, take it back to my Airbnb and spend the night in Lightroom, editing my photos.

Chapter 15
Casey, Berlin

I've spent the workday dealing with artists, catering, deliveries, minor mishaps, and finalising everything for the exhibition opening on Tuesday night. My mind has had no space to dwell on the phone call I need to make to Eva later, but my body carries the stress of it. My shoulders pinch, there's a relentless throb in my temple, and I have no appetite. Now, it's just gone 5.40 pm, and as much as I'd like to keep working so I can avoid that call, we've done all we can for today and Felix wants to leave.

'Call on the weekend if you need me,' I say to Felix as I slip my laptop into its bag. 'I'll be working on the London exhibition anyway.'

'Sure. I'll be here Sunday for the installers. That leaves us two days for any last-minute issues, so I think we're good.'

'I'll come in on Sunday and give you a hand, if you like,' I say.

'Great, thank you. Any plans tonight?'

'Erm...' I massage my temple. 'Have to call Eva. Things to talk about.'

He grimaces. 'Like that, is it?'

I frown. 'Mmm.'

'Sorry to hear that. If you need a friend afterwards, you have my number.'

I hoist my laptop bag onto my shoulder. 'Cheers, Felix. I might take you up on that.'

'Oh.' He jumps up. 'Can you wait a minute? The caterers contacted me with some last-minute changes and I'd like your opinion before I get back to them.'

'Sure,' I say, welcoming the delay.

He heads down the corridor to another office and I lean against the doorframe and check my phone, automatically navigating to Holly's Insta profile, hoping for a new post since her night out on Saturday. Her grid has new photos, but they're outside shots – a park, an old building. I click on the first image and read the caption. *Rain in the Tiergarten.* I push myself off the doorframe, my heart leaping. Does Melbourne have a Tiergarten? I look at the next image and my legs almost buckle. It's the Alte Nationalgalerie, posted twenty-one minutes ago. *Oh, God.* I check the time – 5.49 pm.

'Felix,' I shout. 'I have to go.'

He appears holding a piece of paper. 'Oh, I just need—'

'Get whatever you think. Sorry,' I call over my shoulder as I shoot across the gallery floor and out the doors.

I run to the end of the street, glancing at my watch as I turn onto Tucholskystrasse – 5.52. I switch to a fast walk, darting around people who get in my way. *Why is this road so long?* I reach Oranienburgerstrasse at 5.55. The pedestrian crossing lights are red. 'Hurry up, lights,' I mutter. They change to green and I bolt across the road, then run the rest of the way to the entrance of Monbijoupark. I don't bother with paths this time, just cut across the grass, and then I freeze.

A woman is standing exactly where I was yesterday, her back to me. I squint as I assess her. She has long, wavy, honey-coloured hair. She also has a familiar soft sway of her hip as she takes a few steps forward, and a body shape that looks a lot like the one I mapped with my hands and mouth every moment I could. My gaze lands on a camera cradled in her hand – her *camera*. She points it towards the Berliner Fernsehturm and clicks the shutter.

Move, Casey. One foot in front of the other. But my body won't comply with my brain. Instead, my trembling hands fumble with my phone and I call Jaz.

'Oh, heeyyy,' she answers.

'I think she's here, Jazzy.' My voice is just above a whisper. 'I fucking found her.'

A scream bursts into my eardrum and I hear Chandice in the background say, 'What you screaming at? Is that Casey?'

'Yeah,' Jaz says. 'She's found Holly.'

'No fucking way!' Chandice shrieks.

'Well, I can't be certain, but whoever she is really, really looks like her, and moves like her.'

'Hang on, you said, "she's here". Here where? Are you in the park?' Jaz says.

'Yeah. She posted a photo of the gallery where we first met like, half an hour ago, so I raced over here.'

'Ow, Chandice,' Jaz yells. 'Get the fuck off me.'

'I'm trying to listen!' Chandice retorts.

'Are you sure it was a real-time photo?' Jaz says. 'Not like a photo from years ago she's just posted today?'

'Oh.' My heart sinks. 'I hadn't thought of that.' I try to recall the caption – nothing more than the name of the gallery. 'I guess it could be an old photo. But this person looks just like her.'

'How much does it *actually* look like her?' Chandice interjects. 'You've been staring at her photos on Instagram enough, you should be able to tell.'

'A lot, I s'pose. I can't see her face that clearly from here. But she has a camera, and I remember the way she carried herself – that's the same.' I remember her other Berlin photo. 'She posted a photo of the Tiergarten, too. And that caption said, "Rain in the Tiergarten". It rained here this morning.'

'Well, then,' Jaz says. 'Just walk up and ask, "are you Holly?" And if it's not, walk away, no harm done.'

I rub my stomach. 'I actually feel like I'm going to chuck, though.'

'Just go and fucking talk to her,' Chandice calls out. 'You've spent your entire twenties wanting this moment. Don't ruin it now.'

'How can she not see you?' Jaz asks.

'I'm half hiding behind a tree.'

'Oh my God. What are you like,' Chandice says with a laugh.

The woman tucks her camera away and glances around. She looks my way and does a quick double take, then shakes her head and starts towards the river.

'Oh, fuck. She's leaving,' I say.

'Go! Fucking go!' Jaz says. 'I'm hanging up.'

'Call us back!' Chandice yells.

I slip my phone into my pocket, unglue my feet from the ground and move. She's walking at a fast pace and I'm almost at a jog to catch her. My heart thumps, and the adrenaline coursing through my body makes me jelly-like. When I'm almost caught up, I call, 'Holly?'

She spins, and I gasp. 'It *is* you.'

Chapter 16
Holly, Berlin

My hand flies to my mouth. A person who looks very similar to the image I've carried with me for eleven years stands in front of me. Cropped curly black hair, dark soulful eyes, warm brown skin, tall, lean body. She looks even better with age. I lower my hand to speak, but my tongue feels thick in my mouth, and all that comes out is, 'Casey?'

She nods and awkwardly adjusts the bag strap over her shoulder.

'Oh my God.' I place my palm against my forehead and turn away. 'Oh my God.' I face her again and press my hand to my chest. 'Oh my fucking God.'

'Hiya,' she says.

I give a short, incredulous laugh. 'Hi.' My gut twists and turns. My heart explodes. My limbs weaken. 'You're here. In this spot. On this day. At this time.'

'I am. Although, you're twenty-four hours late...'

I shake my head. 'No, 23 August, 6 pm.'

'22nd,' she says.

I laugh again. 'Well, one of us has the date wrong.'

Casey smiles. 'Seems that way.'

And there's that smile – the one that warms everything around her. I shake my head as though it will help everything make sense. 'Um ... what are you doing here? You're not supposed to be here. That wasn't the plan.'

Her brows lift. 'You had a plan?'

I nod. 'A plan to get you out of my system, but here you are.'

She's silent for an agonising beat. 'You're not supposed to be here either.'

Without taking my eyes off her, I take a few steps off the path and lower myself onto a bench. She joins me, sunbeams breaking through the leaves and highlighting the gloss of her black hair and flawless skin. 'Erm...' I search for words. 'Have you ... you haven't been coming here every year since?' I feel a rush of sadness, picturing her waiting for me every year, my what-if being answered years ago.

She grins. 'No. Have you?'

I relax. 'No.'

'I've been here once before, though,' she says. 'A few years back.' She pauses. 'You weren't here.'

I'm taken aback and suddenly the rejection I've carried all these years doesn't sting as badly. 'I've been here once before too,' I say. 'Three years ago, but not in August.'

We gaze at each other, like we're trying to work out if this is real or a dream. Above us, a bird chirps, breaking the silence and reminding me to speak.

'Do you live in Berlin?' I ask.

'Um...' She blinks like she's been concussed, then finds her voice. 'No. Still in London. I work in an art gallery and we have one here too. I'm here to help with an exhibition.' She points behind her. 'The gallery's just over there actually, on Auguststrasse.'

'Art history,' I say.

'Sorry?'

'You were studying art history at uni.'

She smiles. 'That's right.'

'That's amazing you turned it into a job.'

She nods. 'It is. What about you? Still in Melbourne then.'

'Oh,' I say a little surprised, because that sounded like a statement and not a question. 'Yes. Did you—'

'Your accent,' she says quickly. 'Sounds like you've been in Australia all this time, is all.'

'Ah, yep, still in Melbourne,' I say.

'Are you here for a holiday, or a job?'

'Oh, just a holiday.' I scrunch my nose. 'Kind of lost my job. Redundancy, not because I was shit at it.'

Casey laughs. It's heartfelt, authentic and comforting, and it warms my spirit. 'That's good to know.'

'I wanted to get away from everything. So' – I hold up my camera – 'I decided to travel and take photos.'

'Creative arts. Photography was your favourite.'

I turn gooey. 'You remember that?'

'I do.' Her voice is tinged with nostalgia and she flashes me another smile before she glances around the park. 'Are you here with friends? Family?' A pause. 'Partner?'

I shake my head, my gaze fixed on her, too scared to look away in case she vanishes. She waits for my reply, watching me with those eyes ... those *fucking* eyes. 'Just me.'

There's an imperceptible rise of her brows. Or is that me imagining things? Reading too much into every facial movement?

'Here on your own?' she says. 'Good for you.'

'I take it if you're here for work, you're travelling alone?' It's a question I immediately regret, because I don't want to hear that she's here with her partner. I want this new-found hope to last longer than five minutes.

She breaks eye contact. 'Ah, yeah, just me.'

My heart lifts, and I take the opportunity. 'I was thinking about taking this stuff back to my flat and grabbing some dinner.'

'Yeah?' she says.

Her curious tone encourages me. 'If ... I don't suppose you'd want...' I swallow. 'Do you want to join me?'

A slow smile spreads across her face, making her eyes shine, and I'm right back in that gallery, about to melt to the ground.

'I'd love to.' She points to a large bag by her feet. 'I might drop this off first, though. I don't really want to lug around a laptop. And I've been at work since eight this morning, so it would be good to change.'

I have to stop myself from pouncing on her so she can't leave, like a puppy with separation anxiety. 'Oh. Okay.' I bite down on my lip so I can't say any more, because those two tiny words were loaded with desperation.

She scans my face, like she's trying to read my mind. 'Why don't we exchange numbers and pick somewhere to meet?'

I remember to breathe. We can meet, no need for clinginess. 'Good idea.' I dig into the pocket of my shorts and pull out my phone. 'I'll message you.'

Casey reads out her number, I type it into my contacts and send a message. 'And there's mine.'

Her phone beeps. 'Got it. Where are you staying?'

'In Mitte. Near the Naturkundemuseum. I've got a studio flat thingo for a couple of weeks.'

One side of her mouth lifts and she taps her phone screen. 'A studio flat thingo? Well, let's find somewhere near your thingo,' she says, deliberately pronouncing 'thingo' with a hard G. She opens Maps and zooms in. 'There're some good restaurants in Mitte. We can meet at the end of Friedrichstrasse, near the river. Like, around here.' She leans closer, tilting the screen toward me, and I catch her scent. Still cedarwood. I swallow and stare at her profile, our shoulders only centimetres apart. When I don't respond, she lifts her gaze, eyes piercing mine.

My breath catches and I look down at the screen, heat rising in my cheeks. 'Yeah.' It comes out as a whisper, and I clear my throat. 'Yeah, good. We'll meet there.'

'About seven-thirty?'

I nod.

'Okay, see you soon, then?'

I nod again.

'We should' – she points in the direction of the road – 'like ... leave, if we're going to drop stuff and meet up.'

'Oh. Yes. Yes, we should,' I say with a small laugh, and gather up my bag and camera.

She stands and hoists her laptop bag over her shoulder. 'Call me if, you know, you're late, or change your mind or something.'

'I won't change my mind,' I say quickly.

Her eyes narrow – trying to read my mind again. 'Good.' She gestures diagonally across the park. 'I'm headed that way.'

I point in the opposite direction. 'And I'm that way.'

She starts to walk away, then stops and turns. 'You'll be there, yeah?'

How could she doubt me? 'I will. Call me if I'm not.'

We stare at each other a moment longer. I ache to touch her, to wrap my arms around her, press our bodies together, bury my face in her neck.

'Later, then,' she says and heads off, glancing back over her shoulder, eyes crinkling with a smile just for me.

I watch until she's almost out of the park. 'Holy fuck. Ho-*ly fuck*,' I say far too loudly.

A couple of teenagers sitting on the grass nearby stare at me.

'Can you believe that?' I say to them as though they have any clue what I'm talking about. They shrug and laugh, and I start towards the exit, a huge grin stuck to my face.

Almost ten minutes later, I jog down the stairwell at the U-Bahn station, moving quickly through the crowds just as the bright yellow train comes into view. I squeeze into the carriage crammed with peak-hour commuters. It's been a warm afternoon and the crowded carriage smells of body odour, but nothing can quell the excitement that's sparking inside me right now. I want to tell everyone on the train – the elderly man by the doors rocking gently with the movement of the carriage, the woman trying to pacify her screaming toddler, the two guys sitting side by side giving each other loving looks, the teenagers talking animatedly behind me – anyone who'll listen to this incredible, amazing thing that just happened.

I hop off a stop later and walk the short distance to my studio flat. Dumping my gear on the tiny dining table, I head straight for the fridge and pour myself a glass of riesling, take a large gulp, then jump in the shower. I scrub and shave and wash my hair. 'A bit presumptuous, Holly,' I sing to myself. But deep down, it doesn't feel wildly presumptuous. There was something there – a crackle of unfinished business. It can't have been all one-sided. I can't have misread that.

Washed and dried, I slip on the only sexy underwear I brought with me – a matching cream-coloured bra and underwear set that leaves nothing to the imagination. Then I find some clean jeans and a fresh white T-shirt. It's the best I can do at short notice. I dry my hair, choose a musky perfume and apply some make-up. Suddenly, a panic that Casey might not show up grips me. No, *she* found *me*. Not the other way around. I pump the mascara wand and slick it across my lashes.

She wouldn't have done that just to ghost me again; she wouldn't have told me to call if I changed my mind.

I banish the thought, slip my feet into a pair of black ballet pumps and grab a lightweight jacket. At the door, I turn and survey the flat. The bed's unmade, clothes are strewn around the room and my empty wine glass is on the dining table. Is she likely to come back? I have no time to tidy, but I rush over to the bedside lamp and switch it on. Mood lighting is good, just in case. I switch off the overhead light and head out into a Friday evening filled with new possibilities.

Chapter 17
Casey, Berlin

'Fuck, Jazzy, she's so beautiful,' I say. 'Even more than she was, if that's possible.'

Jaz shakes her head, tight curls filling the screen of my laptop. 'What is it with you and beautiful women? It's like they just look at you and you're gone.'

I extend my leg and tug on a boot. 'Don't know.'

'Don't wear anything that's too hard to take off.'

'We're not having sex. We're just going for dinner.'

Jaz scoffs. 'You're totally having sex, babe; I can tell.'

'I haven't broke it off with Eva yet.' I slip on the other boot, then jump up to grab my jacket from the wardrobe, giving it a quick run over with the iron.

'Look,' Jaz says. 'All I'm saying is, you might never get this chance again, and you can't call Eva, dump her in two minutes and then get off with another woman.'

I lay my jacket over the ironing board and sit back in front of the screen. 'Of course I wouldn't do that. But if I call her now, I'll be on the phone for hours. She'll be going out anyway,'

I add, reasoning with myself as much as Jaz. 'I'll call her when I get back tonight.'

Jaz swigs her wine, her dark eyebrows rising. 'When you get back tonight? With Holly in your bed?'

'She's not going to be in my bed. We're meeting for dinner and a drink.' I shrug. 'Couple of drinks, maybe.'

'Just explain it to Holly tonight and call Eva in the morning.'

I chew my bottom lip.

'Casey, are you for real?' Jaz says. 'Don't fuck this up. Be honest with Holly.'

I nod. 'Totally. I will. I mean, if it comes up, like.'

Jaz rolls her eyes. 'Are you allergic to having proper discussions with people you're shaggin'?'

'It's a—'

'Gemini thing?' Jaz finishes my sentence.

I grin. 'Yeah.' My phone beeps and a message from Eva appears on the screen.

> Going out with Leila. Call you tomorrow xx

'That's Eva now. See, I said she'd be going out.' I reply with 'have fun' but a surge of guilt rises in me.

'Okay, so you're not breaking it off tonight, then. But that doesn't mean you can't tell Holly,' Jaz says.

'I don't want to scare her off when I was going to split with Eva anyway. She might disappear again. I don't want to hurt her, you know?'

'Okay, first of all, she's not the one who disappeared – that was you. And secondly, you don't want to hurt either of them, but someone is going to get hurt. If Holly still likes you after dinner, she won't go anywhere. You've got each other's phone numbers, yeah? And you know where to find her on Insta now.

Hang on, my mum's calling me.' Jaz shouts, 'What?' A pause. She faces the screen again, picks up her wine and walks through the house to the kitchen. 'Tea's almost ready.'

'I need to go anyway,' I say. 'I don't want to keep Holly waiting.'

'Have fun,' Jaz singsongs, sitting down at her parents' dining table. 'Do *everything* I would do.'

'Is that my daughter?' my mum says in the background.

I groan. 'Is my ma at yours?'

Jaz nods and flips the screen. 'So is Chandice and your dad.'

Mum and Jaz's mum are at the table, food platters spread out in front of them. Chandice is in the background with Jaz's dad, transferring chicken pieces from a pan to a plate, while my dad carries over a tray of fish.

'Hiya,' I say to everyone. 'You having a neighbours' feast without me?'

Mum ignores my question and points a fork at the screen. 'Why is Jazzy telling you to do everything she would? Are you up to no good over there?'

'No, Ma. Course not.'

'Why you all dolled up, then?'

My brows furrow and I look down. 'I've got a T-shirt and jeans on.'

'No. You're all fresh and done your hair and got a short-sleeve shirt on to show off your tats. I bet you're smelling all nice, too.'

I sigh. 'I'm just going out for my tea. I'm in a hotel room. I can't cook.'

'With who?'

'Never mind. I have to go.'

'It's Holly,' Chandice says, placing down the plate of chicken and taking a seat.

'Shut it, Chandice,' I say.

Mum gapes at me. She looks at Chandice, then over the top of the screen to Jaz, then back to me. 'She better be winding me up.'

I rub the back of my neck and look away.

'How the fuck has that happened?' Mum's fork clatters onto the table and she throws her hands up. 'Now you've made me swear at the dinner table. You know I don't like swearing at the dinner table.'

I give an incredulous laugh. 'I didn't make you do anything. I've got to go, yeah.'

My dad sticks his head in front of Mum's. 'Hiya, Casey love.'

'Hiya, Dad. You having early birthday celebrations?'

'We are.'

'I'm sorry I'm missing it, but I'll call you Sunday.'

'Okay, love. Enjoy Berlin,' he says.

'Oh, she's bloody enjoying it all right,' Mum hisses.

'I'm having dinner with an old friend. Stop frettin'.'

'But she's not an old friend, is she? She's an old fling that you never got over. What is she even doing there? I told you not to contact her.'

I throw my head back and groan. 'I'm not talking about this now. I'm going to be late.'

'Have you spoke to Eva yet?' Mum asks.

'Jaz,' I call. 'I've got to go.'

'That's a no, then.' Mum shakes her head and stabs a piece of chicken.

'Leave it out, Wendy,' Dad says. 'She's a big girl. She can sort out her own mess.'

Mum shoots Dad a look. 'No, Marvin. I won't leave it out. Someone needs to talk some sense into her.'

'Fuck's sake, Mum,' I mutter, only partly under my breath.

'Oi. Mind your language at the dinner table,' Mum says.

I throw my hands up. 'I ain't at the dinner table!'

'But we are, so watch that mouth.' She tuts. 'I don't know why I'm worried about what's coming out of your mouth; I should be worried about what's going in it!'

'Oh my God, Mum! No need. Jaz!' I call.

Jaz flips the screen around, a mischievous grin on her face.

I hold my hand up in a wave. 'Later.'

She takes a massive bite of chicken and waggles her eyebrows. 'Have a good time,' she says through her mouthful.

'Jasmine!' her mum scolds. 'Don't encourage her.'

'I'm off.' I hang up, grab my jacket and leave the hotel, ready to meet the person who became an integral part of me the moment I first saw her.

Chapter 18
Casey, Berlin

Outside, the bars and restaurants are beginning to fill, and the temperature has dropped enough to slip on my jacket. I wanted to message Holly, to reassure her I was on my way, but thought that might come across as too heavy. Or perhaps she would've liked that? The way she drank me in with those curious blue-grey eyes, unresolved emotions filling the space between us, waiting for us to grab them and run. It took all my strength to stop myself from pulling her to me and saying, 'How could I be so stupid?'

When I round the corner, Holly's waiting, and my breath catches. Her hair is loose and she looks fresh and bright having changed into jeans and a vintage-looking green velvet jacket. I stop to compose myself before crossing the street, clocking the relief on her face when she sees me.

'Hiya. You're here,' I say.

She smiles and my heart swells. She still has the prettiest smile. It's all sunshine and warm ocean breezes and tropical seas.

'Did you think I wouldn't be?'

'Um ... no ... yes ... I don't know.' Fuck. Now I've lost the ability to string a sentence together.

Holly's smile widens.

As I step closer, I catch a soft musky scent. I have the urge to bury my face in her neck and inhale. Then I hear Chandice calling me a creep and quickly dispel all sniffing thoughts. I part my lips to speak, but my tongue fills my mouth. 'You, erm, you look grood.' My face burns as I let out an embarrassed groan. 'Oh my God. I tried to say good and great at the same time.' I take a nervous breath and try again. 'Nice. You look really nice.'

She laughs, the top of her nose crinkling slightly. 'Thanks. So do you.'

I'd forgotten how lovely she is when she laughs, and I can't help but gaze at her.

She points down the street. 'Should we find somewhere to eat?'

It takes a moment for my brain to register what she's said. 'Yes, we should.'

We fall into step side by side, our arms brushing.

'What sort of food do you like?' Holly asks.

I shrug. 'I'm not that fussy. I'll eat most things. You?'

'Same. I can't get enough of German sausages and sauerkraut, though. I'm a tourist cliché and have pretty much been living off them since I arrived. And chips with mayo.'

I moan. 'The chips with mayo are the best, yeah? Especially with onion and tomato sauce.' Eva turning her nose up at German sausage and chips with mayonnaise flashes in my mind, and the guilt hits me again but I swiftly brush it aside. This is dinner with an old friend. No big deal. I stop in front of a restaurant I'm familiar with. 'How about here? I came here the other night with my aunt and uncle. Great food. They're heavy on the meat, though – not ideal if you're vegetarian or vegan.'

She shakes her head. 'I'm not. This looks nice.'

Inside, the restaurant is almost full, but I spot a couple of free tables. A waitperson approaches. '*Guten Abend, Tisch für zwei?*'

I nod. '*Ja, danke.*'

He grabs some menus and leads us through the tables to the back of the restaurant, then lights a candle. 'Date night?'

Holly and I exchange a shy glance.

'Something like that,' Holly says quietly.

'*Möchten Sie Wein?*' the waitperson asks as we sit.

Holly nods and picks up the wine menu. Remembering the wine bar photos she posted, I assume she's better with wine than me and let her choose. She lifts her gaze from the menu. 'Oh, do you drink wine?'

'Sure.'

'The riesling sounds good.' She looks at the waitperson. '*Eine* ... oh, I've only ordered glasses since I've been here. I can't remember the word for bottle.'

He grins. 'It's *Flasche,* and good choice,' he says, switching to English.

He walks away and Holly groans. 'My German is so bad.' She points at the wine menu. 'And it says *Flasche* right there.'

'At least you tried.'

'I attempted a crash course by podcast when I arrived, but not a lot has stuck,' she says, pouring us both some water.

I pick up a menu and hand her one. 'Well, you're about to get a lesson in food, because this menu is in German.'

She opens it and I sneak glances at her while she reads. Her brows are drawn together in concentration, and it's adorable. 'I might need your help,' she says in a hushed voice.

'I'm having the *Kalbsleber* – it's veal liver.'

She grimaces. 'Ugh. Not for me.'

'The *Schweinebauch* is nice,' I say. 'That's what I had the other night. It's pork belly.'

She nods. '*Schwein* ... of course. I should've worked that out. Okay, I'll have that.' She looks at the menu again. 'Oh, some of the sides are in English and they have mash and gravy. I have to have that. It reminds me of my mum.'

'It does?'

She closes the menu and places it on the table. 'Long story.'

'Liver reminds me of my parents.' My face heats. Jesus. What a thing to say. I glance around. Where the hell is that wine?

'Yeah?' she says, actually sounding interested. 'Why's that?'

'Oh, they own a butcher's, so I grew up eating all sorts, but Mum loves liver.'

The waitperson returns, pours our wine and takes our food order.

Once he's gone, I say, 'It's how my parents met. Dad was doing his apprenticeship there and Mum was working in the shop. They liked each other straight away and that was that.' I rush to get it all out, as though I'm compensating for not telling her anything about my family when we first met.

'That's cute,' she says.

I nod as I take a sip. 'It is. They're still kind of cute together.'

'So, you might inherit a butcher's shop one day?'

I shrug. 'Maybe, although my sister and I never got into it like they hoped.' I reach for my glass. Why the fuck am I talking about my parents and butchering? 'Sorry,' I say. 'That's such an uninteresting topic.' She laughs and my stomach flips at how beautiful she looks in the candlelight.

'Well, it's something you never told me the first time we

met, and it's not every day someone has a story about why liver reminds them of their parents.'

I grin. 'I guess not.'

She takes a slow sip of wine, taking me in over the rim of the glass. My body warms and I remove my jacket, placing it over the back of the chair. When I face her again, she's eyeing the tattoos covering my arms, her head tilted. It takes me right back to showing her around galleries – the way she'd always angle her head when looking at a piece of art, as though that was the only way she could make sense of it.

'Sorry,' she says, eyes cutting back to mine. 'Your arms were bare when we ... before. I didn't expect it.' Her gaze drops again. 'They're amazing.'

I extend my left arm and turn it slightly. 'It's taken me years to get to this, but it's my art, I s'pose.'

'You designed them?'

'Some of them.' I lift my T-shirt sleeve and point to a tattoo that circles my upper arm. 'This was the lace design that was on my gran's wedding dress – my dad's mum.' I point to the one underneath – a multicoloured abstract of a woman dancing. 'This is new. It's a watercolour tattoo.'

She takes it in. 'Huh. Looks just like a watercolour painting.'

My first tattoo is hidden under my other sleeve, but I don't want to show her that. Not yet. 'So,' I say, pulling my sleeve down. 'I think you've probably heard enough about my parents and butchers and tattoos. What have you been up to for the past eleven years?'

She gives a short laugh and places her glass on the table. 'Where do I start?'

Please don't start where we ended, I want to say, but I shrug. 'Wherever you like.'

We catch up on each other's lives, from finishing university to our postgraduate degrees, jobs, friends and families. I ache for her when she tells me about her dad dying from testicular cancer, her mum's stroke three months later and the dementia diagnosis. Although I'm desperate to know about her past relationships and that bloke in the photo, she doesn't mention anyone and I don't ask. As the wine bottle empties and the food disappears from our plates, we settle into a lovely ebb and flow of effortless conversation, like we've never lost touch, like it was just this morning our naked bodies were entwined.

Now, she's talking about her brother and his family, and I'm listening but also not, because I'm mesmerised by her kind eyes, the tiny mole to the right of her nose, the freckle on her bottom lip, the soft lilt of her voice. And then I think how nice it is to be with someone who doesn't stop mid-conversation to snap a photo of their meal and upload it to their socials or live stream their night out. It's just great food, nice wine and good conversation about things that matter – family, friends and life.

Holly stops mid-sentence. 'Why are you looking at me like that?' Her face falls. 'I'm talking too much, aren't I? I've barely let you speak. I'm sorry. I've been alone since I left Melbourne and trying to talk German. It's nice to speak to someone—'

I hold up a hand. 'Oh, no. I've talked loads. Sorry. Um, I...' *Fuck, Casey, just speak.* 'You're really beautiful,' I blurt out, heat racing up my neck. 'More than I remember,' I add quietly.

She looks down, but not before I catch the delight in her eyes and a quietly confident smile. It's the type of look that tells me she's heard that compliment before and a shard of jealousy cuts right through me, like I have any right to be jealous.

'You, too,' she says, meeting my gaze. 'More beautiful with age. And your eyes...' She glances away. 'God, I can barely look at them.'

My stomach knots. This is not good. Not good at all.

'Should we go for a walk or something?' she asks.

I nod, under her spell.

Outside, the temperature has dropped further, and we slip on our jackets. It's busier now, the restaurants and bars more lively. We cross the road and walk along the path that runs parallel to the river. Holly slips her hand in mine, and I look down in surprise at our entwined fingers. Her palm is warm and my pulse quickens at the sensation of her skin against mine.

'Is this okay?' She asks the question with such tenderness that I almost crumble.

I gently squeeze her hand. 'Yeah.'

We walk along the river in silence, sneaking disbelieving glances at each other, and stop when we reach a quieter area.

I lean against the rail and look out over the water at the buildings opposite that shimmer with blue lights. 'Such a nice spot.'

Holly stands close to me – so close that I could dip my head and brush my lips against her delicate neck.

'It really is,' she says, reaching into her bag and pulling out a small camera. 'Sorry, I have to take a photo of this.'

'You carry a camera everywhere?'

'Pretty much. My phone takes decent photos but the night mode is better on this and it's small enough to carry around.' She takes a few snaps and shows me the display.

I glance at the image, but I'm distracted by her smell – fresh shampoo and musk. A shiver passes through me. 'Yeah. That's a great shot.' My voice is raspy, and I clear my throat.

She slips the camera back into her bag and faces me. She's inches away and I can almost taste her lips. 'Where did you go that day?' she asks. 'Why didn't you return any of my calls or messages?'

And there it is. The question that's been hanging between

us since we ran into each other this afternoon. I sigh heavily, almost relieved. 'I went home.'

'Home? As in, back to London?'

I nod.

Her brow crinkles. 'Okay. Why? And why not just tell me that?'

I'm silent for a few seconds while I work out the best way to articulate myself. 'I was really struggling here. It was the first time I'd been away from my family and I missed them so much. I didn't gel that well with the people in my course, and apart from absorbing myself in the art scene, I spent most of my time with my aunty and uncle. I was about to go home when I met you, and you gave me a reason to stay. But I fell for you so hard and so fast, it messed with my head.'

I pause to give her space to reply, but she just watches me with questioning eyes, so I continue. 'Before we met up that day in the park, I'd been on the phone to Mum, saying I felt like I was drowning and couldn't cope, then that afternoon you mentioned leaving Australia and your university for me. You were so determined—'

Her face falls. 'So it *was* what I said that day.'

I grab her hand. 'No. That's not what I'm trying to say. It wasn't your fault. It was mine for not coping. I could've opened up to you or talked to my family about it, but I didn't understand it at the time. I was so in awe of you, how you were so sure about things, about us, and I couldn't measure up to that. I couldn't see how I could ever be that person you thought I was, so I took myself away, thinking it would be the best for both of us.'

'I wasn't sure about us, Casey. All I was sure about was that you were special and I wanted to see where that could go. That's all.'

I nod. 'I worked that out after a while. Once I felt better

and had time to process everything. I hated myself for doing that to you.' I shake my head. 'Fuck. My mum gave me the biggest bollocking when I told her.'

Her lips twitch at that comment.

'But I missed you,' I say. 'I thought about you all the time and wished it had worked out differently.'

'I tried to find you,' she says. 'I went back to the park every day for a week. I went to your campus asking for you, went to the galleries, looked online. I've been in London, too. Went from gallery to gallery, hoping I might spot you. It was like you died, Casey, and I had to grieve. If I had known you were okay, it could've been so much easier. I just wanted to know you were okay.'

I bow my head, my heart heavy that despite hurting her so badly, she continued to look for me. 'I did call you back.'

'What? When?'

'In December of that year. You said you weren't going back to Australia until after Christmas, and I rang mid-December, but the number was dead.'

She gives a pained groan. 'Fuck, Casey. I went home at the end of November when lectures finished because it hurt too much to be here.'

'I thought you probably had. I told myself it wasn't meant to be and to leave it because we couldn't be together anyway.'

She rests her arms on the barricade and looks out over the water.

'I've always wanted to tell you how sorry I was,' I say. 'I knew how you felt, and I knew that I hurt you.' I hesitate, uncertain whether I should voice my next thought, but it's pressing on my tongue and I can't stop it. 'I've never forgotten you.'

She turns slowly to face me. 'Never?'

'Never. I've tried to find you too.' I bite my bottom lip. 'Don't be creeped out, right.'

Her brows furrow. 'Oh-kaay.'

'I did find you.'

Her eyes widen. 'What?'

'On Insta. I found you.'

Confusion crosses her face. 'Then why didn't—'

'I mean, like, just in the past week.' I rush to get it all out. 'I wasn't sure about contacting you because I didn't know whether you'd remember me.'

Holly scoffs. 'Not remember you? You crushed me when you vanished, Casey. You were the first person who made me feel like that.' Her brows draw together. 'Did you see my Berlin photos? Is that why you went to the park?'

'Yes and no. I mean, yes, I saw your photos, but I was at the park the day before because I thought our day was the twenty-second. I wanted to feel close to you and I always remembered what I said about meeting there. When I finished work today, I checked your profile, thinking about how to contact you, and there was a photo of the Tiergarten and the gallery, and I hoped the park was your next stop.'

The breeze blows a loose strand of hair across her face. Before I realise what I'm doing, my hand is brushing it away, and my fingers linger behind her ear. She side-eyes my hand, then meets my gaze.

'Sorry,' I say, dropping my hand.

She steps closer. 'It means a lot that you wanted to find me.'

I swallow.

'I've never forgotten your kiss,' she says, inching her face closer to mine. 'The way it made my body hum.'

Oh, God. My trembling hands find her hips. 'Listen, there's something else I should tell—' But my confession about Eva is broken by Holly's lips lightly brushing against my own.

'This okay?' she whispers.

I nod. There's the briefest hesitation before our mouths meet. Her lips are as soft and sweet as I remember. The kiss deepens, and her hands slide under my T-shirt and rest in the small of my back. My body reacts to the memory of her touch and my hands gently clutch her face. Our tongues mingle and my groin burns. We finally break apart, our foreheads touching, our breathing rapid.

'Jesus,' Holly breathes. '*Better* than I remember. Maybe I had forgotten after all.'

'Holy fuck,' I reply. 'Me too.'

She chuckles. 'Are we praying?'

'That was definitely a divine experience.'

'Come back with me,' she murmurs.

I hesitate.

Her lips brush my ear, and a shiver crawls over my skin. 'Please,' she says. 'I've waited so long to find you.'

I link my fingers through hers, no power to stop this, and let her lead the way.

Chapter 19
Holly, Berlin

I click the door shut behind us, peel off my jacket and hang it on the coat rack. My body is too warm and my insides are all over the place. *This is real. This is actually happening.* I don't bother switching on the main light; the mood lighting I set up earlier is perfect.

Casey takes off her coat and hangs it alongside mine. The vision is surreal, and my mind flashes two images simultaneously – one from the past where our jackets were hung side by side in my dorm room, and another set sometime in the future.

'Are you okay?' Casey asks.

I spin. 'Oh, yes. Just thinking.'

She raises a brow but doesn't question me. Instead, she glances around, then crosses the large studio space to the thick glass doors of the balcony, boots tapping lightly on the floorboards. 'Your studio flat *thingo*' – she turns to grin at me – 'is cool. And you've got a view.'

I grab the clothing that's tossed over the small two-seater sofa and the radiator and shove it into a drawer. 'I was amazed when I arrived and it matched the photos.'

'Always a bonus. Looks like you still live like a student, though.' She smiles again, eyes crinkling. 'You were always really messy.'

I laugh. 'Yeah, never broke that habit. I just spend a lot more time cleaning up now.' I move across to the galley kitchen. 'You want a drink? Wine? Water? Tea?' I silently berate myself. *Why the hell am I offering tea? I absolutely do not want to waste time drinking tea.*

'Water's good, thanks. You sure you're only here for a couple of weeks?' Casey gestures over her shoulder. 'Because that looks like a lot of stuff for two weeks.'

I fill a couple of glasses with cold water from the fridge, hand her one and take a large gulp from mine. I didn't talk much about how I came to be here during dinner. 'I did bring plenty with me, because I have an open ticket, actually, and no other home at the moment, so...' I shrug. 'This is it.'

Concern fills Casey's dark eyes, and she places her water on the small dining table. 'None? You're homeless?'

I give that some thought. 'Technically, I guess, yeah. If I went home now, I'd stay with friends or my brother until I found somewhere. And Mum has a house; it's just being rented at the moment.' I move closer to her, eager to move on from casual chat. Maybe she'll be around tomorrow for that, or maybe not, so I'm not wasting any more time. 'I can't believe you're here. Real. In front of me.'

Her mouth curves into a sexy half-smile, and her eyes flare with *that* look. The one I've been searching for. The one that says she wants to devour me. Like she needs to devour me to sustain life, like a vampire needs blood.

Heat clambers over my skin. 'It kills me when you look at me like that.'

She steps closer. Our mouths are a whisper apart, her breath hot on my lips. She flicks out her tongue and runs the tip along my bottom lip, making me shudder. 'I remember your lips,' she says, her voice thick with want. I stumble back against the kitchen bench and she presses her pelvis against me. 'And I remember them all over my body.'

My own body feels like molten lava, and my breaths come fast and shallow. I slide my hands under her T-shirt to skim her stomach, then rest my lips on hers and murmur, 'I remember your soft skin.' I slowly move my hands upward and her nipples harden under my palms. 'And I remember your taste.' I kiss her hard on the mouth and push her backwards, across the studio floor, stopping only to strip off my shirt and delight in her moan as her eyes drop to my lace bra. I rip off Casey's top, and she fumbles with my bra and throws it to the floor.

We kick off shoes and fall onto the bed. My hands find the waistband of her jeans. 'Can I take these off?'

'Go for it.' She watches me with sultry eyes as I peel off her jeans. I hook my thumbs under the elastic of her underwear pausing as my gaze flicks downward.

'Can you please hurry up and take them off? I'm dying here,' she says.

I grin and do what she asks. My body pulses as my eyes travel up her long legs, over the neat patch of dark hair between them, skim her lean torso and erect nipples. She pulls me onto the bed and flips me over, and I let out a squeal of surprised delight.

She gently tugs at my jeans, peering up at me and wiggling her eyebrows.

I nod. 'Take it all off.'

Casey removes my jeans and underwear, releasing a breathy sigh as her eyes scan my body. She drops onto the bed and eases onto me, pausing a moment to stare into my eyes before her delicious lips are on mine again, and my brain is already starting to splinter.

Our kiss becomes more urgent as she grinds her pelvis against mine. I'm dizzy with the sensation of our hot naked bodies fusing together.

Her lips brush my neck before she nips at my collarbone and moves down to my chest, taking my nipple in her mouth.

I moan. 'Slow. I don't want this to end.'

Casey lifts her head. 'Slow?'

I cup her cheek. 'Yeah.'

She whimpers and comes back to my mouth, kissing me slow and deep. I drag my nails down her back and over her arse as her pelvis gently rocks against me. The kiss soon becomes heated again and she moves back to my breasts.

'Okay, don't slow down,' I say.

'No?'

'No.'

Casey's lips skim my torso as she travels down my body, stopping just above my pubic hair line. I let out a frustrated cry and glance down. She smirks and drops to her knees on the floor, slides her arms under my thighs and yanks me down the bed, causing me to gasp. She lifts my leg and places it over her shoulder, then moves her mouth slowly along my inner thigh.

'You're killing me,' I moan. Then her tongue is on me, and I release a long, satisfied sigh. She groans and closes her eyes. 'Don't close your eyes,' I say. 'I need to see your eyes.'

She partially opens them; they're black in the amber lamplight and smoulder up at me as her tongue moves in slow circles.

'Oh, God.' I throw my head back on the mattress, the throb in my body intensifying. 'I can't look at your eyes.' I push myself against her mouth as my back arches and her tongue presses harder against me. Her fingers dig into my hips as my groans grow louder. My body burns as her tongue works faster and I'm gasping her name and grabbing fistfuls of her hair.

Finally, the intensity begins to ease. My skin tingles and becomes sensitive to the touch, and I gently push her head away with a whimper. She lifts my leg off her shoulder, kisses my hipbone and crawls back up the bed, taking me back to the pillows with her.

'I've always remembered *that*,' Casey whispers in my ear.

'Brain, shattered,' I say breathlessly.

She lets out a small laugh. 'What?'

I grin. 'That shattered my brain. It's in pieces. I'm not sure I'll ever think clearly again.'

She hooks her leg over me and pulls me tight against her, like she needs me under her skin. 'I enjoyed shattering your brain.'

I wipe the back of my hand across my clammy forehead. 'I'm all sweaty.'

Casey presses her face against my cheek and murmurs, 'You're gorgeous.'

I push her onto her back and roll on top of her, not wanting to waste time on rest.

She smirks. 'Oh, a bit of force. I like it.'

I kiss her hard and her grip tightens on my hips, then I make my way down her body, sucking at her neck and breasts, enjoying her husky moans and her pelvis pushing up against me. I move further down, and she runs her fingers through my hair, shivering as my lips brush the delicate skin between her thigh and pubic area.

'Oh, God, um...' she says.

'Are you okay?' I ask, peering up at her.

Casey tenderly runs a hand over my head. 'I'm literally about to have an orgasm.'

I laugh and press my face against her thigh.

'Sooo embarrassing,' she says.

I run my tongue between her legs and she gasps. I look up. 'Try and last a few seconds longer. For me?'

With a whimper, she throws her head back.

I press my mouth to her, moaning as my tongue remembers her feel and taste. She rocks against me, her groans becoming louder as my tongue works faster. My body begins to throb again and I need more of her. I slide my hand between her legs and gently insert my finger.

'Fuck, Holly,' she pants and clutches my head. For several seconds her thighs squeeze my shoulders as she breathes my name, then her body deflates with a long, contented sigh.

I stay where I am, feel her throb against my tongue.

'I lasted a few seconds, yeah?' she says, breathless.

I shimmy up her body, pulling the doona over us. 'You did.'

'My body is actually buzzing,' Casey says, her eyelids beginning to droop.

'Mine too.' I prop my head in my palm and trace my fingertip around the outline of a tattoo. It's a globe with only two countries, a crack between them, and what looks like two letters in an elaborate font at the top and bottom. 'What's this?'

Her eyes search my face. 'That's for you.'

My brows furrow. 'What do you mean?'

'It was my first tattoo. I got it in the new year after I came back from Berlin. When I'd missed the chance to see you again.'

My mouth falls open.

'I couldn't get you out of my head and I needed a way to process it all. So I got this.'

My gaze shifts back to her upper arm. I can make out the H near a tiny map of Australia and a C near the map of the UK. 'Fuck, Casey. Seriously?'

She bites her lip and nods.

My eyes fill. 'All this time, I've wondered why you ran off, whether it was me and what I said…'

She rolls onto her side and slips her arm across my waist. 'It was never you. I got myself into a state and couldn't deal with it. You were special to me, and this was my way of keeping that memory.'

A tear trickles down my cheek. 'I love it.'

She brushes it away with her thumb. 'Yeah?'

I nod.

She wraps her arms around me and draws me close, her eyelids closing. 'Sorry, I'm falling asleep.'

'Go to sleep. You've been at work all day.'

Casey covers her mouth as she yawns, then snuggles her head down into the pillow. 'I can stay awake for a bit…'

My own eyelids feel heavy, but I'm not ready to close them yet, just in case she isn't here when I wake up. I don't want to be that needy person I was back then, but if she does leave during the night, then I want to absorb every second of this moment. I press my lips to her tattoo – our tattoo.

'I'm glad you like it,' she says softly.

'You're supposed to be asleep.'

She opens one eye a fraction. 'I can feel you staring at me.'

'I just can't believe you're here, and I don't want this night to end,' I say.

'I'm not going anywhere,' she says with a sleepy smile.

Chapter 20
Casey, Berlin

Sunshine peeks through the gap surrounding the pull-down blind and highlights the honey tones in Holly's hair. Her lashes, black from last night's mascara, are stark against her fair skin. Her chest slowly rises and falls with her gentle breaths. My heart balloons, and I can't wait for her to wake so I can kiss her again. Last night, we drifted in and out of sleep for hours, more sex, more kisses, but it's not enough. I need to be constantly charged with it.

I run a strand of her hair through my fingers. She belongs in a fairytale – a modern-day Sleeping Beauty. Weirdly, I've always had a thing for Sleeping Beauty.

I was seven or eight when I first realised it, sitting at the kitchen table doing homework about fairytales. I'd been staring at the illustration of the prince kissing Sleeping Beauty when Mum said, 'You all right, darlin'? You've been on that page for a long time.'

I lifted my eyes from the book and said matter-of-factly, 'When I grow up, I want to be that prince.'

Mum stared at me for a beat, then put the butter knife

down and walked over to examine the page in my book. She swept her hand over my curls. 'Do you mean that you don't feel like a girl?'

'No. I feel like a girl. I mean, I want to kiss the princess, not the prince.'

'Oh.' She crouched down so that we were eye to eye. 'Have you felt like this with other stories?'

I nodded.

She cupped my face. 'Well, when you're older and ready for that, you can kiss whoever you like and be whoever you want to be. You just make sure you always talk to me or your dad about how you're feeling. And if you can't talk to us for some reason, you find a good friend, okay? Can you promise me that?'

I nodded again then shot down the hallway, book in hand, and out the front door. I was already calling 'Jazzy!' as I hoisted myself over the concrete barricade separating our house from next door, and yelled through the post slot. 'Jaz, open up!' Within seconds, Jaz flung the door open. I raced inside, telling her what had happened.

She grabbed the book from me and pressed her mouth hard against the picture of the prince, and did the same to Sleeping Beauty, making loud 'mmm' noises. 'I want to kiss them both,' she said.

We squealed and collapsed onto her sofa in giggles.

From that day my and Jaz's parents encouraged us to be open with them, so by the time we were teenagers and started understanding our sexuality, we were supported.

Thinking of London reminds me that my phone's been off since dinner last night. I slip out of bed, quietly step across the floorboards to retrieve it from my jacket pocket and switch it on. It vibrates with messages. One from Jaz, desperate for details. Another from Felix saying the last few pieces were delivered this morning. And a third from Chandice, also fishing for details and telling me she has a date tonight. That's too good not to reply to. I tap out a message.

> A date? Who's that then?

> Oh hello, stopped shagging have you? Guy from uni. Going to do my own research for my steamy romance.

> Is he also 28 going on 15 and living with his parents? 😄

> You're in a good mood for someone who's in the shit with two birds.

> I'm sorting it. Tell me how the date goes!

Nothing from Eva, and there's no telling if it's because she had a big night or she's giving me the silent treatment. I stare at the screen, uncertain whether I should call her today, then glance at Holly. Is it so bad to want one day with Holly where we're the only two people in our worlds? I'm not sleeping with Eva and never will again – I am one thousand per cent certain of that. We're over. I'm just delaying the ending-it bit for a very short time. Twenty-four hours, max.

Holly stirs and rolls onto her side, stretching her arm across the empty space beside her. Her eyes shoot open. 'Casey?'

I shove my phone back in my jacket pocket and rush back to the bed, slipping under the duvet. 'Hey, I'm here.'

The flash of panic vanishes from her face and she cuddles into me. 'Mmm, you are real. I wasn't sure if it was a dream.'

I push her hair from her face and kiss her. 'I'm real.'

'And you're still here,' she says.

'Still here.' I kiss her again, her soft lips making me sigh.

'I've been watching you sleep, waiting for you to wake up so I could do that.'

She grins. 'That's very cute.'

My cheeks warm. 'Oh, good. Not creepy?'

'If it is, then I'm also creepy because I was awake for ages last night watching you sleep.' She traces her fingertip over our tattoo. 'I was worried you'd disappear again.'

I tuck my arm under the duvet and bring us closer, slipping my leg between hers. 'I'm not that kid anymore. I went looking for you, didn't I?'

'You did, and I shouldn't start the day by talking about that. Let's start again.' She kisses me with heat, runs her hand up my thigh, over my arse and up my spine. 'Morning,' she breathes when she pulls away.

'That's the best good morning I've ever had,' I say.

She narrows her eyes suspiciously. 'The best?'

'Mmhmm.'

'I've got a feeling other women have heard that.'

I shake my head. 'Only you.' And it's true – at least, I don't recall saying it to anyone else. 'It was the night after we met, and I stayed in your dorm for the first time.'

Her hand moves over my breast as she lightly sucks at my neck.

I swallow. 'And the next morning, you...'

Her mouth trails my chest until her tongue and teeth graze my nipple.

'You, um ... oh, God.' I release a shuddery breath, an urgent throb in my groin.

'Woke you up like this?' Her hand snakes down my stomach and slips between my thighs, and I bite back a gasp. 'Wet,' she whispers before she kisses me hard and my entire body pulses. She straddles my thigh and slowly moves against me, her breath hot on my mouth as her lips hover over mine.

Her fingers soon pick up pace, inviting my pelvis to rock, and she rubs harder against my thigh.

It's warm in the flat with the morning summer sun filtering through the blinds and I throw off the duvet. Moisture builds along my hairline and our bodies are both sticky with sweat. My insides begin to sizzle, and our moans grow louder until we both can't contain it any longer. For a glorious moment, we unravel, loud and breathless, before Holly falls against me with a satisfied sigh as my own body turns to mush.

I bury my face into her neck, my eyes stinging, and my chest fills with a gushing warmth. *Fuck. Fuck. Fuck.*

'Still with me?' she murmurs against my forehead, stroking my back with feathery fingertips.

I look at her and nod, too love struck to speak.

Her brows pull together. 'Are you ... are you crying?'

'Just a little overwhelmed,' I say, my voice thick with emotion.

Concern passes across her face. 'Not too overwhelmed, I hope?'

'No. Just the right amount.'

She pulls away so we're eye to eye. 'Please tell me you don't have to rush off today.'

'No. Day off today.'

'Could we maybe spend the day together?' Her voice is tentative, like she expects me to say no.

I smile. 'Definitely.'

Holly lets out a breath, almost like a sigh of relief. 'Want to take me around some galleries and show off your art knowledge?'

Hearing that she wants to spend time doing one of my favourite things fills me with pure joy. 'Really? You'd want to do that?'

'Uh-huh.' She wrinkles her nose. 'I still don't get some art. I could use a teacher.'

'I always love an opportunity to show off my art knowledge, but staying here all day would be nice, too.' And I don't just mean for sex because the moment we leave, I'll have to face reality, and I can't burst our cocoon yet.

'That would be nice if I wasn't so hungry. The *schweinebauch* and mash wasn't enough to fill me for days, and all I have here is tea, coffee, milk and wine.'

I drop a kiss on her shoulder. 'I guess I'm pretty hungry, too.'

'I'm going for a shower.' She hops out of bed and crosses the room.

My eyes skim her torso, over the curve of her hip, across the soft roundness of her arse and down her delicious thighs. I let out a low wolf whistle.

She glances over her shoulder and gives me a coy smile. 'You're not joining me?'

I rush after her, grabbing a tiny container of hair product from my jacket pocket on the way.

She quirks a brow. 'Someone thought they were getting lucky.'

I give her a knowing grin. 'Says you with the bedside mood lighting.'

She laughs and pulls me into the shower.

Chapter 21
Casey, Berlin

Almost two hours later, after a stop by my hotel room for a change of clothes, we're sitting at a café off Münzstrasse sharing eggs, sausages and French toast with brown butter.

Holly leans back in her chair and stretches her legs, bare from the mid-thigh. 'I feel amazing.'

'You've had about four brain-shattering orgasms in the past twelve hours. I'm not surprised.' I smirk and take a bite of French toast.

Her face splits into a grin, and she has a lovely shimmery glow about her. 'Is that what it is?'

I nod, my mouth full. 'Mmhmm.'

'What about you?' she asks, leaning over to get some French toast for herself.

'I had about five.'

She chuckles. 'I mean, how do you feel?'

I run my hand up her thigh, my fingertips slipping under the hem of her denim skirt. 'Incredible.' I want to say more, tell her how my heart is pounding, how I feel complete in a way I haven't since I first met her, but the words catch in my throat.

She narrows her eyes. 'What are you thinking? You look like you want to say something.'

I gaze at her for a long moment. 'Just how lovely you are. Natural. I like that.' I can't help but compare her to Eva, who'd grunt about eating greasy eggs and fat sausages, and who would've spent hours preening herself before going out, then be glued to her phone or filming herself. There's none of that with Holly. She just has an enthusiasm and curiosity for everything around her, like she's rediscovering herself and life after being tied down the past decade. 'How about you?' I ask. 'What are you thinking?'

She takes the last bite of sausage and considers me while she chews, then pushes the plate away. 'You really want to know?'

'Erm ... I think so?'

'I was thinking that life has put us together twice now, and that's fate. Being in the same city at the same time is fate. Thinking about each other at the same time is fate. So we owe it to ourselves to give this longer than two weeks and to not disappear from each other's lives when it gets too hard.'

My brows rise. 'Wow. Okay. I thought you were going to say you wanted another coffee or something.'

She shrugs. 'I can't wonder about what-ifs anymore, Casey. In a way, you ruined me for everyone else, and I've found you again. I'm sorry if that's too much for you, but I'm thirty-one; I want to find my person. And maybe you're it and maybe you're not, but the way I feel right now is that I want to at least try to work out what you are. So please, *please* don't run away from me this time.'

I blink at her.

She cocks her head. 'Anything to say to that?'

'Um. Ditto.'

Her brows knit, but she laughs. 'Okay. That's how it's going to be. A line from a film that's older than us.'

I shrug. '*Ghost* is Mum's favourite movie, so I heard it a lot growing up. It's a great response to so many things.'

'Mmm, okay, Miss Ditto, but I have your number. I know where your hotel room is. I know the name of the art galleries where you work, and I know your parents have a butcher's shop in Stratford. I'll find you, Casey Vassell.'

'Ah.' I wince. 'About that...'

Her mouth presses into a tight line.

'That's not my last name.'

Her brows shoot up. 'You gave me a false last name?'

'It's not false,' I say quickly. 'It's just not mine. It's my friend's.' I shake my head with a groan. 'That was a stupid thing to do. I think I was trying to be mysterious and cool or something?'

She rolls her eyes. 'Probably. You did a lot of that.'

'Sorry. Mine is Miller-James.'

She watches me and I think she's about to tell me to do one, but she says, 'I was a bit full-on that day. It was too much, especially since we'd only known each other a couple of weeks. I'm not surprised you freaked out.' Her face relaxes. 'You forgot my last name, didn't you? Otherwise, you could've found me before last week.'

I nod. 'Yeah. I vaguely remember you mentioned it when you told me a story about your lecturer, but we'd only known each other a few hours by then, and I was so focused on how lovely you were and how much I wanted to kiss you that I wasn't really listening. It just didn't seem important at the time, you know?'

Holly shakes her head at me, but she has a wry smile. 'Well, what's done is done. And we've got the chance now, Casey Miller-James,' she says, cupping my cheeks. I love the feel of her hands on my face, like they belong, like they've always belonged. Her phone buzzes on the table, and my eyes flick down, but I can't read the name. She picks up her phone, then drops it back on the table with a grunt.

'Everything okay?' I ask.

'Yeah. It's just...' She gives an annoyed huff. 'Stuff at home. I didn't want to talk about it, but—'

'You don't need to tell me anything,' I say, sensing relationship drama that I definitely don't want to discuss today.

'It's just my ex.'

'Oh.' I'm suddenly interested. 'Your *ex*.'

She huffs again. 'He keeps texting, calling, wanting to work things out, trying to get me to go home.'

'Your ex is a he?' The handsome lad called Tom comes to mind.

'Uh-huh. You knew I was bi, right?'

'Yeah, I did. But seriously, you don't have—'

'He just won't get the message it's over.' She bites her bottom lip. 'Doesn't stop me feeling guilty, though.'

I nod, my own guilt rising up. 'I take it you're not rushing home to sort it?'

Holly makes a face. 'God, no. I'm having to be really blunt with him now and I don't like doing that.'

I rub her thigh. 'I'm sorry you're dealing with that. Anything I can do?'

She smiles coyly. 'There's lots you can do, but we'd get arrested if we did that here.'

I giggle. Like, a proper girly giggle. Fucking hell, who am I right now? I clear my throat, try to find my normal adult laugh.

'How about you?' she asks.

'How about me what?'

'Well, we didn't get around to talking much after dinner last night. Any ex drama you want to tell me about?'

I quickly look away, rubbing the back of my neck. *Tell her.* I take a deep breath and shift in my seat so that I'm facing her, ready to tell the truth. She watches me, her eyes wide, and underneath that bravery and determination, there's something so fragile, something just a little bit broken. Like a drinking glass with a tiny chip – you're not sure if it can cope with more use, or if one more knock will turn the chip into a crack. I can't do it. I can't destroy this moment when she looks so vulnerable and hopeful all at once. Not today. 'Nothing I want to tell you about.'

Her shoulders drop and she beams, her face bright and full of possibilities. I snap a mental image for the future, knowing that whatever happens, then at least on this day I didn't break her again.

She holds up her phone. 'You know what? I've been nice enough to Tom now. He needs to deal with it. I don't want him to ruin our day.' Her fingers fly across the screen, ending in a jab. Then she throws it into her bag. 'There. Sorry about that.'

I hang my head, shamefaced. 'No problem.'

'I want to get some good shots today.' She pulls out her camera. 'I might post a couple on Insta.'

My head snaps up. I was so caught up in us I forgot about social media. I point behind me. 'Just need the bathroom, then we'll go, yeah?'

'Sure. No hurry.'

I rush through the busy café to the toilets, lock myself in a cubicle, dig my headphones out of my bag and FaceTime Jaz.

After four rings, she answers with a yawn. 'Hiya.' She's still in her pyjamas, curls popping in all directions. 'Glad you're still alive.'

'I'm alive. I'm very alive. And I've fucked up.'

'Already? It hasn't even been twenty-four hours.'

'It's just been this whirlwind night, and we hardly spoke before we—'

Jaz snorts. 'Fucking hell, Case, you work faster than me.'

'This is different. It was so ... intense. We had dinner, and our past love lives didn't come up, then I went to tell her about Eva, seriously, it was right there, and next thing she's kissing me, and ... well ... you know what happens next.'

'Mate, what is it with you being pussy-whipped? Are you incapable of speaking when you're about to get some?'

'It's a bit of a weakness, I guess.'

She rolls her eyes and swigs from a mug.

I continue. 'Holly just told me about her ex and asked if I had anything to tell her, and I kind of said no,' I say through a wince.

Jaz gapes at me.

'I went to, but she looked so broken. You should've seen her face. She's so beautiful, yeah, and her eyes were all sad, and—'

'Oh, wow,' Jaz says, hand up to stop me talking. 'You have well and truly fucked this up already, girl.'

I groan. 'But we had the most brilliant night and this brilliant morning, and I didn't want to ruin it and break her all over again.'

'You still haven't broke it off with Eva. She's been on Insta with the wedding planner, bangin' on about the chef.'

I grimace. 'Holly just mentioned posting on Insta and now I'm paranoid she'll somehow come across Eva before I've had a chance—'

'Look. I get it,' Jaz says, ignoring me. 'You've lived in the fantasy of what-if for years, and you've just found each other again. You're caught up in the romance of it all. But this bubble ain't reality, mate. And Eva's planning a wedding – a fucking *wedding*. You need to end it quickly. And if things continue with Holly, which I really hope they do for both your sakes, you think she's not going to find out? Enjoy your day, but tell both of them over the weekend at least.' Her eyes are filled with concern, and I don't want to let her down.

'Okay. I will.' An incoming call flashes on my screen. 'Fuck, Eva's calling me now.'

'You might want to take that.' Jaz wiggles her fingers at me. 'Later, lover girl.'

'Later, Jazzy Jaz.' I end the call, take a deep breath and answer. 'Hiya.'

'Hi,' Eva purrs. 'When are you coming home?'

A heaviness lodges in my chest. 'Um ... Thursday or something? The opening isn't until Tuesday night.'

'Thursday? I wanted us to meet up with the chef on Wednesday night.'

This is it. Ending an almost year-and-a-half relationship from a toilet cubicle in another country. 'About that,' I start.

'Oh,' she says. 'Dante's calling. I've been trying to catch them all morning. Have to take this. Talk to you later.'

'Eva, wait!'

But she's gone. I stare at the phone, mouth agape, the words I wanted to say hanging in the stale air of the cubicle. I don't want to talk to her later. I don't want this day interrupted, because who knows what will happen afterwards? It might be my only chance to enjoy this time with Holly. With guilty fingers, I switch off my phone and head back outside.

Holly looks up from her camera, brightening when she sees me. 'Thought you'd crawled out the window or something.'

'Sorry. Was on the phone to my bestie.'

'Oh?'

'Yeah. Jaz – Jasmine. We grew up next door to each other.' I give her a sheepish look. 'Her last name is Vassell.'

'Ah, that's where it comes from. She was your best mate

when we met.' She turns pensive. 'It was one of the few things you told me about yourself.'

There's a tiny crack in my heart that she remembers that. 'I'm sorry I didn't tell you more.'

She gives a rueful shrug and her demeanour shifts. 'Anyway, nice to know she's still your best mate.'

'She's an amazing friend. I think you'll get on.'

She breaks into a smile. 'Does that mean I'm meeting her?'

I give her a soft, lingering kiss. 'I hope so.'

Chapter 22
Holly, Berlin

Casey stretches out on the grass, and I zoom in on her perfect face. Almond-shaped eyes framed by long black lashes and thick eyebrows, soft, defined cheekbones, a well-proportioned nose, and full pouty lips. Not one mark on her skin apart from a tiny mole on the right side of her upper lip. Her gaze flicks to the camera, and she has *that* look. I'm not sure it's even directed at me; it's just who she is. I hold down the shutter as the camera captures several shots.

'When you said you wanted some photos, I didn't think you meant of me,' she says.

I drop down onto the grass beside her. 'The camera loves you.'

'I think it might love you, too.' She takes it from me. 'May I?'

I shrug and rest back on my palms, lifting my face to the early afternoon sun.

She kneels in front of me and clicks. 'You're so beautiful.'

I pull her to me. 'You'd say that to anyone who gave you orgasms all night.'

She grins. 'Fair point.'

I shuffle closer and retrieve the camera. 'Can I take one of us?'

'Sure.'

I set the timer, press the shutter and position the camera. Casey wraps her arms around my waist, pushes her nose against my face and releases a melty sigh. I instinctively lean my head towards her.

The camera clicks, and I look at the display. 'Oh,' I breathe, because the image is everything – brimming with the type of intimacy that only exists between kindred souls. 'I love it.'

Casey rests her chin on my shoulder and peers at the image. 'Mmm,' she says, with an unmistakable dreaminess. 'It's like *Sappho and Erinna*.'

I lift a brow. 'Friends of yours?'

She laughs. 'Kind of. It's one of my favourite paintings.'

'I don't know it. I remember *Italia und Germania*, but a lot of the other art you talked about was lost on me.'

'I didn't know about the *Sappho and Erinna* painting when we met,' Casey says. 'I discovered it in my final year at university and spent a lot of time staring at it online. Then the Tate acquired it and I got to see the real thing.' She faces me, eyes squinting in the sun. 'It brought us alive in my head again. Helped me kind of process things.'

My heart lifts, and it feels so light and free that it could carry me away. 'You're a true romantic.'

She lifts a shoulder. 'The Berlin air...'

I steal a kiss. 'You've used that excuse with me before, but I think it's you.'

'Or maybe it's the Holly effect.' Casey smiles and stretches out, resting her head in her palm.

'Mmm, maybe.' I stretch out beside her. 'You really have to work tomorrow? On a Sunday?'

'I don't have to, but I told Felix I'd be there. The installers messed up, so they've agreed to hang the art tomorrow instead, plus we've still got a bit to do. You should totally come to the opening on Tuesday night, though.'

A buzz of excitement ripples through me. 'Really? You'd want that?'

'I'd love you to. It's a contemporary exhibition of local queer artists – *Queer Perspectives*. It'll be on for a few weeks but opening night is always good.'

'I won't be in your way or anything?'

She shakes her head. 'Not at all. I'll have to chat to some artists and potential buyers but not all night.'

I'm almost lightheaded with the idea of it. 'Okay. It's a date.'

She smiles. 'Yeah. I s'pose it is.'

I roll on my back and tuck my hands under my head. 'Why contemporary?'

'The exhibition?'

'No, your job. When we met you loved historical art and wanted to work in that area. It's all you talked about.'

She rolls onto her back too. 'I still like it. I worked in an art museum for a few years after I graduated, but I wanted to go higher and didn't feel like management took me seriously. It might be better now, but then it was a world filled mainly with old white people, and I think they struggled with a young biracial lesbian, especially one who did her master's in the history of Black art and tried to bring that into their gallery. They weren't all overtly rude or racist, and some colleagues supported me, but it's that inherent bias that's ingrained in so many people – the racist, homophobic, misogynist thing, you know? And class – I think Britain has a real issue with class. I just open my mouth and people make assumptions. I felt that me as the whole package made them uncomfortable, and I couldn't be bothered educating them. Besides, all the artists were dead. So I went contemporary and it's much more diverse – the staff, the art and the artists, who are mostly alive. Although, every now and then one will come along who's so difficult I long for the days of the dead ones.'

I'm sitting up now – I have been since halfway through what she was saying. 'That's bullshit that you couldn't progress in that environment because of who you are.'

'It is, and I was angry about it back then, a lot more than I am now. But it's everywhere, innit? The world over. It must be like that in Australia, too?'

I nod. 'Class not as much, but the other three ... yes, to varying degrees.'

'Anyway, it's my gain, because I love the gallery I'm at now. Josanne – that's my boss – is brilliant. She's got such a great vision and she's the first Black, female boss I've had. Her view is that it's pointless trying to change what exists; instead, create a new reality you want to be part of and eventually old orders in the art world will change. I like being part of that with her and the rest of our staff, including the gallery here.'

'That must be a good feeling, finding the right fit in an area you're passionate about,' I say.

She nods. 'Yeah. Didn't you like your job? Before you got the boot, I mean,' Casey says with a cheeky grin.

I poke her in the ribs. 'Redundancy. I did. I liked working on different projects and seeing them implemented across the campuses and in the community. I'll probably look for the same type of work when I get around to it.'

Casey points to my camera. 'You don't want to do more with that?'

'I'd love to. I charged for my photography for the first time in a while the night after I was made redundant.'

'Yeah?'

'Uh-huh.' I pull out my phone and open a browser. 'I left work as soon as they told me and stopped at a wine bar. Their photographer had pulled out last minute for an event they were having the next night, and Caleb – that's the bloke who owns the bar – noticed my camera and asked if I'd do it.' I bring up the bar's website and pass her my phone.

I rest my chin on Casey's shoulder as she scrolls through the photos, but I'm distracted by her scent and press my nose against her neck, breathing her in. 'God, you smell good.'

'We're going to need to get back to one of our rooms fast if you do that to me,' she murmurs.

I smile and pull away. 'Sorry.'

She chuckles and returns to my phone. 'You took all of these?'

I nod.

'They're good, Holly. Really good.' She points to a photo of the woman who was giving me flirty looks that night. 'She either fancied you, or someone standing right on top of you.'

'Oh,' I say. 'Yeah, she was kind of giving me that look through the night, and I wanted to capture it.'

'You didn't talk to her?' Casey asks. Her tone is hesitant, like she knows she has no right to ask but that she also needs to know.

I shake my head. 'No. I wasn't in a good headspace. Just lost my job, trying to work out what to do, deal with how I felt about Tom.'

Casey's brows shoot up. 'This was the Saturday night before you came over here? As in, last weekend?'

'Uh-huh.'

'Oh,' she says, 'Tom is *that* recent?'

'Yep, we were together three years. The night after I took these photos, I booked my flight, let him go to work the next day so he couldn't talk me out of it, and packed everything up.

When he got home, I was waiting with my suitcase. I told him and left.'

Casey's eyes widen. 'Whoa.'

I wince. 'That's bad, isn't it? An awful thing to do. But at the time, I had to go.'

She shakes her head. 'It's not bad.'

'I should've talked to him sooner, told him how I was feeling, but I didn't fully understand it. You know when you're in a situation and there's something a bit off about it, but you can't work out why or what to do, and it's not until you're alone or away from it that you think, *how fucking stupid was I? Why couldn't I see that then?*'

Casey stares at the ground, picking blades of grass and tossing them to the side. 'That was a really brave thing to do. I wish I could be more like that.'

'I'm not sure I would've been so brave if I wasn't going overseas. But I figured I couldn't just leave without telling him something.'

She nods, but she's silent as she continues to pick at the grass.

I lean forward so I can make eye contact. 'You okay?'

She turns her whole body to me and eyes me intently. Her face carries a pained expression, but it's more than that – it carries a story, too, some history. My heart crashes back down from wherever it had drifted off to. Whatever her story is, I don't want to hear it. Not today. I'm not so naive to think that she doesn't have a past, and probably a present of some kind too, but I can't lose this yet.

Just as her lips part to presumably tell me something, I jump in. 'Tell me about your family.'

Her shoulders drop and her face brightens. 'Ah, my fam. They're the best. Jazzy's too.'

'Your families are besties, too?'

'Yep, next door neighbours for forever – well, since me and Jaz were about four. We were like identikit families. Terraced houses. Black dads. White mums. Jamaican grandparents. Lesbian daughters. Hetero siblings. The only difference is I have a younger sister and Jaz has a twin brother. Oh, and Jaz is a total fem.' She pulls out her phone and switches it on. It buzzes with messages, and she quickly swipes the screen, taps the 'do not disturb' option and opens the photo app.

I don't want to link the action with her pained expression, so I flick it away, like a bug crawling across my skin. Right this minute, we're together and she's focused on me; I'll take that.

'I'll show you some pics.' She scrolls for a few seconds and brings up an image. 'That's Jazzy.'

I take the phone for a closer look. The woman staring back at me has warm brown skin like Casey, lush black curls, cheekbones that glow with a shimmery bronze blush, full lips covered in clear gloss and deep brown eyes. 'Wow. She is very, very attractive. Like, beautiful.'

'And she takes full advantage of that,' Casey says, taking her phone back.

'Does her twin brother look like that too?'

'Uh-huh.' She narrows her eyes. 'Hmm, maybe I don't want you to meet them. You'd totally be both their type. Although, Jazzy has lots of types, and her brother is married with a new baby.' She pulls up another photo. 'That's Mum, Dad and my sis, Chandice.'

I take the phone again and immediately see where she gets her looks from. 'Oh, your dad. He is seriously handsome.' I look at her. 'You have the same features.' I glance at the photo again. 'They're young. Or maybe they just look good for their age. Mine were pretty old when they had me, so everyone's parents look young to me.'

'They are young. Mid-fifties.'

I stare at the photo a moment longer, enjoying learning about this side of Casey's life. 'Your mum is tiny compared to the three of you.'

She smiles fondly. 'What she lacks in size, she makes up for in ferocity. But in an admirable take-no-shit way, know what I mean?'

I nod. 'Must be nice. Having a close family, or two close families, around you.'

Casey's face falls. 'Sorry, I—'

'Don't be. I'm interested.'

'I'd love you to meet them one day.'

I raise my brows. 'I'm meeting your best friend *and* your family? This is moving very fast.'

She glances away shyly, but I catch the smile in her eyes.

I find a photo of my own family and show her. 'Me, Adam, Mum and Dad.'

She stares at it for a few seconds. 'You're very...'

'White?' I say with a grin.

She laughs. 'Well, yeah, but I was going to say similar. You and Adam are a lot like your mum.'

I nod. 'Yep. Dad didn't get too much of a look in, although Adam got his height.'

'It's really nice to see your family,' she says, passing my phone back to me. She points to my camera. 'Speaking of photos, you could do more of this and charge, yeah?'

'I guess. Not sure I could make a full-time living from it, but while I have a year's salary in the bank, I'd like to use the time to do more photography.'

Her eyes widen. 'A year? They paid you out a year?'

I nod. 'Almost a year and a half.'

'That's something, then.' She slips her arm around my shoulder. 'I'm sorry you lost your job, but if you hadn't, we wouldn't be sat here right now.'

I cup her cheeks and hold her face close; it's the most deli-cious sensation and I could sit like this forever. 'Like I said this morning: fate.'

'Mmm. I'm starting to believe that, too.' She kisses me then tweaks my chin affectionately. 'Want to go to another gallery?'

I pull away and come back to reality. 'Sure.'

'Actually, do you want to see mine? The new exhibition isn't fully set up yet, but a few pieces are up, and the current exhibition is still mostly up.' She points behind us. 'It's only about a ten-minute walk that way.'

'Let's go,' I say, jumping up and brushing the grass from my skirt.

Soon, we're stopping at a set of glass doors with 'Mitte Contemporary Galerie' engraved into a large silver plaque beside the entrance. Casey taps in a security code, the door clicks and she holds it open to let me pass. She locks it behind us and flicks a switch that floods the gallery with light. The space is airy, bigger than it seems from the street, with dark wooden floors and white walls covered in various-sized canvases and frames.

'Tomorrow these will be replaced,' she says, pointing to one side of the gallery, then gestures to the opposite wall. 'But some of these are for the new exhibition.'

I run my eye along the display, automatically drawn to the photographs. 'These photos...'

'I thought you'd like those.'

I slowly take them in, one by one. Portraits, street photogra-phy, landscapes.

'Come through to the back. There's a piece I want to show you.'

I follow her, still gazing at the art around me. We pass through a door and into a storeroom. Propped on a large wooden easel is a sizeable canvas that at first glance looks like a photograph, but as I edge closer, I realise it's paint. I spin around, my mouth dropping open. 'This is a painting?'

Casey nods. 'It's incredible, right? You thought it was a photo?'

'I did.' I step closer, squinting as I inspect it. 'Is it oil?'

'Uh-huh.'

It's a naked woman, lying on a bed, her hand resting against her inner thigh, her other arm stretched over her head. Thick, auburn hair falls across one breast. The other is exposed, pink nipple erect. My eyes drift down her torso, over the small rise of her belly, along the sharpness of her hip bone, across the triangle of hair between her legs, and down her shapely legs. The woman has a contented smile, satisfied eyes, and a body that shimmers with an after-sex glow. Her lips are slightly parted, almost like she wants to tell a secret, or maybe she's telling her lover to come back to bed.

My body stirs, and I slowly walk backwards to appreciate it from a distance, tilting my head to take it in.

Casey is leaning on the edge of a desk and wraps her arms around my waist as I rest against her. 'Like it?'

'Mmm.' I run my hands over her forearms. 'It's beautiful. The detail makes it so lifelike, down to the pores in her skin and the hair on her arms.'

Casey brushes her lips against my ear. 'How does it make you feel?'

I swallow as heat pulses between my legs. 'A little turned on. But I guess that's the point.' Her mouth moves to my neck and I tilt my head further to allow her better access.

'Just a little?' she murmurs, her fingers slipping under my T-shirt and skimming my stomach.

My body warms and I steer her hand towards my breast. Over the silk of my bra, she gently squeezes my nipple then slips her fingers under the fabric while her other hand travels up my inner thigh. I'm too hot now, the ache between my legs too intense. I place my hand on hers and guide it inside my underwear.

She releases a soft sigh. 'I love the feel of you.'

My breath quickens as my eyes scan the painting, my fingernails digging into Casey's forearms. Her hand moves faster in response, and I clench my jaw to stop myself calling out.

Within minutes, my legs begin to weaken as ecstasy builds, and when they buckle, Casey holds me up, whispering 'I've got you' in my ear.

For several seconds we stay like that – breathless and stunned with her hand between my legs and her lips pressed against my temple. As my heartrate normalises, I remove her hand and turn to bury my face in her neck. My heart is exploding, turning to liquid and drowning me.

She kisses my forehead. 'You all right?'

I hold her tight and nod, my eyes stinging.

She pulls her head back a little and scans my face. 'Are you crying now?'

'Just a little.'

'Fuck. I'm sorry,' she says. 'Oh, fuck. That was too much, wasn't it? Was that weird? I've weirded you out. I was just taken by the moment.'

I cry-laugh and shake my head. 'No. It was perfect. It was so fucking perfect, and you're so fucking perfect. And this...' I gesture between us. 'This is so fucking perfect, and it blows my mind, and I just wish I knew what you were thinking and feeling because it can't all be one-sided, and—'

Casey swallows the rest of my sentence with a kiss, then says, 'The same, I feel the same, because you ruined me for everyone else, too.'

Chapter 23
Holly, Berlin

I t's opening night of the *Queer Perspectives* exhibition, and I'm giddy with excitement as I walk towards the gallery.

I was still half-asleep when Casey kissed me goodbye early this morning, and I've missed her today. I occupied myself by walking the city, taking some great shots of art on decaying buildings, then shopping for something to wear tonight. I spent hours getting ready – for Casey, for anyone who'll see us together, and for me – sometimes it's nice to have a reason to dress up.

After we left her gallery on Saturday afternoon, we visited another contemporary art gallery, followed by dinner, then back to her hotel room for more brain-shattering sex. The entire time I carried the feeling that I was exactly where I was supposed to be, like everything I had ever experienced had been mapped out for me to arrive in that very moment. After-wards we lazed in bed, naked in fresh white sheets, watching TV and eating milky European chocolate. We parted on Sunday morning when she left for work and I stayed in her hotel bed, her scent lingering, until early afternoon when I floated back to my studio flat to edit photos and talk to Mum, Adam and Nat. That evening, Casey surprised me by showing up at my door with a bottle of wine in one hand, Vietnamese takeaway in another, an overnight bag slung over her shoulder and a coy smile on her lips.

When I arrive at the gallery, I message Casey to tell her I'm outside, and within a minute she's there, pulling me into a kiss that has me sinking into her.

'Hello,' she says, resting her forehead on mine. 'I've been thinking about you all day.'

I brush my nose against hers and breathe her in. She smells like freshly washed skin with a hint of citrus from her perfume. 'Weren't you concentrating on work?'

She smiles. 'I can multitask.' She steps back and gives me a once-over. 'God, look at you. You look amazing.'

I look down at my simple red dress and try to ignore the nagging voice in my head telling me that an unemployed person shouldn't spend over a hundred euros on a piece of material with straps. The material is silk and the dress is fully lined, but a slip of material nonetheless. 'Thought I should dress up a bit. Haven't been to an exhibition opening before.'

Casey runs a strand of my hair through her fingertips. 'And your hair.'

'I just straightened it.' I scrunch my nose. 'Too much?'

'No way. You look beautiful.' She holds out her hand. 'Come on, lovely. Come and meet my colleague before everyone arrives.'

Inside, the gallery has transformed. The walls display the new exhibition pieces, and a small sculpture of two men caught in a tender embrace sits in the centre of the room. The overhead lighting is low, with brighter display lights over the artwork, and soft music trickles through the space.

'Felix,' Casey calls. 'This is Holly.'

A tall, muscular man spins around. His eyes flick to our linked hands, then cut to Casey. He smiles broadly and steps forward to kiss both my cheeks. '*Hallo*, Holly. Nice to meet you.' He waves his hand around. 'Welcome to our gallery.'

'Thank you. Nice to meet you, too.'

He pulls his head back in surprise. 'That's not an English accent.'

'Oh, no. I'm Australian.'

His eyes flick to Casey again and she gives a quick smile. 'Australian?' he says. 'Are you travelling?'

'I am.'

'Well, welcome to Berlin.' A door at the back of the gallery opens and another man emerges with a few bottles of wine. 'That's my husband, Matias. Let me get you a drink.'

He walks off and I help Casey with glasses and alcohol before the guests and artists arrive. As Casey does what she needs to do, I stroll around with a glass of sparkling wine, taking in the incredible art and chatting to Matias, who has cousins in Melbourne. When he goes to get himself another drink, I stop in front of the painting of the naked woman, now hung in the middle of the back wall, and indulge in a luscious memory. Heat rushes to my face and I glance around, certain that people will guess what I've been up to in front of this painting, but they're all busy chatting or looking at art.

'*Hallo*,' says a soft voice beside me.

I startle. 'Oh, hello.'

'*Gefällt Ihnen dieses Gemälde?*' the woman says, pointing to the canvas.

'Oh, sorry, *ich spreche kein Deutsch*.' I grimace. 'Not enough to have a conversation about art anyway.'

She smiles, deep lines framing her eyes. 'Do you like this painting?'

I glance at it again. 'It's incredible. I was trying to work out how the artist used oils to get a photographic finish.'

'Ah, it's tricky. And painstaking. It took years.'

I face her, my eyebrows raised. 'Oh, is this ... are you the artist?'

She smiles again, her face wise and kind. '*Ja.*'

'Wow. Well, it's beautiful.' I look at the plaque but I'm too far away to read her name.

'She is sexy, yes?' the artist says.

My face warms again. 'Very.'

'She is my ex-lover.'

'Oh?' I say. 'Lucky you.'

She grins. 'Indeed. From eight years ago. I took this photo one day, and it was – she was – so exquisite, it would've been selfish of me to keep it to myself.'

'Were you together long?'

She waves her hand dismissively. 'Does she look like a woman you can keep confined in a relationship?'

I glimpse the painting before my gaze drifts to Casey on the other side of the gallery. She's animated, her face aglow with passion, chatting to a couple who are totally engrossed in what she's saying. She wears that same look – a sultry, come-to-bed look – that makes anyone she talks to think they're the only person in her world. 'I guess not,' I say.

'Besides, I am old, and she is young, and I didn't want her to waste her youth on me. I set her free.' She points to the painting. 'But I kept that for myself. I started painting it when we were lovers. She knows it's here.'

'It's incredible,' I repeat, my gaze shifting back to Casey. She catches my eye and gives me a smile that makes my insides vibrate, then deftly weaves her way through the crowd and kisses me briefly on the mouth.

'I see you've met the artist,' Casey says. '*Hallo*, Katarina, *das ist* Holly.'

Katarina kisses both my cheeks. '*Hallo*, Holly.' She greets Casey the same way. 'I was just telling your lover about my lover.'

'Ah, you've heard about the muse?' Casey says to me.

'Holly thinks she's very sexy,' Katarina says.

Casey gives me a knowing look. 'Does she?'

I sip my wine and widen my eyes at Casey.

Katarina waves at someone across the room. 'Excuse me, someone I want to talk to.'

I place my hand against my cheek, which burns under my touch. 'Oh my God. Am I as red as my dress?'

Casey laughs and pulls me close. 'Sorry,' she says, her lips brushing my hairline.

'Mmm. I'll let you off.' I gaze up at her. 'This show is amazing.'

'You like it?'

I nod. 'Looks like you were selling some art over there.'

'Yeah, we've had a lot of interest.'

'I don't think anyone could say no to you.'

'Plenty do.' She kisses me again and then watches me for a long moment.

'What?' I ask.

She runs her fingers over one of my dress's spaghetti straps. 'I'm so glad you're here.'

My heart swells. 'Me too.'

'I just wanted to say hello and check you're okay. I need to catch up with that couple over there,' she says, jutting her chin towards the far corner. 'You'll be okay for a bit?'

'Sure, I still have half the exhibition to look at.' Felix's husband approaches and hands me a fresh glass of wine. 'And Matias is keeping me company.'

'And hydrated,' he says.

'Cheers, Matias,' Casey says, then moves into the crowd, turning heads and drawing people in.

Chapter 24
Casey, Berlin

I've just secured the sale of Katarina's painting when my jeans' pocket vibrates. I excuse myself and pull out my phone to see Eva's name flash on the screen like a warning siren. My stomach drops. I've been calling her for the past three days, wanting to tell her the truth, but she's brushed me off each time with a *hey, babe, busy, busy, speak later*. I scan the gallery and spot Holly still talking to Matias. I feel sick that I haven't been honest with her.

As much as I don't want to have this conversation tonight, I can't leave it any longer. Lying to both Holly and Eva is eating away at me. If Holly can leave an unhappy relationship and fly across the world, I can have a difficult conversation with someone I'm no longer in love with.

By the time I'm in Felix's office, the ringing stops, but within seconds it starts again. I slide the call answer icon. 'Hiya.'

'Hi,' Eva says quietly.

I take a deep breath. 'I've been waiting for you to call me back all day. Eva, I need to talk to y—'

'Daddy's in hospital,' she sniffs.

'What?'

'He was in a car accident.'

'Oh, God. Is he okay?'

She lets out a small sob. 'We're not sure.'

'Shit. What happened?'

'I don't know. We haven't been able to speak to him.'

'But is it serious? Is he conscious?' I ask.

She sniffs again. 'We're waiting to see the doctor.'

I lean my head back against the wall and close my eyes.

'Can you come back, please?' she says. 'You don't have to stay there for the rest of the week, do you?'

'Oh, I'm not sure—'

'Casey, I need you!'

'Um...' *Fuck*. 'It's just that—'

'Oh my God. Seriously?'

I cave. 'Okay. Yes. I'll ... I'll come home.'

'Thank you. See you tomorrow, then.'

'Tomorrow? I'm supposed to be working here tom—'

'Casey! Dad's in hospital! Can't you just support me?'

An ugly twist deep in my gut forces me to sit down. 'Fine. I'll come home tomorrow.'

She sniffs again and there's a murmur as she talks to her mum. 'I need to go. The doctor is calling us.'

My throat is scratchy and dry, blocked with the words I'd rehearsed all day. 'Let me know how he is. I'll sort a flight in the morning.' I drop my phone onto the table and press the heels of my hands to my forehead. 'Fuck.' I throw my head back. 'Fuuuck.' I jump up and pace the office, hoping the movement will spark a solution to my dilemma. Then I stop short; it's clear what I need to do – return to London and tell Eva the truth.

With a sick stomach, I head back out to the gallery. Holly is still chatting with Matias, the glow of the spotlight above giving her a golden aura. I have no idea what this is between us; all I know is that I can't lose her again. I wanted to tell her the truth tonight. I planned to have the conversation with Eva and then tell Holly everything, but I can't tell her now and then leave in the morning. The risk of her disappearing is too great.

I make my way over and Holly's face brightens when she sees me. 'There you are,' she says.

I grab her hand and take her to the side. 'Listen. I ... erm.' I take a breath. 'I need to go home tomorrow.'

Her face falls and she places the wine glass on the table. 'I thought you were here for a few more days at least.'

'So did I. Something's come up with ... with a...' I clear my throat. 'A friend. Their family.'

'Oh. Jaz?'

'No, not Jaz.'

She releases herself from my grip and steps back, confusion and hurt in her eyes. 'Please tell me this isn't it for us.'

I grab her hand again. 'God, no.' I think fast. 'Come to London when your Airbnb is up at the end of the week, yeah? Can you do that? I mean, do you want to do that?'

She softens. 'You want me to be with you in London?'

'Of course. If that's what you want?'

She rolls her eyes. 'I think I've made it very clear what I want.'

Even though I said it on the fly, now the offer is out there, it makes me realise it's exactly what I want, too. 'Brilliant. You've already paid until the end of the week, right?'

'Yep, until Saturday.'

'Then stay and enjoy your time here and come over on the weekend. I'll be at work all week anyway and be working late every night to catch up after being away.'

She beams. 'Okay, Berlin this week, London next.'

I clutch her face and kiss her. 'And we still have tonight.'

She sighs against my mouth. 'And we still have tonight.'

'Hey, lovers,' Felix says, approaching us. 'We're going to a bar afterwards if you want to join us?'

Holly and I exchange a questioning glance and both nod.

'Felix and I will finish up and we'll go enjoy the rest of our night, yeah?' I say to Holly.

She picks up her glass, her eyes dancing and her cheeks flushed. 'We will.'

I see out artists and guests, and peer over at Holly every now and then. She's glowing even more since I asked her to come to London, but my head has started to throb with the stress of what the coming week might bring.

Half an hour later, the four of us are in a bar, nursing drinks and chatting about how well the night went, the artists and the most popular pieces. Holly talks about the photographs, telling us about techniques the photographers used. Felix, and Matias in particular, being a hobbyist photographer, are enthralled.

When Holly goes to the bathroom and Matias goes to the bar, Felix gives me a wry smile across the table.

'What?' I ask, sensing what's coming.

'Now I see why it's complicated.'

My eyes dart around the bar, ensuring the coast is clear. 'Mmhmm.'

'It's not any of my business,' he says with the tone of someone who absolutely thinks it's his business, 'but I'm curious as to why Eva is on Instagram talking about your upcoming wedding, and you're here with another woman.' He pauses. 'One who is obviously completely in love with you, and' – he lifts a brow – 'you look totally besotted yourself.'

I glance towards the bathroom, checking for Holly. 'I'm going home tomorrow and I'm ending it with Eva. Which I had planned to do days ago, but then I ran into Holly. We know each other from years ago and well, I kind of got side-tracked.'

'Holly doesn't know about Eva?'

I shake my head and a guilty, shameful heat crawls over my face. 'I will tell her, but not tonight. I don't want to ruin tonight. I'd really appreciate it if you didn't mention it.'

'Of course I won't; it's not my place. But don't you follow each other on socials?'

I shrug. 'We've been together since Friday night when we ran into each other, so we haven't needed anything but phone numbers. Look, I haven't handled this the best way, and now I wish I'd said something sooner, but seeing Holly again was so unexpected. I've thought about her for years, and, well, it's a long story. I'm not avoiding it; I just need to tell her my way – get the timing right.'

He sips the last of his beer and considers me for a long moment. 'I think you're going to have some fireworks when you get home, and if you like Holly as much as it looks like you do, then...' He grimaces.

'Yeah. Cheers for that reminder.' I spot Holly coming out from the toilets. She stops at the bar to help Matias. 'I'll sort it. Anyway, you got any spliffs? Couldn't exactly bring some in my luggage.'

He reaches into his jacket pocket and pulls out a cigarette packet, sliding it across the table. 'Take two.'

'Ta.' I hand over some euros and tuck two joints into my coat pocket.

When Holly sits, she takes a sip of wine, and a new song begins. 'Oh, I love this track.' She slides her hand over my thigh. 'Dance with me.'

The bar isn't overly crowded, being a Tuesday night, and there isn't a dancefloor, but I take her hand and lead her to the small area in the middle of the tables. I pull her close, wrapping my arms around her hips. She lays her head on my shoulder and slides her hands under my shirt, resting them in the small of my back. I've already become attached to her touch; I don't want to spend any longer than I have to without it.

'I feel lost without you already,' she says.

I dip my head to kiss the bare skin on her shoulder. 'I don't want to leave you. I really don't.'

She replies with a lingering kiss; her tongue finds mine and everything inside me weakens. She pulls away and brushes her lips against my ear. 'I don't care that I only just found you again, I can't ever lose you.' Her voice is so soft that I barely catch it, but then my brain registers her words and my heart crushes.

'Holly. I—'

But she kisses me again and says, 'Let's go.'

Chapter 25
Holly, Berlin

A couple of hours later, we're naked, covered with a doona and lying on the small two-seater sofa that I dragged onto the balcony earlier today. It's a cool evening and the breeze five stories up is fresh, nipping at my exposed skin.

Casey is half sitting up, leaning back against cushions that pad the slanted arm rest, legs stretched the length of the sofa, with me resting between them. Her chest rises as she inhales, then she passes the joint to me as smoke seeps lazily from her lips into the night air.

I inhale until my lungs burn and cough a little as I exhale.

She smiles and takes the joint back. 'Not a big weed smoker anymore, then?'

'Not for a while, no.' I rest my head against her chest. 'These past few days have been amazing.'

'They have,' she says, gazing down at me, her eyes gleaming in the moonlight.

'You have no idea how much I needed this weekend,' I say. 'I felt suffocated at home, not just because of what was going on when I left, but because of all the years leading up to it. All the stress of it.' I pause as I contemplate whether to tell her about Lily, but the thought of going through it all exhausts me, so I forget it for now. 'I had this urge to get away and get some control of my life back, if that makes sense.'

'Makes total sense. I felt like that too. Just didn't realise it until I got here.' She brushes her thumb across my cheekbone. 'We should give this a proper go. See where it goes.'

'You mean us?' I take the joint from her.

'Yeah.'

I release a plume of smoke. 'You think this is more than us needing to get the past out of our system?'

She takes the joint from me, has one last toke and stubs it out, then shimmies down to wrap her arms around me under the covers. They're cool against my warm skin. 'I think it could be more, if we want it to be.'

My finger makes a pattern on her chest. There's something niggling at me from earlier that I've held back, not wanting to scare her off, but I'm loose with alcohol and weed and the words spill. 'When I was talking to Katarina, she said she didn't stay with that woman in the painting because you can't keep a woman like that confined in a relationship.' I look up. 'You have that look about you.'

She cocks her head, a tiny lift of her brow. 'Do I?'

I nod.

Her mouth presses into a tight line as she searches my face. 'I'm not twenty anymore, Holly. I want to find my person too, and I don't have issues being in a relationship when I'm with the right person.' She pauses. 'I don't want tonight to be the last time we see each other. I'd like to give this a go. If that's what you want, like.'

Everything inside me softens and I lay my head against her

chest, listen to the gentle thud of her heart. My own heart wants to tell her I love her, but my head argues that I couldn't possibly know that this soon. Instead, I say, 'I can hear your heartbeat. And you know it's what I want.'

She kisses the top of my head. 'I do, yeah.'

We're silent again for a few minutes until I say, 'On Friday night, at the river, you said you always struggled with feeling overwhelmed. In what way? Is this something I need to worry about if we're going to try having a relationship?'

She stretches across to the coffee table. 'Looks like we're going to need this second spliff.' She lights up, draws deeply and hands it to me, then exhales a long stream of smoke. 'It's just the way I've always been, especially as a kid. I didn't process emotions well. Like, I'd get emotional sensory overload. It's how I got into art, actually.'

I stay quiet to give her the space to talk.

'I was about thirteen, first year at high school and had a fight with this kid in my class. He'd been taunting me for weeks. Little racial digs. And it was a shock because I went to a diverse school, and we had so many non-white kids, but he targeted me. Jazzy and my other mates were like, "Just ignore him." But I couldn't shake it. It felt so personal, and I couldn't handle all the emotions associated with it. One day, he was up in my face saying shit like, "Are you black or are you white? Make up your mind", followed by some racial slur, and I lost it. Smacked him up against a concrete wall, hand around his throat and said, "I'm biracial, you pasty twat".'

I laugh. 'Pasty twat?'

She grins. 'Yeah, not my wittiest comeback, but it's exactly what he was.' She pauses as she tokes and passes the joint to me.

'I thought I'd get a bollocking,' she continues. 'But instead I was put into art therapy and started to learn how art can help you deal with emotions.'

'Huh,' I say. 'I've never thought about art like that.'

'A lot of people don't, not consciously anyway. But art often provokes a reaction of some kind, and your reactions can be a good indicator of what you're feeling and thinking. If you give yourself the space to sit with it, it can really help you process things.'

'What happened to him?' I ask.

'He was put into some sort of therapy program too, and his parents were mortified. They turned up at our house to apologise to me and Mum and Dad. He turned out all right though, and a few years later he said sorry to me, and we had a good talk about it.'

I stub out the joint and cuddle back into her.

'That event kind of changed the course of my life, I think,' she says. 'I can't imagine not being involved in art now.' She dips her head to kiss me, her mouth smoky from the weed. 'So, to answer your question, I've learnt a lot about myself since we first met, and no, you don't need to be worried. When things become too much, I find ways to deal with them. Usually involves tattoos and paintings, but that's what works for me.'

I gaze at her, a little stunned. 'I think we could be really happy together.'

She smiles. 'Agreed.'

~

'Holly?'

'Mmm,' I say, floating in that space between asleep and awake.

'I have to go.'

My eyes flutter open. 'Already?' I prop myself up on my elbows and glance around, the sheet dropping to my waist.

Casey's gaze drops to my naked chest.

'Stop staring at my boobs,' I yawn.

She grins and meets my eyes. 'Sorry. You'll definitely come over at the weekend?'

I nod. 'I'll leave Saturday?'

'Cool. I'll come meet you at Heathrow.'

'I can get the tube on my own. I'm a big girl.'

'It's not to babysit you; it's because I want to.' She looks around. 'And to help with all this gear that I have no idea how you'll fit in your luggage.'

I sit up fully, my gut prickling with anxiety, and stare at her.

'What's up?' she asks.

I hesitate a beat. 'If you don't show and don't answer your phone, I'll be back here sitting in that park for the rest of my life waiting for you.'

She grabs my phone from the side table and passes it to me. 'I knew you'd feel like that, so I've messaged you where I work, my address, my email, my parents' address and the butcher's. You have many, many options to find me.' She gently hooks a finger under my chin and lifts my face. 'I'm not running away. And if you can't find me at any of those places, across from my gallery is a pub; you'll find me in there – usually on a Friday after work with Jaz. Okay?'

I scroll the details, glancing between her and my screen. 'You're serious about this? About us?'

She nods. 'Aren't you?'

I roll my eyes. 'I came straight to Berlin from Australia just to go to our park again. What do you think?'

She smiles. 'I think that means yes.'

I widen my eyes. 'Uh-huh.'

'That's sorted, then.' She makes a sad face. 'But now, I have to go.' She kisses me goodbye, but when she starts to pull back, I hold her there, letting the kiss linger. She moans and runs her hand up my back.

I release her and reach into the drawer beside the bed. 'Before you go, I have something for you.' I pass her a small photo.

She takes it from me and gasps. 'This is the one you took that night.'

'Yep.'

Casey holds her hand to her chest. 'Look at us. How perfect do we look together?'

I pull my knees up. 'I know.'

She shakes her head. 'It was so obvious how I felt.' She clears her throat and swipes a finger across her cheek.

'Keep that; it's yours. I always wanted you to have copy.'

She holds it to her heart. 'I love it.' She tucks it away and pulls me into a tight embrace. 'I'm going to miss you.'

'I'll miss you too, but Saturday is only three days away.'

Casey grins. 'What are we like?' She hops up and heads for the door.

'Oh, wait,' I call as she grabs the door handle. 'You didn't give me your socials. You must be on something. Insta?'

'Erm ... I don't use socials much.'

My brows rise. 'Still?'

'I'm on Instagram – with my full name, and the profile pic at the mo is a photo of the *Sappho and Erinna* painting.'

'Ah, a painting.' I shake my head. 'Never thought to look for a painting as your profile pic.'

'I'll take you to the Tate next week to see it.' She pulls open the door. 'See you in London town,' she says with a wink.

The door clicks shut, and an emptiness consumes me. I open Instagram and search for her. Her account is private, so I send a request and hop out of bed. By the time I make coffee and hop back in bed, my phone pings with a notification that she's accepted. I send a message.

Miss you already x

She replies with a quick video clip. 'Miss you more,' she says to the camera and blows me a kiss.

Chapter 26
Casey, Berlin

Once my bag is checked, I pass through security, grab a double-strength black coffee and head for gate C7. Eva hasn't responded to my messages asking after her dad, so I assume she's occupied at the hospital. I take a seat by the window with a view of planes parked along the tarmac. My eyes feel dry from little sleep. After Holly drifted off, I tossed and turned, unable to ignore the tightening in my chest and the thoughts racing around my head. I hate that I've lied to Holly, I hate that I've lied to Eva, and I hate the worst part that's still to come – breaking up with Eva while her dad is in hospital. I attempt to rehearse the speech I put together in the middle of the night, but a knot of anxiety forms in my stomach, so I call Jaz instead.

'All right, mate,' she says. 'Can't chat long, got a big meeting with a potential new account in a bit. Where are you?'

'At Brandenburg Airport.'

'Ah, you're coming home.'

'Yep. Eva finally called me back last night. I was just about to tell her when she says her dad's in hospital, had a car accident.'

'Shit. Is he okay?'

'She didn't know anything at the time, and I haven't heard from her since. But she wanted me to come home, and well, obviously I couldn't tell her then, could I?'

'No. That would've been a bit rough.'

A sigh slips out. 'It's killing me doing this to Holly.'

I hear Jaz choke on a drink. 'Whoa. You haven't told Holly yet?'

'No,' I say in a small voice.

'Fucking hell, Case. I told you not to mess this up. That meant you needed to tell Holly as soon as.'

My defences rise. 'It was never the right time.'

'There must have been *one* time. You've literally been stuck together since Friday night, that's...' She pauses and I imagine her counting the days on her fingers. 'Five nights. There must have been a moment to slip it in. What, did you just shag the whole time and not speak?'

'Erm ... we shagged a lot, yeah.' I huff. 'And I've been working full-time since Sunday, so we haven't had *that* much time together.'

She tuts. 'You didn't talk about your pasts at all? What you've both been up to for eleven years?'

'We did, just not a lot about relationships. More family and jobs, and ... *us*, I guess, and what was I going to say after I'd already had sex with her? "That was amazing, but I have a fiancée in London who I don't plan on marrying because I'm going to break it off and it's not because of you, I was actually going to break it off anyway; you just happened to turn up at the same time"?'

'Yeah. Exactly that,' Jaz says.

I groan. 'It's not that simple.'

'Fuck, Casey. Does all anyone need to do with you is shove their pussy in your face and you're a mess?'

'Um...'

'Jesus Christ. Don't answer that.' She sighs. 'Look, I'm hardly one to lecture on stable relationships, but—'

I cut in. 'I absolutely will tell Holly. She's coming over on the weekend. I'll sit her down and explain everything. It'll be easier in London.'

'You still haven't broke it off with Eva!'

More people have arrived at the departure gate, and I lower my voice. 'I'm doing that the minute I get back. Which reminds me, she'll totally kick me out, so can I have your couch for a bit? It's just closer to work than Mum and Dad's.'

'You're in luck because my flatmate is about to move out.'

'No way. Why?'

'Moving to Manchester. Just been offered a new job up there.'

'Brilliant. Thanks. Catch up later for a bevvy?'

'Yeah. Meet me after work about half five, at the Pig and Butcher near my place,' she says.

'You're the best, Jazzy. Good luck with your meeting.' I hang up and check the overhead screen. A few minutes to spare until boarding, so I stick in my headphones and FaceTime Holly.

'Hello, you,' she says with a broad, beautiful smile. Her hair is damp and clinging to her bare shoulders. 'Calling me already?'

'I miss you,' I say, my voice tinged with longing. 'Are you naked?'

Holly angles the camera to show the towel wrapped around her chest. 'Not quite.' She returns the camera to her face. 'When's your flight?'

I glance up at the departures screen. 'Leaves in about

twenty minutes and boarding very soon. What are you doing today?'

'I might go to some museums. I haven't done that yet, so...' She shrugs. 'And I need to find somewhere to stay in London.' She sits on the bed. 'Are you okay with me staying close to where you are? Islington, right? Is that cramping your space?'

'Of course I don't mind.' I've already given her Jaz's address, thinking I'd be staying on her couch, not moving in. 'And it will be nice if you have somewhere close, because I'm about to move in with Jaz, and you do not want to be in the flat when she brings someone back. So if we've got somewhere else to go, that will be good.

She laughs. 'I'm looking forward to meeting Jaz.' Her brows knit. 'Why are you about to move in with her?'

I swallow. *Shit.* 'Oh, long story. I'll tell you about it at the weekend.' A voice crackles over the loudspeaker. 'Hey, I've got to board. Maybe we can catch up later? If you'll be about...'

'Where else would I be?'

I shrug. 'Out.'

She shakes her head. 'Other than getting food, I'll be here. I want to call Mum.'

I stand and get in line. 'I'm meeting Jazzy for a drink after work, but I'll call when I'm home.'

'Okay.' She blows me a kiss. 'I can't wait for the weekend.'

'I can't either.' I hang up and release a drawn-out breath, my stomach churning over what's waiting at my destination.

Chapter 27
Casey, London

When I walk into the flat, I'm surprised to hear the sound of the telly drift from the sitting room. Instantly my hackles rise that Eva couldn't be arsed replying to my messages asking after her dad. I leave my case by the door and head into the sitting room. 'Hello,' I say. 'You're here.'

Eva is on the sofa, one foot up on a towel, nail polish in hand. 'Finally, you're back.' She strokes the brush over a toenail, places the polish on the side table and walks over to me. We exchange an awkward half-cheek, half corner-of-mouth kiss before she resumes her position, pulling up the other foot and grabbing a nail file.

'Why haven't you replied to me?' I ask. 'Is your dad okay?'

She sighs a dramatic sigh. 'Sorry. I was really stressed, and I've been with Mum and Dad most of the time. A stupid driver ran a red light and smashed into the side of Dad's car.'

'Shit,' I say, perching at the opposite end of the sofa. 'Is he badly hurt?'

She waves the nail file. 'Oh, no. They hit the back

passenger door. He was just in shock and hit his head, and the seatbelt cut across his neck. He's home now.'

I stiffen. 'He's out and he's okay?'

'Yes.'

'When did he go home?'

She shrugs. 'A few hours ago.'

'Eva, I asked you to let me know if anything changed. I raced back here and he's fine? Why didn't you tell me?'

She drops her foot to the carpet, her brows pulling together in an angry frown. 'I had a lot on my mind, and you were coming home anyway. Besides, you were on the plane before I knew he was getting out of hospital.'

'But you must've known last night or this morning it wasn't that serious. You could've told me that at least.' I release a frustrated huff. 'And I wasn't coming home anyway. Josanne expected me to stay a couple days after the exhibition. Felix is alone again this week – he needed help.'

'Well, it was an emergency, and I needed you more.'

'It wasn't an emergency though, was it?' I say, my tone harsh.

She flinches. 'Sorry for wanting my fiancée back.' She pouts and slides over to me, leaning forward to reach my mouth. 'I missed you.'

I jerk my head back. 'Don't.'

Confusion settles in her green eyes. 'Don't what? Kiss my fiancée, who I haven't seen for a week?'

I sigh heavily. This is it. 'We need to talk.'

Her eyes widen. 'Talk?'

I clear my throat, trying to ignore the nerves firing in my stomach. 'I wanted to talk to you while I was away. Remember on Saturday when you called me? I said I wanted to tell you something, then you rushed off to speak to Dante.'

She shakes her head. 'No. I don't remember you saying that.'

'Well, I did. I also tried calling Sunday and Monday, and you replied that you were too busy. I also called yesterday specifically asking you to call me back, and you didn't.'

Her face hardens. 'Sorry, but between organising our wedding and my job, I've been flat out. Then I had to rush to the hospital. You're not the only one who has a busy life, you know.'

'I know that, Eva, but you could've at least taken my call – or returned one.'

She folds her arms. 'Well. We're talking now, so out with it.'

I lean forward and place my elbows on my knees, my gut twisting. The afternoon news begins on TV and I glance up, suddenly interested in what's happening in the world, but the screen blacks out and Eva drops the remote on the coffee table. I take a deep breath and face her. 'I'm sorry, Eva, but I can't do this.'

Her eyes turn icy. 'What's *this* exactly?'

I pick at a bit of dry skin near my thumbnail. 'Us. Marriage. I can't do it.'

She gives a disbelieving scoff. 'You're not serious?'

I meet her gaze; it's turned from icy to burning and brutal. 'It's taken me a while to—'

She holds up a hand. 'Last week we were getting married and now you're finishing with me? *You're* finishing with *me?*' She points to herself as though I need a reminder of exactly who it is I'm dumping.

I mutter a pathetic, 'Sorry.'

'Why?'

I fiddle with my watch strap – unclasp, clasp, unclasp. 'I've been unhappy for a while. And the wedding...' I shake my head. 'It's too much.'

'It's a wedding, Casey,' she spits. 'All weddings are stressful to organise.'

'They don't need to be that intense. You've become a different person the past few months, and I was never part of it.'

Her expression softens. 'That's not true. We're having the reception at your gallery – that was your decision.'

'No, Eva. It was yours and I got caught up in it.' I pause to catch my breath. 'It's not just the wedding. It's me. I wanted this to work, I really did, which is why it's taken time to figure out I'm not happy. *We're* not happy.'

'We are,' she pleads. 'We've just both had a lot going on.'

Now that I've started, the words are desperate to escape. 'I don't love you like I should,' I say. 'And I don't feel that you love me like you should either. We bicker and argue all the time – we have for months, ever since we moved in together.'

She scoots across the sofa and grabs my hand, her diamond solitaire glinting up at me. 'That's because things have been stressful. Of course I love you. The wedding will be over in a few weeks and we can be us again.'

She leans in to kiss me, a move that's always worked in the past, but Holly is right there in my head and I pull away. 'There's someone else.' The sentence is out before I've registered what's coming, and it hangs between us, three little words that can cause so much havoc and heart ache.

Her jaw tenses and she retreats. 'I fucking *knew* going out with Jaz last weekend—'

'I didn't sleep with anyone when I went out with Jaz.'

'Then who? When?' She throws up her hands. 'You're always at work, here, with Jaz or with your family.' She narrows her eyes. 'Unless it *is* Jaz. I've always been suspicious about you two.'

'Don't be fucking stupid. Of course it's not Jaz!'

'Then who? I want to know.'

I crumble under the pressure. 'It was in Berlin.'

Her brows shoot up. 'Berlin? As in the trip you've just been on?'

My cheeks burn and I nod.

'You were there for a week for work. How is that possible?'

I chew my bottom lip.

'Go on, then. I'm waiting.' When the silence stretches, she says, 'So, you're breaking it off with me and ruining our amazing wedding because of someone you shagged in Berlin?'

I drop my head into my hands. 'No. Yes. No. It's not because of that.' I look up. 'I was going to end it anyway. It's just a coincidence that I met someone, and I've been struggling with how to tell you—'

'A *coincidence*? I'll ask again. Who is it?'

I stare ahead at the black television screen knowing I can't avoid this. 'Her name is Holly.'

'Holly? As in "deck the halls with boughs of *holly*"?'

'Erm...' Of all the things she could have said, that's what she goes with? 'I don't think she was named after a line in a Christmas car—'

'Well, fa la la la fucking la. How de*light*ful for you both. Did you have a nice time shagging while I was organising our wedding that's happening in four weeks? Four fucking weeks! I assume you *have* been shagging? Knowing your history, I'd say you moved pretty fast to get your head between her legs.'

'I'm sorry, Eva. I really am. I should've told you sooner—'

'Oh, you think?'

I ignore the dig and push on with my reasoning. 'I didn't understand what was going on with me, and I didn't know how to tell you.'

'Everything is booked. How is it going to look when it's all cancelled? I have over one hundred thousand followers who are waiting for us to get married.'

Anger rises that that's her main concern, and I glower at her. 'I don't care how it looks. I can't marry you just because it'll look bad not to.'

She jumps up and starts pacing. 'Have you any idea how much my wedding dress cost? It's a Phillipa Lepley!' she screeches. 'I look fucking amazing in it!'

'I don't know what else to say to you, Eva.'

'So, we're not even going to try and work this out? You're just going to leave *this*' – she gestures up and down her body, followed by a wave around the flat – 'and *this*, for a woman you've just met?'

'She's not the reason I'm leaving. I'd be doing this anyway.'

'Sure,' she scoffs, then her expression changes, like something has just occurred to her. She considers me through narrowed eyes. 'I don't get it. How on earth could you meet someone on a work trip and become so enamoured that you're already telling me about her?'

I bounce my leg and look away. 'We ... we already know each other.'

'Oh, this was planned? You went there to meet her?'

'No. It wasn't like that.'

'Then what was it like, Casey? Tell me!'

I stand. 'It doesn't matter. This isn't about Holly. It's about us, and me not wanting to be in this relationship any longer. It's a really, really shitty thing to do, and I wish I'd worked it out sooner.' I point to the bedroom. 'I'm going to get some of my stuff, and I'm going to stay with Jaz.' I stride out of the sitting room towards the bedroom. I know I owe her a better explanation, but if I stay she'll grind me down and I need to protect myself, and Holly.

Eva scurries after me. 'Did it occur to you that you didn't do this sooner because you love me?'

'Of course I love you, Eva. I wouldn't have been with you if

I didn't. But it's not the right kind of love anymore.' I take a travel bag from the top of the wardrobe and throw in some underwear.

'Then why did you say yes to marrying me?'

'Because...' I stop myself. 'Because I did.'

'You hesitated. Go on. Why?'

I throw in some T-shirts. 'Because you asked me at our housewarming and you fucking live streamed it. I didn't want to hurt you by saying no in front of everyone, okay?'

She gasps and her eyes well with tears.

I give a remorseful groan. 'See, that's why I didn't want to say.'

'That's the only reason?' she asks softly. 'Why didn't you say afterwards?'

I drag my hands over my face. 'No. It's not the only reason. Maybe at first, but I loved you and I wanted to be with you. Getting married was important to you, and I got carried away with it. By the time I worked out there might be an issue, we were too far in.'

She grabs my arm. 'Please don't do this. We can postpone the wedding.'

'I tried to postpone before I went to Berlin. You threw a tantrum.' I shake my head. 'Besides, I don't want...' I gesture between us. 'I don't want this.'

'Okay, so you had a fling; we can work that out.' She wraps her arms around my waist.

'Please don't, Eva. I feel bad enough.' I peel her off and walk away to grab some work clothes.

'So I get no say in this?'

I zip up my bag. 'No say? You can't force me to be in a relationship with you.'

Her face hardens again. 'Have you any idea what you're giving up? You've done all right for yourself being with me,

The working-class girl from East London who done good, yeah?' she says, mimicking my accent.

I curl my lip in disgust. 'You're a fucking classist cow. And you've just made me feel much better about dumping you.' I throw the bag over my shoulder, storm down the hall and grab the handle of my suitcase. 'I'll be in touch to get the rest of my stuff.' I gesture to the walls. 'And don't think you're keeping any of my art either.'

'And don't think you're getting your ring back!' she screams.

I slam the door behind me. My pulse is racing and my skin burns from the anger coursing through me. I wave down a black cab, give the gallery address and don't look back.

Chapter 28
Holly, Berlin

The night after Casey leaves, I pour myself a glass of wine and take it to the couch, ready to edit some photos. My favourite shot from today is a cartoon bunny painted on the side of a decaying building. I fix the exposure so that the cracks and dents in the concrete are more defined, then enhance the pale-yellow bunny to a vibrant lemon, which makes her pop like a 3D image.

The vibration of my phone buzzing against the glass coffee table breaks my concentration, and my heart flutters when I see Casey's image light up the screen. She said she was working late and would call once she was home, but given it's nearly nine, I had lost hope. 'Hello, you,' I say.

She gives me a slow smile, her eyelids heavy with weariness. 'Hiya. Am I calling too late?'

I shake my head. 'Nope. Are you only getting home from work now?'

She nods and covers her mouth as she yawns. 'Mmhmm. On catch-up after being away last week. And it's only eight here – you're an hour ahead.' She pauses to take a sip of water. 'Feel like I haven't seen you for ages.'

It was only yesterday morning that she left, but time has dragged. 'I feel like that too, but it's only been two days.'

She grins. 'I know, but I miss you. Even after only a short week together, it just felt right.'

A warmth gushes through me. 'Yeah, it did.' We gaze at each other for a few seconds before we both give a shy chuckle and I change topic. 'Everything okay with your friend?'

'Oh.' She suddenly seems more awake and waves a hand. 'Yeah. Her dad was in a car accident but turns out he's okay. She, um...' Casey scratches the back of her neck. 'She's a little dramatic sometimes, but all good.' She looks at the screen again. 'Are you all right? What did you do today?'

I want to ask more questions about who this dramatic friend is that she needed to rush back for, but instinct tells me to drop it for now. 'I walked around and took photos. Look at this.' I flip the view on my camera and show her the bunny on my laptop. 'The street art in this city is amazing.'

She squints at the small image. 'Ooh, very nice.'

There's a clatter in the background and Casey turns her head. 'Sounds like Jazzy's home.'

'All right, mate,' says a rich, smooth voice off-screen.

Casey points to the screen. 'Just talking to Holly.'

A second later, Jaz's face blocks Casey's and she beams at me, bright and beautiful. 'Holly! Oh my God. I finally get to meet you. Kind of.'

'Hi, Jaz,' I say. 'And I finally get to meet you.'

'Eleven fucking years I've been waiting,' Jaz says.

The pure joy of knowing Casey's talked about me over the years makes my head spin and I can't wipe the smile from my face.

'Don't mind her.' Casey says, shoving Jaz away. 'You sort somewhere to stay in London?' she asks me.

'Uh-huh. In Angel. It's on ... hang on, I'll check.' I bring up the booking on my laptop. 'Cruden Street.'

Casey grabs another device and scrolls. 'Okay, that's on the other side of Essex Road. Not far.'

'It's a studio flat.'

'Ah, another studio flat thingo,' she says.

We smile at each other, and in the background, Jaz calls, 'Jesus Christ, you two, what are you like?'

We both laugh and I move the conversation on, telling Casey about the photos I took today and giving her an update on Mum and Adam. She tells me about work and an artist she's booked for their winter exhibition, until her eyelids start to droop.

'I need to let you go. You've had a long day,' I say.

'No,' she pleads. 'Keep talking. I can take you into bed with me.'

'You're very cute, but we can talk tomorrow and we'll see each other on Saturday.'

She makes a sad face. 'Guess I could use an early night.' She presses her fingertips to her lips, then places them on the screen. 'Can't wait until the weekend.'

'Me either.' I blow her a kiss and end the call.

I can't doubt her interest in me, her commitment to seeing if we can work. And the friend she had to rush back for? Probably an ex that she doesn't want to talk about, like I don't want to talk about Tom or Lily. Nothing wrong with that. Loads of people are friends with their exes. But as I think this, a niggling in my gut stirs. *What is that? Jealousy? Distrust?* I need to shake it. I don't want to be the suspicious person I was when I was with Lily, and I don't want to ever pressure Casey again. But she misses me, and I miss her. We're alone in separate cities when we don't need to be, and Saturday feels too far away.

I log into the website for my London accommodation to check if it's free tomorrow night. It is, so I amend the booking, then bring my flight forward a day. Buzzing with excitement, I pour myself another wine and start packing up my messy flat.

Chapter 29
Casey, London

Finally, Friday afternoon arrives, and there's only one more night before Holly's with me again. I'm desperate to tell her the truth about Eva so we can start afresh with no secrets.

Last night Jaz and I were up late brainstorming how to explain my situation to Holly. Jaz took her part seriously and threw various scenarios at me, which made me crumble in a heap, but eventually we came up with the simple plan that I'll meet Holly at Heathrow, take her to where she's staying and tell her the truth. She'll be upset, but if I can tell her when we're alone, take the time to properly explain, she'll understand, even if she needs space to process it.

I glance at my watch – just gone five-thirty. Eva's been messaging me non-stop the past two days, everything from she hates me to she loves me to she's glad we're finished to begging me to come back. The latest is she's glad we're done and wants my keys to the flat. I offered to post them, but she insisted on meeting up, and since I still feel shitty about what I did to her, I agreed to meet at the pub across from work.

I leave my laptop on and my jacket over the back of my

office chair, since I'm not done for the day, and head across the road. Through the window, I spot Eva perched on a bar stool at one of the high tables. She gives me a wave through the glass, and I give an upward nod in return and head inside.

'All right,' I say when I reach her.

'Hello,' she replies, a frosty edge to her voice. She slips off the stool and tilts her face upward to kiss me. I don't want to make a show in the pub, so I offer my cheek, but she deliberately catches my mouth.

I recoil and glare at her.

'Calm down, it was just a peck hello.' She sits and points to a glass on the table. 'Got you a pint.'

'I just came to give you the keys,' I say.

'You can't have a drink with me?'

'No. I need to get back to work.'

'It's five-thirty on a Friday afternoon and you need to get back to work?' she asks, with a disbelieving arch of her brow.

'Yeah, I'm busy.'

She points to the glass. 'You're going to let a pint go to waste just to avoid me?'

I sigh. 'Fine. One drink.' I place her keys on the table followed by my phone and wallet. 'There're your keys. I'll stop by on the weekend to get the rest of my things.'

Eva sips her champagne, and I'm relieved to see her engagement ring finger is bare. 'I'm not sure when I'll be home.'

'Then I'll keep these,' I say, picking up the keys, 'and give them back when I'm done.'

She snatches them from me and drops them into her handbag. 'No, you won't. It's my flat, and I don't want someone who doesn't live there having keys.'

'Well, I want my stuff, so if you can't be there can you please get one of your friends to let me in?'

'Fine. I'll ask Leila.' She glances out the window and then back to me. 'I take it you've not had second thoughts, then.'

I cock my head. 'I'm surprised you want to be with a working-class girl from the East End.'

She rolls her eyes. 'I didn't mean it. I was upset.'

But she did mean it; she always carried an air of superiority, thinking she was just that little bit better than me – that she had the upper hand, not only in our relationship, but in life. 'No. I haven't changed my mind.'

She looks away again, her jaw tight, then takes a sip of her drink and places it calmly on the table. 'Where's this new girlfriend of yours, then? I haven't seen you with her.'

I narrow my eyes. 'What do you mean you haven't seen me with her? Have you been following me?'

She gives a casual shrug. 'I've been following you on socials and about the place. You've not been with anyone.'

'Don't do that, please.'

'Well, where is she? There's only one Holly following you on Instagram, so I assume that's her.'

I stiffen. 'You better not have messaged her.' My mind quickly computes the last contact with Holly. It was this morning and she seemed like herself. Actually, she sounded even happier than she normally does.

'And why would that be a problem?' Eva says.

Now my jaw tightens. 'Because us splitting up has nothing to do with Holly.'

'You know...' Eva says, fiddling with the stem of her glass. 'I'm surprised she was okay with shagging someone who was supposed to be getting married in a few weeks. What sort of person does that? She looks quite sweet and innocent in her photos. Doesn't really have a wedding-wrecker vibe about her.'

I shake my head and stand to leave. 'I can't be doing with this, Eva.'

'Unless you didn't tell her.'

I take one step and freeze.

'You didn't, did you? She doesn't know what a piece of work you are.'

I turn to face her. 'What we talked about has nothing to do with you.'

'Oh.' She leans forward so she's inches from my face, green eyes blazing. 'I think my fiancée sleeping with someone else has *everything* to do with me.'

I let out a frustrated sigh, then sit back down and take a gulp of ale. 'I struggled with how to tell you because I didn't want to hurt you. And by the time I felt I could tell you, I met Holly.'

'Go on, then. Where is she?'

'She's still in Berlin. She's coming to London tomorrow.'

'Aw.' She gives an exaggerated pout. 'Isn't that sweet.'

I look out the window to the grey sky.

'She must be having a lovely time on her travels from Australia.'

I whip to face her. 'Stay out of Holly's socials, Eva, for fuck's sake.'

'How could you possibly meet up with someone from Australia in Berlin by coincidence? How could that happen?'

'It doesn't matter.'

'It matters to me, and I want to know. You owe me that.'

I bristle but I feel like I do owe her an explanation, so I answer. 'We met in Berlin when we were exchange students at university. We lost touch, and we ran into each other again.'

'In Berlin? You just happened to both be there at the same time? Her from Australia and you from London?'

'Yes.'

Her eyes flick to my upper arm and she jabs my tattoo, hard. '*That* makes sense now.'

'Ow,' I say, rubbing my arm. 'I never lied about that. I told you it was about someone in my past.'

'You didn't let on that you'd never stopped thinking about her!'

'I'm sorry, Eva. I really am.'

She scoffs and necks the last mouthful of champagne, then plants her glass on the table with more force than necessary. 'Your round.'

I stand. 'No. We're done here.'

'Oh, go on. I'm winding you up. Of course I haven't been in touch with your little Christmas carol. One more drink.'

I snatch up my wallet. 'I'll get you one, then I'm leaving. What do you want?'

'Another glass of Moët – the 2013 vintage, not the other one.'

'Vintage Moët? It's about thirty quid a glass.'

'And?'

'And I'm not fucking paying thirty quid for something that will be gone in three mouthfuls.'

She gives a delicate little grunt. 'I'm not a heathen; I sip champagne. It will take at least six.'

'You're getting sparkling wine or standard wine. Take your pick, otherwise, I'm gone.'

She huffs. 'Fine. I'll have a chardonnay, but make sure it's *not* Australian.'

I roll my eyes and head for the bar.

Chapter 30
Holly, London

It's just past five forty, and the glass doors of the Soho Contemporary Gallery are locked. Casey said she'd probably work late today, and I wanted to get here early to surprise her, but a delayed flight and sorting out keys for the Airbnb means I'm an hour later than planned. Across the narrow street, there's a pub called The Regency and a bar on the corner. Did she say she goes to the pub across from the gallery after work, or the bar? I peer through the gallery doors. The lights are on, but how long before she comes out? I put in my AirPods. The surprise will have to be via FaceTime. After three rings, the call picks up and a woman with sleek dark hair and fine features appears on the screen.

'Hello,' she says, with a tone that suggests she knows me.

'Oh. Hi. I was after Casey, but I must have the wrong—'

'This is Casey's phone.'

A prickle of unease passes through me. 'Is she ... is she there?'

'She's at the bar buying me a drink.' The woman narrows her heavily made-up eyes. 'That background's familiar. Almost like you're in front of Casey's gallery.' Her eyes lift from the screen as she looks around.

I glance up and down the street and across at the pub, trying to identify her location. 'Yes, I am. I came to meet Casey, but the gallery is closed. I thought she might be at the pub?'

'I think I can see you,' the woman says.

I scan the bodies in the pub window, and a woman matching the one on the screen wiggles her fingers at me.

'You must be Holly.'

My eyes flick between my screen and the pub window. 'I am.'

'Well, Casey's just at the bar. Why don't you come over? I'm Eva, by the way.'

My shoulders drop and the murkiness in my belly dissipates. 'Okay.' I step off the footpath and cross the road. 'Are you a friend?'

She glances over her shoulder, then back to the screen. 'You could say that.'

I spot Casey returning to the table with a glass of wine. My heart leaps and I start towards the door.

'I'm her fiancée,' Eva says.

I freeze. My hand drops to my side, but the call is still connected and coming through my headphones. 'Sorry?' I say, staring at her through the glass.

'Her fee-ance-ay.' She pronounces each syllable clearly and slowly. 'You speak English in Australia, don't you?'

The narrow street closes in on me as my disbelieving gaze shifts to Casey. Her eyes are wide, and she shakes her head at me before she rips the phone from Eva's hands, and I hear, 'Fuck you, Eva.'

My fingers tremble as I end the call, shove the headphones back in their case and race off, alternating between a jog and a fast walk.

'Holly, wait!' Seconds later, a hand grips my shoulder. 'Please.'

I spin and wipe my face. 'Your fiancée?'

Casey's face crumples. 'I'm sorry.'

I clutch my hand to my chest as though I'm trying to stop my heart from falling out. 'Your *fiancée*.' It's not a question now; it's a bitter accusation.

She shakes her head. 'She's not.'

'No?'

'No.' She places her palm against her forehead and screws her eyes shut. 'Not anymore.'

'When did she stop being your fiancée? Like, months ago?' I wait, willing her to say yes.

She looks down at the footpath and shakes her head.

I swallow. 'Weeks ago?'

She meets my gaze and shakes her head again.

I close my eyes not wanting to look at her because in my heart, I know the answer to my next question. 'Was she still your fiancée on the weekend?' Reluctantly, I open my eyes.

She bites her bottom lip and nods.

'Fuck, Casey.'

'I wanted to tell you.'

'Then why didn't you?'

'Because, well, she wasn't in my head. Like, I mean, it was over for me and I was about to tell her, and I met you and things happened so fast and it was so brilliant, and I didn't want to hurt you, and I...'

'What?'

She clasps her hands behind her head, a pained expression on her face. She's only in a T-shirt, and her arms are covered in goosebumps from the cool air. Despite my hurt and anger, I'm desperate to pull her close and keep her warm. But I restrain myself because I've been here before with Lily. I won't fall for it again.

'How could it be over if she was still your fiancée? And she clearly doesn't think it's over.'

'It *is* over. Now.' Casey shakes her head. 'No. Then. It was over then. I was going to tell her on the Friday night. I was going back to my room straight after work to tell her, but instead I found you. We got on so well and you kissed me—'

'I kissed you? That's your reason for not telling me?'

People navigate around us, throwing curious looks. Casey steps closer and lowers her voice. 'No. All I meant was, when you kissed me, I didn't want to stop.'

'I asked you that first morning when we were out for breakfast. I told you about Tom and asked if there was anyone recent. You said no.'

Casey hangs her head.

'You could've told me then. That would've been the perfect time to tell me. Yes, I would've been upset, but I would've let you explain.'

'I wanted to. The words were right there, but you looked so ... so broken, and I couldn't do it. It's over with Eva; I promise you. I told her as soon as I got back on Wednesday, and I was going to tell you the truth this weekend. You were supposed to be here tomorrow, and I was going to tell you everything.'

My eyes fill again. 'I trusted you, Casey. I thought last week was something special.'

She grabs my hand. 'It was. I fucked up not telling you straight away, but the more time I spent with you, the harder it became.'

'Have you been sleeping with Eva since you got back? Did you hop off the phone to me and into bed with her?'

'What? No!' She looks genuinely outraged. 'From the

airport, I went straight to her flat, we broke up and I moved to Jaz's place. I also told her about you at the same time.'

'How am I supposed to believe that when you lied to me for almost a week? And I assume, lied to her.'

She opens her mouth to speak, but I cut her off.

'Did you sleep with her the same week you slept with me? Before you went to Berlin?'

Her brows pull together and she stays silent.

A rush of nausea hits me, and I turn away with a disgusted grunt.

'The weekend before I went to Berlin...' she says. 'I didn't know then that—'

'So you went from having sex with your fiancée one weekend, not knowing you wanted to end it, to having sex with me the following weekend knowing it was over with her?'

Her brows furrow deeper. 'Well, it sounds bad when you say it like that.'

I start to walk away, but she grabs my arm.

'I did have doubts about Eva then. I have for months. But I was trying to make it work.' She releases me and takes a deep breath. 'Okay, this is what happened. We were together the Saturday before I went to Berlin. I was having serious doubts. We went to her parents' in the afternoon and I was struggling, so I left and went to my own parents' and stayed the night. It was over for me then and I did *not* sleep with her again. I tried talking to her about the wedding, but she broke down and I couldn't handle it, so I went to Berlin the following day instead. But I swear to you I didn't have sex with her again.'

I want to believe her, but my head is swimming with memories of finding out about Lily's affair, and my heart cracks from the familiar hurt and rejection, except this time, the crack feels so much deeper.

Casey continues. 'It wasn't until I got to Berlin and had some time alone that I knew I couldn't go on like that. But work was so busy, and if I told her then I would've been up all night dealing with it. So I planned to tell her on the Friday night instead, when I didn't have work the next day and could spend the time to talk to her properly, but then I found you. Please, Holly, you have to believe me. I can't lose you a second time.'

I frown. 'I'll never be able to trust you.'

She takes my hand. 'Of course you can.'

'We were so intimate, so close. How could you be like that with me, yet be in a relationship with someone else?'

'Because I don't love her and I knew we were done.'

'Except you forgot to tell her.' I pull my hand free and start walking.

She keeps pace beside me. 'Let's go somewhere. We can talk.'

'Leave me alone.'

She grabs my arm and I yank it free. 'I said, leave. Me. Alone. This can't work. I was stupid to think last week meant anything to you.'

'It meant everything to me.'

I stride away, then stop and turn. 'Don't follow me. You can watch me walk away like I watched you walk away, and you can fucking hurt like I hurt then and like I hurt now.' My tears spill again. 'Fuck you for doing this to me.'

'Holly!' she calls, but her voice dissolves into the sounds of London, and the ache in my heart is even deeper and more painful than the first time she let me down.

I reach Oxford Circus tube station, fly down the escalator and escape underground.

∼

Back at the Airbnb, I screw the top off a wine bottle and hunt for a glass. It doesn't take long – the kitchen is tiny, and I only have a choice of four cupboard doors. I take a large swig, then splash more in my glass and slump against the bench, fresh tears spilling. The flat suddenly feels too small and I can't breathe. Desperate for fresh air, I drag a dining chair over to the window and hoist it up, gulping in the cool evening breeze.

My phone rings. I don't bother checking it. Casey has been calling since I left her standing on Regent Street. I was tempted to switch it off, but I want her to know how it feels to have your calls ignored. Eva enters my head, perched on the bar stool, perfect and poised, cool and calm, ready to protect her prized possession. Even through the thick glass, the fiery determination in her eyes was clear. Then my brain conjures up an image of Casey and Eva in bed, and a bitter jealousy rips through me.

I reach for more wine, desperate to wash away the vision, but instead it's replaced with a reel of Casey and me the past week. Five nights together, skin on skin, lips on lips, hands and mouths trailing over each other's bodies. To me, it was more than physical; our souls were connected. I thought she felt that too. What did she say that afternoon we were in her gallery? I stare at the darkening street and search my mind ... *The same, I feel the same, because you ruined me for everyone else too.* I scoff. *God, I'm an idiot.* Stupid for letting myself get caught up in something so unrealistic, for spending my entire twenties thinking about her, for putting her in this idealistic bubble of perfection, for comparing all my relationships to this person I'd made her out to be.

'So. Fucking. Stupid!' My words vanish into the night sky, just like the relationship I thought I was about to embark on. The silence in the flat is too loud. I slam the window shut, turn on the TV and collapse on the couch. My phone rings again.

Casey's image flashes up at me. I turn up the volume on the TV and drown her out.

Chapter 31
Holly, London

A buzzing on the bedside table wakes me. The left side of my head throbs and my skin is clammy and hot. I throw off the doona and reach for the glass of water I don't recall pouring. As I drain it, memories of last night filter into my mind. I turned the heating up at some point and forgot to turn it down. That, combined with the sunshine beating against the windows, makes the flat feel like a hot yoga studio. My phone stops and starts again a second later. I grab it, expecting it to be Casey, but it's Adam. I bolt upright – it's 7 pm in Melbourne on a Saturday evening and he wouldn't normally call at this time.

'Adam?' I say, my voice urgent.

'Hi, Hols.'

His tone is heavy and I stiffen. 'Is it Mum?'

'Yeah.'

I close my eyes and lean my head back against the wall.

'They think she's had a stroke. About an hour ago. She's okay; don't freak out. It was small, apparently, but she's in the ambulance to the Royal Melbourne. She'll need to have MRIs and stuff because, well, you know what another stroke could mean for her.'

My body relaxes with the relief that it's not worse news. 'I'll come home as quick as I can.'

'You don't need to. I just wanted you to know. We can maybe call you later, once she's settled into a room or something?'

'Yes please, but I'm coming. I'll check flights now. Let her know I'm on my way.'

'Are you sure? You only just got there, and it'll be expensive to get a ticket at short notice, won't it?'

'That doesn't matter.'

'Righto. I'll call when I know more.'

I hang up, take two painkillers, make coffee and hop back in bed with my laptop to search flights. The first available isn't until early tomorrow morning. I book it and message Adam the details.

Then there's that silence again, the enormity of it swallowing me. I peer at the empty space beside me where Casey should be. Would she be sleeping peacefully? Maybe she'd be walking around naked or in the shower, singing. No, she'd be holding me close, murmuring caring words in my ear, keeping me calm about what's happened and urging me to return home as quickly as I can. The thought makes my chest ache, and I jump out of bed to prevent myself from curling into a pathetic, miserable ball. I can't visit my relatives because they're out of London this weekend, but I can't be alone in here all day. I switch on the TV for background noise while I shower and dress, then head out with my camera.

On the tube, I read through the string of messages Casey sent last night. Short messages pleading for me to give her a chance. Long, rambling sentences explaining herself. I read the last one she sent at 2 am.

> Please let me explain. Please forgive me. I love you.

I run my thumb across those last three words. I didn't want her to tell me that in a message. I wanted her to whisper it in my ear while we were entwined in bed, or as we walked the streets of London hand in hand, or when we were drinking nice wine in a bar. But most of all, I wanted her to tell me at the right time, if and when we reached that point, not because she thinks she needs to.

I shove my phone back into my bag, burying the reminder of her, and get off at Westminster. Above ground, I grab a triple-shot black coffee and a savoury croissant and wander to the Abbey – one of Mum's favourite landmarks. I lose myself taking a series of wide shots capturing the magnificence of the building and the contrast of stone against blue sky, and close-ups of the intricate carvings of martyrs framing the entrance. Next to me, a group of teenagers snap each other on phones, trying to get themselves all in the frame. I intervene to help them out, circulating their phones for different photos, and for a short while, the joy of what I'm doing numbs my heartache.

Once they're gone, and I'm happy with my own photos, I take my time walking through St James's Park and the old London streets until I find myself in Trafalgar Square and stop for more food. While I eat, I select a few images and upload them to Instagram, knowing that Casey will see them. Maybe Eva will too. Maybe they'll see them together, back in their shared home, wherever that is. A sourness rises in my throat, but I force it down and focus on the shots I've taken today, scrolling image after image.

In the afternoon I walk around central London, absorbing the architecture. I want to go into the National Gallery and the Tate but the idea of seeing art without Casey hurts too much, so I head back to my Airbnb to hopefully sleep ahead of a 5 am journey back to Heathrow, not even forty-eight hours after I've arrived. I take the tube to Angel. The bus would've been nicer, but I crave the darkness of the underground, the tight tunnels, the rocking carriage, and the anonymity of a crowd.

Back at the flat, I heat up a chicken curry ready-meal that I grabbed at the Tesco Metro on the corner and sort out my clothes and luggage for the morning. My phone rings and my stomach lurches when I see Casey's image flash on the screen. She hasn't called all day and I had started to think if she'd given up that easily, then I really meant nothing to her. My head tells me not to answer but my heart overrules, and my hand shoots out to snatch up the phone. 'What?'

'Oh God, you answered. Can I see you?'

'No.'

'Please. I'm outside.'

'What?' I walk over to the window and lift it open.

She's on the footpath looking up. 'You told me during the week where you were staying, remember?'

'I've got nothing to say.'

'But I have, if you'll let me,' she says.

Even from this height, the despair on her face crushes me. 'Fine. I'm on the second floor – 2A.' I buzz her in, unlock the flat door and lean against the frame until she appears, bounding up the stairs two at a time. Seeing her turns my legs weak, but I steel myself.

'Can I come in?' she says.

I walk inside and sit at the small dining table. Casey shuts the door behind her and tentatively sits across from me. Her eyes are heavy and red-rimmed, and I'm glad.

'Thanks.' She looks around. 'This is nice.'

'What do you want, Casey?'

She takes a deep breath. 'Not telling you the truth was

stupid. But it all happened so fast, and I got swept away in it – in us. I've spent a decade wondering what happened to you and suddenly there you were. I didn't want anything to spoil that, and I knew it was over with Eva.'

'Then why didn't you tell her?' My voice wobbles, but I won't let her see me crack.

'My head was a mess about our relationship. She was fixated on the wedding, and I thought I should try to make it work, but as the date got closer, I struggled. I couldn't think straight. She was in my ear constantly about the wedding. Mum and Jaz were at me to sort it. When I wasn't dealing with that, work was stupid busy. It wasn't until I was on my own in Berlin that it became clear to me. I went to the park the day before we met, and that's when I knew for certain I couldn't stay with Eva. It was partly because I remembered being there with you and how much you meant to me, and I couldn't marry Eva when I had unresolved feelings for someone else. It's true that I told her when I got back from Berlin. She did that little performance yesterday to hurt me because I hurt her.'

Casey takes my hand and my body warms from her touch. 'When you and I went for dinner that first night, we didn't talk about other relationships. And at the river, I was about to tell you – the words were right there – but then we kissed and it felt so right, like I'd found something I thought I'd lost forever. I didn't want to spoil it.'

I look away because the pleading in her eyes is wearing me down. I intentionally avoided talking about Tom or Lily at dinner, but I don't recall hesitancy from her before we kissed. Still, she had the choice to tell me afterwards, and she didn't.

Her thumb skims over my knuckles. 'I wanted to tell you on Saturday,' she says. 'When we were in the park and you told me about leaving Tom. I was so close to telling you.'

Despite the hurt she's caused me, a guilty heat spreads over my face. I knew she wanted to tell me something that day and I wouldn't let her. 'I would've dealt with it, Casey. I would've understood. But to lie to me, then spend another four nights with me, ask me to come to London, pretending I was the only person in your life...' I shake my head. 'I'm not some fragile little thing who can't cope with the truth.'

'I know you're not. It was a shitty thing to do. To you and to Eva. I was trying not to hurt either of you.'

Envy ripples through me that she wanted to protect Eva, but then I check myself because why wouldn't she? If what she's saying is true, she must have loved Eva at some point to get engaged. 'Having to come back here suddenly, that was because of Eva, wasn't it?'

Casey nods. 'Her dad had a car accident. I called her all day on Tuesday so I could tell her it was over, and when she finally called me back, she told me about her dad. I couldn't tell her then, so I came home. But when I arrived, he was fine. She hadn't told me because she wanted me to come back early.'

I retract my hand. I've heard enough. 'This can't work for us, Casey. It's too late.'

'Of course it's not too late.'

'How do I know you won't do the same to me in the future? How do I know you're not still sleeping with Eva? I mean, she's a beautiful woman.'

She strokes my cheek. 'So are you, and I swear to you that I'm not sleeping with her.'

'You were at the pub with her, buying her a drink.' I shrug. 'You weren't expecting me until the next day.'

'I met her to give her back the keys to the flat. I was getting her a drink because she'd bought me one then I was going back to work.'

'You couldn't return the keys some other way?'

'I wanted to, but Eva's pushy; she insisted, and the pub is right across from work.'

'When were you going to tell me?'

'Today. I was going to meet you at Heathrow, bring you here and tell you the truth.'

'Here? So you were going to fuck me first and then tell me?'

Shock flashes in her eyes. 'God, Holly, no. Of course not. I didn't want to tell you over the phone with you in Berlin and me here.'

'Anyway, none of this matters,' I say. 'Because I'm going home tomorrow.'

Casey's eyes widen. 'To Melbourne?'

I nod.

Her swallow is audible. 'Please don't.'

'I have to.' My voice cracks, and I take a deep breath to get through the next sentence. 'Mum had a stroke and she's in hospital.'

Casey slumps back in the chair, defeated.

My heart aches for us, for what we could've been. I want to pull her close. To kiss her lovely mouth. To wrap my arms and legs around her and stay like that until the morning. But that would be too painful because once I'm home, I don't know that I'll ever come back.

She wipes a tear from her cheek. 'I guess it's too soon to ask if there's any chance of you coming back?'

'I don't know. I need to be there for Mum.'

Casey nods, a deep sadness etched on her face.

I stand, needing her to leave before I relent. 'I have to be up early, so you should go.'

She stands too and fixes me with an intense stare, like she senses my urge to hold her one last time. 'Let me stay. I'll go with you to Heathrow in the morning.'

I hesitate, desperate for that, but no, we were never meant

to be. I can't trust her, this stranger I thought I could love, this fantasy I'd created and built in my head. 'No, Casey. This is over.' I force myself to walk to the door and hold it open.

She steps in front of me and cups my cheek, and I instinctively lean into her palm.

'Please try and forgive me,' she says. 'I am so, *so* sorry I hurt you. I'll always regret it and I've always loved you.'

Those words about love again. I squeeze my eyes shut as a tear escapes. When I open them, she's still there, so close. I tilt my head forward, and then her lips are on mine, sweet and warm. I let out a sob and clutch her face as our kiss deepens.

She rests her forehead against mine and places her hand flat against my chest. 'I know you feel the same.'

'Goodbye, Casey,' I choke.

But she doesn't respond, just kisses me one last time and jogs down the stairs.

I race to the window, waiting for her to appear. She steps out onto the footpath and glances up, gives me a sad smile, and disappears around the corner. And for a second time, my heart collapses as I watch her walk away.

Chapter 32
Casey, London

I round the corner and slump against the side of the end terrace, the deep pang of regret anchoring me to the spot. How could I fuck this up so badly? I'm desperate to roll back time and tell Holly the truth that first night. It would have been so easy. As soon as she closed the space between us, all I had to say was, 'There's something I need you to know.' She would've stepped away, looked out over the river, asked questions, and I would've said, *I don't love Eva. It's over between us. I need to call her right now to tell her, but once I've done that, please give me a chance because you've always been in my heart and now here you are.*

I lean my head back against the brick and choke out a sob.

'You all right, love?' a man says, approaching me.

I wipe my face. 'Yeah.'

'You're not hurt?' He stops in front of me. He has kind eyes and a gentle voice like my dad.

I shake my head. 'No, all good.'

'If you're sure, then?'

'Yeah. Ta.' It's the push I need to keep going, and I walk

up to Essex Road, pass by the green to Upper Street and head home. The bars and restaurants are alive, crowded with people, laughing and drinking. Holly and I should be among them enjoying her first weekend in London, sitting side-by-side, bodies pressed together, exchanging loving glances, eager to fall into bed and wake up entwined, naked and content.

Back in the flat, I toss my keys on the table in the foyer and head into the lounge where Jaz is in the same position as when I left her – cross-legged on the sofa, tapping at her laptop, working on a big presentation for Monday, telly loud, wine on the side.

'Hey, mate,' she says, staring at her screen. 'How'd it g—' Her sentence stalls when she looks up. 'Oh.'

I drop beside her and bury my face in my hands. 'I'm so fucking stupid.' When I drop my hands, she's staring at me, her mouth a tight line. 'Don't say it.'

'I didn't say a word,' she says.

'You didn't have to.'

She sighs and places her laptop on the coffee table. 'Well, what do you want me to say? Fuck's sake, Casey. I gave you enough warnings.'

I throw my head back against the sofa and let her rant.

'You never fucking listen. You know what Eva is like. Did you think she'd act any other way? Why did you tell her about Holly anyway? You should've just ended it and left it at that.'

I give her a side glance, my head still resting on the back of the sofa. 'I told you, it was the only way to shut her down. She would've kept at me to stay together. I couldn't handle it.'

She gives me an unimpressed look as she hops up, then leaves the room, returning with a bottle of lager. 'Here,' she says.

'Ta.' I take it and give it a good swig.

She gets comfy on the sofa again. 'Right. I've said my bit. What happened just now, then?'

I give her the rundown, that I repeated everything I told Holly yesterday at the pub, but with more cohesion and detail, and tell her about Holly's mum. When I'm finished, I say, 'I thought I was getting somewhere. She didn't pull away when I held her hand. She wanted to believe me – I could feel it. But when she told me what happened to her mum, I knew she had to go. Her family is too important to her.'

Jaz frowns. 'I'm sorry, mate. That's rough.'

'I can't hassle her when her mum's not well, can I. A stroke? That's serious, innit? What choice does she have but to go home?'

'Yeah, she has to,' Jaz says.

'If I had handled things differently, I'd be with her tonight, supporting her. She must be hurting so bad and feeling so alone. She needs me, you know? I could've taken her to the airport in the morning. Called her as soon as she arrived home. Fuck, I could've even gone with her.' I close my eyes, the pain of missed opportunities washing over me.

'I don't know what to say,' Jaz says, 'other than you're going to need to give her some space and maybe some time, yeah?'

'But she'll be so worried and desperate to get home, and that kills me. I know she still cares. We kissed. That means something.' I reach for my phone.

'Don't,' Jaz says. 'Just leave it. At least for a bit.'

I look at her, then back to my phone, unsure what to do. But since making my own decisions has gotten me into this mess, I hand over my phone. 'Tell me if she messages though, yeah?'

She takes it from me. 'Course I will.'

~

It's Monday morning, 8 am and I'm already at my desk. I'm never at work this early, but I woke at five, wondering where Holly was at that precise moment. Lying in my dark bedroom, I checked departures, arrivals and flight paths, trying to figure out which flight she was on. Then I remembered the time difference. She would've already arrived, back with her friends and family. Back to the handsome lad called Tom.

I bite into the ham and cheese croissant I grabbed on the way. Flakes of pastry stick to my lips and fall onto my desk. I wipe my greasy fingers on a napkin and check my phone, hoping a message from Holly has appeared since I checked five minutes ago – a change of heart, a desire to talk – but the only new message is one from Eva late last night asking if we could meet. I delete it, then open my work emails and scan the long chain of messages I still need to get to from last week, and the incoming ones from the weekend.

Deciding where to start is too hard, so I grab my coffee and head into the gallery. It's grey outside, and the space is still in darkness. I flick on the display lights for the artwork and immediately my energy shifts. Being in here alone gives me perspective sometimes, helps me organise my thoughts. Slowly, I walk from piece to piece, losing myself in stories told through vibrant paint, brushstrokes, subject matter, photographs. How many of these artists created these while heartbroken or full of regret over a bad decision?

I stop in front of one of my favourites – an oil painting of a woman partially submerged in the ocean. A sheer white dress clings to her body, stark against her black skin. She stares at the viewer, raw emotion in her dark eyes, lips painted red and parted like she's about to speak. Is she about to duck her head under? Does she want to say one final word? Or is she emerging from the water? Opening her mouth because she's found her voice?

Every time I look at this painting, I see and feel something different. This is why I love art; it's about reflection and relatability. I step back to fully absorb it, let myself feel the ache spreading through me, close my eyes as the tears build. When I open them, I see a woman trapped, overwhelmed and half drowning.

My chest feels hollow and my vision is blurred, but I continue through the gallery, taking in the rest of our summer display. It will come down in a couple of weeks to be replaced by the autumn exhibition we planned months ago. Work is all I have now, and this needs to be my focus.

I head back to my little office, gaze up at the Jamaican beach on the wall, let the serenity of it wash over me, then get to work on putting together a cracking winter exhibition.

Chapter 33
Holly, Melbourne

Jetlag drags at my body as I walk the brightly lit corridors of the Royal Melbourne Hospital stroke unit, searching for Mum's ward. When I find it, she's asleep, frail and delicate, a gentle rise and fall of her chest. I take the seat by the bed and pick up her hand. Her wedding ring is looser than it was when I left.

'Hi, Mum.'

Her eyelids slowly open and she blinks at me.

'It's Holly. I'm here.'

Her brows furrow, but then recognition fills her eyes. She holds her hand up to my face. 'Lovely girl,' she says, her voice hoarse. She glances around and licks her lips.

'Are you thirsty?' I pour her a glass of water from the carafe on the bedside table.

She sits up and takes a few sips. 'That's better.' She places the glass on the tray table and opens her arms for me.

My body relaxes in her embrace. 'I missed you.'

'It hasn't been that long since I've seen you, has it?' she says.

I take a seat. 'Maybe that's because we've had lots of video calls.'

'Yes, but at the care home ... didn't I see you in person...' She shakes her head, forehead crinkling.

I don't want her distressed, so I go along with it. 'I was there two weeks ago – not long at all.'

'I thought so,' she says, lying back against the pillow.

'I went to Berlin. But I'm home now.'

Her eyes widen. 'Berlin?'

I'm about to remind her of the conversations we had when I was there, but it's pointless, so I just nod. 'Uh-huh. For a holiday.'

Mum's eyes flick behind me, and I spin to see Adam. He breaks into a wide grin. 'Hey, you.'

I jump up and rush to him. The stress of the past few days hits me, and I let out a small sob against his chest. 'Missed you.'

'Missed you, too.' He steps back and holds me at arm's length. 'You were only gone a couple of weeks. Why the tears?'

I wipe my cheeks. 'Long story. I'll tell you later.'

He gives me a perplexed look and walks around to the other side of the bed, giving Mum's shin a light pat. 'Hi, Mum.'

She smiles at him and opens her mouth to answer, but nothing comes.

'It's Adam,' he says. 'Your son.'

She tsks. 'I know who you are.'

'Sorry.' He bends down to kiss her cheek before pulling up a chair. 'How was the flight?' he asks me. 'You must be tired.'

'Flight was long, and I barely slept, so yeah, exhausted.' I glance at Mum, who's shifted lower in the bed and closed her eyes. 'Any updates on what's happening?' I whisper to Adam.

He keeps his voice low. 'Apparently it was a transient ischaemic attack – a ministroke. It has similar symptoms to a regular stroke, which is why the care home called an ambulance straight away. The doctor says the effects usually aren't as major, but they need to monitor her for a few days. They did an MRI today but no results yet.' He looks at Mum. 'She seems okay. She's eating. Her memory doesn't appear any worse. Says she has some aches and pains, but that's about it.'

'I can hear you,' Mum says, opening one eyelid.

Adam laughs. 'I know you can, Mum. I'm just giving Holly an update.'

'So if everything is okay after a couple of days, she can be discharged?' I ask.

He nods. 'Yep, as long as the MRI is okay.'

I fall back against the chair with a relieved sigh.

'Sorry you rushed back,' Adam says. 'I had no idea what was going on when the care home called me.'

'It's fine.' I try not to let the heartache of what happened show. 'I didn't want to be so far away with Mum in hospital.' Keen to change tack, I pick up a novel on the bed table, flipping it over to read the back cover blurb. 'You bring this?'

'Meg did.'

'You love a British crime, Mum,' I say.

She opens her eyes. 'I certainly do, and now I'm forgetting things, I can watch and read the same ones over and over.'

I smile. 'Silver linings.'

Adam stands. 'I'll go grab us a cup of coffee, hey?'

'That sounds great, thank you,' I say. 'I'll need some sugar in mine.'

'I'll get you a nice cup of strong tea, Mum,' he says.

He leaves the room, and I open the book to where it's been bookmarked with a scrap of paper. 'Want me to read you some of this story, Mum?'

'Lovely,' she says, closing her eyes again.

Just as I begin to read, my phone pings in my bag. I reach for it expecting a text from Nat, and my heart jumps when it's from Casey. She hasn't contacted me since she left the flat on Saturday night. I kept my phone close all night, thinking she'd keep trying, that she'd turn up at Heathrow, that she'd fight harder for me.

With a shaky hand, I open the message.

> I hope you're home safely and your mum is okay. Haven't stopped thinking about you.

I read the message again, aloud this time, and say, 'What do you think about that, Mum?'

Mum's eyes twitch under the thin skin of her lids, already asleep.

My finger hovers over the screen, itching to reply, but I stop myself. My head is foggy with jetlag; I'm not of sound mind. I switch off my phone, return to the book and focus on the reason I came home.

~

Three days later, I'm back at the hospital.

Apart from a solid twelve-hour sleep on the night of my return, the time has been filled with hospital visits, sorting out what to do with Mum's house now that the tenants have left, and ferrying my nephews to and from school. Tom has messaged, way too enthusiastic about me being back in the country. Not that I told him I was home. Presumably he found out through Nat's husband.

The jetlag has finally lifted, but my heartache hasn't. If anything, it's worse. As I exit the lift on Mum's ward, I stare at the second message Casey has sent me since I've been home and a confusing mix of longing, hurt and anger lodges in my chest.

> I know you don't want to hear from me and
> you have more important things going on, but
> I just want you to know you're on my mind
> and I hope your mum is doing okay.

Part of me, a very large part, wants to call her, to tell her that I miss her, and that I'm desperate for her support. But then I see Eva perched on that bar stool with rage in her eyes, the word 'fiancée' echoing in my ears, Casey's guilt-ridden face, and my heart hardens. As I walk into Mum's room, I type out a perfunctory message.

> Home okay. Mum's still in hospital. Thanks for
> checking.

What else is there to say?

Mum's eyes open as I sit by her bed. 'Hi, Mum.'

She blinks slowly before her pale eyes scan the room then focus on me.

'How're you feeling?' I ask.

'A little fuzzy.' She rubs her chest. 'Chest feels a bit tight.'

'Are you in pain? Do you want me to get the doctor?'

She shakes her head. 'No, it's probably just a cough coming on.'

'You don't want to get a cold. I can get the nurse.'

She pats my hand. 'It's fine ... erm...'

I give her a few seconds, but when nothing comes, I say, 'Holly.'

She frowns. 'Holly. I do remember you; I just can't get names sometimes.'

'It's okay, Mum.'

The nurse who's been on duty the past few days comes in and greets me with a warm smile. 'Hi there, Holly.' He moves to the monitor on the other side of Mum's bed.

'Any word on the MRI results?' I ask him.

'Nothing yet, but they can take a few days. Hopefully later today.' He finishes what he needs to do and starts for the doorway. 'I'll be back a bit later with your lunch, Elaine.'

She grunts as he leaves the room. 'He says that like it's something to look forward to.'

I chuckle. 'I can get you something downstairs if it's that bad.'

She waves her hand. 'I'm just having a moan. Besides, I should be out of here once that MRI is back. They don't seem overly concerned about me.'

'That's true. Hopefully tomorrow.' I take a seat. 'Would you like to see some photos from my trip?' I wanted to show her yesterday, but the doctors took her away for more tests and I didn't get the chance.

Her eyebrows pull together. 'Your trip? Have you been somewhere?'

I nod. 'I went overseas. To Berlin and London.'

Her face brightens. 'London? And you have photos?'

'Yep.' I pull out my phone and open the photo app, my pulse quickening as I land on the photo of Casey and me on Saturday afternoon in Berlin. 'You remember Casey?' I say. 'The one from London I told you about?'

Mum shakes her head.

'Well, we found each other. I thought it was fate, until she broke my heart again.' My voice wobbles. 'How could she do that to me?'

Mum shuffles up the bed and offers me her hand. 'Oh, my lovely girl, I don't know what you're talking about, but I don't like it when you're upset.'

I run my thumb across the delicate skin over her knuckles. 'You always told me to aim for the best, not to settle. To be with someone who makes my soul sing, like you and Dad. I've always searched for that. I thought I finally found it.' A tear falls onto our linked hands. 'But Casey had that with someone else at the same time.' Mum watches me as I wipe my face. 'Sorry. Seeing the photos is hard. We need to focus on you, not me.'

'No, you don't need to focus on me. That's why I'm here, so the hospital can look after me.'

I blow my nose. 'Thanks, Mum.' I find the London photos and pass her my phone. 'I took some of Westminster Abbey for you.'

'Oh,' she breathes, staring at the screen. 'So beautiful. London is so clear in my mind. Why is that? Why can't I remember your name or what you said ten minutes ago, but I remember something from so long ago?'

My heart aches for her. 'That's just your condition, Mum.'

She rubs her chest again and passes my phone back.

'Are you sure you don't want me to get the doctor?'

'No, don't bother them,' she says. 'It's nothing.'

There's a rattle by the door as the nurse from earlier takes a food tray from the trolley and brings it into the room. 'Here you go, Elaine.' He places her lunch down and helps Mum to sit up.

'Maybe I'll go and get something to eat, too,' I say, leaning down to kiss her forehead. 'I'll be back soon. I love you.'

'Love you too.' She gives me a quick smile before she focuses on the tray of sandwiches in front of her.

I catch the nurse as he's heading back to the trolley to fetch Mum a cup of tea. 'Mum says her chest feels a bit tight. She said it's probably a cough, but I thought I should mention it. She looked like she was in a bit of pain.'

Concern fills his eyes. 'Right. Okay. I'll let the doctor know right away.'

'Thanks.'

I head downstairs to the hospital café, grab a chicken salad sandwich and a coffee, then head outside to sit in the spring sunshine. I take a bite and open Instagram, automatically going to Casey's profile. The last photo is still of her and Jaz on a night out the week before we met in Berlin. I click on the list of people who've liked it and scroll, looking for a name. And there it is – *Eva Rossi*. I've told myself I'm not interested in what she's about, but I can't shift her and Casey's relationship from my mind.

I click Eva's profile, my eyes widening when I see her follower count. Her latest post is from yesterday – a reel talking about evening eye make-up and fluttering her lids to show off a glittery golden olive eyeshadow. I scroll her time-line and find a post from the weekend Casey and I were in Berlin – it's Eva with the wedding planner. What were Casey and I doing at that very moment? My face warms as I picture us in her gallery, looking at a painting of a naked woman, having sex while her fiancée was in another country planning a wedding.

I grunt my disgust, toss my sandwich in the bin and head back into the hospital.

When I step out of the elevator, nurses rush past me, shouting medical terms to one another. I head to Mum's ward, but a nurse stops me.

'Holly, I'm sorry, but you can't go in,' she says. 'The doctor's with your mum. We'll need you to wait out here.'

My pulse spikes. 'Mum said her chest was tight. Is that it?'

'We'll be with you soon,' she says, her expression grave, then disappears into Mum's room.

I stand in the middle of the corridor helplessly staring at the closed door, my vision growing blurry. A hand grips my elbow and guides me to a waiting lounge, where a staff member sits me down and makes me tea.

'Holly,' she says, placing a mug in front of me on the coffee table. 'Do you want to call your brother?'

I stare at her while I process the question and then grab my phone, my fingers trembling as I hit Adam's number.

'Hey, Hols. What's up?' Adam say, his voice rising over construction in the background.

'It's Mum.'

'Hang on...' The background noise becomes muted. 'Mum, did you say?'

'Something's happened,' I say in a shaky voice. 'They're in her room and they won't let me in.' My eyes fill. 'She was fine, Adam. I just went to get some lunch and when I came back everything had changed.'

'You're still at the hospital?'

'Yes.'

'On my way.'

He hangs up and I'm alone again. I go back out into the corridor, but the door to Mum's room is still closed. I press my ear against it, try to listen, but the same nurse catches me and leads me back to the waiting room.

'The doctor will come and speak to you as soon as he can,' she says.

I stare out the window at the trams trundling along, the cars passing, early afternoon dog walkers. It's not fair that time continues for them when it's stopped for me.

Adam arrives, dusty from work, and I launch myself at him. 'I won't be able to pick up Eli and Cooper from school,' I sob into his chest.

'Don't be silly. I've called Meg. She'll deal with it.' He sits and pulls me down beside him. 'Tell me exactly what happened.'

When I'm finished, he says, 'Well, it doesn't mean it's anything bad. It might just be another one of those TIA things. People have ministrokes in a row sometimes, don't they? That happens, right?' There's a panicked edge to his voice.

'I don't know,' I say softly.

We sit in silence as time stretches until eventually, a tall, thin man with a thick head of grey hair walks in and we both jump up.

'Holly and Adam?' He gestures to the couch. 'Please, take a seat.'

We exchange a worried glance and sit. He closes the door and drags a chair closer. 'I'm Dr Wren.' He looks down at the carpet and takes a deep breath before he meets our eyes, and I see it – the anguish of having to deliver bad news. It's in the heaviness of his expression, the lines in his forehead, the downward pull of his mouth, and before he's even spoken my hand is over my mouth and I'm screwing my eyes shut to make this moment go away. Adam slips his arm around me.

'Your mother had a heart attack,' Dr Wren says.

Adam's fingers dig into my shoulder.

'I'm so sorry. We tried everything to revive her.'

I open my eyes to look at the doctor. 'But she was okay.' I turn to Adam. 'She was okay.'

Tears streak his dusty cheeks. He opens his mouth to speak, but nothing comes out. I pull him to me and hold him tight as he sobs.

I stare at the doctor, my own tears falling. 'She was okay,' I whisper.

Chapter 34
Casey, London

I trudge across the road to the pub, a light mist of rain falling on my face. When I walk in, Jaz pokes her head out from a booth seat and gives me a wave.

'All right, mate,' she says as I slip into the seat across from her. 'Got you a half, since you're cutting back on the drink and all.'

'Cheers.' I strip off my jacket and take a long sip of ale, which means half of my half is already gone.

Jaz frowns and glances at the glass as I place it on the table. 'I should've known you'd need a pint. Not heard from her, then?'

'One reply,' I say sulkily.

'Well, that's better than none, innit?' she says, using the overly enthusiastic tone she's adopted with me recently.

I grab my phone and read Holly's message. 'Home okay. Mum's still in hospital. Thanks for checking.'

Jaz grimaces.

'Exactly. What sort of message is that? "Thanks for checking"? What's that about?'

'She won't be thinking straight,' Jaz says. 'She's got a lot going on with her mum's health and dealing with what happened between you two.'

I sigh. 'I just want her to know how much she means to me. How sorry I am. Like, it can't be over just like that.'

'I get that you're hurting but listen to me, right, don't crowd her. Imagine how you'd feel in her situation. Your heart is broken, your mum in hospital, and you have to race back to the other side of the world.'

'Okay. I hear you.' I hold up my phone. 'Am I crowding her if I reply to this, then? If I ignore it, she'll think I don't care. I feel like I can't win.'

'Just say, "I'm sorry about your mum".'

'And?'

'And nothing. Leave it at that.'

'But that doesn't seem right. Like, shouldn't I offer something else?'

'As long as you don't make it about you. It needs to be about her, yeah?'

'About her...' I tap out a message. 'How about this. "I'm sorry to hear about your mum. If there's anything I can do—"'

'Anything you can do? I think you've done enough for the minute, don't you, Miss fucking Lover Girl.' She huffs and shakes her head. 'Just say, "If you want to talk about it, I'm here".'

'Yeah, that's good.' I type, then pause. 'Should I not end with "I love you" or something?'

Jaz chokes on her wine. 'Are you for real? You've known each other five minutes.'

I make a face. 'Eleven years.'

'Okay, then, you've known *of* each other for eleven years. You've shagged for a few weeks total during that whole time.

And what part of "don't make this about you" didn't you understand?'

'All right, keep your fucking hair on.' I press send. 'There. No love confessions. Happy?'

She rolls her eyes. A few seconds later, she leans forwards and says in a hushed voice, 'Three o'clock.'

My brows furrow and I peer at the wall.

Jaz snorts. 'Oh my God. My three o'clock. Your nine o'clock.'

I chuckle and look towards the bar, my smile vanishing when I spot a familiar figure waiting for a drink – tan heeled boots, tight blue jeans, sleek black hair falling past her shoulder blades. I groan. 'For fuck's sake. She knows we come here on a Friday.'

'Of course she does. But she is with Leila,' Jaz says. 'Hel-*lo*, Leila.'

'No, Jazzy. You are not starting anything with Leila.'

'But she's well fit, and she fancies me. Don't spoil my fun.'

'You can have anyone.'

'But I want her.' She gives a little growl and claws the air, then gives her sultriest smile as they approach our table. 'Hi, Leila,' she purrs, followed by a frosty, 'Hello, Eva.'

Leila gushes, 'Hiya. Mind if we join you?'

Jaz scoots over like she's been shot out of a canon. 'Not at all.'

I stare at Jaz, but she's too busy making gooey eyes at Leila. I sigh and shift over.

'Thanks,' Eva says, taking a seat and placing her champagne glass on the table.

We haven't spoken since she answered Holly's call, but we did exchange some catty messages in the days following.

'So, how are you?' Eva asks me. 'Still sulking, I take it, since I've not heard from you.'

I sip my ale and calmly put my glass down. 'Why would you hear from me, Eva? We're not exactly friends. But since we're talking now, did you enjoy hurting Holly like that?'

She smiles smugly. 'I enjoyed hurting you.'

Leila and Jaz exchange an awkward glance.

'I'm surprised you haven't called, though,' Eva continues. 'I thought you might have had second thoughts now that your little Christmas carol has gone back to Australia.'

I narrow my eyes. 'How would you know that?'

Eva cocks her head. 'Because her Instagram account is public, and she's posted about being back in Melbourne.'

I face Jaz. 'I reckon I might head off. Ta for the drink.'

Eva places her hand on my thigh and squeezes. 'Why don't I come with you?'

I pluck her hand off my thigh, my anger rising, not only over what she did to Holly, but because she always has to have the upper hand. 'Can you move, please.'

She stays put, her jaw tight.

'For fuck's sake, Eva. Move.'

She scoffs. 'You're seriously turning me down? For what? A bland Australian Blake Lively lookalike who's on another continent?'

My face burns as my anger reaches its peak.

'Ooh, I don't think you want to say that about Holly,' Jaz interjects. 'And Blake Lively's well beautiful.'

'Yeah, she totally is,' Leila says.

Eva shoots Leila a look. 'Sure, if bland blondes are your thing.'

My eyes sting and I take a deep breath to halt the tears. 'Holly is one of the most amazing people I've ever met,' I spit at Eva. 'She's passionate and intelligent and creative and brave.'

Eva's cheeks grow pink.

'And she has a smile like sunshine,' Jaz says.

I give Jaz a grateful nod and turn back to Eva. 'She has a smile like sunshine, and I've been in love with her since I was twenty years old.'

Eva's nostrils flare but she stands to let me out.

'Nice to see you, Leila,' I say, sliding out of the booth. 'See you at home, Jaz.'

I storm out of the pub and head for Oxford Circus, wild heat coursing through me, hot tears threatening to spill.

'Casey, wait up!'

I spin to see Jaz jogging towards me. She slips her arm around my waist. 'Come on. I'll buy you a laksa for tea at that nice Malaysian place near ours.'

'What about Leila?'

She shrugs. 'My best mate is more important.'

I give her some sceptical side-eye. 'And you running off will make her more keen?'

She grins. 'No, mate. I'm totally thinking about you.'

I ruffle her hair, my anger dissipating slightly. 'What are you like.' I rest my arm across her shoulder. 'Fucking Eva.'

Jaz peers at me, mouth tucked in on one side, assessing what I need from her. 'She's a total cow. And there's nothing bland about Holly.'

I give her a squeeze, grateful that she's loyal to the core. 'Cheers, mate.'

Chapter 35
Holly, Melbourne

I stir sugar into a mug of tea and pass it to Nat.

'I was going to do that,' she says, taking it from me.

'I can make a cup of tea.' My tone is sharp, my voice unrecognisable, and I immediately let out a remorseful sigh. 'I'm sorry. I know you're just trying to help.'

Nat gives me a sad smile. 'It's fine.' She gazes out at Adam and Meg's backyard, where a small gathering of people dressed in black dot the lawn. 'It was a nice service.'

'It was,' I say.

The funeral was a small affair in a chapel near Adam and Meg's place with relatives and some close family friends. Mum's truly gone and there's nothing left of my heart. It's shattered, an empty shell, a hole in my chest. I'm a thirty-one-year-old orphan, with only Adam and his family here and no relationship of my own. There is something so terribly sad about that, it almost floors me.

That fated day at the hospital, after Dr Wren explained that Mum had had a heart attack and the hospital staff had given us the obligatory support resources, we drove back to

Adam's in separate cars. He took himself to bed, and I curled up in the spare room, with Meg tending to us both late into the night. The days that followed were dark and painful, Adam and I flitting between dealing with our own grief and holding the other up. I raged with the unfairness of it, while he stayed grateful Mum didn't have to cope with deteriorating further. At least arranging the funeral gave us something to focus on and a chance to spend time together to celebrate the memory of our parents.

Casey messaged me the day after Mum passed, unaware of what had happened. I sent a short reply to tell her – I couldn't cope with continuous messages asking how Mum was. My FaceTime lit up immediately, but I declined it; seeing Casey's face would've ended me. I sent another message a few days later to explain I couldn't talk and that we'd set a date for the funeral.

Nat rubs my back, reminding me I'm not alone. 'I'm just going to check on Archie.' She leans closer. 'Tom's on his way over.'

She heads inside as Tom approaches me. Other than a few messages to tell him about Mum and a quick nod across the chapel, we haven't spoken.

Tom gives me a tentative smile and slips his hands into his suit pockets. 'Good to see you, Hols. I'm really sorry about your mum.'

I nod. 'Thank you. How are you?'

He shrugs. 'Okay.'

The late afternoon breeze has turned cool, and I rub my bare arms. 'How's Jack?'

'Oh, he's pretty good. Getting used to spending time with me.' His eyes scan my face. 'You look really well.'

I've hardly slept for two weeks, so I know that's not true, but he's never been comfortable in these situations and he'll be struggling to make conversation. I glance down at my shoes, sensible black flats that I once joked would only be good for a funeral.

'Did you have a nice holiday?' he asks.

I almost scoff at that. 'Nice' doesn't even come close. Incredible. Mind-blowing. Life-changing. Heart-breaking. But it feels so long ago now. 'I did.'

'I saw some of your photos on Instagram. Berlin looks like a beautiful city.'

My head snaps up. Since when is Tom on Instagram? My mind goes to the photos of Casey and me that I posted after she returned to London. Our Sappho and Erinna photo, she'd called it, and I feel my cheeks colour. 'It is a beautiful city. It was good to go back.'

'Looked like you met some friends while you were there?' he says, his tone curious.

I nod. 'An old friend from when I was there for uni.'

His eyes narrow slightly before he says, 'Didn't realise you had friends there.'

I give a half shrug.

His smile is tight. 'I'm glad you didn't spend the whole time alone. I was worried about you.'

'I'm a big girl, Tom.'

He gives a curt nod. 'So, you're home to stay now?'

'I guess so.'

'Maybe we could catch up? Have dinner or something?'

'I ... erm...'

'Just as friends.'

'Oh. Friends. Maybe. Bit hard to think about anything past today at the moment.'

His cheeks redden. 'Yes, sorry. Of course. I meant...' He shakes his head. 'Sorry.'

'It's okay.' I point across the backyard. 'I should probably see how Adam's doing.'

'Sure. And again, I'm so sorry about your mum.' He reaches for my hand. 'If you need someone to talk to...'

'Bye, Tom,' I say, retracting my hand and stepping off the deck into the garden. 'Hey,' I say to Adam when I reach him. 'Are you doing okay?'

He nods gravely. 'You?'

I swallow. 'Numb.'

'Yep. Me too.'

I give his arm a rub. 'I'll go and say hello to a few more people and then we can wrap it up, hey?'

'Yes, please.'

Adam, Meg and I spend another hour or so chatting to guests until everyone eventually leaves. As the sun sets, we move inside to the lounge, eyes red and scratchy, and share stories of Mum and Dad. Meg controls our wine intake, and Eli and Cooper sit on our laps, dabbing at our tears, while we show them photos and videos of their grandparents. Soon, exhaustion sets in and I take myself off to my room.

Tucked in bed, I pull my phone from my bag to find a message from Casey, and my heart stutters.

> I couldn't let today pass without contacting you. I'm thinking of you and your family today and hope the day goes as well as it can. If you ever want or need to talk, I'm here for you. Always xx

I clutch the phone to my chest. 'What have I done, Mum? Have I made a mistake?' I wait for some kind of sign – a flickering light, a photo frame flying off the chest of drawers – but the only sounds are Adam and Meg shuffling around the house, getting ready for bed. I read Casey's message again and my resolve weakens. I reply.

Funeral went okay. Thinking of you too.

Immediately, Casey's image flashes on my screen. My heart leaps and my finger automatically joins the FaceTime call. And there she is, radiant and beautiful. 'Hello,' I say.

Casey gasps. 'You answered. I totally didn't expect that.'

I give a tired smile.

'You all right?' She shakes her head. 'Sorry, that was stupid. I meant, are you doing okay?'

A tear falls and I nod.

Her eyes widen. 'You're not. Of course you're not.'

I wipe my cheek. 'It was a difficult day. Mum was unwell for so long, and it's not just grief, but everything. The stress and shock of it all.'

Casey nods, her eyes filled with compassion.

'At least the last words I said to her were "I love you" – and she said it back to me. And I got to see her in person, rather than being over there when it happened. I will always have that.' I choke back a sob.

Casey's eyes well and she clears her throat. 'That's really special. I'm glad you got to see her too.'

We're silent as I brush away a few more tears, then she says, 'You want me to hop on a plane after work? I totally will.'

Yes, my heart screams, but I give a weary shake of my head. 'I'll be okay.' A heavy pause follows, filled with everything we need and want to say to one another, but that's too much right now, so I ask, 'Are you at work?'

She glances around. 'Yep. This is my little office.' She switches the view and does a quick scan. I glimpse white walls and a bright painting of a beach before she flips it back to her.

'I've been working a lot, curating the winter exhibition. Opens mid-December.'

What I'd give to be there right now, sharing her excitement about a new exhibition and looking forward to going to another opening with her.

She chews her bottom lip, then says, 'I miss you, Holly.'

I hesitate, uncertain whether I should open up, but I'm raw and vulnerable, my guard down. 'I miss you too.'

She brightens. 'You do?'

I nod.

'But I'm here and you're there,' she says sadly.

I slip further down into the bed and lay my head on the pillow, my eyelids drooping. I want to fall asleep with her beside me.

'You look tired,' she says.

'It's been a long few weeks.'

'I'll let you go,' she says. 'Do you think we could talk again? Try and...' She shrugs. 'Just talk again?'

'Mmm. Maybe. Night, Casey.' I hold my finger to the screen to end the call.

'Wait.' She stares at me, those dark eyes digging into my soul. 'I...' She shakes her head. 'Nothing. Night.'

Chapter 36
Casey, London

Through the windows of the gallery, the pub taunts me. Holly staring at me through the glass, her face a blend of shock, confusion and hurt. I release a heavy breath and stare at her latest message. I thought the conversation we had would lead to another – the start of us being on speaking terms again. Two days after her mum's funeral, I messaged to see how she was, asked if she needed someone to talk to. She replied that she felt okay and was spending time with her brother and his wife. That was five days ago and this morning when I woke, a new message was waiting for me.

> I'm sorry if I gave you false hope. It was a difficult day. I received your messages, but I think it's best we forget about each other and move on. It's pointless when we're in different countries and I won't be returning to the UK anytime soon. I'm glad we found one another and had our questions answered. But we were never meant to be.

I sent a desperate response, assuring her that I didn't want anything except to be in contact, but she left me on read.

Now, reading the message again, my eyes prickle, and I rush back to my office before Michaela catches me crying in the gallery.

'Why didn't I just tell her when I had the chance,' I mutter as I walk into my office.

There's a tap at my door and I spin around to see Josanne. 'Are you on the phone?' she whispers.

'No,' I say sitting at my desk. 'Just talking to myself.'

She takes a seat and considers me thoughtfully. 'Are you okay, Casey?'

I swallow the emotion that's edging up my throat and start rearranging the Post-it notes stuck to my monitor. 'Yep.'

She's quiet as she watches me. 'I'm sorry that you and Eva broke up.'

'I'm not.'

Her brows rise. 'Oh. Like that, is it?'

'Mmhmm.'

'Okay, well if it's not that, then something else is bothering you because you've gone into work overdrive, and you only do that when you're upset.'

I arrange the Post-its neatly across my desk. 'There's just a lot on.'

She takes a moment before she says, 'I don't think that's the reason you're overworking.'

I slouch in my chair, no energy to keep pretending. 'It's someone else. Someone I really cared about, and I fucked it up. She found out about Eva before I told her. Even worse, Eva was the one to tell her.'

Surprise flickers across Josanne's face but it's quickly replaced by concern. 'Oh, Casey. No wonder you're stressed. How did this all come about?'

'Long story. But the quick version is, and it sounds bad when I say it out loud, but I was going to finish with Eva, then I met up with Holly in Berlin, and well...' I shrug. 'Things happened. I did break it off with Eva, I just didn't get the chance to tell Holly myself. Now she's gone back to Australia. She wants nothing to do with me, and the most horrible thing happened after she'd been home a few days – her mum passed away from a heart attack.'

'Oh,' Josanne says, placing her hand to her chest.

All the emotion I've tried to contain since I read Holly's message this morning starts to seep out of me. 'We finally spoke the night of her mum's funeral, and I thought we'd keep talking,' I say with a wobbly voice. 'But now she's messaged to say it's pointless, and I feel like I can't keep contacting her or fighting for her because of what she's going through.'

Josanne nods. 'Yes. That's a difficult situation.'

My eyes begin to water. 'I'm so angry at myself. It was a shitty thing to do to Eva, and it was my second chance with Holly and I blew it.'

'Your second chance? I didn't realise you had an ex in Berlin.'

'Not an ex. We met when we were exchange students and lost touch. Neither of us had any idea the other would be in Berlin – we had this silly meeting-point thing and we found each other.'

'Well, that sounds like fate to me,' Josanne says.

'That's what Holly said, before I messed everything up.'

'Maybe she just needs some time? And maybe you're being too hard on yourself? We all make mistakes and love makes us do stupid things sometimes.'

'More like lust, I think.'

She nods. 'That too. You can take some time if you need.'

'No.' I say. 'Thank you. I need to work, if that's okay. It's the only thing that helps. Being around art helps.'

'Of course. Just don't want you overdoing it.' She pauses a moment. 'Speaking of work, there was something else I wanted to talk to you about.'

'Oh?'

'There are going to be some staff changes in the Berlin gallery, so it's a good opportunity for us to appoint a director – just for a year, at this stage. Felix isn't interested, and while I don't want to lose you, you would be perfect for it.'

I sit back in my chair, brows raised in surprise. 'Wow. Okay. When do you need to know?'

She shrugs. 'It's a big decision, so take time to think about it. We have a few weeks before we'd need to move ahead with recruitment.'

I light up my phone screen with a tap, glance at Holly's message. Maybe she's right. Maybe we weren't meant to be. Maybe our fate was a brief reconciliation so that we could both move on. I flip my phone over and say to Josanne, 'I'll definitely think about it.'

Even though it's a Sunday, I've spent the morning at work. Now I'm wandering through Soho, contemplating the job offer – other than Holly, it's all I've been able to think about since Josanne mentioned it on Friday. Not that I need more reminders of Holly, but at least our time together in Berlin was special, unlike here, where I need to look at the pub every time I go to work.

I find myself outside the bar Jazzy and I go to. A pint sounds good right now. Inside, I settle on a bar stool, order an ale and pull out my phone, hoping to find a reply from Holly, but there's nothing. Just like there wasn't an hour ago, or eight hours ago, or twenty-four hours ago. I reread the garbled reply I sent her on Friday.

> It doesn't matter we're in different countries. I don't want anything from you other than to stay in touch. It's not pointless and you're wrong we weren't meant to be. You said it was fate and I believe that.

I want to retrieve the message so I don't look like a pathetic sap, but she's read it.

'Hi, Casey,' says a familiar voice beside me.

My head snaps up to see Eva, and I groan.

She holds her hands up. 'Don't storm off or have a go, just let me...' She points to the empty stool beside me. 'Can I sit for a minute?'

I consider telling her to go away, but there's not much fight in me these days, and the guilt about what I did to her continues to weigh heavy on me. I pull the stool out for her.

She orders me another drink and two glasses of white wine, then pushes the half pint of ale in front of me.

'Thanks.' I gesture to her drinks. 'Thirsty?'

She picks up one of the wine glasses and points behind me. 'I'm here with someone. Give me a second. Don't leave.'

I casually glance around as she walks away, curious to see who she's with. She places the glass on the table and bends down to give them a brief kiss on the mouth, then heads back my way. She doesn't like to waste time being single, our Eva.

She sits and watches me a moment, nervously fiddling with her earring. 'I ... I wanted to say sorry.'

My brows shoot up. That I did not expect.

She takes a deep breath. 'I shouldn't have done that to you

or to Holly. I was hurt and angry, and it wasn't fair.' She pauses. 'On either of you.'

I stare at her, stunned. This is the Eva I first met. More genuine, more compassionate. All my defences crumble. 'Thanks, Eva. That means a lot.'

I give myself a moment before I speak again, because I'm a little choked up. 'It was my fault. I put you in that situation and I hate myself for it. I'm sorry too.' I shake my head. 'I handled the whole thing so badly. I should've talked to you well before, told you how I felt, but I was so confused.' I take a breath. 'I *did* love you. Marriage just wasn't what I wanted, and I let it go on too long before I figured it out.'

She nods, a flicker of sadness in her eyes. 'Some things aren't meant to be, I guess, and it leaves the door open for other stuff, right?'

'That's one way to look at it. I'm sorry your parents spent so much money on the wedding, and that I haven't seen them again—'

She cuts me off with a wave of her hand. 'Don't worry. Mum got most of it back. And, um...' She fiddles with her necklace. 'They gave me a good talking-to. Told me to grow up and apologise to you.'

That makes me smile. 'I always liked them.'

'They liked you too. Thought you were good for me.'

'We were good for each other once.'

'Until we weren't,' she says.

I nod my agreement. 'Until we weren't.'

'It sounds like no one can compete with Holly anyway. You would've kept searching until you found her.'

I peer into the amber liquid of my glass, shame nipping at me. Not only over what I did to Eva, but what I said to her in the pub the other week.

'Sorry. That came out wrong,' she says. 'I just meant, you

obviously have a strong connection with her, and she would've always been in your head no matter what. She's stunning by the way, not bland at all. I was jealous.'

Her eyes flit around nervously, and I feel sick that I've put her in this position. 'I shouldn't have said that stuff to you in the pub. I didn't mean you weren't all those things. You are.'

She swallows and glances away. 'Forget it. I pushed you.' She takes a breath and composes herself. 'Anyway, Holly isn't here with you, and you look miserable. I take it things didn't work out?'

I shake my head. 'She had to go home.' My voice wobbles. 'Her mum had a stroke and then she died of a heart attack not long after Holly got back, so we haven't had a chance to talk much.'

Eva's face falls. 'Oh, that's really sad. I'm sorry to hear that.'

'Yeah.' I point behind me, keen to change topic. 'You've met someone, then?'

She looks over my shoulder, her face turning dreamy. 'Her name's Frankie.'

'You happy?'

She smiles. 'I am, and I haven't popped the question yet, so all good.'

I grin. 'Haven't seen you splash it all over Insta.'

'No, Frankie's not into it much, and well, neither am I these days.'

'You're good at it, no reason not to keep going with the influencer stuff,' I say.

'Yeah, but for now I'm doing some other things for a bit. That make-up line thing I've been working on came through, so...'

Her own make-up line has been a long-standing dream, and I'm genuinely happy for her. 'Eva, that's brilliant. Good for you.'

'Thanks.'

I gesture towards her new partner. 'You should probably be getting back to Frankie. Can't imagine she'll be too pleased about you sitting here with your ex.'

She slips off the stool. 'I've told her everything, including what a cow I was.'

'And what a cow I was?'

She grins. 'That too.' She reaches into her pocket and slides a small felt box towards me. 'Thought I should return this.'

I push it back towards her. 'Keep it.'

'Seriously, Casey. As much as I love it, I'm not going to wear it again, am I? Even if I do get engaged to someone else. Take it.'

I slip it into my pocket. 'Thanks.'

She gives my forearm an affectionate squeeze. 'I hope it works out with Holly. I can call her if you like—'

'No! No. It's fine. I'll sort it.'

'Okay, well, I'm glad we ran into each other,' Eva says. 'I would've contacted you at some point anyway. Might be hard to avoid each other now that Jaz and Leila seem to be a thing.' She pauses. 'They're kind of cute, I guess.'

I smile. 'They are.'

As she walks back to Frankie, I sip my ale and feel a slight shift, the apathy I've been lugging around beginning to dissolve. I call Jaz.

'Mate,' she says. 'Where are you? Got the shock of my life when I got up and didn't see your miserable face moping about the flat. I'm not sure whether to be worried or happy.'

'Fancied a change of Sunday scene, so I went to work for a bit and now I'm having a pint in Soho.'

'I'll come meet you.'

I neck the last of my ale. 'How about we go to the pub near

ours? Eva's here with her new partner, so I think I should get out of their space.'

'Ha, no way. Right. Meet you at the Pig and Butcher in about half an hour, then.'

I slip my phone away and give Eva and Frankie a wave goodbye. They both wave back, and Frankie gives me a genuine smile. Very cool.

As I head for the door, I accidentally knock shoulders with someone. 'Shit, sorry.' Then I make eye contact and inwardly cringe. For such a huge city, London is really fucking small sometimes, and it needs more lesbian bars.

The vet nurse's eyes narrow. 'I remember you.'

'Do you?' I say, playing dumb.

'Yeah.' She points to the far wall. 'Over there.' She folds her arms. 'Easy to remember such blatant rejection. I thought you were going to take me home, but you scarpered.'

My cheeks warm. 'Yeah, sorry about that. I was wired that night.'

'Ah, so you do remember.' She cocks her head and her eyes shamelessly roam my body. She steps closer. 'No reason we can't pick up where we left off.'

The desire in her eyes and the want in her voice tells me there's a night of sex on offer. I dig about for the old me, the one who'd have a drink with this woman and dive into bed with her without a second thought.

'Rum and orange, wasn't it?' she says.

'Erm...' I look down at my phone, at my unanswered message. Holly has made herself clear, so why am I stalling? I could definitely use a good shag, no question. But that old me is nowhere to be found today because the thought of being with someone who isn't Holly makes me feel dead inside. 'Thanks,' I say. 'But my best mate's got a bevvy waiting for me elsewhere.'

Her eyebrows shoot up and she shakes her head. 'Wow. Rejected twice. You sure know how to make a girl feel good about herself.'

'Sorry.' And with that, I head for Islington feeling pretty bloody proud of myself for saying no for once.

Chapter 37
Holly, Melbourne

'What are you doing today?' Adam asks, rinsing his cereal bowl and placing it in the dishwasher.

I shrug.

He gives me a fed-up sigh and crosses his arms.

I make a face. 'What?'

'You can't stay indoors and mope every day, Holly. The funeral was a month ago, and you've barely stepped outside.'

'I've been out,' I shoot back.

'You went to the shop on Monday to grab some milk and that's only because Meg and I were frantic with the kids.'

'Well, sorry for being devastated that Mum died.'

He stares at me a beat, like he can't believe I said that. 'I'm devastated too. She was also my mum. But Meg and I have a lot of stuff to deal with – the business, the kids, Meg's job, the house. None of that stops because Mum isn't here anymore. If you're going to stay here, we need you to help.'

I open my mouth to defend myself, but he continues.

'Maybe you need to talk to someone to help you deal with what's happened. I need to deal with it by getting on with things.' He grabs his car keys from the bench. 'And whatever happened with that chick in Berlin or London or wherever, bloody sort it out. And while you're at it, can you reply to Tom? I'm sick of getting messages from him every five minutes asking about you.' He raises his eyebrows expectantly.

Chastised, I bow my head. 'No need to rip me to shreds. It's been a hard time, okay?'

'It has for all of us, Holly. But sitting around staring at your phone isn't going to make it easier or make the hurt go away.' His tone doesn't soften. 'We've been leaving you alone because you've had a tough time, but we can't keep looking after you like this. We're falling apart too. Can you do some stuff to help out today, please?'

'What do you want me to do?' I ask in a small voice.

'First, if you need to, speak to someone about Mum or book an appointment with a therapist or something. You know I'm not good with that stuff. I can't help. Then, can you go to the real estate and see what's happening with Mum's house? It was supposed to go on the market this week. And we need some groceries.' He jerks his chin towards a piece of paper on the kitchen bench. 'There's the list.'

'Righto. Geez.'

'See you tonight, and you'll be helping with dinner.' He heads for the back door as Meg walks into the kitchen pulling her hair up into a top knot and glancing between us. 'And fucken call that English chick so you stop being miserable,' Adam says. 'Or if you're sticking around here, look for a job.'

'Adam...' Meg says, but he leaves, slamming the door behind him.

I gape out the window as he strides across the backyard towards the garage. Has it been a month since the funeral? Have I been that obvious about Casey? I search my mind for evidence that I've been helping Adam and Meg and getting on with my life, but the only image is me lying in bed or on the couch, dressed in pyjamas or the same old pair of grey track-pants, scrolling through photos of Mum and Dad or Casey and stalking Eva's Instagram.

I face Meg. 'I'm sorry.'

She rushes over to me, pulling me into a hug. 'He's just upset and trying to deal with things his own way.'

I cling to her. 'I'm in the way.'

'You're not.' She releases me. 'You're welcome here as long as you want.'

'He's right, though. I probably need to look for a job. Find someone to talk to about Mum.'

'Only if you're ready,' she says.

The thought of getting on with life makes my body deflate. 'Everything's so hard and unfair.'

'You'll be okay, Holly. You just need some time,' Meg says gently.

Time. The answer to everything. 'I'll get those groceries for you.'

'Leave it. I'll grab some stuff on the way home.'

'No, let me do it. It'll be good for me to get out of the house.'

She gives a grateful smile, and I shuffle off to the shower. After I'm washed and dressed, I scan the grief resources that the hospital gave us and make an appointment to speak with a therapist. Then I add some items to the shopping list so I can cook dinner. I grab my camera, which I haven't touched for weeks, and my car keys, and head out into the bright sunshine.

As I start the engine, my phone rings. I sigh when I see the caller, but answer. 'Hi, Tom.'

'Holly! Are you okay?'

I click in my seatbelt. 'I'm fine. Sorry I haven't replied to you. I've just been a bit down.'

'Of course you have.'

'I got your text about dinner tomorrow night,' I say. 'I'm free if you still wanted to go somewhere.'

'Yes! Great. I'll find somewhere and let you know.'

I'm disheartened by the excitement in his voice. 'Okay. I was just heading out, so I'll see you tomorrow night.'

'Look forward to it.'

I hang up and set off towards the city, muttering, 'Don't look forward to it, Tom.'

Half an hour later, I'm in the botanic gardens walking towards the lake where Mum and Dad took me for my tenth birthday. It's a weekday morning, so this section of the gardens is quiet and I'm grateful for the solitude. I dump my bag and wander along the water, looking for potential photo subjects. That's what Dad taught me that day – look for the photo potential in the ordinary things. I spot a leaf on the ground and bend down to inspect it. At first glance, it's just a pale green leaf that's recently fallen. But a closer look reveals a fine silver thread weaving a symmetrical pattern through the leaf. I take it to a bench and set it in position. Through the lens, the silver thread catches the sun, giving the leaf an ethereal glow, and the edges blur into the soft morning light.

'That's for you, Mum and Dad.' I close my eyes and hold the leaf to my heart, releasing some tears to ease the heart ache. I feel my parents' presence and it comforts me.

I open my eyes and take in the lake, the trees, the city buildings in the distance. I do love Melbourne, and I still have Adam and his family and my friends. Maybe I should be more positive about setting up a new life here. I had my what-if answered. Casey is alive and well and we were never meant to be. I'll be fine on my own, my camera for company. At least it never lets me down.

The following night, locked in the restaurant bathroom, I pull out my phone and stare at Casey's message.

> It doesn't matter we're in different countries. I don't want anything from you other than to stay in touch. It's not pointless and you're wrong we weren't meant to be. You said it was fate and I believe that.

It's the reply she sent a week after Mum's funeral, and there hasn't been another since. Yesterday, after deciding to get on with life in Melbourne, I stayed on the park bench for a while longer and deleted her messages, bar this one. Even though she's sent me pleading messages for weeks, there's something about this one that almost cuts through the barrier between us. Almost. I take a deep breath, swipe delete and head back to the table.

Tom brightens when I reappear and tops up my wine. 'It's nice here, don't you think?'

I glance around the restaurant. It's small and busy, sleek furniture, exposed brick, hipster staff, overpriced food. The kind of place Tom never would've suggested going to when we were together. 'Yeah. It is.'

As though he knows what I'm thinking, he says, 'I'm sorry we didn't do this more.'

I shrug. 'Just the way it was.'

He gazes at me like a lost puppy. 'I'm sorry about a lot of things.'

I shake my head. 'Don't, Tom. It wasn't all you.'

'I didn't appreciate you enough.'

I fiddle with the cloth napkin in front of me. He opens his mouth to speak again, but I reach across the table and give his hand a friendly pat. 'Seriously, it wasn't all you.' He glances down and hope blooms on his face. I slowly retract my hand, gripping my wine glass instead. 'I'm sorry I left the way I did. That wasn't the right way to handle it. I feel guilty about that – and about how much that would've hurt you.'

'Okay, I wasn't sure you wanted to talk about that, but since you've brought it up – yeah, you leaving hurt like hell, and I struggled.'

My guilt flares, but I also feel the urge to defend myself. 'I'm sorry, Tom, but I felt suffocated here. Not just us, but Mum needing so much care, my job, the past few years ... it all became too much, and I had to get away.'

'I know. And expecting you to take on Jack...' He shakes his head. 'That was a big ask. I don't think I even discussed it properly with you.' He reaches for my hand again. 'I'll do better if we try again.'

My stomach tightens. 'Oh, I thought this was a friends' dinner.'

His face falls and he releases my hand.

'Sorry, that was insensitive,' I say.

He breaks eye contact and adjusts his glasses. 'No, you're right. I did mention the F word.'

Our meals arrive and he picks up his cutlery, giving me a resigned smile. 'Tell me about your trip? We haven't talked about that. Your photos are amazing.'

I tense at the mention of my travels, but I want to be honest with him. 'I met someone, Tom.'

He stops chewing for a moment as he looks at me with wounded eyes, then resumes eating. He swallows. 'And here I am trying to woo you back.' He clears his throat. 'I really do misread things sometimes.'

'We're not together. It didn't work out and they're in the UK. I just wanted to be honest with you.'

'In the UK. Okay, well, I'm not going to pretend I'm not

happy it hasn't worked out, but I can see you're upset about it, so...'

I suck in a sharp breath, and he lets out a remorseful sigh. 'Now I'm being insensitive. I'm sorry you're not happy. This person it didn't work out with ... it's the woman in the photo with you, isn't it? The one on your Instagram?'

I nod. 'Casey is her name.'

There's a strained silence as he takes a sip of wine. 'As soon as I saw that photo, I knew I could never compete.'

'Please don't think that. It's not a competition.'

'I meant, how you were looking at each other. You seemed so happy. I don't remember you ever looking at me like that.'

I hang my head guiltily and murmur, 'Sorry.'

He leans forward and ducks his head so he can meet my eyes. 'I wasn't after an apology. It was just an observation, and it was nice to see you happy.' He sits back. 'Did you meet in Berlin? I'm confused about how you could be like that with someone you'd only just met.'

'It's a long story,' I say and take a bite of salmon, regretting my decision to be honest.

He shrugs. 'I haven't got anywhere else to be.'

'Really? You want to hear about this?'

'If it's important to you, of course.'

So, as we eat and drink another glass of wine, I tell him the whole story, starting with my uni exchange in Berlin and meeting Casey in the Alte Nationalgalerie. I tell him about our fleeting time together, leaving out the details of our intense connection, about Monbijoupark, the time and day and place thing, how Casey ran off and we lost contact, and finally, finding each other again in the park when I returned.

'Well, that explains why you were keen to get there so quickly,' he says.

'Not because I thought she'd be there. It was something I

needed to do for myself, to forget the idea of her and move on. I wanted closure because I had spent a decade thinking about her, wondering what had happened and creating this ideal person and relationship in my head. But in the end, it wasn't meant to be.'

'Why not?'

I tell him about Eva, watching him closely to gauge his reaction, but his face is unreadable. 'So that's it,' I say finally. 'And now I'm home, trying to build a new life.'

He pushes his plate to the side and picks up his glass. 'You know, Hols, people aren't perfect. Relationships aren't perfect. You do have high expectations, and sometimes it's a little hard to meet them.'

A slow heat crawls up my neck. 'Geez, Tom. Say what you think.'

He gives a short laugh. 'Well, we're friends, right? Did you listen to her side before you wrote her off?'

'Her side? She lied to me, and to Eva. They were getting married in a matter of weeks.' I know this from going through Eva's Instagram page. I down the last mouthful of wine, angry he's siding with someone he's never met. Besides, Casey not only lied, she and Eva were still having sex right up until she left for Berlin. They probably had sex before Casey ended it, too. *Thanks for the shag, Eva. By the way, the wedding's off and I've been sleeping with this Australian bird called Holly in Berlin. Later.* Is that how it went?

Tom leans forward. 'I didn't mean to upset you.'

'Yes, she told me her side, and I didn't believe it, so...'

'So...' he says, his eyebrows rising above the frame of his glasses. 'She did something human and that's it? Someone who looks at you like *that*? Someone you searched the world for and who searched for you?'

'I didn't know she had a fiancée,' I argue. 'I thought—'

'What?' he says abruptly. 'That she was perfect? You're always going to be disappointed if you're looking for perfection, Holly.'

My face warms. 'Okay. Thanks for your insights, I guess.'

'I don't mean to be harsh—'

'Ha, you and Adam with the "I don't mean to be harsh" talk.'

He smiles. 'I don't want you to be unhappy. If we can't be together, then I'd like to think it's because you're with the one.' He raises his wine glass. 'Friends?'

I pick up mine and clink, but the sting of his words lingers, because the truth cuts deep.

Chapter 38
Casey, London

'So, you're just going to run away again?' Mum says, plonking a mug of tea in front of me.

'I'm not fucking running away.'

Dad swats my arm with a tea towel. 'Don't swear at your mother.'

I glare between them. 'I'm not running away. I'm getting on with my life, there's a difference.'

Chandice saunters into the kitchen, a towel wrapped around her head. 'You're moving to Berlin so you don't have to look at the pub every time you arrive and leave work. Sounds like running away to me.'

'Fuck off,' I say.

'Oooh, I've a touched a nerve.' Chandice pulls the towel off her head and hangs it over the back of the dining chair.

'Leave it out, Chandice,' Dad says.

'Excuse me for being triggered every time I go to work over something that was quite traumatic!' I say.

'Traumatic?' Mum says, her eyes bulging. 'You had two birds on the go. They're the ones who'll be traumatised.'

'I didn't have two birds on the go!' I protest.

Dad pats my hand. 'You kind of did, love.'

I shoot him a look. 'Well I didn't fucking mean it, did I?'

He shakes his head and takes his empty mug to the sink.

'Like you won't be triggered in Berlin,' Chandice says. 'You spent more time with Holly there than here.'

'Yeah, but here is where it all went wrong, innit? At least there I have some nice memories. And it's an opportunity to head a gallery on my own. I'd be stupid not to take it.'

'In normal circumstances, yes,' Mum says. 'But you love your job and life here and—'

'No – I *loved* my life here. Past tense. Anyway, I'll get to spend time with Aunty Linda and Uncle Dave. It's not like I won't have family around me.'

Mum jabs a finger at me. 'They don't want you moping about.'

'I'm not going to be moping about.' I stand and Mum pushes me back down.

'Don't think you can run away from us, either. You're hurting and we're going to talk about this.'

'I'm all right, Mum. I've had bad break-ups before. I just want to get on with it.'

Chandice sits across from me with a mug of tea. 'For God's sake, Casey, just call Holly.'

Mum gestures to Chandice as though a master of sage relationship advice has just spoken. 'Listen to your sister.'

'What's the point of calling her when she won't even respond to a message?' I say. 'Keep up.'

'A message is different,' Chandice says. 'Have you actually dialled her number, left a voicemail, sent an email so you can get more words in, and not given up because she didn't reply?'

I glance out the window, my jaw tight. It's a typical grey, miserable mid-October day. 'I called her a couple days after the funeral. She didn't answer. My last message was weeks ago, and she didn't answer that either.' I face Chandice. 'She's getting on with her life and I'm getting on with mine.'

'Jesus, Casey,' Chandice says. 'Maybe she's had other things on her mind since the funeral, like grieving. It's not all about you, you know.'

'I didn't say it was, but I thought she was open to talking again. Next thing, I'm getting a message not to contact her. And before you have a go about me giving up, I responded to that.'

'She's lost her mum, love,' Dad says. 'Her head will be all over the place.'

'Yeah, and if I was important to her, she would've let me be there for her,' I shoot back. But my cheeks burn with shame over my lack of compassion, and underneath my hurt, my heart breaks for Holly's loss and what she must be going through.

'That aside, it's not the time to be racing off and getting up to God-knows-what in another country,' Mum says. 'I think you need to stop here and get through this.'

I drop my head into my hands and let out a frustrated groan. 'You lot are doing my fucking head in.'

'Ours and all,' Chandice says.

I jump up and head for the front door.

'Where are you going?' Mum shouts after me.

I grab my coat off the hook in the hallway and slam the door behind me.

An hour later, at the Tate Britain, I head straight for the 1800s room. My strides are long and heavy, carrying my anger at Mum and Chandice for having a go, and at Dad for agreeing with them. It's a busy Saturday morning in the gallery, but as I walk into the room I want, a couple of people exit and I'm alone. I sit on the bench and gaze at *Sappho and Erinna in a Garden at Mytilene.* The tension in my body eases as I become lost in their story. Sappho clinging to Erinna, painful longing on her face, their lips a breath apart. Erinna leaning against her, the dress slipping off her shoulder, soft eyes gazing straight ahead, daring the viewer to ask questions.

The first time I saw this painting I was in my third year at university. After being surrounded by classic art, I finally found a historical painting I connected with. I related to Sappho's longing for Erinna, her darker skin and more androgynous features, but mostly it made me feel close to the memory of Holly and me. Every time I looked at it, I'd work through another layer of emotions, and the ache would shift.

And now, as I lose myself in the connection between the two women, my longing for Holly surfaces. I dig into my pocket for the photo she gave me the morning I left Berlin and a sadness consumes me. I run my fingertip over the image, remembering Holly showing it to me the night she took it. How confronting it was to see that intensity between us reflected back at me at a time when I struggled to understand what it all meant.

I lean forward, elbows on knees, head in my hands, trying to work through the confusing thoughts in my head. Am I running away? Would Sappho and Erinna run from each other? Or would they run towards each other? Holly leaving Australia and heading straight for Berlin wasn't running away; it was facing her emotions head on, reclaiming that city for herself. Maybe that's what I need to do. Run towards Holly, run towards dealing with it. What's stopping me going to Australia? She'd have to talk to me if I were on her doorstep. But I also don't want to force her to talk to me if that's not what she wants.

There's movement beside me as someone sits, followed by a

familiar scent of leathery aftershave. I lift my head and sigh. 'For fuck's sake, Dad. What you doing here?'

'Oh, that's nice, innit? Don't let your gran hear you talking like that.'

'Sorry. Didn't mean to swear at you, but you're supposed to be at work.'

He's changed out of his work gear and into jeans and a jumper. 'Give myself the day off sometimes. Especially when my little girl is heartbroken,' he says, scooting across the bench.

I hang my head. 'Just hurts, you know?'

He wraps his arm around me and draws me tight against him, kissing my temple. 'I know it does, love.'

I lie my head on his shoulder. 'How could I mess this up so badly?'

He rubs my upper arm. 'You're being too hard on yourself.'

'That's not what you said this morning.'

'You didn't give me a chance to say anything else before you stormed off.'

'All of you were right, though. I didn't listen and it went wrong, and I hurt people.'

'I don't think we said that. We're just trying to say that Holly might need time, yeah? Some space to work things out. And losing her Mum can't be easy.'

I nod against his chest, a tear escaping. 'I know. But I care about her. Pretty sure I love her, and I should've been with her through that.'

He gives me a supportive squeeze.

I sit up and wipe my cheek. 'How'd you know I was here anyway?'

'I called Jazzy and she said you'd likely be moping about a gallery somewhere.' He points to the canvas. 'You've sulked over that plenty of times, so call it a lucky guess.'

'You're wasted in butchering, you. You want to move into detective work.'

He grins.

'Where's Mum and Chandice then?' I ask.

'Outside.'

'They're doing my head in.'

'Mine and all,' he says.

I laugh through my sniffles.

'I gave them a talking-to on the tube after they ran after me.' He gives my shoulder a nudge with his. 'Since I've got the day off, how about the four of us go for lunch at that nice Caribbean place across the river you've taken me to before? The one that does the rum cocktails.'

I stare at the painting. 'I s'pose.'

'I can wander around if you need more time with Sappho and Erinna.'

'I'm good. I can always come back.'

He pulls me close again and gives me another kiss on the temple. 'It'll work out, don't you worry.' Such a dad thing to say, but he'll want to fix me, so I stay quiet and let him be my dad. 'Come on,' he says, helping me up and slipping his arm around me.

Outside, Mum and Chandice are leaning against the concrete pillar at the bottom of the steps.

As soon as Mum spots me, she holds her arms open for me. 'I'm sorry, darlin'.'

'You're all right, Ma,' I say, hugging her.

Chandice gives me a sheepish smile and a hug. 'Sorry.'

I kiss her cheek. 'Forget it.'

We head along Millbank, then cross Vauxhall Bridge. I can't remember the last time we had a family outing like this. The mood is jovial and Mum stops in the middle of the bridge to snap a selfie of the four of us. Then she and Chandice have a spat over almost dropping Chandice's phone into the Thames, which just makes Dad and me laugh.

Twenty minutes later, we're seated outside at the restaurant. After we place an order for a massive feast of jerk wings, saltfish fritters, mutton curry, buns and rum cocktails, I force myself out my own head and focus on my family.

'So,' I say to Chandice. 'What's happening with this fella of yours, then?'

Chandice smiles coyly. 'Going out tonight.'

'You should see him,' Mum says, picking up a napkin and fanning herself. 'He is something else.'

I laugh. 'Jesus Christ, Mum.'

'Mum,' Chandice whines. 'Please don't stare at him when he stops by to pick me up tonight.'

'I have to admit,' Dad says, 'I was taken aback by his looks.'

'Give us a gander, then,' I say to Chandice.

She grabs her phone, taps the screen and passes it to me. It's an Instagram post, and I enlarge the photo. A broody-looking man stares back at me. His skin is a smooth, deep brown. Eyes so dark they're almost black. Chiselled jaw. Hair lining his upper lip and chin. Black-framed glasses and closely cropped hair.

'He's well fit,' I say.

'I know,' Chandice says, all bashful.

Mum places her hand on Dad's. 'He's a bit like your dad.'

Chandice scoffs. 'He so isn't and don't say that, it's weird.'

Mum screws up her face. 'Your dad's fit, you know. Especially when he was younger. He looked exactly like that.'

'He so didn't,' Chandice says. 'Way to turn me off my new boyfriend, Mum.'

I snort with laughter. 'I knew you had daddy issues.'

Chandice glares at me. 'Fuck off. You're one to talk, pining after the pretty white blonde. Talk about mummy issues.'

'Pack it in, you two,' Mum hisses. 'What have I said about swearing at the dinner table?'

Dad gives a fed-up sigh and shakes his head. 'Nobody has mummy or daddy issues, okay? Chandice, your lad is very handsome and doesn't look a thing like me now or when I was young. And Casey, Holly is beautiful and looks nothing like—'

Mum turns to him, brows shooting up towards her hairline.

'I didn't mean you're not beautiful, love. I'll start again. Casey, Holly looks nothing like your mum. They're both beautiful in their own way.'

Mum rolls her eyes. 'Where are those cocktails? I need a drink.'

Dad's eyes dart between the three of us. 'Can we just have a nice lunch now, please?'

'S'pose so,' Chandice says.

'Right,' I say, taking her phone. 'Let me look at his grid, then.'

Chandice rests her chin on my shoulder as I scroll, sighing at every photo.

Our cocktails arrive, soon followed by the food, and for the next hour I numb my heartache and stay present with my family.

Chapter 39
Holly, Melbourne

A week after my dinner with Tom, I'm at Caleb's Wine Bar. It's a busy Saturday night, loud with conversation and jazz music. Nat's late and I've already finished my first glass of wine. Caleb has just opened a new bottle and put two fresh glasses in front of me when Nat hurries in, forehead puckered with stress.

'Sorry I'm so late,' she says, giving me a quick hug. 'Archie's sick.'

'Why didn't you call? We could've cancelled.'

She waves a hand and hops onto a bar stool. 'No. He's settled now. I needed to get out and I wanted to see you.'

I give her a grateful smile and point to the bottle. 'My friend Caleb chose this for us.'

'Oh, I remember him,' she says and gives him a wave.

'How are you?' I ask, pouring her wine. 'Other than Archie being sick.'

She takes a sip and nods. 'Busy. Always busy.' She frowns and pats my knee. 'But that's not important. How are you? You sounded pretty down during the week.'

My mouth twists into what I hope is a smile and I give an overly enthusiastic nod. 'I'm fine.'

She tilts her head. 'Really?'

I fiddle with the stem of my glass. 'Ah, you know. Getting there.'

Nat is silent for a beat, then says, 'With what?'

I look up, confused. 'Sorry?'

'Getting there with what?' she says gently. 'Because I feel like you're really struggling, Hols.'

I swallow back the burn in my throat. 'I've been busy this week, helping out with Eli and Cooper, cooking meals, sorted out everything with the real estate. I've talked to a grief coun-sellor. Even applied for some jobs.'

'Okay. That's good.' She pauses. 'Have you contacted Casey? Replied to her last message?'

I shake my head. 'Deleted it.'

She raises her brows. 'You don't even want to try talking to her again?'

'It was torture to see it on my phone every day, okay?'

Nat's mouth pulls downward and her eyes narrow – the look she gives when contemplating whether or not to give her opinion. 'You're torturing yourself.'

'That's because talking to her, seeing her face, it's too much,' I say.

'Remind me again why you're not going to try and figure this out when you're both single and you have no reason to be here?'

Nat got the whole sorry story when I arrived home, but with losing Mum, we haven't delved too much into the Casey situation. 'Because she was sleeping with me in one city while her fiancée was planning a wedding in another!'

Nat nods. 'Ah, that's right. A fiancée she told you she was planning to break it off with before she met you again.'

'Well, that's what she *told* me. Anyway, that's not the point. We were together for days, literally stuck together, and she didn't tell me about her.'

'Maybe it's not that straightforward?'

I roll my eyes. 'It's not hard. Just say it. Geez, what's with everyone being Team Casey?'

She laughs. 'I'm not Team Casey. I'm team "I want to see you happy". Look at it this way. What if you hadn't split with Tom before you went away—'

'But I did—'

Nat holds up a hand. 'What if you hadn't? You just went for a holiday on your own, and you met her. You were all swept up in the romance of it, went for dinner and went home together. Would you have told her about Tom?'

'Yes.'

Nat raises a questioning brow. 'Before you slept with her or after?'

I purse my lips. 'After, maybe.'

'Okay, and how long before you would've told Tom?'

I shoot her a look. 'Did you just come here to grill me? Did Adam put you up to this?'

'Answer the question.'

'Fine. I would've told him at some point.'

'Exactly. At some point. You can't say for certain.'

I swig my drink.

She taps my arm to force me to look at her. 'Hey, I'm just trying to make you see things from a different perspective.'

'Okay, yes, I would have slept with her if I was still with Tom. But I would've told her about him, and then I would've contacted Tom and told him.'

'Well, from what you've told me, Casey was going to do that. She just got the timing off. You have to admit, it's an odd situation, you two suddenly meeting again like that. I'm guessing neither of you were thinking logically.'

'She slept with Eva the week before she slept with me!'

Nat sips her wine and considers me. 'So, you and Tom weren't having sex before you split? What was the timeframe between sex with him and you leaving?'

I blink at her, my face growing hot. The last time was our anniversary. Five days before I broke it off and flew to Berlin. I close my eyes a moment as the realisation sets in. 'Okay, point taken.'

Nat sighs. 'You're miserable, Holly. When I spoke to you in Berlin, you were the happiest I've heard you in years, even before you ran into Casey. You were so excited to be there. What have you got here? No job. No relationship. Adam is flat out with his family and business. I'm so swamped I barely get to spend time with you. And...' She grabs my hand. 'Bless your lovely mum, she's at peace.'

Her comment triggers my self-pity. Everyone getting on with their lives but me. 'I can't trust Casey now. What if she does what Lily did? How do I know these messages she's sent aren't messages she's sending to other people? To Eva?'

'Come on. Do you truly believe that? Wouldn't Eva broadcast that on her Instagram? From what you told me, Eva posted everything else about their relationship.'

Nat has a point. Eva has only been posting make-up tips. Nothing about Casey or the wedding, despite people filling her comments with questions.

Nat continues, 'Casey was in Berlin, wasn't she?'

'Yeah, for work!'

'But she didn't have to go to the park after work, did she? She didn't have to find you on Instagram and watch what you were up to. Would she seriously do that for anyone? She wants you, Holly. She went there looking for you.'

I open my mouth to protest, but she hasn't finished.

'And no one can predict the future. There is not one person alive who knows what the next minute holds.' She glances around the bar. 'Look at all these people. Who's to say I won't meet someone I'd leave my husband for in the next five minutes.'

I roll my eyes. 'Unlikely.'

Nat smiles. 'Yeah, unlikely. But my point is, no one really knows. You can't live your life assuming every woman you're with will be like Lily. Go back to the UK. Give Casey a chance.'

I frown. 'She's probably slept with a hundred people by now.'

'Maybe. Maybe not.' She sighs. 'I love you, Hols, but I don't want to see you miserable. Go. And if it doesn't work out with Casey, spend time with your aunty and cousin, have an adventure, travel around with your camera, create new memories. You might even meet someone else.'

I dare to let the possibility of what she's suggesting sink in. 'You really think I should go back?'

She nods. 'Please. I can't bear to see you moping around Melbourne any longer.' She's about to pour herself another wine when her phone rings. 'It's Marc.'

She answers, and I mull over what she's said. My heart urges me to return, my gut telling me that the next part of my life was just about to begin. But my head is crammed with everything that could go wrong and the fear of being hurt again.

Nat hangs up. 'Archie won't settle.'

'It's fine. Go.'

'Do you want to share a cab?'

I shake my head. 'I'll stay a bit longer. Finish this glass.'

She stands and gives me a quick hug. 'Why don't you come

over tomorrow for lunch? We can have a proper chat. Promise I won't lecture you again.'

I give a small smile. 'That sounds nice.'

She leaves and I top up my wine, contemplating her comments, but I can't imagine Casey hasn't been sleeping with other people. It's been almost two months since we were together. Can she even go that long without sex?

'Hello,' a soft voice beside me says.

I turn and it takes a few seconds to register that it's the woman I photographed the night Caleb hired me.

'Mind if I sit here? I think your friend has left,' she says.

'Um, sure. Yes, she has.'

She smiles her pretty smile. 'I'm Rochelle.'

'Holly.'

'I'd offer to buy you a drink, but I think you're good,' she says, gesturing to the bottle.

'I am. You don't have one, though,' I say. 'You're welcome to some of this.'

'Thanks.'

She takes Nat's stool, and I ask for a clean glass, then fill it to the halfway mark. We spend the next hour or so talking. She's interesting and vibrant and attentive, and I lap it up.

Over the course of our chat, the bar has become more crowded, so she's standing now and leaning in so we can hear each other over the noise. She smells good – a subtle floral perfume. I lift my mouth to her ear to speak, but she shifts to face me and our lips brush. I pull my head back. I want to kiss her, but whether it's genuine attraction or wanting to pay Casey back for all the sleeping around she's doing, I'm not sure. Either way, I press my lips to Rochelle's and she responds. She tastes white-wine sweet, and for a few beats of my pulse, I lose myself. Until a vision of Casey's face swims into my mind, and I'm painfully aware these lips aren't hers.

I move away and touch my fingertips to my mouth. 'I'm sorry. I can't.'

Her eyes search my face. 'Someone else?'

I nod. 'I thought I could. I wanted to.' I stand and grip the bar, swaying.

She catches me by the elbow. 'Do you want me to get you a cab or walk you somewhere?'

'No. Thank you. It was nice to meet you. I'm ... I'm sorry.' I push my way through the crowd, stumble down the concrete step and gulp in the fresh evening air, but my chest is so tight I feel like I can't get any into my lungs.

Tears spill down my cheeks as I walk along Little Bourke Street. I want to call Casey, but I won't cope if she's with someone else. I rest against a shopfront, pull out my phone and open Instagram, then go to my follower list, find who I'm looking for and press the video call icon. After a few rings, the call connects.

'Holly?' Jaz's dark brows pull together, daylight flooding the space behind her.

'Hi, Jaz,' I say with a sob.

'Oh, babe.'

I wipe my cheek. 'I miss her so much.'

'She totally misses you, too.'

'Really?'

Her eyes widen. 'You have no idea.'

'She hasn't met someone else?'

Jaz makes a face. 'Serious? She goes to work, comes home and mopes about the flat, and if she does go out, it's to mope about art galleries. She's a total sad fuck. It's doing my head in. Will you come back, please? Is that possible? I can't be doing with her crying anymore.'

'Crying?'

'Yes, crying.' Jaz pauses. 'Hang on, let me go over here.' She walks a few steps and leans against a building. 'She fucked up, but that's because she was all confused.'

I sniff. 'She's not back with Eva?'

'No, mate. And I promise you, she was about to end it with Eva when she met you. She wasn't happy; it just took her a while to get there, yeah?'

'She hasn't...' I swallow, not certain I'm ready to hear the answer to my question. 'Slept with anyone else?'

Jaz gapes at me, outraged. 'What? No, babe. Course she hasn't.'

My heart lifts and then crashes when I remember I've just kissed someone.

'Can you maybe call her or something?' Jaz asks. 'She's just messaged me. She was moping about the Tate and her family found her and took her out for lunch.'

The Tate. *Sappho and Erinna* is there. Hope blooms that maybe it's not too late. 'I don't want to interrupt them.'

'You won't. Believe me, they all want you to call her right now.'

'If you're sure?'

Her face splits into a broad grin. 'Brilliant.'

I wipe my face again and notice hordes of people behind her. 'Sorry, I called you in the middle of something.'

'You're all right. I'm on Oxford Street looking for an outfit. Got a hot date tonight.' She winks.

'Lucky her,' I say.

'Lucky me, I think. Now, stop stalling, Holly girl, and call Casey.'

I inhale and release it in a shuddery breath. 'Okay. Bye.'

'Later, lovely.'

I hang up, open FaceTime and hit Casey's number before I can talk myself out of it. Within two rings, her face fills the screen and my tears start again.

'Holly? Oh my God. Hiya.'

'Hi,' I sniff.

'Where are you? It's dark and you're crying.' Her eyes widen. 'Are you in danger?'

I shake my head. 'No. I'm fine. I miss you.'

Her shoulders drop. 'I miss you too.'

Chapter 40
Casey, London

I power down my work laptop and check my phone with a frown. Since Holly called me on Saturday, we've spoken in some form every day – thirteen days of solid contact – so I'm fretting about not hearing from her for well over twenty-four hours. We've mostly talked about her loss and how the grief therapist has been a good outlet for her. She and Adam are in a better place and while they've always been close, sorting through their parents' belongings and preparing their house for sale has helped them form a stronger bond. She's nurturing the relationship with her relatives in London, and she told me more about her time with Tom and Lily.

I was happy to keep quiet and listen, but yesterday morning she said, 'We've spent most of our time talking about me. I'm ready for you to tell me everything about Eva.'

My eyes widened in surprise.

She chuckled. 'Sorry, but I needed to build up to it. If you don't want—'

'No. I'm glad you want to talk about it. I think it's important.' I started at the beginning – how we met, sleeping with other people when we briefly split, the cracks in the relationship when we moved in together, the proposal, the wedding plans, how I got swept away with it all until one day my instincts told me something wasn't right, but that I owed it to Eva to try. I told Holly about the weeks leading up to me going to Berlin and how I thought about her then more than I ever had. She was quiet as I spoke, her face impassive.

When I finally finished, she said, 'You must have really loved her.'

I felt uneasy discussing my former relationship openly with Holly, but I also didn't want to keep anything from her. 'I did, but in the end it wasn't the right kind of love.'

'Mmm, sometimes we can't see that until we're out.' Holly was lying on her bed and rolled onto her side, propping her head up with her hand. 'Maybe I would've done something similar in your situation.'

I gave her a grateful smile, knowing she was trying to make me feel less guilty. 'I've been waiting for you to tell me, but can I ask what happened with Lily?'

'Oh, sure.' She took a deep breath. 'She was sleeping with someone she worked with.' Her gaze shifted from the screen, and when it came back to me, I could see the hurt in her eyes. 'I was suspicious for a while, just the way she spoke about this woman, the way her face would change when they talked; they seemed more than friends. I questioned her, but she brushed it off, told me I was being silly. I believed her, and I believed that she loved me too much to do anything like that. Then one day I went to meet her for lunch at work. It was her birthday. I wanted to surprise her, and I saw them together in a café next to her office.' She paused. 'They were sitting so close. Talking and laughing. And I knew. I confronted her that night and she admitted they'd been seeing each other for months.'

'Shit, Holly,' I said. 'That must've hurt so bad.'

She bit her bottom lip and nodded. 'I was devastated. I left that night, and she didn't try to stop me. I think that hurt just as much. It was like she was relieved I finally knew, like it saved her having to tell me.'

My own guilt rose. 'God, and I did the same thing to you.'

She shook her head. 'It's a different situation.'

'Just so you know, I had never cheated on a partner before,' I said. 'Yes, I've slept around, but only when I was single. With Eva, we'd split when I slept with someone else, until you. I lost my head because it was you, but you can trust me, Holly.'

She gave a tentative nod. 'I want to trust you.'

'And I want to prove to you that you can.'

'I know you do.' After a beat, she said, 'Let's talk about something else, hey.'

'Sure. What would you like to talk about?'

'Tell me about work.'

I told her about Josanne's job offer. She encouraged me to take it, but I had already decided it wasn't the right time for me. If there was any chance of Holly and I building a life together, then I wanted that to be my focus. Job offers would come and go, but I'd never get another shot at us. I saw a shift in her when I said that. Her face relaxed, and she broke into a broad, beautiful smile that made her eyes sparkle.

Since that conversation, all I've had is a message saying that she was off to bed and she'd be busy the following day sorting the sale of her Mum's house. I send her another text, grab my gear and lock the gallery doors behind me. It's just gone six-thirty, but it's already dark since the clocks went back last weekend. There's an early November chill in the air, but since I'm only crossing the road to the pub I don't bother putting on my jacket.

Inside, I'm surprised to not see Jaz's head pop out from

somewhere. I buy us drinks and head for a table by the window. I'm about to sit when Jaz rushes in and cuts in front of me.

'All right, mate,' she says, taking the seat facing the window.

I put the drinks down and take the seat opposite. 'Okay, then. I guess you want to sit there.'

'Cheers.' She takes a gulp of wine. 'Ahh, nice. I got a right thirst on, racing here.'

'Where you been? You're never late,' I say.

'Oh.' She glances out the window, her eyes darting left and right. 'You know, busy at work with the new job.'

I look outside and then back to her. 'Why you being shifty?'

She scrunches her face. 'I'm not.'

'You are, but whatever.' I clink her glass. 'Cheers.'

Jaz raises her brows. 'You're chipper compared to this morning when you were sulking because Holly hadn't replied to you.'

'I've kept myself busy today, but she still hasn't replied.' I frown. 'Bit worried all the past relationships talk the other night has scared her off. She hasn't replied to any of my messages.'

'How many have you sent?'

I scratch the back of my head. 'Like, four ... maybe five.'

'Five in twenty-four hours with no replies? Fuck me, mate. I never took you for one of them clingy types.'

'I'm not. It's just that she would've normally replied by now and I'm worried she's changed her mind about, I don't know, whatever it is we are.'

'Well, don't start crying again. Does my head in.'

'So much compassion,' I say.

'I'm plenty compassionate, it just has limits, is all.' Her phone pings. She snatches it up, grins, then taps the screen.

I gesture to her phone. 'That's Leila, I take it. Thought you were going out tonight.'

Jaz's eyes flick up from the screen and she gives a sly smile.

'We're catching up later.' She places her phone face-down on the table.

I look at it, and then at her. 'You're definitely being shifty. I'm not going to read your dirty texts, if that's what you're worried about.'

She laughs. 'I am worried about that. You'll get excited. You must be gaggin' for it by now.'

My phone vibrates on the table and Holly's image flashes on the screen. My heart skyrockets and I hit the answer icon. 'Hiya.'

Her lovely face and warm-tropical-seas smile fill the screen.

Chapter 41
Holly, London

'How are you?' Casey asks.

From my vantage point across the road, I casually look over the top of my phone to the pub windows. Jaz just texted to say they were at the table fourth window from the door. I spot them and my stomach flips. 'Good. I think.'

'You think?'

My smile widens and I focus on the screen again. 'I'm never sure these days.'

'Where have you been? I've not heard from you. I was getting ... well, I was worried.'

A lovely warmth spreads through me hearing that, especially since I was so nervous about showing up unannounced, but Jaz assured me Casey would be ecstatic. If Casey and I are going to do this, then I want it to happen in the same city. So I spent two weeks plotting my arrival with Jaz, packing, and saying tearful goodbyes. 'I've been travelling.'

'Travelling?' Confusion flitters across Casey's face. 'I thought your Mum's house was in Melbourne. Did you have to go somewhere to sort it?'

I step out of the doorway, check for traffic and cross the road, keeping the phone close to my face in an attempt to disguise my location. 'It is in Melbourne, and all dealt with. I meant, I couldn't reply to you because I was offline while travelling across the world.'

Her brow furrows as the comment processes. 'Across the world? Like ... a fair way across?'

'You could say that.' I hover outside the door to the pub, pulling the phone away so that the background is visible.

She gasps. 'Wait, are you...'

I take a few steps along the footpath so that I'm closer to where she and Jaz are sitting. 'Maybe you should look out the window.'

She spins and I hold up my hand in a wave. The shock on her face will stay with me forever. Behind her Jaz beams and gives me a wave.

'Oh my God,' Casey says, dropping the phone and rushing out.

I tuck my phone and headphones away as she stops short in front of me, her mouth open. 'Hi,' I say.

She lets out a short laugh. 'Hiya.'

We both take a tentative step forward and then she swoops me up, crushing me against her body. I laugh-cry as she kisses my forehead, my temple, my cheek, and then finally my mouth, and my body dissolves at the touch of her lips.

She grips my face. 'You're here. You're actually here. Does this mean you've forgiven me?'

'I'm getting there.'

She kisses me hard then, and a group outside the pub 'aww' in unison.

When we part, she rests her forehead against mine. 'I can't believe you're here,' she whispers. 'I swear I was about to book a flight to Melbourne.' She grabs my hand and guides me inside.

Jaz jumps up and opens her arms wide. 'Holly! Finally, I get to meet you in person.' We hug hello and when she pulls away, she looks me up and down. 'You're even more beautiful in the flesh.'

I grin. 'I was just thinking that about you.'

Jaz raises her brows at Casey. 'Did you hear that? You might have some competition.'

Casey laughs and jerks her thumb in Jaz's direction. 'Watch her,' she says to me, then addresses Jaz. 'You have something to do with this? That why you were late and being all shifty?'

Jaz gives a satisfied smirk. 'Maybe.' She sits and tugs at our hands to join her and points to two glasses on the table. 'I got you both a glass of champagne to celebrate while you were canoodling on the footpath.'

'Aw, Jazzy,' Casey says. 'That's sweet.'

Jaz presses her hand to her chest. 'I'm a true romantic deep down.' She hands a glass to me and gives one to Casey, then clinks us. 'To long-lost lovers.'

'To lost and found lovers,' I say, brushing my lips against Casey's cheek.

'And to new beginnings,' Casey says, catching my mouth.

Jaz grunts. 'When I said I was a true romantic, I didn't mean I want it shoved in my face. You two are sickening. Is this what I'm going to have to put up with?' She looks between us, then breaks into a grin.

'Yep,' Casey says, gazing at me and pushing a strand of hair from my face. 'Are you tired?' she asks. 'When did you get here? Have you slept? Are you hungry?'

'For fuck's sake, Casey,' Jaz says. 'Stop mollycoddling her.'

I laugh. 'Yes, I'm tired. I arrived a few hours ago. No sleep and I need food.'

Casey gives a bashful smile. 'Sorry. I'm just excited. You're here for longer than a holiday, right? You've still got that British passport and dual citizenship?'

I nod. 'Still got it.'

'Brilliant.'

Jaz drains her last mouthful of wine and stands.

'You're not staying?' I ask.

Jaz shakes her head. 'No can do, Holly darlin'. I've got a date.'

'Another one?' I ask.

'Yes, another one, but with the same person,' Jaz says.

Casey raises her eyebrows at me. 'It's getting serious.'

Jaz points at Casey. 'I'll see you when I see you. I take it you'll be in bed all weekend at wherever Holly is staying, and good thing, because our flat will be a-rockin'.'

'The whole flat?' I ask.

Jaz gives a slow, sly smile and her eyes smoulder. 'Oh, you have no idea.'

Casey rolls her eyes. 'Dear God.' Then she looks at me. 'Your timing is perfect.'

'Later, lovers,' Jaz says and breezes off.

'Wow,' I say, watching her saunter out. 'She's something.'

Casey laughs. 'That's one way to describe her. She's also the best mate anyone could have.' She turns serious. 'Just so you know – I don't want any secrets – the person she's seeing is Leila, who's a good friend of Eva's.'

I didn't expect to hear Casey mutter Eva's name so soon after arriving, and I try not to react to the jealously rippling through me. 'Oh. Does that mean Eva's in your circle of friends now?'

Casey shakes her head. 'No. She's busy with her life and her new partner.'

'I saw her post last week that she's met someone,' I say sheepishly.

Casey's brows shoot up. 'You've been cyberstalking her?'

I scrunch my nose. 'A bit. She actually has some really good make-up tips, although she doesn't post as much as she did.'

'No. She's giving it a rest for a while, she said. Busy getting a make-up line going and—'

'I kissed someone,' I blurt out.

Casey's face falls.

'I know we had that big conversation about everything, but I wanted to tell you in person so we could talk about it if you wanted to.' I pause to let her speak, but she stays silent. 'I don't know why I did it; it really meant nothing. I'm sorry.'

'You have nothing to be sorry for.'

'It was—'

'You don't owe me any explanations,' she says, taking my hand.

'I don't want us to get back into this with any secrets,' I say.

She nods. 'Okay.'

'It was that woman from the wine bar. The one in the photo I showed you in Berlin.'

She pulls her head back slightly. 'Oh. She found you again. Or you found her...'

'I was at the same wine bar. Had too much to drink. I was convinced you'd be sleeping with heaps of people. She was there, recognised me...'

Casey swallows. 'It's none of my business, but ... was it just a kiss?' She cowers a little, waiting for my answer.

'Yes. A brief one at that, because all I could see was you. That made me cry and I ran off and called Jaz.'

Her eyebrows pull together and she gives a short laugh. 'What?'

'I called Jaz, and then I called you. It was when you were out for lunch with your family.'

'Ah, that's why you were upset.' She pauses. 'I deserve it, I guess. I haven't, just so you know, kissed anyone or been with anyone since you.'

'I know. Jaz told me.'

'You asked Jaz *that*?'

I nod. 'I needed to know.' I take Casey's hand, her skin warm, and it feels so right to be touching her again. When I look up, she's gazing at me, her eyes soft. 'Should we maybe forget everything in the past and start again?' I ask.

Casey nods. 'Mmm. I won't let you down this time.'

'You might.'

She frowns. 'True, but I'll try really hard not to. Is that better?'

I kiss her. 'Better. And I'll try really hard not to let you down.'

We finish the champagne, and I stand holding out my hand for her. 'Want to come home with me?'

She presses my fingers to her lips, closes her eyes and breathes me in. 'There is nothing I want more.'

We leave the pub and walk hand in hand in comfortable silence, glancing at each other every few seconds. I pull her closer to me. 'I think we might need to talk about this "I love you" thing.'

Casey winces. 'Yeah.'

'A bit soon, maybe?' I say.

She nods. 'I was desperate. I do love you though, in some capacity.'

I slip my arm around her waist. 'How about for now we just love getting to know each other better and commit to seeing if this can work?'

She stops in the middle of the footpath and faces me, cupping my cheeks in her hands. 'I am all in.'

Chapter 42
Holly, London
Six weeks later

'Babe, are you almost here? I'm desperate to see you,' Casey says from the other end of the line.

I skim the hordes of people outside Oxford Circus tube station. 'I'm desperate to see you too, but I told Jaz and Leila I'd wait for them here.' Further along Oxford Street, I spot them rushing towards me, hand in hand. 'Oh, here they come ... see you soon.'

'Sorry, Holly,' Jaz says, giving me a quick hug. 'I bet that was Casey on the phone hurrying you up.'

Leila squeezes my hand, the wool of her gloves warm against my skin. 'It's my fault. I told Jazzy she should leave without me and come meet you,' she says.

'It's fine. We've got time. You know how nervous Casey gets before an exhibition opening.'

'Yep, she'll be hyped,' Jaz says, then looks down at my legs as we head along Regent Street. 'Ooh, what are you wearing?'

I stop, untie the belt of my coat and hold it open to reveal a sleeveless, silver-sequinned jumpsuit that clings to my body, then quickly close it again to protect myself from the cold air.

Leila groans her appreciation. 'Oh, Holly. I love it.' Leila works in retail and constantly groans over clothes, especially when they sparkle.

Jaz lets out a whistle. 'You look hot. Has Casey seen you in this? She's going to love it.'

'Not yet.' Despite the winter chill, my cheeks flush. Casey has been so busy with work the past few weeks, we haven't seen each other as much as normal, and I wanted to keep my exhibition outfit a surprise because I love the way she looks at me when I dress up.

Leila links her arm through mine and says excitedly, 'It's your big night.'

'Oh.' I scrunch my nose. 'It's not really *my* big night...'

'Babe. It totally is,' Jaz says. 'You've got three photos in an art exhibition. It's huge.'

'It's Casey being kind,' I say.

Jaz gives me a playful nudge with her shoulder. 'Stop being so modest. You know as well as I do Casey doesn't show anything in the gallery that's not up to scratch.'

I stand a little taller. 'I guess.'

We continue towards the gallery. It's early evening on a Wednesday and Regent Street is bustling with people leaving work or stopping for a drink, a sense of merriment about them. The magnificent Christmas angels hover mid-air, their wings spanning the width of the street. Cold air vapour seeps from my lips and it reminds me of winter at home. A pang of longing rises for Adam, Meg and the boys, and Nat and her family.

Jaz wraps her arm around my waist as we turn the corner. 'You okay?'

'Yeah. I'm thinking about home. Melbourne's cold like this in winter, and...' I swallow back the emotion. 'Miss it sometimes.'

Jaz gives me a sympathetic smile. 'They'll all be so proud of you. Your Mum and Dad especially.'

I nod. 'Just wish they could be here.'

Leila slides a supportive arm across my shoulder.

'Your aunty and cousin will be here,' Jaz says. 'And Adam, Meg and Nat are going to follow the live stream…'

I give her a grateful smile. 'You're right. Just having a moment.'

We arrive at the gallery and Jaz knocks on the glass doors.

Casey's face lights up and she rushes out. 'You're here!' She makes a beeline for me and kisses me. Her lips are soft and warm on my cold face, her hands gentle on my neck, and it feels like forever since our last kiss. 'Hello, lovely,' she says.

I brush my nose against hers. 'Hello.'

'For God's sake, you two,' Jaz says. 'It's freezing out here. Do your canoodling inside.'

Casey ushers us in and we unravel scarves and shrug off coats. Her mouth drops open as she looks me up and down. 'Babe.'

I raise a suggestive brow. 'Like it?'

She throws her head back and moans. 'How am I going to concentrate on work when you look like *that*?'

'What did I say?' Jaz says with a sly grin, then waves a finger between us. 'I do not want to walk into the toilets and hear you two shaggin' in a cubicle.'

I laugh. 'I think we can control ourselves.'

Casey kisses my neck, her hand sliding down my back. 'I don't think I can. You look incredible.'

My body sizzles under her touch and I giggle as she nuzzles my neck.

'Ahem.' Josanne is watching us with raised eyebrows, her lips twitching. 'I don't think that's the kind of exhibition people are coming to see.'

Casey grins. 'Sorry.'

Josanne's eyes flick over me. 'I can't blame her. You look amazing, Holly.' She turns to Jaz and Leila, who both look stunning. Jaz is dressed in a black, glimmery suit and Leila is in a slinky emerald-green dress – the same one she's wearing in one of my photos. 'And you two, just gorgeous.' She gives Casey a tap on the arm. 'Well, get your friends and girlfriend' – she turns to me – 'sorry, *artist*, a drink, Casey.'

'On it,' Casey says and crosses the floor, vanishing through the staff entrance with her colleague Michaela.

The gallery looks spectacular. There's a huge Christmas tree in the window decorated with gold baubles and twinkling lights. Large, shimmering stars and mistletoe hangs from the ceiling. Artwork for the new exhibition is spaciously displayed in the main gallery, and through the doorway into the smaller, side gallery, I glimpse the digital art display. My eyes cut to the back wall and I breathe in sharply.

Josanne gives my back a maternal rub. 'Your photos are beautiful, Holly. I hope you're ready to take on some portrait work after tonight.'

I break into a grin. 'I am. Thank you for letting me be part of this.'

She points to Casey, who's approaching us with a tray of champagne flutes. 'Thank your superstar curator girlfriend. This is her exhibition and I trust her judgement.'

My heart swells. I'm only in the exhibition because an artist pulled out and Casey needed to fill the space fast, but I also know she could've found someone else if she really wanted to. I already knew about the theme for the exhibition, which had inspired some photo ideas. So when the opportunity arose, I gave Casey and Josanne a proposal and they both loved it. Luckily for me, I was able to execute my ideas better than I imagined.

'Here you go,' Casey says, handing me the champagne.

I thank her with a lingering kiss.

When we part, she touches the H pendant of my necklace. 'I am so proud of you.'

'Mmm. I could do nothing and you'd be proud of me.'

She smiles. 'True. But tonight I'm extra proud.'

We're interrupted by the gallery doors opening, Casey and Jaz's families piling in, laughing, talking, oozing joy and love. There are bear hugs and cheek kisses like it's been months since we've all seen each other rather than just last weekend.

Minutes later, my aunty and cousin arrive. My cousin Kate, who is a couple of years younger than me, is also my flatmate, so I give her a quick, 'Hey, Katie,' before she rushes off to talk to Chandice. But I haven't seen my aunty for a couple of weeks. I pull her close, breathing in her comforting, familiar scent. 'Hi, Aunty Carol. I'm so glad you could make it.'

We step apart and she beams at me. It's like looking at a younger, healthier version of Mum. 'I wouldn't miss it,' she says. 'Plus, Katie and I are in one of these photos, aren't we?'

'You certainly are.'

Casey appears and gives Carol a warm embrace. 'Hi, Aunty Carol.'

'Hello, Casey, love,' she says, returning the hug. She holds Casey's hand in hers and glances around the gallery. 'Look at this. So beautiful.'

Casey points to the back wall. 'Your niece's photographs are over there.'

Aunty Carol squints as she focuses. 'Oh, Holly.' She touches a hand to her chest and faces me with watery eyes and a look that says, 'Your parents would be so proud', but she knows if she voices it, we'll both be in tears.

I give her another squeeze. 'Thank you for being here.'

Casey and Michaela fetch everyone drinks, and for the next

half an hour, we have the gallery to ourselves. Although my contribution to the exhibition is tiny compared to the feature artists, Casey insisted on making a fuss over me, ensuring our friends and families were here first to help celebrate.

'Webcam is on,' Michaela says, pointing across the gallery. 'And your family and friends have joined us. Give them a wave.'

I do and within seconds, my phone beeps with a message from Adam.

> Proud of you little sis. Love you.

I walk over to the webcam and blow a kiss, even though I can't see them. Another message arrives from Nat.

> Hols, look at you. So happy for you. That jumpsuit is sizzling.

I do a little twirl in front of the webcam for her, and say, 'Miss you all.'

Casey's voice drifts across the gallery, pulling me back into the event. 'Hello, my dear friends and family,' she says, standing by the Christmas tree. The twinkling lights flicker across her face, giving her an angelic glow. 'Thank you for coming along to the opening of our winter exhibition, *Beyond the Ordinary*. You're surrounded by some incredible art that explores the everyday moments of people's lives. At first glance, what you see might appear mundane and ordinary, but look closely and you'll find moving and thought-provoking stories about human connections. Our artists and guests will arrive soon and the exhibition will be officially open, but first, a very special toast to my beautiful, talented, creative, brave...' She stops and beams at me. 'Did I mention beautiful?'

'Yes,' Chandice and Kate groan.

Casey laughs and continues. 'Partner.' She gestures for me to join her, and I nestle into her side. 'Holly has three incredible photos here tonight, and while she won't let us sell them because she wants to keep them for herself, I have no doubt they'll generate interest and new clients for her in the future.' She gazes at me. 'I'm so proud of her.' She looks at everyone else. 'And who knew some of you lot would feature in one of my exhibitions?'

Everyone cheers and raises their glasses.

'Feel free to say something, if you like,' Casey says to me, loud enough for everyone to hear, and they all quieten down.

'I'm lost for words,' I say, projecting my voice so that Adam and Nat can hear me through the webcam. 'It truly is a dream to spend my time on photography and to have my photos displayed in a gallery. Thank you to my willing subjects who let me follow them around for weeks with my camera. Thank you to Josanne for supporting aspiring artists.' I turn to Casey. 'And of course, thank you to my amazing partner.' I press my lips to hers and everyone cheers again.

Then the doors are open. Artists and guests flow in, and the space fills with chatter, music and laughter. Catering staff circulate with drinks and finger food, people slowly roam the gallery, taking in paintings, photographs and digital art, and Casey gives an official opening speech.

I'm enjoying the atmosphere and soaking up the compliments, when I come face-to-face with Eva. I knew she'd be here but I didn't allow myself to think about it. Now I'm suddenly very aware that the wedding reception was meant to have been held in this room, and her ex-fiancée is here celebrating another event with another woman.

'Hi, Holly,' Eva says, her voice softer and kinder than last time we spoke – the only time we've spoken.

I give a small, cautious smile. 'Hi, Eva.'

She points towards the back of the gallery. 'Congratulations on your photos. You've really captured the essence of everyone's personalities, especially Leila.'

My defences start to lower. 'Thanks.'

Her eyes flick downward. 'Amazing jumpsuit, too.'

My smile is more genuine now and I run my hands over the smooth sequins. 'It is amazing, isn't it?'

Eva nods. She looks stunning, with her glossy black hair and perfectly made-up face, a diamond pendant glistening at her throat. She lowers her gaze. 'I, um ... wanted to apologise to you.'

My brows shoot up. 'Oh?'

She bites her lip. 'That was a horrible thing to do to you that day at the pub. I regret it and I'm sorry. Casey broke up with me the minute she returned from Berlin and she told me about you.' Her cheeks redden. 'I was trying to hurt her, and maybe you a bit, but mostly her.'

I feel a wave of empathy for her, having been there myself. 'I understand.' I want to tell her that I would've stayed away from Casey if I knew, but I'm not certain that's true. Casey's pull on me was too strong. I would've tried; I would've encouraged Casey to speak to Eva sooner, but stay away completely? Unlikely. Instead, I say, 'I really should thank you because if that hadn't happened, I wouldn't have gone home and had the chance to say goodbye to my mum in person.'

Her eyes fill with compassion. 'Casey told me about that. I am so sorry about your mum.'

I shift my gaze and take a deep breath before I give her a smile. 'Thank you.' I point to Aunty Carol, who's talking to Casey's parents. 'Mum's younger sister is here tonight, so that's nice.'

A soft, protective hand touches my back and Casey is by my side. 'Eva.'

Eva's jaw tenses. 'Don't worry, I was just apologising.'

'And complimenting my photos,' I say, feeling the need to defend Eva.

Eva gives me a grateful nod. 'Yeah, that too.'

'Thanks for coming,' Casey says, her tone softening.

Eva points behind her where Frankie is gazing at a painting. 'Thank Frankie. She's the art lover.' She gives a little shrug. 'And I couldn't miss the photo of my girl Leila.' Her eyes dart between us. 'Well, I'll leave you to it.'

'Okay?' Casey asks once Eva has moved away.

I release a relieved sigh. 'Yes. I was more worried about seeing her than I realised.' I give Casey a little shove. 'Go on. Get back to work.'

Casey returns her attention to artists and buyers, and I get back into celebratory mode, squealing with delight when I see Felix and Matias walk through the door. Matias and I have become great friends, bonding over photography.

'I thought you couldn't make it,' I say, giving them both a hug.

'Last-minute change of plans,' Felix says.

'I couldn't miss your gorgeous photos,' Matias adds.

A waitperson appears and we each grab a glass of champagne and catch up on life in London and Berlin.

Eventually, I'm alone in front my photographs.

The first is of Casey, Chandice and their parents working together in the butcher's. We'd stayed at Casey's parents' place one Friday night and a staff member called in sick the next day, so Casey had reluctantly helped them out. I arrived with my camera as they were closing. I liked what I'd snapped at the time, but it wasn't until I examined the images closely on a larger screen that I found one I loved.

They're mid-activity, a lyrical flow to their movements, an unbreakable bond between the four of them. Marvin's hands are busy covering meat trays while he watches his daughters with a bemused smile, adoration in his dark eyes. Wendy's mouth is open in a joyous laugh as she wipes down a counter. Chandice and Casey are bent over a single mop handle, using it as a makeshift microphone. Chandice's arm is flung in the air, a cleaning cloth dangling from her fingers. Casey's eyes are partially closed, her mouth open, belting out a song in her white butcher's apron. It's the most perfect shot and Casey had a tear in her eye when she saw the final product. It's hers after the exhibition finishes.

I move to the next photo. Jazzy and Leila, taken late one afternoon when we were all at Jaz and Casey's. Leila had come straight from work, arriving with bags of new purchases from her store. She disappeared, returning to the lounge room five minutes later in a long, slinky dress with a split that ran to the top of her thigh. The silk was taut across her breasts and clung to the curve of her waist and hips. On her feet were a pair of glittery, strappy heels that set off her golden skin. Jaz fell to her knees with a whimper and crawled across the carpet. I lifted my camera as she knelt in front of Leila, gazing up with smouldering eyes. Leila had one foot placed against Jaz's shoulder, the heel of her shoe denting Jaz's skin, a wicked smirk on her face and one slick eyebrow raised. They were completely caught up in each other, oblivious to me swiftly moving around them to capture the moment. The image sizzles from the chemistry between them.

'The woman who literally brings me to my knees,' Jaz says, appearing beside me.

I smile. 'There's a lot of heat and connection in that photo, Jazzy.'

'Mmm. I think I might actually love her.'

'Oh, you think? It's not like it's obvious or anything,' I say with a laugh.

Across the gallery, Leila is dancing with Eva. She catches us watching her and blows Jaz a kiss.

Jaz's cheeks flush. 'I know.'

'You should probably tell her instead of me, though.'

'Oh, like how you and Casey tell me instead of each other, you mean?'

I chuckle. 'Yeah, something like that.'

Jaz heads back to Leila, and I look at my final photo. Aunty Carol and Kate sharing a pot of tea and a lemon drizzle cake on a wet Sunday afternoon. Kate gazes at her mother lovingly as Carol talks about her week. The window behind them is splattered with rain drops and it adds a depth of coziness to the image. It's a tender moment – a strong mother and daughter bond that's reminiscent of Mum and me.

An ache rises in my chest. 'This one's for you, Mum,' I whisper. A shiver runs over my skin and I rub my arms, blinking back tears.

I sense someone behind me. Even without turning around I know it's Casey. Her woody scent, her warm touch, the way my body hums in response.

She wraps her arms around my waist from behind and kisses my temple. 'Happy?'

I continue gazing at my photos. 'So happy. Thank you for doing this for me.'

'I just gave you some well-deserved wall space. The rest was you.'

I turn to take her in. She looks beautiful. She always looks beautiful, but tonight she has something extra about her – a brighter glow, proud, content, comfortable in her skin – and I feel myself falling for her all over again. 'You're glowing tonight,' I say.

She laughs and lowers her lips to mine, then says, 'I'm so

glad you're here with me. In London. In the gallery. In my life. I want moments like this together forever.'

Words I've been holding off saying press on my tongue – words I didn't want to say because I thought it was too soon – but when you know, you know. 'I want moments like this forever, too, because I love you.'

She stares at me in disbelief then grins. 'You said it.'

'I did.'

'Maybe you should say it one more time to make sure I heard right?'

'I love you, Casey Miller-James.'

'Ditto, Holly Craddock.'

Then she kisses me.

I sink into her and the magic of this moment, surrounded by inspiring art, our wonderful friends and families, twinkling decorations and Christmas music, and I know this is exactly where I'm meant to be.

Epilogue
Casey, London

Eight months later

Holly and I have been lugging boxes and furniture up and down stairs for the past couple of hours, moving it all into our new home – a new block full of modern one and two-bedroom flats in Bethnal Green.

Eight months is my record for moving in with someone, but why wait when we're both certain? I even asked Holly to marry me one night when we were at Mum and Dad's and I'd had too many rum cocktails. She laughed and said, 'Don't be stupid.'

My face fell and Holly's mouth dropped open. 'Oh, God. You're serious?'

I shook my head. 'Not really. I just thought you might want that.'

She slipped onto my lap and held my face. 'No. I think we're good how we are. Don't you?'

I kissed her, heady with rum and love, my mum cooing at us across the kitchen table. 'I do,' I said. 'But how about we …

maybe, if you want, like ... move in together? We spend most nights together anyway.'

Holly stroked my cheek. 'That's exactly what I want.'

Mum dabbed the corner of her eye. 'You two.'

'Are you for real, Mum?' Chandice said. 'They're just moving in together, not having a baby.'

'It's beautiful, though, innit?' Mum said. 'What they went through to get to this point.'

Chandice rolled her eyes. 'You better shed a tear when me and Joseph move in together.'

'If you're not careful, I'll bloody move in with Joseph,' Mum said. 'I wouldn't mind a bit of him.'

Chandice stormed off, horrified, and Holly collapsed into giggles. We spent the rest of the night searching flats online and planning our next chapter together.

Up to the moving-in decision, Holly and I flitted between each other's flats, getting to know one another properly, living in the real world. Me learning more about her habits and quirks, like her messiness and the contrasting behaviour of organising groceries neatly in the shopping trolley, and her putting up with mine – like working too much, stressing about my exhibitions not being perfect, and making sure every item of clothing I put on is freshly ironed. We talked more about the relationships we'd each had over the years, and it took time to fully earn her trust again, to assure her I really was working late, to call and message as much as possible to prove my commitment. It paid off and we eventually reached a comfortable place.

She found herself a part-time project manager role at a local council and set up a small photography business, which has taken off, so she'll soon be giving up the part-time job.

My and Jaz's families have taken her in as their own, their hearts breaking over her losing both her parents at such a young age. She's tried all the spicy Jamaican dishes Dad and Jaz's dad have served up for her; eaten the black pudding and liver Mum's given her to try; spent time at the butcher's; read drafts of Chandice's steamy romances; and constantly listened to Jazzy gush over Leila.

And now, here we are, in our new flat, purchased with Holly's share of the sale of her parents' house and a sizeable mortgage for my half.

Holly dumps a box on the lounge-room floor. 'That's it. The last one.'

I groan and fall onto the sofa. 'Thank God. Up and down those stairs all afternoon has done me in.'

Holly leans against the doorframe. 'Don't relax. Jaz and Leila will be here for dinner soon.'

'Tell me you're jokin'?'

'Jaz said it's British tradition to invite people over on the first night in a new place, so I invited them.'

I raise my brows. 'And you fell for that?'

Holly scrunches her nose. 'That's not a thing?'

I give a short laugh. 'No. She's takin' the piss.'

'Well, I guess we have dinner guests now. I have no idea where the plates are, and we have no food, so it'll be takeaway.'

'The cheek of her,' I say with a grin.

Holly opens a box and pulls out some sofa cushions, throwing them over to me.

I pile them at the end of the couch. 'Come and lie here with me for a bit, since we're not going to get the night to ourselves.'

Holly's eyes flick up from the box. 'They'll leave at some point.'

'Yeah, but we'll be tired and pissed up by then.'

She walks over and pushes me back, stretching out on top of me. 'Better?'

'Mmm.' I lift my head to kiss her and sigh as her lips make

the day's stress drain away. 'What time will they be here?' I murmur.

She pushes her pelvis against me and kisses my neck. 'Seven.'

I grab my phone from the floor and glance at the screen. 'Half an hour.'

Holly kisses me again. 'Plenty of time.'

I wrap my arms around her waist and flip her over, delighting in her shriek. 'I've got a present for you.'

She lifts a questioning brow. 'Is that what we're calling it now?'

I grin and jump up. 'Sex is a gift I like to give you, but I've got something else. Close your eyes.'

'Ooh, a gift.' She sits up. 'Okay. Closed.'

'Keep them shut,' I call as I dash into the bedroom and grab a canvas Dad and I placed under the bed earlier while Mum and Chandice distracted Holly. I carry it along the short hall back to the lounge. 'Still shut?'

'Yep.'

I pad across the carpet and rest it on the mantel, then strip off the covering. 'Okay. Open.'

Holly opens her eyes and gasps, then stands and walks over to me. 'No.'

I grin, dead pleased with myself. 'Yes.'

She slides her arm around my waist and gazes at the painting. 'Oh,' she breathes. 'I love it. But how?'

I wrap my arm around her shoulder and look at the painting of Holly and me lying on her bed in a Berlin university dorm, staring into each other's eyes. 'Katarina did it.'

Holly's mouth drops open. 'Katarina? The artist who did that incredible painting for your Berlin exhibition?'

'Uh-huh. As soon as you showed me that photo I knew I

wanted it as a painting, and when you came back to London, I contacted Katarina straight away and she—'

Holly kisses me. 'I love it.'

The doorbell rings.

I groan. 'Jazzy's always early.'

'I'll get it,' Holly says, heading to kitchen to buzz them in. After a few seconds, she wanders back in, still smiling.

'What?' I say.

'You.' She pulls me to her and gives me a lingering kiss.

I moan and slip my fingertips under the waistband of her jeans.

'Oops. Soz,' Jaz says. 'Want us to come back in five?'

I grunt and pull away. 'Why are you always fucking early, Jazzy?'

'Don't mind us,' Leila says, trailing behind Jaz. 'We'll just go in the kitchen and have a drink.'

'Won't take you long, yeah?' Jaz says. 'A few minutes?'

Holly laughs. 'More like a few hours.'

'Sure, Hols,' Jaz says.

'She can wait,' Holly says. 'Come in. Sit down. You'll have to use boxes as tables.' Holly empties the rest of the cushions and turns a box upside down, pushing it towards the sofa.

Leila sits and looks about. 'This is really nice.' She clocks the painting. 'Oh my God, is that' – she gestures to Holly and me – 'you two?'

'Aw,' Jaz says. 'It turned out amazing.'

Leila looks at her, and Jaz nods towards the painting. 'That's when they first met all those years ago. It's been painted from one of Holly's photos. Look how in love they were.'

Leila clutches her chest. 'Naw. I love love stories.'

I grin at Jaz who gives a bashful smile. She's well love struck.

Holly returns from the kitchen holding up some plastic tumblers. 'It's all I can find.'

'That'll do,' Jaz says, unscrewing the cap from a wine bottle and filling the cups. She passes them around and holds one up. 'Cheers to your new home.'

Leila holds up her cup. 'And to the next stage of your life together.'

Holly and I exchange a loving glance. 'We'll drink to that.'

The hours pass as we drink, talk and eat takeaway. I look at the painting leaning against the wall, the memory of Holly photographing us still vivid in my mind. I see the connection that she wanted to capture forever – a connection I could never truly run from. My being fills with joy and peace and love – for life, for Holly and for our future, whatever that looks like.

Acknowledgments

The development of this novel feels serendipitous. From the moment I had the idea of two people losing touch and reuniting in a foreign city, right through to publication, everything flowed to make it happen. A huge thanks to the following people for helping me get this story into the world.

Claire Furniss for the beta read at very short notice, her always helpful suggestions, her continued support and for following my writing journey with such enthusiasm.

Sophia Blackwell for the developmental edit. I feel very fortunate to have come across Sophia when I was looking for a UK editor. She was a pleasure to work with and gave me some great insights on the plot and characters, and some excellent suggestions for additional scenes (and scrapping scenes).

Stephanie Davy for the sensitivity read. After weeks of struggling to find a sensitivity reader to suit my story and characters, I remembered a Facebook group I'd joined years earlier. I posted a request and someone replied recommending Stephanie. Not only was she perfect for my characters, she gave me confidence in my ability to write a character very different from myself. She's also become a valued friend. Steph – I'm so glad our paths crossed.

Jess McFarlane for her beta read and proofread, her support and friendship. It's a pleasure to share the writing journey with you, Jess, and meeting you is without a doubt the best thing to come from our early publishing experiences. Can't wait for your future novels to be out in the world.

Suzanne O'Sullivan for the great title, a variation of my original title, yet not one I thought of! Sorry we couldn't work together on this novel, Suzanne, maybe in the future.

Samantha Sanderson-Marshall for the beautiful cover design and artwork. I'd been looking for a cover designer for weeks when, as a last resort, I thought I'd try Reedsy (where I'd found Sophia). Sam was the only person who replied to my request and as luck would have it, she was the perfect choice. All I told her was that I wanted Holly and Casey to be illustrated on the cover and she did the rest, including coming up with a concept that mirrored both a scene and a painting referenced in the story. I hope we have many more covers together, Sam.

Penny Carroll for the copy edit. Another fortuitous meeting when I decided to take a workshop at the 2023 Romance Writers of Australia conference being co-run by Penny. As soon as I realised she was a freelance editor, I knew I wanted to work with her on one of my novels – just a feeling I had! As it transpired, I did need an editor for this novel. I'm grateful I had the opportunity to work with Penny because she's a fantastic editor who helped tighten up my tilts and tuts and glances and gazes, among other things. Definitely more stories coming your way, Penny.

To my friends and family for their continued belief in me, and of course to my wife for thinking I'm the best author who has ever lived and for giving me the space and time I need to live my dream.

And finally, to you, the reader. I hope you've enjoyed this story and love Holly and Casey as much as I do.

About the Author

Samantha L. Valentine is an Australian author of contemporary sapphic fiction, both life lit and romance. She is passionate about diversity in fiction and would love the world to read more diverse Australian stories. She graduated with first class honours in English Language and Linguistics from the University of Westminster (London) and holds a Masters in Writing, Editing and Publishing from The University of Queensland (Brisbane). In her early twenties, Samantha went to the UK for a one-year working holiday that turned into twelve years living in London and Oxford. She now lives in Brisbane with her wife and their two Boston terriers. She is the author of three published novels, two published short stories and many unpublished drafts.

If you'd like to stay up to date, you can sign up to her monthly newsletter at www.samvalentine.com.au and follow her on Instagram or TikTok.

www.ingramcontent.com/pod-product-compliance
Lightning Source LLC
Chambersburg PA
CBHW030520120726
47904CB00005B/1548